The Last Breath

A novel

by

Darrel VanDyke

ISBN: 978-0-578-66782-9

CONTACT: DARRELVAN@GMAIL.COM

A heartfelt thanks to Carolyn Henderson, Mary Lee Long, Francesca Ruth Johnson, and Carolyn Moore who provided much needed "you really should change..." comments and other suggestions.

Also, without the edits from Carolyn Moore and her company, Wordsworth, Inc., this book would have breathed its "last breath" years ago.

My daughter, Alex Moore-VanDyke, has been an inspiration to not only me but to others to help change the world's thinking for a sustainable future for all people. With her and young people like Greta Thunberg raising their voices for change, maybe someday the world will listen.

Year 1

April – Antarctica

Whether one lives or dies depends on the skills of others at McMurdo Station, and during the winter months it is doubly so. Anything pliable under normal circumstances yields itself into a different state in a manner of seconds – minutes at most – including human tissue. Many bodies of intrepid explorers to both poles have been found where they dropped. When blood freezes in a body and starts the evaporation process, the skin blackens – so much so that the covering makes the corpse barely recognizable as a former human being.

The winds can be calm to non-existent one minute, and within seconds come roaring across the barren landscape. Those who temporarily live in Antarctica have learned to recognize signs of an impending windstorm, and they know when to pull up their research tents and head to safety. If a scientist is asked to explain these signs, he will give myriad answers like, "The sun looks different" or "The hills seem all blown around today" or "The snow is crunchier." All the answers are based on experience from living in a world where signs are a matter of survival, and when the command "Pack up now!" is given, it means for everyone to heed that advice immediately.

Antarctica, like Mars, is a deadly place where it makes no sense for people to live. Yet, people go to this godforsaken place for a reason – namely scientific research and as support personnel for the scientists. Environmental monitors, sociologists, and even archaeologists set aside months or sometimes years out of their lives for the opportunity to research everything from ice thickness to temperatures, wind speeds, ice sheet cracks, and environmental data. And all this for just a nominal salary.

Spring in Antarctica is nothing more than a way to assign a name to more sunlight hours and temperatures warmer than the minus fifty degrees Celsius designated as winter. Many scientists, though, are concerned about the trend in higher temperatures year-round, and April is when William Moore arrived. Along with other scientists, his job is to set out new stratosphere monitoring equipment and to try to verify the data from older equipment that had been in place for ten years.

William's journey to Antarctica was as circuitous as others who had preceded him. A unique decision chosen at random, an interaction with someone, or something as simple as the weather changing, alters every person's journey in life, and so it was with William. William's background had been strictly academic. He wrote his required technical papers while earning his MS degree and finally his PhD in oceanic and environmental studies. Before graduation he had had two job offers with oil companies, but his professor had mentioned a possible opening coming up with the U.S. Department of Oceanic Studies for Antarctica. The more he asked about the job and the answers he got, the less interested he became in the position. "The South Pole," he would say to his school friends. "Can you imagine that? Not me – I'm just fine in the U.S."

He also enjoyed dating as much as the next guy and driving on open highways between his home in North Texas and his university near Houston. Both activities, he predicted, would be seriously curtailed by working in a place where he was pretty sure there were few roads and definitely no Porsches. Yet… something in the back of his mind kept telling him that it could be fun before he settled down for a career. After all, who could say they had worked in Antarctica? He imagined this could be a great pick-up line somewhere down the road. As he ponders the application that his professor had forwarded to him, he decides to fill it out with a "What the hell – it won't hurt – I can always tell them no" attitude of ambivalence.

One oil company had interviewed him twice and was ready to make him an offer, but he was hoping for a reply from the U.S. agency before he committed to the large corporation. William's finances are in bad shape after years of trying to make ends meet by working at part-time jobs around campus. Having a large salary – in fact having any salary – waved in front of him would tilt his decision. In his last conversation with the oil company, he had delayed a direct answer with "Let me give you an answer in a week." He knows that if all goes well, he can see himself retired in another forty years with this company and hopefully contributing to both the company itself and to the environment. He has strong ideals about how the world needs to be more observant and less cavalier in handling pollutants, and his thesis provided excellent research on that topic. Sitting in a local coffee shop half-way between his apartment and campus (as he has done on a regular basis for the past five years) he knows the waitstaff by name – and they know him.

There are few places in America where one can discuss politics, hear about husbands and wives and relationships, and in general find out about the mood of the country than at a local diner. William had found Pete's during his first year of grad school, and since then had settled into being a "regular." This unofficial title allowed him to sit in a secluded corner that let him face the counter and glance at the random people between studying – all while sipping a bottomless cup of coffee. When any of the staff saw him coming down the street, they automatically drew a hot cup of dark roast. He gave a cheery "top of the morning" no matter what time of the day it was when he walked in. During school semesters, his only reading had been a textbook. Today, he opens the daily newspaper as the coffee aroma focuses his attention in front of him.

"Thanks, Mary," he says to his favorite server – who seems to actually enjoy her job. He had seen other servers come and go, and maybe a third of them never did anything more than grunt at him. Why they were in a field of work that required them to interact with people when it was obvious they didn't like most in the human race was perplexing to him. He always thought that his life's work would be something he truly enjoyed – not something he had to pretend to like.

While parsing the headlines and trying to decide on what article to start reading, his cell phone rings. The unknown area code from the caller-ID number makes him think twice about answering it. It rings again, and he studies the number more closely. On the third ring, he answers, "This is William."

"Good morning, William. My name is Samantha Coryell. I work at the Department of the Interior. We got your resume and application form, and I have to tell you, you are exactly the sort of person we are looking for. Would you be able to fly to Denver next Monday for an interview?"

At first William thinks it could be a prank from one of his buddies. He asks a series of questions: "Who are you again?" "What department are you in?" "When did you get my resume?" The voice on the other end provides all the answers to satisfy his queries, and satisfied that that Ms. Coryell is on the up-and-up, he agrees to the interview for two reasons; mainly because he has never been to Denver and has heard it is a hip city for younger folks, and second, he is curious about meeting someone face-to-face who hopefully can answer specific questions about life at the South Pole. Hanging up, he starts making a list of questions. "How long do I have to stay?" He underlines it three times. Then writes, "How much do they pay?!"

"Yup, gotta earn some money, but what can I spend it on at the South Pole? Nothing – so this could be good." He ponders the consequences of saving a year's salary, then puts down the pencil, and nods.

Over the next few days he sleeps way too many hours – he knows that staying in bed until almost noon might be construed by many as being lazy, but he justifies it by telling himself that he has earned a nice rest from his academic work. Plus, he does have one real job offer, and if the Denver interview goes well, he'll have two to consider. Sunday evening, he double-checks his flight times for the following day, and for the first time thinks about what to wear for an interview.

"Shit." He only has one suit, and maybe four ties – although the term "used to own" seems more appropriate as two have disappeared over the past months. He notices that neither of his good white shirts are hanging in the closet. He looks around his bedroom and goes to his clean pile of clothes. Rummaging through them, he comes up with nothing. He walks to the other pile – the dirty ones that he is going to wash one of these days. Pushing aside a few on the top, he spots his quarry. He yanks it out as if the vertical effect will fix the wrinkles. The stains on the front remind him of the reason it was in the pile to begin with. Digging some more he pulls out the other white shirt, but after a comparison review, he lays the latter one back on the heap. He contemplates washing the one he is holding and then ironing it. Walking to his closet he picks out a blue plaid shirt with a button-

6

down collar. He holds a solid blue tie up to it. His eyes dart from one shirt to the other. Finally, he tosses the white shirt back on the pile.

He flies to Denver the next day, and the interview goes well with him asking only the two questions he had written down – money and length of time commitment. Those are answered quickly, but the interviewers keep steering him to talk about how he gets along with others – actually they never come right out and ask overtly by using those exact words, but rather more subtly with questions like, "So tell us about your childhood friends," or "When you were doing research for your PhD, did you work closely with deans and classmates?"

They tell him they will get back to him soon, and he tells them that he has another job offer to which he has committed to providing an answer within another few days.

"William, it just doesn't work that fast here. The best I can say is that maybe in a month you'll hear from us. We hope you can wait for us to get back with you, but if you feel you have to take the other job, then we certainly understand." They depart with a handshake and William returns to his hotel. His flight isn't until the following morning, so he grabs a cab and heads to downtown Denver. He wanders a few streets before deciding on a bar bustling with a young crowd his own age. Noticing an empty seat at the bar, he sits down and orders a local beer. He looks around the room at the mingling people, and wonders if beer is even allowed at the South Pole? He sips his beer, then has another along with a Denver Devil sandwich that the bartender recommended. William takes a cab back to his hotel, and that night tosses and turns as he evaluates his work options. "Better for my career," he mumbles as he stares at the blinking red smoke detector light. "Yup, the oil company it is."

Still, something keeps drawing him back to how adventurous it would be to actually get paid to stay at the South Pole for two years. Then he laughs thinking about how even though he tried to enjoy a night out in Denver after his interview, he wasn't a nightlife type of guy – so what does this say for his actual sense of adventure?

Right on schedule and as promised, the oil company calls and presents him with his offer. Earlier in the day FedEx arrived with a package whose contents read almost verbatim to what the personnel director was reading over the phone. William offers excuses about an illness in his family that is requiring his time, but that he appreciates their offer and promises to get back with them soon. A week later the oil company calls again, and William tells them he is too busy to talk at the moment, but that he will call them back. A day, then two, three, and another week goes by, and with every day, guilt builds for not returning their call. William sits in his small apartment staring at the generous offer laying in front of him. He looks at his bank account balance and shakes his head at the paltry $1,832 balance. He can pay the rent in a few days, and then what? He knows that he needs to get on with his life. He decides that the following Monday he will accept the job offer from the oil company.

At 8:00 Saturday morning, his phone rings.

After introductions, the government person on the other end of the line says they were pleased with his interview and asks if he wants the job working at McMurdo Station. William had stayed up late the previous night at Pete's drinking coffee and talking with his old friends from campus, thereby contributing to the lack of clarity of the words being heard.

"Sorry, who is this again?" he asks. The man introduces himself again and reminds William of the interview in Denver. "Yes, yes I remember the meeting. I know you guys said you move slowly on these jobs things, but any idea as to when a decision can be made on your end?"

"William, a decision has been made. You're our guy. Ready to start?" came the reply. William takes in a deep breath, then time stops as his mind races.

"William – you still there?"

"Absolutely. Why not?" Pausing, "I meant that question to me – not you. Yes, I'll take the job."

"Great – I'll be back in touch soon. Enjoy your Saturday. Goodbye for now."

William looks at the clock, then falls back on his bed. "What the fuck did I just commit to?" he says out loud.

He starts thinking about all of the stuff he has to buy to live at the South Pole. It is sinking in that, yes, he is actually going where it is cold not just some months, but every month. He goes to several sporting goods stores and checks out their parkas and boots and makes notes on their cost and more importantly their descriptions such as "Good to 20 degrees." He laughs at those labels as he figures that twenty degrees will be on a warm day.

The following Monday another FedEx package arrives, but this one brings the government letter showing a very respectable salary and giving him his itinerary and plane tickets from Houston, Texas, to Ushuaia, Argentina. Studying the letter more closely, he sees that once there, he will be given all the necessary garments, and he will spend two weeks of intensive "pre-acclimation" – described as a seminar on what to expect for toilets, food, entertainment, medical emergencies, sex, and in general what life is like at literally the end of the Earth. William sinks back into his chair and looks out the window. The parking lot below is full of colorful cars and trucks of all makes and, as far as he can see, there are scruffy little houses that owners have rented to students for the last forty years, and with a little paint and even smaller repairs, they continue to be rented to the unsuspecting students. Randomly intermixed are new brick apartments where he always figured the wealthy students lived. He wonders what it would all look like covered in nothing but snow and walking between them in a spacesuit type of parka. He studies the letter once more, then picks up his phone and dials the personnel guy at the oil company who answers, "Hello – Thomas here."

"Thomas, this is William Moore. I received a job offer from the company, and I apologize for not getting back to you sooner. I appreciate the generous offer, but I have to decline. I've decided to take a couple of years to do some research."

"William, thank you for your call. We wish you the best, and at the end of your research, keep in contact and I will let you know if we might have any openings then. The best to you."

"And to you too, Thomas. Bye." William feels confident in his decision, even though his stomach is in knots understanding what he just turned down and not knowing what lies ahead.

A month later he has returned his apartment to his landlord, said goodbye to his friends with a promise to send pictures from the South Pole, and has boarded his flight to Argentina – his jumping-off point before flying on to Antarctica. His connections take him to via Santiago, Chile, then to Punta Arenas, Peru, where a small commuter, two-engine prop plane takes him the rest of the way. The altitude is thinner than what he is used to, and even though he considers himself in good shape, he can tell his breathing is a little shallow. The flights are grueling just from the time spent in airports, in airline seats, and dealing with customs agents. He understands "Pasaporte, por favor" – which is enough to get him from plane to plane.

The Last Breath

William looks out of the plane window and sees only a smattering of lights flickering across miles of country. Every now and then, with the aid of a few cars' headlights, William makes out a highway that snakes around the mountains. The plane turns and William sees an airport blazing with runway lights. Gradually, the engines are throttled back and the plane lines up to land. The touchdown is smooth – a testament to these pilots' skills from flying through valleys and around mountains. Considering the distance travelled and flights he has had to connect to, his arrival time into Argentina is only a little over two hours late.

Gathering his bags, he watches other passengers head to a door marked "SALIR" and follows them. After presenting his passport, William finds himself in the open air. At the curb is a man holding a sign with William's name on it.

William waves to him, and with no words exchanged he gets in, trusting his driver to deliver him to wherever he is supposed to go. The hotel has his reservation, and the front desk clerk hands him his room key. Throwing his bags on the floor and giving his teeth an overdue and thorough brushing, he flops on the bed – which is so soft that it almost flops back at him. He laughs at the springiness of his mattress, pulls a blanket over his body, curls up, and falls asleep.

Awakening after some unknown hours, he looks at his watch. He has no idea what time it is locally, but the sun is shining brightly.

Walking downstairs, the man behind the desk is waving an envelope and yelling, "Señor Moore. Por favor."

William retrieves the envelope and utters "Gracias," one of the few Spanish words he knows, then walks outside into the fresh Argentinian air. The cold air surprises him, as he recalls it wasn't like this when he was at the airport. He ducks back inside and reads the note. It tells him where and when to meet and get his gear for his next stop – McMurdo Station.

Stepping outside again, he looks up and down the street to get his bearings, then back at the map included in the note. He fetches his jacket from his room, and as directed, walks west one block, then south for three more and finds himself at the address given to him. Inside, William shows a man his paperwork with a list of gear. The man nods and returns with parkas, gloves, hats, face masks, pants, and packages of specially insulated underwear that could theoretically keep someone alive at minus thirty degrees Fahrenheit for several hours according to the large print on labels attached to them – although on a small label behind the first one the issuers admit that no one has actually tried this. The gear is sized properly and stuffed into two large duffle bags that are handed to him. "What the fuck am I getting myself into?" races through his mind several times.

Carrying (but mostly dragging) the equipment back to the hotel, William heads up to his room and for several minutes sits on the edge of the bed staring at the bag of gear. He dumps out the contents of the bags. "Maybe they'll let me keep this when I leave – this stuff is worth a fortune," he thinks.

His growling stomach reminds him that he hasn't had a meal in many hours, so he grabs a quick meal in the hotel lobby dining area. After finishing his meal, he returns to his room and climbs back into bed.

When he wakes, a small lamp is on, and he looks around the room wondering how long he has slept. He looks at his watch out of habit, then pulls back the curtains. It is nighttime, and only a few streetlamps provide any sign of life. All is quiet. Is it three a.m.? Four? Five? He doesn't have a clue, except that the only thing he is one hundred percent certain of is that it is not daytime. His body clock tells him to be awake – his myopic existence in the lower forty-eight states has not prepared him for this thing called jet lag. He is tired, but he can't sleep. A look in the mirror after splashing cold water on his face focuses him on the coldness – not the drowsiness. A shave and a shower with tepid water awakens him even more. He turns on the TV, and stares at the characters speaking words he can't understand. He stares some more at it imagining what the plot is to this show. Turning on his laptop to catch up on world news, he lets out both a groan and laugh as he sees that there is no signal for an internet connection, so he turns to his packing.

As he stares at the packing he has to do, he again questions what he is doing. He's going into brutally cold conditions with none of his friends around, no going out on weekends and catching the latest movie, and confronting a fear of the unknown, among other things. With a sigh of acceptance, he rolls up the garments and stuffs them as tight as he can into two large duffle bags.

As he checks his watch, a small pickup pulls up right on time, and waits for him to throw his bags in the back. Jumping into the front seat, the driver starts the truck and deftly makes his way down the cobblestone streets. In a mile (maybe more, as the jarring from the road and the slow speed made the distance hard to judge) a runway appears. In front of a dilapidated building, which at one time could have been hangar, sits a two-prop plane and three helicopters that look like remnants of the Korean War. William's driver waves to a man sitting by the gate, and a small wooden gate is lifted to allow the truck through – no checking of credentials or inspecting the truck. As the truck proceeds to the plane, William makes out "United States Navy" stenciled in large white letters on the side of the plane.

As William gets out and unloads his baggage, a man and woman walk over to him. They introduce themselves as U.S. Navy officers. Everyone but the truck driver pitches in to throw the bags on board, and as soon as the woman gives him some U.S. money, he drives away.

"Yeah, they like Yankee dollars more than their pesos. Who knows, maybe they trade it to other travelers – not a clue. We just pay them, and they're happy."

The Navy man points to the waiting plane. "Time to go. Buckle up in any seat you find. You're our only guy today, so stretch your legs out and we'll keep you posted as we get airborne." Sticking his head into the body of the plane, William picks out a seat toward the middle of the plane. In a half-bent stance, he walks to it and sits back to look out the window at the mountains in the distance. The woman pulls up the back door, and while she secures it, the engines crank over. After some minutes of preflight checks and the noise of the engines increasing, the plane taxis to the end of the runway, makes a U-turn, and is airborne within less than a minute.

After over two hours in the air, William awakes from a nap to hear the motors slow. Almost like it's gliding, he can barely hear the engines running it seems, and the ground appears to be getting closer. Within five minutes the plane lands on an icy runway. In the near distance are a few houses – the only color added to a colorless world as far as he can see. That wasn't too bad, William thinks. And it doesn't look that terribly harsh. He stands up the best he can with the low ceiling height and starts for the door when the pilot hollers from the front, "Don't go too far. We're only here until they top off the tanks."

"Huh?" William asks.

"We have another three hours. There are some extra sandwiches up here – grab one if you get hungry. Forgot to tell you earlier."

William sits down like someone had just punched him the stomach. "Three more hours," he mumbles out loud. "Holy crap."

He looks out the window at the desolation and cranes his neck to look out the door's window on the opposite side – the view is the same. Who are these people that live in this godforsaken place? How in the fuck did they get fuel to fill up our plane? Was it fuel left over from WWII? William laughs again to himself, but he can only imagine what lay ahead if this was only half-way.

"Ready?" the pilot shouts as the other pilot closes the door and heads to the cockpit.

The engines rev higher, and within a few minutes of the pre-flight check, the plane heads out onto the snow and gains speeds. The bumpiness causes William to be slightly on edge, but the jostling disappears suddenly, and he relaxes into his seat. He opens up a book that he had tucked into his shoulder bag and gets absorbed in the story. He glances out the window every now and then, then back to the pages. The cycle repeats itself over the span of the flight.

Daily life

Acclimation to the way of life at what many call the end of the world comes quickly for William. Eight months of sometimes long days and even longer darkness goes by in spurts – some days are slow and boring, and some days are so full of excitement that he only sleeps a few hours before jumping back into the thick of experiments he is learning to do on his own. Just as he had been warned in a pre-briefing, personality differences make everything certainly much more interesting. Some people are easygoing, and some people need very little to push them into downright rudeness. William gets along with almost everyone, and he simply avoids or has little contact with the ones he knows he can't win over.

He has gotten used to everything, like taking two-minute showers, watching movies multiple times and still finding them entertaining, eating pretty much the same menu items week after week, and basically settling into a routine of life at the bottom of the world.

One of the things that William discovers is that there is cold as one might find on a ski slope in Colorado in January, and then there is super-cold – which happens here – consistently and almost constantly. Most of the time the temperature hovers around ten degrees Fahrenheit in the daytime – "balmy" for those accustomed to life here. Sometimes the temperature reaches a high of twenty degrees, but quickly settles back into the low single digits at night. Three days a month before he landed, the temperature had risen to over fifty degrees Fahrenheit – unheard of by anyone before. Then, the temperature returned to the usual coldness, and to this day no one can explain the temperature anomaly that occurred.

The relentless cold makes anyone adapt and learn. While some basic things can be taught, many things have to be learned on one's own, and those learned by failures, if survived, are the most important ones of all. A woman who had been there for over a year, and should have known better, got caught in a blizzard and either lost her grip on the routing lines that connect the buildings – or she simply lost track of where the line was. She was found within thirty minutes by a rescue team; the doctor said that within another five minutes, at most, her heart would have stopped. She recovered, but it is a lesson that everyone at the station will never forget.

William, when not doing analysis on the data he and the others have collected, learns to keep occupied doing something – anything – because boredom and aloneness here is a one-way path to disaster for anyone. Hours are spent reading and playing endless games of Monopoly with whomever is found in the game room. Everyone, it seems, has brought some sort of electronic gadget with games on it they could play by themselves, but those increase the isolation, and it usually doesn't take long for most to put those aside and enjoy the interaction of sitting down with others. As with games of any nature, someone tries to win, but here, few really care.

William lives in one of three huts, all of which are enclosed within a larger dome. To the person who designed this back in Washington, D.C., it must have made sense, but the reality is that cold easily penetrates all structures. No matter how many walls between his room and his hut doors, he never gets warm enough to walk around in sandals, shorts, and a t-shirt as he would prefer back in Texas.

Each hut holds a special function. Two huts hold, in addition to some bunking rooms, research labs, a hospital, a library, food services, or other common areas. He soon discovered that sleeping in long underwear and a t-shirt really does help stave off the cold when in bed. Another thing not taught was how one's body clock functions – or ceases to function. Waking up from sleep, his clock reads four a.m., although time has little relevance in August this far south. People work all kinds of strange hours, and the sun (too much at times and too little at others) plays havoc with everyone's circadian sleep patterns.

He has settled into life here, and as he glances at his calendar to see his two-year end date, he is startled by a muffled boom. It wasn't loud, but yet it was, well, different from the creaks and doors shutting that he had gotten used to. Hearing something like this in any major city would be ignored, but not here. Everyone comes to know every sound that should happen, and this sound was not ordinary. He puts on his shoes, insulated bibs, and jacket, and hurries down the hallway where other people are gathered in similar attire.

"What the hell was that?" he asks to no one in particular as he approaches them.

"Beats the shit out of me, eh," said his friend, Bob, a Canadian who thought that he needed a temporary change in his life but is now in his fifth year here.

Someone at the front opens the door that leads out into the large covered area, and men (or what appear to be men, but in reality could be any gender since the bulky clothes do a great job of hiding all hint of gender) are seen running toward the back of the facility. A startled, but not quite panicked, look comes over those in the hallway, as they all can quickly guess what has happened – the large system that provides heat to the building has a problem. William, Bob, and the others know they can offer little help, as the people heading to the massive heating system are maintenance specialists. In William's first few days at the station, he (along with every new person who has ever arrived there) was given the basics of how to repair something in case a primary person was incapacitated or could not be found quickly. William had also been told that without heat, the life expectancy of a person could be less than twenty-four hours in a winter month. Everyone standing with William knows instinctively that people are feverishly trying to get the massive heating machine back in working order, and unless requested by someone working on the furnace, all they can do is wait.

The hallway door has two small windows in it, and everyone cranes his or her neck to see any signs of the repair people returning. Everyone has an issued radio, but only one person picked hers up to listen for any chatter from the maintenance crew.

Twenty minutes go by, and all can feel the temperature start to creep lower. "Should we go help?" someone asks. Before anyone can answer, a voice from the radio crackles, "We got this antique pile of crap fixed. Spread the word in case anyone is excited or worrying their frozen brain over it."

William and the others have a nervous laugh and breathe a silent sigh of relief while mumbling, "Good job," as they disperse and head back to their rooms. The door opens and Earl, who works as the maintenance lead, sticks his head in.

"I saw you all standing here," he hollers down the hallway. "Fucking oil line froze up, and it caused the fucking burners to stop. Contraction of the hot metal caused the noise, thank god, or we might have missed this until we all froze in our fucking beds. We replaced the fucking valve – it shouldn't have stuck. Just too fucking cold, I guess. Oh well – shit happens. It'll warm back up for you in a little while."

"Thanks, Earl, for the fucking update," Bob says with a laugh.

"Sure, that's my job – fixing this twenty-year-old equipment that should have been replaced nineteen fucking years ago."

William returns to his room and since his adrenalin is running higher than usual, he turns to his laptop and opens up the current data logs that had been transmitted from the environmental sensors this station was responsible for monitoring and maintaining. He had meant to look at the logs earlier but got busy with several hands of cribbage and set the work aside. It was boring going through them, so he had not been in a hurry to do a manual analysis of them, as this was usually an easy task done by computers. William, though, wants to make sure the calibration and algorithms are correct, so a manual inspection of the data is the only way to make sure things are functioning as needed. Sensors had been placed at various sites within five miles of McMurdo Station, and part of William's duties is to make sure they are alive and sending data. His primary job, though, is to gather the data once it is received and to make sure it is properly formatted as it's logged into the collection server. The last step in his duties is to fill out a form and send it to his supervisor that all is well with the sensors. He wants more responsibility to run more analysis on the data, but so far, has been told, "We'll get you more comfortable with the base operations first." This frustrates William, as it sounds like a parent saying to a child, "When you're older, we'll tell you more."

On his own, William has started to study the reported data by himself, and not rely on the computer to run its preprogrammed analysis. As William looks at the latest download, the pollutants parts per million (known to everyone working with these sensors as simply PPM) seem high, but the reports being generated indicate they are lower. Before he can make any judgment as to what is causing this discrepancy, he has to pull up data from years past. With a few keystrokes on his laptop, he goes poking around database files looking for the information he wants, and locating the data, he starts comparing older sensor readings and graphs to the current readings. Looking closely at the screen, he sits back in his chair and scratches his head.

"This can't be. It's six times what it was last year." He studies the screen again. "I must be doing something wrong," he mumbles as he types an email to his supervisor asking him to meet tomorrow after lunch. William folds up the laptop, crawls under his blanket for those extra degrees of warmth, and within minutes, he is dozing and snoring soundly – much to the chagrin of those in the rooms in the near vicinity.

Awakening when his alarm alerts him to 8 a.m., he stumbles out the door to the common bathroom and throws water on his face. He looks in the mirror and thinks about shaving, but shrugs that it can wait another month. At the canteen where everyone congregates for food several times a day, he spots his supervisor, Chris.

"Did you get my email?" William asks.

"Yes. Now regarding your message, I think you did one of your analyses incorrectly – that's the only explanation, as those monitors have performed flawlessly given the cold. I suppose one could be flaky, but not all of them. I was told they could withstand down to minus one hundred fifty degrees Fahrenheit. I'll look into it, though. Come on, let's have some of that great Australian soup made out of kangaroo or whatever they claim is meat."

"Had some – it wasn't bad. I heard a fresh load of veggies and meat is coming in overland next week. About time. Back to those numbers just a minute, though. Probably a malfunctioning sensor throwing things off. Want me to take a look at it?"

Chris replied, "Not in this weather, you're not. Just before you got here, we had a guy walk no more than two hundred yards from the main building. Still not sure what happened. His hand was clenched tight around the guide rope when they found him frozen to death. Maybe he just gave up. Too cold to go on. No one knows. Shame, though. You should have seen his face. It was so shriveled and brown you would have thought he had been out there for months."

"Yeah, the welcoming committee told me that story. And about ten others. I think they wanted to scare me – and it worked! I got their message straightaway."

"We'll go out in a couple of months when the temperature reaches a more comfortable temperature."

"You don't have to convince me – it can wait," William concluded.

Over the next weeks, William carefully looks at the daily collected data Chris provides him, and like a hound dog on a trail that won't give up his prey, he keeps running his own analysis on the data – and still the PPM is consistently showing a six-fold increase from the previous years. He wants to ignore it, but his scientific curiosity is getting the better of him. And each time he broaches the topic with his supervisor, he is told to focus on something else – that in time they will figure out what is going on with one or more of the sensors.

Each sensor keeps raw data in its memory in addition to transmitting it. If the memory agrees with the received transmission, then the sensor is obviously bad. If, on the other hand, the memory conflicts with the received data, then the problem lies elsewhere. It could be something as simple as the receiver scrambling the data, the sender being buggy, and myriad other technical and electronic problems. The data is certainly an anomaly and the answer has to be somewhere. Given William's engineering and analytical mind, it is just a matter of tracking it all down to the source causing the problem. As William walks over to the library to pick out a book to read, he spots Earl.

Earl is a guy that most ignore, mostly because Earl ignores you first. Earl has been at the station for more than five years and has found his niche – mainly he fixes things – like when the furnace chooses to stop running in the middle of the might. For all of Earl's quirks, though, everyone stays warm, has fresh water, and the electricity works.

"Hey, Earl, want to give me a hand with something?" William asks tentatively, as Earl is known to be quite the rough individual if he doesn't want to take the time to deal with you.

"What?" Earl replies tersely as if even the words annoyed him, let alone someone daring to ask him for help.

William continues, "I need to check some sensors. Maybe just one – just to calibrate it and make sure it's okay."

"Dr. Moore, do you know how fucking dangerous it is out there?"

"Yup. But I really need to replace a sensor. It's driving me bonkers. It's giving us bad readings, and I have to see what's up with it. Every time I tell Chris the data seems to be bad, he tells me to 'wait'. Look, I've got nothing to do until I verify if a sensor is weird or not. Come on…we'll be out there and back before anyone knows we left. It'll be an adventure."

Earl looks William in the eye and can't figure out if William is fucking with him or is serious.

"Are you sure you want to do this?"

"Yes, man! One of the sensors is driving me nuts."

Earl stares at him for a few seconds while neither one says anything. "Fuck, why not. We can take two snow cats, but I don't go anywhere outside the dome without a backup plan. Can you drive one?" Earl asks.

"Yeah, they gave us instructions, plus I drove one a little last fall. I'll be fine. I'll just follow you. I'll give you the GPS coordinates."

"You scientists think everything is fucking easy out there – well, it isn't. There's no such thing as 'out and back before you know it.' Damn, didn't they tell you that?" He pauses, then grins. "When do you want to go?"

"How about tomorrow?"

"How far is this sensor?" Earl asks.

"Max five miles – I think – or close to it. I have the exact coordinates."

Earl stares at William for a moment. "Five miles? You've been here too long already – you're crazy." Then he grins again. "Be at the snow cat shed at ten a.m. It's going to be an all-day drive there and back, so bring a snack. What can they do? Fire me?" He laughs.

William smiles and says, "See you then – thanks."

Back in the lab, William picks out a brand-new, still-in-the-box, model 78431-AMS sensor.

The next morning, William has the replacement sensor packed, along with a new battery, in his backpack. He hasn't totally ignored telling his supervisor of his plan, but on the other hand he has not gone out of the way to tell him what he is up to. He has checked and double-checked that it is in perfect working condition. He puts on his two pairs of mittens and cold-weather layers of parkas and face masks, then meets Earl at the agreed-on place. Earl already has two snow cats running.

"Ready?" Earl asks.

"Yup. I've got everything I need. I've plugged in the coordinates to the sensor. Here – the GPS is all yours. You lead, and I'll be right behind," William replies as he jumps into his snow cat and gets accustomed to the controls. It's warm from the heater blowing full blast, so he takes off his gloves to feel the knobs and switches better.

A small door to the side of the large main door goes up, and slowly they pull away from their home. Once both are clear of the door, the safety of the station shuts behind them. William knows that his life is in Earl's hands and feels his heart race as he sets out into the white.

During his whole time at the station William has stayed within sight of the main buildings, and this is the first time he will have ventured so far that the station will not be a point of reference. His mind drifts to what it must be like to take a spacewalk away from the security and comfort of a spaceship, and the fear in the astronauts as they take the first step. This is what it is like for him as the buildings become a blur and the tracks of their machines kick up snow behind him. Focusing once again on Earl, he feels his breathing calm and looks all around him to see the absolute serenity of Antarctica. The landscape is as if a white sheet has been laid upon the landscape. He thinks of how he will describe it when he talks to his friends back in the States.

"What will I say? Peaceful, quiet, white, boring?" The hum of the snow cat makes him laugh at the term "quiet." But it is quiet here – no cars, no people, no jets overhead, and no barking dogs.

Even though his watch reads 10:45 a.m., the light they had when they took off has slowly dimmed and faded to darkness. The only light they have now is from their snow cats' headlights. The going is slow; snow cats only have a top speed of about five mph in good conditions – and Earl is not one to take chances. William would honk the horn to make him speed up, but he knows that the snow cats have no such device, and even if they did and he honked it, Earl would probably stop and come back to rip the horn from the dash. Biding his time and glancing at the controls, William settles in watching the reflection of his headlights on the back of Earl's snow cat.

The little convoy takes over an hour more to reach the coordinates where the sensor should be. The headlights only light up a narrowly focused area extending no more than about fifty feet. In perfect conditions, a sensor – although on a tall platform and painted bright red to conflict with the background – can be difficult to spot simply because of its size compared to the overall vastness. Now, though, the snow is blowing, and he knows that it won't be easy to find right away.

Earl knows the sensor should be in sight if the GPS coordinates were accurate, so he slows his machine even more and makes it turn by holding one track steady. William slows also and tries to stay about twenty feet behind so he can see what is going on. Fifteen minutes pass as Earl slowly scans the landscape looking for the elusive sensor. William sits in his idling snow cat waiting to see what Earl tells him to do next.

"Found it, college boy. Ain't nothing but fucking white. Do you see it?" breaks the silence, startling William from the near trance he was in watching the snow and feeling the warmth from the small heater.

"Where? I can't see it," William answers. "Shit, I hope you didn't run over it."

"Very funny," Earl snarls.

Earl puts his foot on the right brake and gives the snow cat gas to increase the engine speed. Slowly, the snow cat rotates to the right with the left track providing the momentum.

"There – see it?" Earl hollers into the radio. William turns his snow cat in the direction of Earl's headlights and goes slowly forward until he is within fifteen feet of the sensor.

"Yup – I got it."

He puts on his gloves, picks up the backpack, and opens the door. Too late he realizes that he hadn't pulled up his face mask. A body will automatically react to danger by throwing its resources to protect that part or a vital organ like the brain or heart. The frigid air is so cold that his lungs seem to have shut down while blocking out the frigid cold. William can't breathe, and he coughs hard several times in an attempt to clear his airway. He turns away from the wind and grabs over and over for his face mask with his mittened hands. With a desperate yank he pulls the mask up so that his eyes are the only exposed part of this face. He gulps for air. His lungs react slowly as warmer air is allowed in. Calming himself down, he turns back into the wind and makes his way toward the sensor over the crunchy snow. Reaching the unit, he undoes its latch, and replaces it with the new sensor and battery pack. He hits the "on" switch, watches it start to blink to

31

acknowledge being alive, and returns as fast as he can with the old sensor to the protection of the snow-cat cab.

"Earl, I've got it. Let's head back – or as you would say, 'It's fuckin' cold out here.' I'm right behind you."

"On my way, college boy," Earl says as he plugs in the base camp's coordinates and rotates his snow cat in the right direction.

The relentless wind has covered the tracks laid down on their way out, so going back won't be quite as easy as Earl had hoped. Still, as long as satellites fly and communicate to his GPS, he knows he can find his way back. Visibility is now less than five feet, and Earl finds himself gripping the controls hard in response to the stress of keeping an eye on the GPS and watching the gauges of the snow cat. Feeling his hands go slightly numb, he lets go of the steering handles and eases his foot from the gas pedal to make himself relax. In that fraction of a moment, he forgets that William is close behind him. A snow cat cannot coast like a car, but rather it slows abruptly. William's mind is on the sensor analysis to be done, and before it can register that Earl has come to a stop, his snow cat's treads start to climb over Earl's vehicle.

The sounds of metal on metal startle both drivers and, before William can put on the brakes, he is wedged at a 30-degree incline over Earl's vehicle, pushing it deep into the powdery snow. William puts the snow cat in reverse and attempts to back off, but all this is doing is driving his snow cat deep into the snow at an angle and denting the hell out of Earl's snow cat.

32

"Get the fuck off of me!" Earl screams into radio. "You break my window and I'm dead!"

William pulls on the brake levers as hard as he can. Earl tries to move forward, but with the added weight of William's snow cat on his, he doesn't have enough power to pull them both. Instinctively, Earl gets on the radio and tries to raise someone at McMurdo – nothing but static.

"Are you okay back there?" Earl asks.

"I'm fine. I wasn't paying attention – let's leave it at that." Pausing, William continues in a calm but apprehensive voice, "What do we do now?"

"Well, we either get them going or we die. I prefer we get them going." Earl pauses and looks over his shoulder at William's snow cat perched on the back of his. "Don't do anything – let me do the driving."

Earl pushes on the left brake pedal while at simultaneously pushing on the throttle. His snow cat groans under the weight of the extra snow cat, but slowly it turns. Finally, he rotates his vehicle enough so that William's snow cat is now only hanging on by the left tread. As Earl continues to rotate his snow cat, William's snow cat comes loose. William is jarred as the snow cat drops, but because of the twisting angle, his snow cat falls on its side. Earl swings around to see the undercarriage of William's snow cat.

"You got your radio?" Earl screams over the noise of his engine. Nothing. "Hey moron, you okay?" Nothing. "Shit," Earl mutters to himself.

He is about to get out and head to William's overturned snow cat when he sees a door flop back, and then William is pulling himself out. William reaches back inside to grab the sensor. In an ungraceful rolling maneuver, he falls backward, expecting to land on his back in nothing but soft snow. Unfortunately, William's left pants leg catches on one of the treads. Instead of falling as planned, he plunges headfirst into the crusty snow, and his head takes the brunt of the fall. The dive isn't but a few feet, but the fall still makes him groggy. He grabs his neck by reflex, but at the same time feels a brutal stinging in his leg.

"Shit, did I break it?" he wonders.

He looks down through the howling and blowing wind and can't make out what is hurting. By instinct and from fear of freezing, he stands up to make a dash for the other snow cat. Both legs hold him upright, which actually surprises him, as he knows from the pain that a bone must be fractured. Through the blowing snow he sees the cause of the pain – his naked skin is exposed from a large gash in his parka and through his long underwear. He tries to gather the material and hold it shut, but it's difficult while trying to hold on to the sensor. He struggles to Earl's snow cat, opens the door, and pulls himself inside.

"My god, it's cold out there," he yells as the howling wind blows the door shut behind him. "And my leg! Will I get frostbite and have to have it amputated?"

Instead of sympathy, the first thing William hears is Earl howling in laughter. When Earl assesses the situation and sees that, indeed, William will live through the ordeal, he finally says, "No, you'll be fine. The only thing that should be amputated is your head."

After a shared laugh, Earl checks the GPS once more, and revs up for home base. William is relieved that his leg will be fine, and he has the satisfaction of knowing that the old sensor is secure on his lap.

"I'm glad I could lighten up your night with some humor. Sorry about the snow cat. I was staying too close – I didn't want to lose you."

"Put your leg next to the heater, college boy. As for the snow cat, hell, that's all it is – a fucking snow cat. It'll be here tomorrow, don't worry about it. Granted, it might be under ten fucking feet of snow, but we'll find it. Let's get back before something happens to this one, and then we're really fucked."

Almost three hours have gone by since they left the protection of the dome, and others are about to send out a search party when they see the lights of a lone snow cat approach. Earl hits the button to open the snow cat garage door, pulls in quickly, and shuts the door behind him so the little warmth inside will not dissipate so quickly.

"Okay, doc – I hope it was worth it."

"We'll see. Thanks for the ride." William steps out into the safety of the cavernous dome and turns to say thanks once more to his driver, but Earl is already driving away to put the snow cat to bed.

William walks to his room and throws off his parka. Settling in with his precious sensor, he connects an interface cable to it and turns it on. He stares at the marvelous engineering that allowed it to function in the coldest air on Earth and now in the relative warmth of his lab.

"Why can't they build cars this way?" he muses.

The sensor makes no noise, and the only way William can tell it has powered up is by the blinking red light on top. From his computer keyboard he types in commands that cause the sensor to start downloading data that it has stored for the past thirty days. His eyes are tired from the stress he just experienced, his neck still aches, and his leg has a small scratch. One part of him wants to go the First Aid station, but another part of him says it will be fine. He rubs his leg and returns to watching as his computer counts the number of bits; the number grows as the data is transferred from the sensor to the computer's hard drive. He has trouble focusing, and he wants to be doubly sure that his work is one hundred percent accurate. He walks over to his bed, and lies back, thinking about the past few hours. Remembering that Earl's calmness out in the snow probably saved his life, he looks down at his shaking hands and realizes how close he came to a serious injury or even death. He slows his breathing and closes his eyes.

For the next six hours William sleeps restlessly, dreaming of freezing to death or being left all alone at the station. He awakes unrested and is anxious to see what the sensor downloaded. William gathers up his laptop and walks down the chilly hallway to the lab room.

"Good morning, Dr. Chris," William calls out as he enters the room.

"Good morning to you, Dr. William. I heard you had a little scare last evening. So, tell me…you okay?"

"Yeah, still unthawing though. Holy shit, it sucks out there. If I ever suggest doing that again, just hit me over the head with something to make me come to my senses."

"A person can die out there in an instant. I told you we could get those sensors later when the temperature warmed a bit – no need for the rush. Why did you go against my request to wait?"

William replied, "Sorry, Chris. Yeah, I should have listened. You were busy, I was bored, and I thought it would be a short drive – out and back. Gave me something to do – the weird data was driving me crazy."

Chris continued, "Look, no one gets fired here. You are my responsibility, that's all I'm saying. When people do silly stuff, we just reduce their work and give them less to do – and it can get real boring real fast. You're a smart guy, William – just don't do something that stupid again. We have everything running nice and tidy here, and we can figure out stuff without putting ourselves in unnecessary risks." He pauses to read William's reactions, then asks, "I assume you got what you were after?"

William nods and says, "It probably wasn't worth it, but here's the sensor I was after."

"Have you had a chance to look at the data? If so, let's see what it tells us."

William plugs in his laptop to a central computer and transfers the sensor data to it. Chris opens up the new data along with the data gathered from all sensors for the past year, and a graph is displayed representing all of the data on one sheet. The PPM for all sensors except one shows a flat line, with an occasion blip that returns to a straight line again. The exception is the data that William had retrieved last evening. This data reports significantly higher PPM than the other data.

"That's strange," William says as he points to the screen to draw Chris' attention to it.

Chris replies, "Very strange. But surely that can't be right. Look at the other numbers. Why are they completely flat-lined at one-third of this silly sensor? That's just crazy. That is one odd sensor, that's for sure."

"Chris, we've eliminated any other contamination and corruption that could be happening. If these numbers are correct, this could mean that all kinds of particles are being detected. But why? Shit, the ozone must be going crazy over us," William says.

Stopping to realize the stupidity of his own questions, he continues, "Either the magnetic poles are increasing their strength somehow, or the pollutants are simply... out of the norm. Obviously, the magnetic attractiveness is not increasing, so that leaves only one thing– but where could these added pollutants be coming from all of a sudden?"

"It could just be a calibration problem with the sensor," Chris replies. "You said you had eliminated all other contamination factors, but I disagree. Let me get the specs on it and do some testing. I'll also write up a report and email it to Dr. MacLean back at his lab in the States. He's the state's "go-to guy" for all atmospheric data capture and analysis. He has years of sensor data not only from here, but also from other places, at his fingertips. He can get to the bottom of this. I have a suspicion, though, that it's still a sensor problem somewhere – they do go bad, especially when exposed to minus twenty degrees or more for weeks and months on end. But, even assuming it is correct, this doesn't explain why the other sensors are reporting nothing out of the ordinary. It just doesn't make sense. I'll keep you posted."

"It's all yours. Let me know what the other guy says, please. I'll be glad to check out the sensor if you want. Hell, after thawing

I'm ready to go back out and get another one if you think it will help."

"No, no, that's okay. You've enough excitement for a while. I'm sure Earl is back out there trying to get the cat on its feet and back to base. Plus, playing with the data will give me something to do. You can do something for me, though. I'm swamped with other analysis I'm trying to get done – would you mind writing up the findings and emailing them to me? I'll forward them and copy you."

"Sure, Chris, I'll be glad to do that. I'll stick around now – might as well do it while my mind is on it. It'll be short and to the point – is that okay?"

"Certainly, William. The more to the point, the easier reading by everyone."

William continues his analysis into the next day, only stopping sporadically to rest his eyes and for a quick snack. When the analysis is completed, he sends the email as requested. The next day, Dr. Chris Walker forwards the email to Dr. Bob MacLean at his university in the middle of Texas along with a message: "Call me."

"Call me" was a code between Dr. Walker and Dr. MacLean that meant exactly that – do not send a reply email, but instead pick up the phone and call the private satellite phone located in Dr. Walker's room.

William spends time in the rec room where he once was just another scientist putting in his time – but now he has stories with which to regale anyone who wants to listen. "We almost died out there!" is his answer to the simplest of questions about his trip to the sensor. He feels like he has passed some initiation to the McMurdo club – an imaginary circle of people who have adventures under their belt. His confidence in his abilities to survive at the station has exceeded what he first thought he could do when he first contemplated taking this job.

Back in the quiet of his room, he grabs a book from a shelf, lies back on his bunk and starts reading while letting the words on the pages take him far away from the cold outside and the reality of the humdrum daily routine.

Fifty yards and many walls away, a satellite phone rings. "Hello – Chris here. Is that you, Bob?"

"Yes. Good to hear from you. What's the urgency?"

"You haven't had a chance to look at the report I sent, I'm sure, but when you do, you'll see some new findings by a new scientist we brought on board. It's the typical stuff that we've seen before."

"I'll take care of it," Dr. MacLean replies without a pause. "Thanks for the heads-up on this. We've got a funding issue here at the university that I'm dealing with, plus I'm sure you would like new equipment down there. I'm working on getting that for you, and I'm going to put in a nice raise for you along with my proposal. Don't let this data or that new guy worry you. All that extra PPM in the air will settle down. The drilling will stop and the fracking or whatever they are doing will be over. Hell, I know for a fact it's winding down. Look, the poles are just pulling this in, that's all – its nature's big-ass vacuum cleaner. Hell, you know that."

Chris interjects, "Did you see the latest satellite data from the poles? They show the holes are huge, and we can't hide this data too much longer – people are going to start questioning what we have been reporting when they start doing their own analysis. Right now, they take our word for this, but..."

"Chris, Chris, relax. I said I'd take care of it. Maybe their analysis was flawed? Whose word are they going to take? We have the data to show what we want it to say. And what if the ozone holes are a little bigger. History is the key – they will fill back in over time. Have you ever seen it when they didn't? What's the worst that could happen? The ice caps completely melt?" Bob laughs into the phone. "It ain't gonna happen. And what if they did melt some? Those bleeding hearts who want their cars and air conditioning while complaining about the ozone had better tighten up their sphincters and learn to live with it. They can't have it both ways. Have you seen any signs of melting other than a normal floe or two breaking away?"

"Not really, but it is winter here and damn cold."

"So, it's cold, huh? No global warming? I think we're fine, Chris."

Silence.

"Chris? Still there?"

"Yeah, just thinking about what you said. I'm fine. I'm okay with this. Just don't ask me to continue this much longer. I will keep watching the real data, though. If things go worse, we'll need to talk. And thanks again for the funding. And I didn't miss what you said about my raise – thanks very much for that too. Good talking to you, Bob. Remember, I've only got six more months in this hell hole, so don't forget you owe me. Keep a spot open for me back in your department."

"You're number one on my list. I'll scrub this data, so it'll look like the old data. It's all under control, and you can tell your new scientist buddy that the U.S. Government is investigating it. Take care, Chris." Silence fills the earpiece.

Chris pauses and looks at the phone. "Yeah, good talking to you too, Bob."

Chris thinks about the challenges he has had to endure, and the experiences he has had with his work. But he knows that when his contract is up, his loyalty to his buddy back in the U.S. will reward him with a nice job where it's much, much warmer.

William has learned to sleep when he is tired and not according to any clock time. He remembers his first day at the station and asking someone what time it was. The person laughed and said, "Watch me." The man slowly turned in a circle and counted off 1 to 24, then said, "There, all 24 hours and time zones were just accounted for. We do have a clock that people set their watches by, but it's up to you to set your own internal clock to whatever you want – we are at zero o'clock here. Well, not really, I suppose – that's only true at the exact South Pole position. But we're close enough that people just ignore most clocks and go about their business without paying too much attention to them."

William is tired but can't sleep. Something is troubling him about the sensor data. He gets dressed and puts on a parka. He looks at his watch – 4 a.m. He could take his normal circuitous route down hallways that will eventually lead him to the lab room, but instead decides to take a more direct route by cutting across the open-air, but enclosed, part of the complex. He opens the door to the cavernous dome and closes it quickly behind him. A huge temperature gauge reads fifteen degrees. He quickens his pace to the entrance of a hut across the cold expanse. He reaches the door and tugs on it, but it doesn't budge. Shit, he thinks – is it locked? For just a brief moment he thinks about his snow cat episode and how close he came to freezing. He tugs again. Nothing. He gives it one more tug, and it opens. He makes a mental note to tell Earl to look into fixing this, but his mind is focused on what he wants to work on in the lab.

He likes being in the lab for quite a few reasons – primarily that it gives him a focus on something to do rather than wander about the area meeting the same people and playing yet another game of Scrabble. A side benefit of working in the lab, though, is the heat. Computer chips generate heat, and their cooling fans circulate that heat throughout the room. It's not hot, but a toasty sixty degrees is always warmer than almost all parts of the other enclosures. He makes himself comfortable in front of a screen and logs on to the system. He wants to poke around the sensor data more – both past and present – and he has nothing but time.

"Now, what's going on?" he mumbles to himself. All sensor data should be unsecured, as all data is only analyzed by one of two people – himself and his supervisor. He finds it strange that some files are secured so that he can't access them. He makes a note of the file names along with a heading 'Discuss with Chris.' He enters a command to read the new sensor data and waits. From this room, a command is sent to a computer somewhere in New Zealand, then to another computer somewhere in the United States, and onward to a satellite uplink also in the United States, where it is intercepted by one of many orbiting satellites set aside for government work. The message, or more precisely a command, is then sent to the sensor telling it to send its data to the requester. The sensor eventually acknowledges this request, and proceeds to upload data that it has collected for the past thirty days. All of this could take thirty minutes to an hour, because once the data begins transmitting, it is bundled and finally presented to William as one huge file. William has done this many times in the past, so he knows it will take some time for the data transfer to occur. He grabs a book off a shelf, looks for a bookmark he had stuck in it sometime before and, as he waits, starts reading.

He dozes off, and wakes to a beep from the computer announcing a message for him. He looks at the screen, which says: "File cannot be transmitted."

"Shit!" he yells. Laying down the book, he enters the command again telling the sensor to transmit its data. He picks up his book once again. Thirty minutes later, the computer once again beeps with the same message.

"Goddamn you, sensors – all you do is cause me grief!" He thinks about whether he turned on the sensor correctly, and the thought of travelling back again to the sensor is not something he relishes. He is in no mood to spend another hour trying to get the sensor data, so instead he sends an email to Chris asking him to see if can retrieve the data for him. He puts the bookmark back into the book and places the book back on the shelf. Wide awake now with his mind full of ideas, William puts on his parka and wanders over to the diner shed where, although it is open twenty-four hours a day, meals are officially prepared and served three times a day. People work odd hours at the station, plus some people never get on the same awake schedule with others no matter how hard they try. Instead, everyone leaves their sleep/awake times to adjust themselves as best they can. In William's case, he has pretty much adjusted to a regular schedule when most are awake, but on nights like this, he can usually find someone in the lounge to talk with, or simply play a computer game by himself.

The meal room is empty of others, but as always, coffee, pastries, and fruit are there for anyone to consume. He sits at one of the tables after making himself a cup of Earl Grey, lays his head on his arms, and falls asleep. He doesn't know how long he has slept as the chatter of others about the room rouse him. William looks at the clock. He rubs his eyes, and looks at the cold cup of tea, then pours it out, makes himself a new one, and walks back over to the computer lab.

Chris is sitting next to computer screen when he hears William open the door.

"William – good morning. Working late, I see. I got your email, and tried dumping the sensor data when I came in. Guess what? All is good. Must have been a satellite or server problem somewhere. I've got it in a file ready for you to analyze. I'm going for breakfast – want to join me?"

"No thanks – I'm not that hungry at the moment."

"Come on, William – we need to chat anyway – we've both been busy and there's nothing like good conversation over a plate of fake eggs and potatoes. The data can wait – it will always be here for you when you're ready to jump into it."

"Pretend eggs it is. Or is it 'are'? Never mind – I'm right behind you."

As both settle with their plates of food, William moves the grub from one side to another. He takes a bite, then moves the food around some more.

"William, everything alright? I mean, not with this sensor stuff, but life in general. We don't get a chance to talk very much, but let's face it – about ninety percent of the people aren't really sociable anyway – that's why they're here, I suppose. I remember reading your profile and interview notes. As I seem to recall on your application, you wrote, 'I have never been to Antarctica and this is a great opportunity to visit there and get paid' – or something like that."

William laughs and says, "Yeah, that's about it."

"So, how are you finding life here at the bottom of the world?"

"Well, a bit challenging at times. Let's see – where do I start? Lack of plumbing that works all the time. Being able to lie on a deck outside staring up at the stars and not dying within two minutes. Hmm, and no one told me about body odor. I can go on, but let's just say it's been one hell of a learning experience that I'll never forget."

"Ah, yes – those are certainly things to challenge anyone. But we usually get used to them pretty quickly. How do you find the work?"

"Frankly, Chris, it's a little boring. I know someone has to do it, but I think most of the data collection could be automated more."

"Yes, I know what you mean. I've been thinking about that too. But, on the positive side, how we collect and analyze the data has brought you here for an adventure of a lifetime. As for me, my time is up within the year, and I think I'm going to go into academia. An assistant dean position is opening up that I've applied for, and I've been told that the job is essentially mine if I want it. Please don't tell anyone this, as I just want to keep this between you and me – just our secret."

Chris waits to see William's reaction to him offering this bit of confidentiality.

"Your secret is safe with me. Who can I tell anyway – Earl? He'd probably just tell me to go fuck myself." Both laugh, knowing Earl's disposition.

"William, I have another secret – and it's a little embarrassing. Recall how you said you get bored at times? Well, every now and then I have some formulas I developed to play a 'what if' type of scenario with the data. I tweak any pollutant and then see what effect it has on the overall data. And one time, I accidently transmitted my 'play' data by mistake back to the central site in the States – you should have heard the 'Crap, the sky is falling' wailing. I admitted to them the data I sent was in error, and immediately sent them the correct data – but boy, did I catch hell. And here is my big apology to you. I was swamped with work when you said you were going to go out to replace the sensor, and it didn't dawn on me that you must have been looking at my modified data and not the real data. William, I am so sorry to have put you through that."

"You're kidding me! So, the data I looked at was your play data and all the sensor data are fine?"

"Absolutely, William. I uploaded the data a couple of hours ago, and you are welcome to look over it. I can tell from my first pass at it though that things look quite good."

"Good to hear – I was worried that something was going on in the upper atmosphere. One of the things I have learned here is that we really are on the front lines of protecting Earth."

"You are absolutely right – this is what drives me daily. But all is good, and again, my apologies for putting you through so much hassle."

"So, I can upload the data any time I need to directly from the sensor?"

"I don't see why not – go crazy. Wait, bad choice of words here at the station. Go for it."

September – Mexico

As she has done almost every day of her adult life, Claudia De La Cruz awakens early to make her husband his breakfast before he goes to work. Santa Maria Del Oro, a town nestled in the hills of central Mexico and so small that most maps don't even show it, has been her home, her parents' home, her husband's parents' home, and many of their families' generations before that. It has been a hard life for her and her family, as there never seems to be enough money to buy the things she sees on her small TV. She notices fine things worn by the tourists who come to play in the mountain lake every summer, and she knows she can never afford these. But her demands are simple, and bright clothes and fancy cars are for others – not her.

The very faint light appearing toward the eastern dark sky means it is time for another day for her work to start. No words are spoken as her husband Joel climbs out of bed to the smell of fresh coffee wafting through the air. By instinct from his many years in this small four-room house, he feels his way into the tiny kitchen and sits down at the table. He yawns and rubs his eyes. His eyesight is not as good as it once was, not only from the effect of time on a body, but from the sawdust and other grit that irritate his eyes daily. He had a pair of goggles once that someone gave him, but they got lost many years ago and he told himself, "Ah, I don't need those anyway. What's a little sawdust?"

When a visitor once asked Claudia what she ate for breakfast, she was perplexed and had to ask what that word meant. To Claudia and her husband, there were never choices like expensive cereal or pancakes. Scrambled eggs over a tortilla with hot coffee to wash it down was the only option, and to them it was just a "meal."

After Joel finishes his tortillas and huevos with his dosage of hot sauce, he gives Claudia her see-you-later kiss as he goes about gathering what he will need for his work today. He grabs a clean shirt from their small wardrobe. He never takes his tools out of the bed of his truck, as there is never any crime after the tourists leave. A wave and "see you in a few hours" get him a smile and wave in return as he walks to his truck and drives off down the graveled road.

Claudia washes the dishes and stares through the window at the bright sunny day awaiting her. She slips on a pair of sandals and walks down the road toward the azure-blue mountain lake water. As if drawn by its magical properties, the lake is her refuge – her safety place – her comfortable place where she can sit and watch the wind make ripples, and she can be alone with her thoughts. The small surrounding mountains have formed a natural funnel to catch rain and, as a result, the water is so blue that visitors can't believe how beautiful it is. Most of them come back year after year, and she has gotten to know many of them through their frequent visits.

The tourists who were here all summer are now gone. They usually leave all manner of trash in the houses, campgrounds, and the lake – which gives it back by washing it to shore. Plastic Pepsi bottles bob here and there, and Claudia shakes her head in disgust.

Claudia thinks of her childhood with her father and mother counting, "uno, dos, tres" and jumping into the water with her. It makes her grin as she bends over to touch the water. She misses her parents, who died a few years ago, but the image of them and the beautiful lake in her mind make her smile.

The lake and the simplicity of the nature that surrounds her is hard for her to describe to her distant cousins who have never visited, so she has given up and simply tells them, "Oh, it's a nice little lake." In reality, it is much more than that for Claudia. Legend has it that the lake used to be a volcano that a Mayan priest could beckon forth when needed. The reality is that simple geology and erosion created it, but still, the legend makes for good stories to the tourists.

The sun is high enough to start warming the air. Summer has gone, fall is on them, and soon the rains will come, along with the chilly, high-altitude weather. Claudia's family owns two rental houses that provide her family with a little income until the following summer rolls around…plus she is hired by the city to help keep the lake clean. It doesn't pay much, but it helps provide her with enough money so that she doesn't feel as poor as others in her town.

Growing up with little money and working hard all her life is taking a toll on her body, and she struggles more these days walking down the road from her house to the lake.

"If only I was younger," she mumbles and breathes hard as she sits down. The rock that makes her seat has been there for many more years than she or her ancestors. Many boulders border the lake, but this is her favorite one. It has wedged itself in perfectly with lesser boulders, and its almost flat surface is perfect for sitting and watching boaters, birds, or nothing. Everyone should have a peaceful place to go to when they can, and this one is hers.

As she surveys the trash that's been left, she realizes that intermixed with the trash are numerous dead fish. It isn't uncommon to see an occasional dead fish floating next to shore, but this morning is different. In fact, she has never seen so many fish with their white bellies bobbing skyward. She studies the dead fish a little closer and considers for a brief moment about scooping the bigger ones up and taking them back for a meal.

"Was it pesticides that killed them?" she wonders. Maybe someone on the other side of the lake – the rich area where the big homes are – did something. But her husband would be aware of that, surely. Or those damned tourists? Yes, that must be it – they are careless every summer they come here. They don't care. A group rents a house, parties all night, and spills their petrol casually as they fuel their boats.

"And who suffers? You poor fish," she says as if others under the water can hear her.

"Hola, Señora Claudia. What about your fish friends? Are you sad for them?" Claudia knows the voice. It is Peter, who retired here from Germany about ten years ago. She turns and smiles.

"And a guten morgan to you, Peter. Come – I want to show you this." Peter stands next to Claudia and looks at the shoreline scattered with dead fish.

"Ja, I have seen this before, but not so many."

"Si – oder sagan, 'ja'?" as she laughs at their German, Spanish, English easily intermixed. Claudia and Peter have gotten to know each other well, as their houses are a little more than fifty meters apart. Peter and his wife Evelyn moved here more than fifteen years ago. Rumors started that they were part of Hitler's youth program during WWII, or that they robbed a bank, or other stories that invoked whispers. The reality is that both of them retired from the German high taxes, and with their pensions, they are living quite nicely in a community of nice people. Everyone in this community knows everyone, and even outsiders who move in from other places are accepted after the normal sniffing period. Because of the tourists, even though both have their own native languages, both Peter and Claudia have learned English well enough to make conversations understood.

Peter takes a stick and rakes a larger fish to the shore. "See, its mouth is open as if it can't breathe. Someone has polluted the water, velleicht."

Pushing herself down off her perch, Claudia is standing next to Peter watching him turn the fish over to see if he can see any other signs of problems with the fish.

"Yes, it must be that someone has put something into our beautiful lake. We probably should not eat them. Let the birds and turtles have them – they'll have them cleaned up soon."

Peter sits down on a rock nearby and looks across the lake.

"Do you miss Germany?" asks Claudia.

"Ja, much at times, but not too much at other times. Evelyn's health is so much better here – her doctors were worried about her in Friedrichsdorf, but you see her now – she is healthy, si?"

"Si, she is." Then Claudia pauses and adds, "I'm glad you moved here. You've been nice neighbors to us."

Peter smiles and responds, "We are glad we are here auch."

"Also," Claudia scolds him with a smile. "The word is also or también."

"Ja, ja – also. I think my Spanish is better than my English," he laughs.

"I'm heading back – you?" Claudia asks.

"No, I'm going to walk some more for some exercise. I'll see you

56

später," he says as he gives her a grin and a wave and heads away.

"Adios, Herr Peter." Claudia looks back at the water.

She knows that her job tomorrow and the rest of this week will be to start removing the dead fish if the scavengers have not done their work by then. Her eyes focus on a particularly large fish with its mouth wide open. She picks up a stick laying close by and pulls the fish closer to shore. She puts the stick into its mouth and slowly rotates it to see if there are noticeable wounds that could have killed it – but there are none.

"What happened to you, my old friend? You and I have lived here for years, and today you died." She looks down the shoreline at the other bobbing bodies and shakes her head in disgust at how someone could have been so careless as to dump something in the water to kill so many of nature's creatures.

She starts her walk up from the bank and stops after about twenty meters to catch her breath. The climb is no steeper than it ever was, but today she finds herself taking in big breaths. Her body responds quickly to the inflow of oxygen, and immediately she feels more comfortable. Am I having a heart attack, she asks herself? No, it isn't that, because she realizes that by making herself calm down and take in deep breaths, she feels normal once more. What is wrong with me? Am I getting old? I'm only 60 – that's not old, she thinks to herself.

She continues her walk back to her house, but at a slower pace and taking in big, deep gulps of air with her mouth. She sits down on her porch and looks out on the meadow, then over to one corner where she has her broom. I'll sweep tomorrow, she says to herself, and closes her eyes to rest.

The hours go by quickly when, "Claudia – wake up," startles her. She smiles to see the face of her husband walking up to her. "Are you okay? You never take naps in the morning," Joel says.

"I'm fine. I was just tired from walking."

"What is that smell?" he asks?

"Fish – many, many of them. The sun is cooking them for us. Tomorrow, I'll help clean them up if the turtles and birds don't get them," she replies.

"How many?" Joel asks?

"Many. I think it is the rich people on the north side. They don't care what they dump into the lake."

"They are nice people. They care about our lake like we do. I don't think they caused it."

Changing the subject to allow her time to think about other causes of the dead fish, she says, "How is the garage coming?"

"Very good. About two more weeks until I'm done. Then he promises me more work. He's a fine man who pays me well – and on time. Here…" he says as he lays down ten thousand pesos on the kitchen table.

"Joel, that will help us a lot! I feel rich when you show me so much money!"

Joel laughs, "We are rich. Look at our nice house – and the lake. Who says we are not rich?"

"No one," Claudia says as she smiles at him. "You are right."

Joel and Claudia enjoy a lunch that she quickly prepares for them. It is simple by many standards – some tortillas with some fresh tomatoes and lettuce from their garden, and rice –her meals are always served with rice that she proudly has ready at any time. She gets a bowl from the refrigerator and sets out the chicken, which she killed, dressed, and cooked yesterday. She paid a local farmer forty-five pesos for a nice plump hen, and she will make it last for several meals. With an "Adios – see you this evening," Joel gives her a hug and drives back to his work.

The rest of her day is quiet as Claudia relaxes on her porch reading an English novel that a tourist had left. She doesn't understand the story very well, but she enjoys trying to sound out the words and remember what they mean. The idioms always give her problems, as most make no sense literally translated, but it always makes her smile when she reasons them out. She falls asleep and wakes up abruptly with a sense of having a hard time breathing. Sweat is pouring from her forehead as she feels her pulse beat faster.

"Relax," she tells herself in an effort to calm down. She gulps big breaths again and feels the calmness return throughout her body. She stares out into the meadow and thinks of her husband. What if I die? No, I can't. I'm fine; I'm just old and need to slow down. Her eyes drift to her right toward the sun reflecting off the lake in the distance. She takes in a deep breath and can feel her anxiety ebb slowly.

"Ah, the beautiful lake, my old friend – we will both get better tomorrow."

Joel returns later than usual from his work, and Claudia has waited patiently for him as she has sat and read, taking it easy after her morning health scare. As she hears his truck come down the road, she goes into their kitchen to prepare their evening meal and a cold beer. Later that evening she contemplates telling Joel about her panic and breathing attacks today, but she doesn't. "Why should I worry him?" she asks herself several times throughout the evening and as she prepares for bed.

In the wee hours of the morning, when there is no sound and all is calm in their little community of houses, Claudia gasps for air once again and abruptly sits up in bed. Sweating again, she takes in large gulps of air.

She gets out of bed while trying to draw in as much air as she can, and she can feel her body ever so slightly calm down. Joel sleeps well after a day of hard work, and he doesn't usually know if Claudia has gotten up. Claudia is scared and shaking as she sits in her living room.

"Am I having a heart attack? Yes, this must be what it is like." She gets up and walks onto their porch, and as she moves a chair in the dark, her broom falls over and makes a thwack sound as it hits the small concrete slab. The sound rouses Joel from his sleep, and as he gets up to investigate the noise, he finds Claudia crying.

"What's the matter?" he asks.

"Oh Joel, I'm scared. I think I'm having a heart attack. I can't breathe very well."

"Put on your coat – I'll drive you to the clinic."

"They're closed. The hospital in Tepic is the closest, but it's so far away. Give me a minute – I'm breathing better now. Maybe it wasn't a heart attack."

"Or maybe it was. Come on, let's go."

"No, Joel. I can feel my heart slow down – it was beating fast when I got out of bed. Is that a sign of a heart attack?"

"Maybe."

"Let me relax for a minute, then we'll see." Pausing as she takes in deeper breaths, and asks, "Can fish have heart attacks?"

Joel laughs at the question. Claudia smiles and laughs along, but she thinks about how the fish could have died.

"You are a silly wife."

"I have been thinking about the dead fish Peter and I saw today – they looked like they couldn't breathe, either. Joel, do you think the rich people gave me something like they gave the fish?"

"I don't think so. Did you eat any of the fish?"

61

"No."

"Then I'm not sure what it could have been. I have never seen anything thrown in the water from the north side. I think the fish just died – it happens sometimes. Claudia, I don't care about the fish – I am worried about you."

"I'm worried too, Joel. It happened this morning, but it went away. Now, when it happened again …I don't know what to do." She inhales deeply. "I'm feeling better now. Let me sit out here – you go back to bed. I'll be fine."

"No, if we don't go the hospital tonight, I'll sit here with you. Tomorrow you go to the clinic. It will open in a few hours, and I want to make sure you are okay."

Joel holds her hand and watches as Claudia gradually falls asleep. As he observes her heavy breathing, he closes his eyes and rests the best he can until daylight.

When Claudia wakes up, she finds a note on the kitchen table that says "You were sleeping well, so I decided not to wake you. I promised Mr. Martinez that I would finish something this morning. It should not take long, and I will be right back. Call Peter if you need to go to the clinic before I get back – don't wait if you are feeling bad. Call me at the Martinez house if you need me."

She must have been so tired that she didn't hear his old truck start.

She smiles at the thought of him leaving her this note but is also angry at him for leaving her.

There is only one road from Claudia's house to the top of the hill that surrounds the lake. She has only walked this road a few times in the past, and each time it took over an hour – and she was very tired when she got to the top. But she was younger. Today, if no one can pick her up at her house, she cannot imagine making the long climb to the top to catch a bus. She feels alone. She is feeling much better than last evening, and she doesn't want to bother Joel at his work. She walks onto the porch just as Peter pulls up in his truck.

"Claudia, Joel left me a note asking for me to take you to the clinic. Let's go!" he commands as he opens the car door for her. "So, what is wrong with my favorite Claudia?"

"My breathing is hard."

"Well, you must see to that. I cannot afford to have you ill – who would teach me Español?"

"Ja, das ist richtig," she replies in German and smiles as she sits in his car.

The road winds back and forth up the face of the hill, and she thinks how hard it would have been to walk it, then wait for a bus that is so irregular in its schedule. After ten minutes of driving, they reach the top and the road merges into a straight paved highway for a short drive into the town center.

"This is fine, Peter, danke," she says, as Peter's truck pulls up in front of the city clinic.

"I'm going to pick up some lumber. Shouldn't take long. I'll come back to the clinic for you."

"Thank you, Peter." As Claudia enters the clinic, she sees many familiar faces.

"Why so many patients?" she wonders as she looks around the small room. Claudia patiently waits her turn to see the nurse who opens the clinic every day. When it's her turn, the nurse calls her name, and both go into a small examining room.

"So, Claudia, what can I help you with today?"

"I thought I might have had a heart attack last night. I am having trouble breathing."

"You look so healthy. Tell me what happened."

"I almost passed out – I could not breathe. I was sweating, and I could feel my heart beat like it was going to jump from my chest."

"I have heard this a lot today, and yesterday, and the days before that. I think there is something in the air. Do you have a cold? Sniffles?"

"No, I feel fine except for my breathing."

As the nurse performs her cursory examination, she says, "Your heart sounds fine and your lungs clear. Let me give you a few pills to help you relax. I do not have many left, but the Pharmacia has more. That should help you. But if you still feel ill in a few days, come back and we'll get you to a doctor in Tepic."

Claudia thanks her and walks next door to get her prescription filled. Then, she finds some shade covering the low stone wall that surrounds the plaza and waits for Peter. She takes one pill along with some water from the bottle that she has brought with her from home. Several cars pass, and with each one's approach, she anticipates it is Peter so that she can get back to her house. She smiles as she spies Peter's blue pickup.

"How are you, my Claudia," Peter asks as he rolls to a stop and throws open her door.

"The nurse gave me some pills that are supposed to help me. She didn't find anything wrong."

Claudia says no more as she stares out the window on their ride back to her house. When Peter turns to head down the hill from the main road, the mountain lake comes into view. Claudia smiles as her old friend beckons her home. As the truck pulls to a stop at her house, she thanks Peter, and he gives her a wave as he drives back down the dusty lane.

Joel has been waiting for her and rises from the chair on the porch, anxious to hear about her health.

October – United States

The temperature hits an all-time high of one hundred fifteen degrees in Central Texas. Dr. Marsha Oliver looks around her classroom, and even though it is five minutes past start time, several students are absent for the second time this week. Since these students usually walked into class with a bicycle helmet under an arm, she assumes they're now looking for alternative modes of transportation because of the heat. It reminds her of her poor college days when a bicycle is all she could afford for transportation. Now, when she rides her bike, it's for exercise, and although she usually enjoys the ride, the past several months have necessitated that she forgo that pleasure for her air-conditioned car. Her rationalization not to walk or bike was, and continues to be, that it isn't worth the thirty minutes or more that it takes her to cool down from the excessive heat. Even after a cool shower, her body temperature stays high and makes her uncomfortable to lecture to her classes.

It's always hot this time of the year, but no one, including Dr. Oliver, has seen these lingering high temperatures drag on for so long. For the past thirty days the temperature has been over one hundred degrees, with the nights cooling off only slightly. It is an oppressive heat, but the anticipation of fall bringing cooler weather keeps everyone saying, "Just wait. This heat won't last forever – then we'll complain about something else."

She focuses on her first class. Soon the hour is up, and she leaves them with their assignment. As she is pulling her notes together and the last student is leaving, she hears, "Hi, Dr. Mac," echoing from the hallway. Her dean, who heads up the Geosciences Department, is Dr. Bob MacLean, but students and most teachers alike simply call him "Dr. Mac." Dr. MacLean and Dr. Oliver have been friends for more than five years when he hired her after she graduated with her PhD in environmental studies. She looks toward the door and sees a familiar figure enter.

"Hi, Bob. What brings you around?"

"I got an email yesterday from a fellow, Dr. Sanjay Krishna, at the University of Technology in Pune, India. He remembered me from a conference on global climate change that we attended in Hawaii in March. He wants to discuss some observations he and some others have uncovered, and I thought you might want to listen in. Are you okay to chat with them at four o'clock this afternoon? Don't worry, though – whatever he's up to, I won't let him hire you away from me. We need you here – just remember that – and the tenure slot is all yours next year. Keep that in mind also."

"I'm not going anywhere, so don't worry. And, yes, I'm counting on the little bump in pay and more job security, so next year can't come fast enough. I will be glad to join the call."

"See you then. Thanks."

"What conference room?" Marsha hollers as he starts to walk away.

"My office," he replies while continuing to head down the hall. He stops and returns to Marsha's classroom. "They requested that no one else be in the room, but I told them I was inviting you, as you were my right-hand professor. They agreed without any problem. I'm sure he wants you or me to speak at some conference in Southeast Asia soon. As for me, I refuse to make any more twenty-hour plane trips – so if that's their request, please be my guest. It will look good on your resume."

Marsha smiled and replied, "I've got a few more classes and some homework to review, but I'll be there at four."

Marsha types in "time zones" on her laptop, and a quick glance shows that Pune appears to be twelve hours and one day ahead. They sure are a dedicated bunch, Marsha thinks as she double-checks her time-zone computation.

"Damn, that's the middle of their night. Whatever it is they want to talk about must be important to them."

She shrugs it off, wraps up her notes, and heads back to her office, which is only three floors up; she usually takes the stairs to save the excruciatingly slow elevator ride. She is proud of herself for being in good shape with tennis twice a week, a gym workout at least three other days, and riding her bike when she can. As she exits into the hallway after the climb up the stairs, she is breathing heavier than she knows she should.

"I've got to work a little harder in the gym," she says out loud hoping that no one is within listening range. As she walks by a glass case of minerals, she glances sideways to look at her figure. She feels fine being around one hundred fifty pounds, which fits her almost six-foot frame perfectly. She puts a hand on her belly to push in her little pooch, but she struts on thinking, "Not bad for forty-one."

She lays her notes on the desk and sits in her squeaky, thirty-year old chair that has been handed down and moved from office to office to make a final landing where it now sits. Even though her school has a large enrollment every semester, and their endowment is huge, as shown by the added buildings bearing the names of wealthy people or companies, professors seem to be at the bottom of the list for office improvements and salary increases.

She tries to turn her old chair around. This can be hard to do since, at random times, the rollers lock and irritate her to the point that she sometimes stands to do her work. This time, though, after jiggling the chair a few times to release the stuck roller, the squeaks continue but at least the chair is rolling. She digs into her lunch that she packed from home.

As she usually does while eating, she spends the time either catching up on emails or looking at data and statistics so she can share the latest information with her students. Marsha has access

69

to environmental data because of the university's grant from the federal government. She also has been granted special access to the U.S. space mission data. One of the intriguing things that she came across last week was buried in a science journal telling of oxygen being discovered in deep space – not only in the Orion nebula, but as close as a few hundred thousand miles on the other side of Mars. While detecting oxygen molecules fifteen hundred light-years from Earth proved earlier theories about how the universe was formed, no theory exists as to why oxygen was discovered so close to our own planet – and being the inquisitive sort, this article struck her as something interesting to explore. She researched other articles on this topic, and while theories abounded as to why this was so, most came to the conclusion that the Herschel Observatory was out of kilter that day – that it was either a programming error or an error in transmission of the data back to Earth.

Atmospheric changes had intrigued Marsha since she first started her undergrad degree program, and her PhD dissertation on "Biogenic Variances of Volatile Organic Compounds to the Atmosphere" earned her credibility for the teaching post she now holds. She picks up the article and rereads it. She recalls another scientist she met who heads up the European Space Agency and has been wanting to email him asking for more data – but her busy schedule has kept her from doing that. She lays the magazine back on a pile of other literature and says, "Next week perhaps."

Glancing at her watch, she realized why she had sensed something was amiss when she said she could meet Bob at four o'clock. "Shit…Megan's piano lessons."

She grabs her cell phone. While dialing in her husband's phone number, her thoughts drift to wondering how her daughter's day at school went and how she can't wait to catch up on anything Megan wants to talk about. It's an evening ritual she has with her daughter and helps them keep their relationship strong. She thinks how lucky she is to have such a wonderful child, but with a slight raising of the eyebrows, she acknowledges that all parents probably feel the same way about their kids. She knows she is overprotective at times, but that is her job – to get her safely through these next years and then into adulthood.

Her husband John answers, "Hey, what's up?"

"Bob asked me to join him on a conference call this afternoon at four o'clock and I said 'yes,' forgetting about Megan's piano lesson. Can you take her, please?"

"Sure. Four o'clock at the conservatory. I'll make sure she's there in plenty of time. And I'll make sure she takes her inhaler with her – her attacks recently are starting to worry me. So, how's your day going?"

"Typical stuff. About Megan…I think we have to see the doctor about getting something stronger for her. On a sort of related topic…I've got to go to the gym some more. I was breathing a little too hard after climbing the stairs today. And if I go, then you have to get your butt in there with me. Deal?"

"Let's talk about this when you get home? I don't do it when it's just me, but if you want me to make you go, then consider it done. I will be relentless."

"Very funny. No, I'm serious. I was sweating like a pig after just three flights of stairs. Am I really that out of shape?"

"You don't really want me to answer that, do you?" he said, laughing. "You look great – trust me."

"You had better say that. Okay, see you as soon as I can get off the call. Probably around five o'clock or so. We'll eat in, so find something in the freezer."

"Sounds good. See you then. Bye."

"Bye – and thanks again."

As she logs on to the university's website to grade papers, her mind travels to a memory of her and Megan camping out with Megan's Girl Scout troop two years ago. Megan had been having breathing problems, and the doctor had prescribed an inhaler to help keep her airway open, as well as a second, backup inhaler that was to be kept close by – in her locker or her mother's purse – just in case. Kids forget things, but it was usually something that could be easily corrected like missing lunch money or no shoes for gym class. On that camping trip, though, an incident happened that still causes Marsha's heart to race.

It was early July. Megan was supposed to check that she had her inhaler. She said that she did, and Marsha can, to this day, still close her eyes and picture it inside her bag where she double-checked that it was where it should have been. Arriving late to the campsite, the tent was set up and after a rousing round of campfire songs and brushing of teeth at the bathroom, all settled in for what should have been a nice, cool night in the woods.

All of the girls slept in a common room, with the moms in their own tents or some even sleeping in the cars. Around one a.m., a coughing fit that someone in the girls' tent was having triggered Marsha awake. A mother always knows the sound of her own daughter, and Marsha immediately ran out of her tent toward the sound. The noise turned into a wheezing as if someone was trying to catch their breath and couldn't.

Instinctively, Marsha rummaged through Megan's bag, found her inhaler, and handed it to her. She breathed deeply, but the wheezing didn't stop. Between deep breaths, Marsha remembered going ashen when Megan uttered, "Mom, I can't breathe." Even today those words send chills through her, and memories of shaking the small plastic container are vividly implanted in her mind. An inhaler only weighs a few ounces and is light to the touch, but on that night, it had no weight. A quick but thorough examination of Megan's bag produced no backup inhaler.

Scooping her up, Marsha ran to the first aid tent that had been set up to handle minor emergencies. Time slowed down as each white, metal box was opened one by one – no inhaler was found in any of them. Marsha remembers vividly how she yelled help as loud as she could while she ran to her car. Megan was now in a panic herself, as she could barely breathe. She clawed and swung her arms in the air for something to cling to – anything, and all Marsha could do was hold her close. She placed Megan in the passenger seat and groped for the keys she had left under the floor mat. Other mothers were running toward them, but all was a blur as the car started. She can still see Megan lying in the seat with her head hanging at an odd angle.

Somehow in Marsha's panic she had called out, "My daughter has asthma and needs an inhaler," and because of that, she probably saved Megan's life. Just as she was ready to pull away, a hand slapped against her window. It was clinched around an inhaler. She slammed on the brakes and opened the door. Grabbing it, she put it in Megan's mouth and told her to breathe deep – please God, let her breathe. Megan's arms knocked her mother's arm away, but instinctively Marsha's other hand kept the inhaler on her mouth, forcing her to suck in on it hard. Within a few seconds, Megan had relaxed and was taking deep breaths without the inhaler. Shaking turned into crying. Another woman touched Marsha as if to say, "It's okay" – and it was. Megan's doctors could only speculate about what brought on the attack – maybe it was pollen or something as innocuous as dust. Over the recent years Megan's symptoms lessened, but two full inhalers are now always close by – just in case.

Marsha returns to the present. She refocuses on the website she was starting to access. She types a search for the "Astrophysical

74

Journal" website, and once there, she reads the full article about the oxygen molecule detection.

"Professor, do you have some time?" Charlotte, a student in her first-period geology class, asks, interrupting her reading.

Looking up from the screen, Marsha answers, "Absolutely. Come on in. What's up?"

She doesn't want to appear rude to Charlotte, but her interest has been piqued by the article she had just started to read. Half listening, she hopes the student will leave shortly so that she can continue her reading. When the interruption ends, Marsha turns back to her computer only to notice that it has now logged her off.

"Crap," she mumbles to herself, and then hears, "May I come in?" from another student.

Marsha smiles at the screen as if to tell it, 'I'll get back to you.' She turns around and says, "Certainly. What can I help you with?"

The afternoon disappears with students dropping by for grade and homework discussions. Marsha wants to get back to her reading, but the time steals away as she looks at the time on her phone and says to no one, "It's already 3:50! Damn." Having missed her usual quiet lunch time with no interruptions, she grabs a package of trail-mix from her purse, locks the door behind her, and heads to Dr. MacLean's office.

"Hi, Bob. Got them on the line yet?"

"No, they were going to dial me, so I'm just waiting. Anything new in the world of geophysics?"

Marsha rolls her eyes. "I wish. Not today. Same-o, same-o. I have a great bunch of students this semester – very inquisitive, but they sure can take a toll on my downtime. Hey, did you see the article on the Herschel Observatory? Some interesting findings both in deep space and near space. Did you have a…"

The phone ringing interrupts her. "This is Bob MacLean." He puts the phone on speaker.

"Hi, Dr. MacLean. This is Dr. Krishna, and in my room, I have Doctors Armrigharaj, Duraipandi, and Kumar. Thank you for taking my call."

"It's my pleasure. Good to hear from you again. I have you on speaker phone as I have Dr. Marsha Oliver in the room with me. So, what can I help you with, Dr. Krishna?"

"As you are aware, India is in the middle of a massive heat wave. Mumbai has stayed at a constant one hundred to one hundred fifteen degrees Fahrenheit, even though our autumn has started. Three days ago, it reached one hundred twenty-five. I'm sure you have seen this on the news. Our ministry of agriculture is reporting significant crop failures with little water to irrigate. This affects many things, including our country's GNP, as we usually export hundreds of tons of rice each year. Other countries are feeling the same pressure, which means that the tons we import have been reduced by over fifty percent. To be concise, we are facing political, monetary, and food crises." He pauses. "Again, I'm sure this has made the world news, but I wanted you to hear this personally. From what we have heard, the U.S. is also having drought and extreme heat issues." Silence ensued for a few seconds.

"Dr. Krishna – are you there?" Dr. MacLean asks.

"Yes, yes. So sorry. My question to you is this – have you seen any data that supports why this might be happening?"

"What, specifically, are you asking, Dr. Krishna? What data, and are you talking political issues, or climate issues?"

"Climate issues – this is why I have called. My department has some excellent people working on it, and they have combed through your data that you made available online. It looks very much the same comparing it to past years' data. Is there something we are overlooking?"

"Well, you are correct – we are experiencing heat also – a very stifling heat…but weather like this is expected this time of year here in Texas. Dr. Krishna, we all know that some climate change appears to be real, but this is gradual, and most studies I have read, and even published, acknowledge this. It takes a lot of fossil fuels to provide countries' needs, and the U.S. is doing all it can to reasonably reduce any pollutants. I think your real question is how long can we sustain this, or when can we expect it to change so we can expect more normalcy? Is that your question?"

There is a pause on the line again, so Dr. MacLean follows up, "Dr. Krishna, did you hear my question?"

"Yes, I understood your question," Dr. Krishna replies.

Dr. Oliver joins in. "Dr. Krishna, this is Dr. Oliver. May I ask what other specific anomalies you might be experiencing in your climate?"

"I am not sure I understand your question, Dr. Oliver. Can you be more specific?"

"Certainly. The temperatures on most continents are up significantly this year and even last year. Do you see this as a trend? Have you been able to attribute these temperature increases to a cause? Or maybe multiple causes?"

Dr. Krishna replies, "Yes, temperatures seem to be up from all reports I have seen. To address your question on how long you might expect this climate change, from what we can tell at this time, historical data shows that this is a fairly cyclical event in nature, and with the normal wobble of the Earth, this heat and drought will eventually change to a wetter, colder climate. We don't have a timeline for this, so obviously we all have to adapt for this temporary change we are experiencing. I will say that all of the data we are collecting from the poles show nothing unusual. So other than what I stated earlier, we don't see any other cause – at least not at this time, but we are always keeping an eye out for anything suspicious."

"Thank you, Dr. Oliver. I want to add that in addition to the oppressive heat, our water tables have been reduced substantially from the water demand, and ironically our coasts have too much water – unfortunately, it is saltwater that we can't drink or use on crops." He pauses, and Marsha and Bob hear discussions going on that are barely discernable over the phone. "That is all we wanted to discuss for now. May we call you again sometime if we have more questions? Thank you very much for your answers."

"Of course, you can always contact me," Dr. MacLean responds. "Any time." They all say goodbye.

Marsha looks at Bob and says, "Well, Bob, that was an interesting call – I'm not sure what they wanted from you. Just to verify that the pole data is up to date? It's damn hot here, that's for sure. I've been following world temps, and they are a little odd, but hot happens. Anything you want me to take a look at in specific?"

"I don't think so, Marsha. All of the raw data is there for anyone to inspect, so if someone can pick something strange out of it, then let them go at it. As for me, I've looked at it many times, and I'm not worried. The sensor data is well within the norm."

Year 2

The Last Breath

April – Nepal

Kwan Ly, along with several hundred of the three thousand residents of Lukla, are at the airport waiting for the arrival of an airplane that is bringing food, construction materials, beer, and supplies, and sometimes people. Each arrival is an excuse for the people of this town to gather and marvel at the incoming flight. In most places in the world, a plane landing is not a big deal, but in Lukla, it's different. It's cold here – not Antarctica cold, but even on a sunny day, the air is thin and chilly. In the old days, before outsiders came, people made their coats out of an animal's hide. Rarely was an animal slain for any reason, but animals do die – and when they did, nothing went to waste. The bone, hooves, meat, and even the intestines and brains were made into a delicacy that only the local people had learned to enjoy from centuries of passed down recipes. Animal skins from horses, yaks, and other small animals made excellent coats. Sometimes they had bartered for quilted coats with Chinese traders who came to the river below them. In today's time, though, airplanes bring in supplies that are exchanged for money – money earned from performing services for the rich outsiders who wanted to climb their mountains.

Kwan, one of the best guides Lukla has ever produced, has been hired by an arriving group to take them to the ultimate in mountaineering – the peak of Mt. Everest. In return they will provide him with a nice stack of U.S. dollars, which he will then use to purchase warmer clothes and other modern conveniences for him and his family. Unlike many in his area who subsist on rations doled out by the government or make a meager living from doing odd jobs around town, Kwan's skills at mountain-climbing have allowed him to make a good living.

The passengers arriving are climbers coming from Germany for their first attempt at climbing Mt. Everest. Ever since Tibet sanctioned an Everest expedition on January 11, 1921, by Englishmen with no sense of the misery that truly high-altitude climbing could cause, thousands of people have tried to climb what is simply known as "Everest." Some climbers turn around after a few days, as they cannot withstand the cold nor the thin atmosphere. The good ones – the ones who have climbed similar mountains and are in good shape – are driven by a personal goal to go on.

Out of those, one out of twenty who attempt the ascent will die – it is simply a mathematical fact. Many dead climbers lie where they fall. Sometimes the blowing snow uncovers such a body. Kwan has passed several on his way up and down the summit, and each time he stops and says a prayer for them. If it was up to the Sherpas, the dead would lie where they died out of respect for their corpses, their families, and even to the mountains themselves. Sometimes families want their relative's body brought down – and sometimes this work results in even more deaths. No trip up or down the mountains is to be taken lightly. Even though Kwan and his family have never spoken about him dying on the mountain, he knows that if he does, his family will leave his body where it falls, and each day they will look up to the mountains and say a prayer for him.

Each year since 1921, the starting point has inched closer and closer to the summit itself, with Lukla now making Everest a much easier journey – at least for those who know the terrain and weather conditions. In the early days, climbers would spend months making their way through valleys dotted with monasteries, past hermits living in caves, through rivers that were so cold it took a day or longer to thaw out if you got wet, and finally to glaciers that doomed men before they had even started an assault on the mountain itself.

Today, the sun is bright, and Kwan scans the sky and looks at the mountains. Sometimes, when it rains or a mist rolls in, it can foretell a monsoon that started somewhere hundreds of miles away at sea level. Today, the sky is clear, and the air is clean like no other place on Earth. On a sunny day like today, though, the sun is relentless. Many Tibetans squint to let in as little light as possible, but Kwan learned early in life that a good pair of sunglasses is essential to work comfortably on the mountains.

He scans the horizon to the south, as this is the only approach an airplane can safely make into the Tenzing-Hillary Airport. At busy airports, aircraft list their times of arrival and departure. At Kwan's airport, a board simply reports "today" for an arriving plane. After more careful watching, he and others see a glimmer of sunlight reflect off of something shiny in the sky; it can be nothing other than the old unpressurized, propeller-driven Twin Otter that is bringing him his climbers. Closer to sea level the sound would give away the nearing plane, but at this altitude, sounds, whether coming from an airplane or an avalanche, are muffled until the source is almost upon you.

The single runway is very short and narrow, and slopes dramatically at one end. A pilot has to have many flights into the airport as a copilot before he is given full control to land or take off here. As a pilot makes the final approach, he has to keep power at full throttle and take in many factors while focusing on the small runway. Because of the juxtaposition of the airport to the mountains surrounding it, once you pass the river, which is about a mile away, there is almost no way to abort the landing – the plane, pilot, and any passengers are fully committed to making a landing. If a pilot misjudges the wind or air speed, or a mist rolls in, there is no turning around.

Wreckage from a crash two years earlier still lays only fifty yards from the side of the runway – a testament to what could occur if anything goes wrong. If the same events happened in most other airports almost anywhere in the world, the pilot could easily recover – but not here. In the past accident, eight people were killed when a pilot tried to land, and the plane flipped and caught fire. Investigators blamed the pilot for trying to land in a fog about which he had been warned earlier; that, with an added slight side draft, proved fatal. On the sides of the nearby mountains are the remains of other crashes – a reminder to pilots that death could occur at any moment if their concentration fails even for a split second.

Kwan watches the plane line up for its landing, and as soon as the wheels hit the runway and the plane taxis to the waiting area, the people watching applaud. For most on the ground their entertainment for the day is over. They show their admiration only because everyone survived thus far, and once the plane shuts off its engines, most of the spectators disperse to go about their day. It is possible to get here another way, but that involves flying or taking a train to Kathmandu, and then walking five more days. But the climbers are always in a hurry, so they rarely take the slower journey.

Saying a quick prayer for the health of the people walking out of the plane, Kwan walks toward them. He is in awe of how life must be in Europe and in the United States where everyone is rich and takes vacations. He has no concept of a vacation or holiday, as each day of his life is filled with trying to provide a better life for his wife and two daughters.

Because of the airport, Sherpas who used to eke out a living by herding sheep or other menial jobs now wait for each plane so they can herd foreigners up into the snow. Kwan does not have to wait like the other Sherpas because he learned English when he was a boy and has made many friends with past climbers. By word of mouth his reputation has grown as a trusted guide, and climbers reserve his talents before they arrive. Kwan has named his company the Adventure Tour Climbing Company, and he anxiously waits for his first clients of the climbing season. When winter comes to Nepal, no mountain is worth the risk of climbing, but with the warmer-than-usual weather, it was decided by most locals that winter was officially over, and climbing could begin.

The altitude in Lukla is nine thousand four hundred twelve feet above sea level. Everyone living here has adjusted to the thinner oxygen level, and Kwan prides himself for being in better condition than the other Sherpas because of his training routine. Lately, though, he has found himself struggling at times at the higher climbing altitudes. Even though he is only thirty-three, he admits to his friends that his best climbing days might be behind him.

As he waits in the reception room for his guests, he looks around at the tourists who are waiting for their return flight. Other guides had taken them, and word spread fast through the other Sherpas regarding how badly their climb went. No one died, but two had serious frostbite – to the point that some toes and fingers probably would be lost. These people had returned from their climbing early, but they will have to wait at least two days and be treated at the small medical clinic, as the Twin Otter is already reserved by Kwan. Between now and departure, the plane will be checked from one end to the other before the pilot trusts it to attempt a take-off – and even then, the weather and wind have to be near ideal.

He looks for a familiar face that matches the picture mailed to him as the first arriving passengers walk through the wooden door under a sign that reads "Arriving and Departing" in both Chinese and English. Then he sees him – Frans Jongma, the leader and coordinator for the German climbers.

"Frans, over here," Kwan calls. Frans waves back, and he and his fellow climbers walk over to Kwan.

As is the custom here, Sherpas only use their first name except in very formal instances. As he greets Kwan, Frans says, "So good to finally meet you, Kwan. Thank you for arranging this. Is everything set?"

"Yes, Frans, I have guides and porters set. Everything is arranged. You get rested at the hotel and we will talk tomorrow. The drivers are waiting outside for you. I will wait to make sure you receive your luggage and then escort you to the hotel."

As Frans and the others are waiting for their luggage to be brought in, Kwan notices some are already breathing heavily through their mouths, not through their noses as people in good shape tend to do.

"I don't know if they can do it," he says to his personal driver standing close by. "Look at them. How can they survive on our Everest?"

Nothing is done quickly when it comes to paperwork, as proper documentation must be sent to others for approval – and thus, Kwan must call his superior in Kathmandu to tell him the exact arrival time, the names of the people arriving, a description of them, where they will be staying each night, and the expected departure date and time. He receives the approval. Kwan and the other Sherpas know it is just a formality, as no one has ever not been approved. Still, they do it because it is the rule. This same routine had been done at each stop the Germans made along the way.

The next morning, in punctuality dictated by his superiors for his role as host to foreigners, Kwan is in the lobby at exactly eight o'clock. Usually, the Grand InterContinental Hotel is at least half-full of visitors, but with the exception of his German guests, he cannot see anyone except for local people.

"Good morning, Mr. Jongma," Kwan says as he approaches the group.

"Wu an," Frans replies. He gets a smile from Kwan and is proud he remembered his Chinese from his studies.

"How did you sleep last night?" Kwan inquires.

"We slept well, thank you. We had breakfast already, and I think we are ready to head out."

"Yes, yes, all is set. The plane is waiting at the airport to fly us to Phakding."

All of the gear was reloaded along with yet more supplies that Kwan prepared. The pilots have rebalanced the gear precisely and even told the passengers who should sit on what side and either in front or back, as this is one less worry for take-off and for gaining altitude. Petrol is precious at this high altitude because of the cost to get it here. Sometimes it is brought in by caravan in ten-gallon jugs, but other times a plane arrives carrying nothing but cans of the precious liquid. Flying a plane with such cargo scares a pilot more than anything; if he crashes with a normal load of passengers, there is a slim chance that he could survive. If he crashes carrying a load of petrol, his plane will surely explode in an inferno. In whatever way petrol reaches this high altitude, it is very expensive. And the cost of the fuel, as part of the agreement with the climbers, will be added to the final bill. Both the pilot and copilot walk around the plane doing one last visual inspection before climbing into the cockpit. Baggage is positioned and repositioned again to make sure the weight is as evenly distributed as possible.

There is no door separating the cockpit from the passengers, so all in the back can hear the pilot radio the control tower asking for wind information. The day is as perfect as it could be. The sky is clear, with only a whisper of a breeze. The plane is started, and the pilots go over their checklist. Everyone is buckled in and anxious for takeoff. Although the wind is slight, it is coming from the north, so there is no option but to take off from the south end of the runway. The pilot guides the plane over the slope and out of sight from the villagers who have come to watch the plane take off – or maybe to watch it crash. The pilot stands on the brakes, applies as much throttle as he can, then releases the brakes. From the north end of the runway, people can see the Twin Otter appear over the crest and head toward them. The pilot is past the point of aborting his takeoff as he nears the end of the short runway, and in an instant the plane rears up and is flying. The people on the ground (as well as the people onboard) applaud the success and then disperse. There will be no crash today.

Once airborne the pilot deftly flies between the mountain ranges. From his experience he knows the exact path that will take him safely between the mountain peaks. The airport at Phakding is at only ninety-four hundred feet, so the plane can safely fly below twelve thousand feet without needing oxygen pumped into the cabin. Sometimes, though, the pilot has to maneuver up to clear a mountain, and Frans and his climbing mates begin to feel the effect of the higher altitude. Frans catches himself breathing heavily, taking in big gulps of air. They do this instinctively from years of climbing at high altitudes. The climbers' breathing does not go unnoticed by Kwan.

The distance between the two towns is not far by air, but it would take weeks to make the journey by foot. As the plane settles into an approach, all eyes are peering out the small windows hoping to catch a glance of Everest. Everyone, including Kwan, is now more excited with anticipation about their days to come in the mountains.

After landing, the plane is unloaded and after doing preflight checks, immediately takes off to pick up the other anxious returning climbers back at Tenzing-Hillary Airport. Waiting trucks and drivers pack all of the supplies and await word from Kwan that all is ready for them to depart. From the time the Germans landed, Kwan is in charge of everything. Kwan is the most important man now to the local support crew and to the climbers. He makes sure all the climbers are comfortable as best they can be in the 1980s era Datsuns, and they head out to Namche, which is only about nine miles away.

Although Namche is close, the drive takes hours due to the curving and potholed roads. Namche will serve as their initial camp site from which all of the supplies will be packed onto small horses, and then porters will start leading them toward Everest. As the old, dilapidated trucks make their way, Kwan again notices the labored breathing of some of the climbers. Although Namche is at seventeen thousand feet, this should not be a problem for climbers who think of themselves in shape for the quest of Everest.

Kwan has climbed Everest twelve times, and with this, he has earned the distinction of being an expert climber and guide. Reaching the absolute apex of Mount Everest is called a full-climb, and he has never attempted one of these in what is considered the winter. On his last winter climb, the previous climbers had only wanted to go to about twenty thousand feet. They snapped their photographs and held up their hands in triumph, and they were happy and tipped him well.

Kwan was surprised by the warmer than normal conditions he had found on that climb. He feels that with the warmer weather they are experiencing, and with spring coming soon, this current climb should not be a problem. He prides himself that, even though a few accidents have occurred, no one has ever lost his or her life under his guidance. Although he feels comfortable with the weather, he's worried about how the weather can change within hours or minutes on the mountain. He looks at the clear blue sky all around him. It is a beautiful day in the Himalayas.

Halfway to Namche, the trucks stop as the lead driver hollers out "toilet." The Germans are confused as there are no facilities, and Frans ask Kwan where to go. Kwan laughs, and points in all directions. He explains to Frans that people are free to use any location for any privacy one can find. Frans communicates this to the other Germans, and slowly they wander about trying to find the perfect place to relieve themselves. One of the climbers, who had walked back down the road and is now walking uphill to the trucks, abruptly sits on the ground sweating profusely and trying to breathe in as much air as he can. Kwan's experience in working with climbers helps him recognize the man's condition, and he quickly rummages through the back of a nearby truck for an oxygen tank and mask. Putting the mask on the man and turning on the valve slowly, the man breathes deeply and gives a thumbs up.

"Sorry. I don't know what is wrong. I felt fine until I started back."

Kwan offers, "Take your time, take your time. We are around fourteen thousand feet here, with another three thousand to go until we get to Namche. You will get used to it – you are a climber, right? Of course, you are! Keep the tank and use it as you need to. We have plenty."

The man smiles. "Yes, but of course. I will be fine. Thank you." Others have gathered around, and, with a little encouragement, the man is back on his feet. Returning to their seats, the little convoy resumes its journey.

When there is at least a half-moon in the Himalayas, the reflection from the snow gives off a pleasant glow. When there is a full moon, it seems like daytime. When the convoy of trucks arrives in Namche, it is a new moon and darkness makes the city seem foreboding – almost eerie. Unpacking is done by flashlight, as the only streetlights come from windows giving off an opaque and muted light. The itinerary calls for them to spend two days here acclimating themselves to the higher altitude before they push on through the other nineteen miles to the Everest summit. As the Germans are shown to their tent sites, Kwan keeps a close eye on his group to see how they were adapting to the high-altitude environment. To his pleasant surprise, no one, including the man who needed oxygen earlier, exhibits any outward signs of labored breathing.

"This will be a fine climb. I will make it a perfect climb for them," Kwan says to a friend of his who is on his sixth trip to the top.

Kwan finds his tent, which has been set up for him, and after a short prayer to his family and to the mountain, he crawls into his sleeping bag for a night of rest.

The journey from Namche to Everest is arduous; nothing is direct in the mountains. The nineteen miles will turn into twenty-seven as the group will follow rivers and previously made trails. Except for the last five miles, horses carry all of the climbing gear, oxygen tanks, tents, and food. The last miles will be focused one step at a time, with the porters and the climbers carrying everything they need to survive the climb to the summit and to return safely. Some climbers, after paying their thousands of dollars to climb Everest, give up either after or during the hike to the next base camp. They are humbly worn out.

Although Kwan was once wary of the Germans' conditioning, they seem to be adapting well to the high altitude by pacing their actions slowly and breathing properly to ensure every molecule of oxygen can reach the deep recesses of their lungs.

Fatigue, cold, inadequate sleep, diet, and lack of oxygen all contribute to altitude sickness, and sometimes even the best climbers can succumb to this ailment. Every climber has spent well over thirty thousand dollars to be here, so they all want to climb even though their bodies might tell them otherwise. Altitude sickness can make a person sick at twelve thousand feet for those unaccustomed to higher altitudes, but at twenty thousand feet, it can be deadly. A person experiencing mountain sickness can develop cyanosis, which causes a person's extremities to turn blue. A person can also experience malaise, lassitude, loss of memory and mental acuity, nausea, loss of appetite, and acutely paralyzing headaches. Any one of these can cause injury not only to the person, but also possibly to others as they have to take care of the ailing person. There is a reason many trekkers call climbing above twenty-four thousand feet the "dead zone."

At the twenty-nine-thousand-foot summit of Everest, atmospheric pressure is one-third of that at sea level; if a climber breathed normally, he or she would absorb only a third of the normal oxygen requirement, so altitude sickness was not uncommon even for the most experienced climber. But it rarely affects the Sherpas, who spend their whole lives living at high altitudes. Kwan knows the symptoms, though, and this is why he pays such close attention to every climber in his group – even his own guides.

They have come to where their first official base camp will be created, and it is from this point onward that all gear will be carried by people rather than horses. The Nepalese porters are well compensated for their work, and without exception, all have made at least three ascents to the last base camp – with some achieving five or more. Kwan feels good about the porters that are provided to him.

On the morning of the first stage of their ascent to the Everest summit, Kwan calls out, "Frans, are you and your group ready?"

"Yes, I checked and double-checked with everyone to make sure they have their own equipment ready. Then I asked each to check someone else's, und alles ist gut. We are ready!" Frans exclaims so that his climbers hear him. In return they shout, "EVEREST!"

Their first route will position them five thousand feet higher at a stone causeway where they will pass some small silver fir trees. Although Kwan has made this exact trek many times, he is always amazed by the colors of the flowering rhododendrons that bloom this time of year and throw off their colors of crimson, white, yellow, magenta, and mauve. He looks into the distance and takes a deep breath. How beautifully everything fits together cannot be described in words – and certainly not in the photographs that so many climbers want to take.

Never forgetting the custom that has been ingrained in him for all his climbing years, Kwan, along with the other Sherpas, ties a prayer flag to a rope stretched between two poles nearby. Prayer flags represent the five elements of existence to a Sherpa: yellow for earth, green for water, red for fire, white for air that gives life, and blue for space that is everywhere. With each breeze, the Sherpas believe that their prayers are carried out into the universe to protect them. Today, Kwan has chosen white for his flag.

He prays silently, and then returns to Frans and the others. "Let us go. The guides in front know the way. I will follow behind until the last night, and then I will lead the final ascent."

Frans nods, and they set out walking another two miles where they establish another camp site. Even though the distance was not far, carrying any extra weight can be troublesome if you're not used to it. Additionally, for these two miles they will be climbing another two thousand feet in altitude. One of the Germans, named Cor, falls to his knees. A porter quickly helps him up, but Cor falls to his back and looks as if he is about to pass out. The porter yells for assistance, and Kwan runs to them. Kwan orders oxygen to be brought quickly, and a small container about the size of a small Thermos bottle arrives from one of the porters. He places the attached mask over the man's nose and mouth and turns on the valve. The man gasps but quickly relaxes with the pleasure of oxygen filling his lungs. Kwan looks into the man's eyes and can see the panic still manifesting itself within him. He leaves the man with the oxygen container and walks over to Frans.

"This is not good. This man cannot go on. I will have a porter escort him back to Namche. He cannot continue."

"Ja, ich verstehen – sorry, yes, I agree," Frans answers back.

Frans and the ailing man have a discussion, and an argument ensues between the two, as Cor wants to go on. When Frans explains to Cor that he could die, he finally agrees to return to a lower elevation promptly. "We'll climb another mountain together, but not this one," Frans says.

Cor stands up, nods in agreement, and all of his climbing buddies come over to shake his hand and pat him on the back as if to say, "Good decision, old friend." As a porter escorts the ailing man back down the mountain, the remaining group sets up camp for the night. They brew hot tea on small burners and pass around sandwiches and energy bars. The porters clean up the cups and any paper and return to their tents. Kwan bids Frans and the others a good night, and then makes his way to one of the porters' tents. Frans and the other Germans have been told what is to be expected camping at this elevation, so one by one they brush their teeth with as little water as possible, and one by one, with as much privacy as possible, take turns using the toilet bucket. The last man using it has the job of taking it outside and dumping the contents away from the campsite – and out of sight for the next climbers making their way up Everest.

After a few hours of restless sleep, a strong wind starts beating on their tents. Because of their weight inside the tent, it is rare that wind actually picks up a tent, but it has happened. All of the climbers and Sherpas stay awake, ready to jump from the tent if they feel it being lifted off of the snow. After two hours, the wind suddenly stops as quickly as it came up. This is life on the side of a mountain twenty thousand feet high – and Kwan knows that the weather can get worse the higher they get. All occupants settle in to try and catch some sleep before the next day's climb.

Before sunrise, the guides, along with Kwan, are up making tea and a hot breakfast for all. Energy is what the body needs. Kwan calls out, "Breakfast – get ready for the climb!"

Slowly the Germans exit their tents, enjoy the prepared food and drink, and then return to their tents to put on more warm clothing.

After a quick cleanup, the tents are rolled up, everything is loaded and secured, and they are off again. The Nepalese make a good pace, while the Germans start to lag with smaller steps and labored breathing. Still, all continue another two thousand feet in elevation where they pass trash left behind by other climbers. Kwan used to help clean up messes like this when he came across them, but they have since become so numerous that Kwan now just shakes his head and offers a prayer to the mountain to forgive them. Kwan calls for everyone to stop and take in the beauty of the mountain range and for all to concentrate on Everest, which is getting nearer. The thought of climbing to the top excites every one of the Germans, and all raise their walking poles and let out a shout.

Within two hours they come upon a monastery that Kwan reveres because of the Buddhism he has followed since he was a boy. He remembers his study of Buddha and recalls the four noble truths – that all life is suffering, that the cause of suffering is ignorance, that ignorance can be overcome, and that if these beliefs are accepted, there is a promise to end suffering and to liberate and transform the human heart. Kwan feels at peace as he passes this place.

A massive, wooden prayer wheel is everyone's focus as they pass the central entrance to the monastery. It is mounted so that it reaches to twice a man's height and approaches six feet in diameter. Inside the wheel are papers that are inscribed with thousands of prayers and, with each rotation of the wheel, a bell sounds indicating that the prayers are ascending into the sky. They all stop, and Kwan asks Frans to turn the wheel. Silently and respectfully Frans does as requested. The wheel turns slowly, but that is enough momentum for it to make a few revolutions – and with each one, the prayers make their way out and up into the air where they float out of sight.

Even though Kwan has passed this way many times before, it is never the same. The wind, although not constant, is indeed consistent in its fury when it does appear. Drifts form, snow melts, ice forms, and rocks protrude where there had been none even a week before – all these acts of nature keep every climbing group aware of how dangerous the mountain can be. After a hard day of climbing, Kwan points to some spaces that appear solid and flat considering they are high on a mountainside, and the Sherpas lay out the tents once more. Frans and the other climbers assist by pegging the ends of their tents and popping them up with a single twist of the poles. Taking off their crampons, the men throw their backpacks inside, then follow quickly to get out of the chilly wind.

Tonight, each tent's occupants will eat by themselves, as it too cold to sit outside in a circle and tell stories of the day's climb. The men open up some packets of high-protein pastas and sauces and place them in small pans on top of their burners. Meals are eaten while wearing their heavy, down jackets, as the cold is now biting. Darkness falls quickly on their side of the mountain, and one by one each retires into his sleeping bag to keep warm. As Frans and his tent-mates warm up, their conversation turns to rehearsing what they will do on the climb toward the summit and retell stories of past climbs together in the Alps. As each grows silent and settles in for sleep, the only noise any of them hear is from the wind that is now blowing harder.

The next morning, the porters announce themselves at each tent. They unzip the tent and set inside a pot of food that has the consistency of porridge and tells them to prepare for the day's climb. As the climbers file out in their heavy parkas, Kwan asks each of them to join him in hanging a prayer cloth on the rope that previous climbers have stretched specifically for this ritual. Frans and the men walk over to the rope to watch and listen as Kwan pays homage to the mountain and nature. Kwan looks at cloths that he previously hung, and although they are tattered from the wind, the sight of them makes him smile and feel confident for this climb.

The group heads out with the porters – now called guides as they lead others over crevasses and rocks. Frans thinks, "It is not that high, and I am out of breath. Why is it so hard here?" Looking around, he sees that, except for the guides, all of his troupe are also having labored breathing – but all are relaxed and seem ready for the climb. In a short but grueling distance, the group stops to eat some food in a secure place the guides know well from previous climbs. Everyone eats and drinks in silence, with the occasional, "Unbelievable – what a sight."

With direction from Kwan that the break is over, they push on, making less distance than Kwan is used to. "This is the last time I take Germans – they are not in shape," he mumbles to himself and sometimes in Chinese to other guides who are close by.

Frans stops at Kwan and asks how many more miles they need to go, and Kwan laughs.

"We do not measure distance in miles but in time. See over there?" he says as he points to range of mountains. "I don't know how far they are, but I know that it would take me three days to get there." Frans nods and walks back to the other climbers.

At camp that evening, Kwan feels he has to ask Frans a difficult question. "Frans, do you think you can climb two more days? Today was nothing compared to what we have in front of us, and we have barely crossed twenty-two thousand feet. Tomorrow will be much harder, and the final day will be the hardest."

"Kwan, I know you are concerned, but all of us are experienced climbers who have practiced hard for this. We run several miles a day, so every man feels he is in good shape to continue. I have watched them too, and I have talked with them. We are ready." Kwan knows that the Frans' crew aren't accustomed to the thinner air as he and his compatriots are, but still he thinks that it shouldn't be as difficult breathing as they are showing.

Kwan accepts the answer and smiles. "Very well. Tomorrow we get closer!"

Another uneventful night comes and goes, with the sun breaking over the far range of mountains as the next climbing starts. Kwan and the guides have prepared more hot food and hot tea for the long day ahead of them, and they set it inside each tent after a quick announcement. If all goes well, tomorrow we will reach the summit, Kwan promises himself. He sets another cloth on the prayer rope and returns to the group.

"Today, we must tie each other together. It is too dangerous if one slips. He will fall and die if others cannot hold him. Watch your steps today and stay in our trail, and you will be fine. Check your oxygen tanks. Everyone should have three. Use them. Do you have any questions?"

There is no response from anyone. Kwan takes this silence as an agreement to continue up the mountain. Namgya, the lead guide, takes off slowly and the others follow. Tomorrow, Kwan will take the lead. All of the Sherpas feel rested and ready to make the climb – the thought of knowing they will be given bonuses by the Germans once back at the bottom keeps smiles on their faces. Through each man's belt runs a long rope that is latched loosely to each other via a clip called an ascender. Additionally, each man carries an axe and crampons to hold himself onto the ice and snow in case of danger. The lead guide comes to a steep part of the trail, and he looks back to see if everyone is ready. He gives a thumbs-up signal, and everyone behind him signals back in kind.

Standing at a spot known as the Pang la Summit, the clouds roll out and Kwan stares around. From this one place he can see four of the six tallest mountains on Earth. Kwan wants to tell each man to enjoy the moment and beauty of the country, but as he takes inventory of the men's climbing, he knows they are too focused on climbing to enjoy what he is seeing on the horizon. He has trusted Frans to provide excellent climbers, and instead, they are now struggling. Kwan knows that even the smallest of the four mountains within his sight is at least ten thousand feet taller than Mt. Blanc, the tallest mountain in Europe, where Frans and the others must have practiced. He watches those ahead of him struggle as he sinks his ax into the crusty snow and pulls himself upward closer to the summit.

Kwan follows slowly up a steep wall looming in front of them and is very meticulous and precise about each step. He reaches the top of the outcrop and looks ahead at one of the Germans. The lead guide has stopped and is observing the labored steps of the Germans, and for just a moment he thinks about going back down to help them. Even though each man is struggling some, each is still making very slow progress upward. Then, as the guide watches, one of the men stops and tries to breathe using his tank, but he cannot get enough oxygen and is panicking – and now calling out for help. Kwan, who is fifty yards back and before sound has had time to form or take on meaning, sees there is trouble but can't understand what is happening. And then he sees the man go limp and fall. The next German, who had also been struggling and is out of breath, cannot hold the falling man and now both fall. Four hundred fifty pounds are now pulling on the rope, and in succession each man loses his footing and falls. The guides try to dig in to stem the falling, but the weight is too much, and they are also pulled over the edge.

Kwan instinctively thrusts his ax into the snow, then struggles to undo the ascender to release the rope, but the rope jerks him quickly from his feet. He tries to hold onto the ax with both hands, but the sheet of snow under it breaks free. He sees blue sky above as he feels a cool, white, powdery mix hit his face. He relaxes his grip on the rope and prays to the mountain and heavens to protect his family as he realizes this will be the last minute of his life.

June – Greenland

The world is changing. Ice shelves larger than a square kilometer break off at least once a year at both poles. The effect is not only more icebergs then forming, but scientists monitor sea levels rising – and they are worried that this speed-up they are witnessing will have other effects on Earth's climate patterns. Since Europeans first set foot in North America, businesses and shipping companies have been on a quest to shorten the voyage from Europe to Asia. Drilling tests at several sites confirm that multi-year ice – the kind that has never been breakable because of its depth – have grown thinner than ever recorded. The Cape of Good Hope and Terra Del Fuego were long and dangerous, and the Panama Canal now contributes immense savings of weeks to travel between the Atlantic and Pacific Oceans. But what if there was another way – another passage? In the mid-1800s it was thought that the North Pole was surrounded by warm water from the currents flowing north, and that once a ship broke through a narrow band of ice, all would be clear sailing. Hundreds of sailors and explorers lost their lives believing in such folly and, to date, no one has been able to navigate across the place known as the Arctic. The Canadian icebreaker, the Royal Griffen, is setting out to change all that.

Now, a ship is being pushed out to sea by tug captains who know how to guide a large ship out of shallow waters into the deeper water surrounding Thule Air Base in northwest Greenland. This ship, the Griffen, is a masterpiece of engineering. While only three hundred fifty feet in length, it displaces over eleven thousand long tons and has the ability to break through ice ten feet thick at three knots. It carries a crew of seventeen officers, twelve chief petty officers, and eighty other crew members. The Griffen has one function – to break ice. It is equipped with two lounges, a library, a gym, and a ship's store. It has scientific research laboratories for areas of geology, oceanography, volcanology, sea-ice physics, and a lot of "toys" that are of interest to scientists.

Within a short distance from the dock, the cold sea quickly increases from a mere fifty feet in depth to over four hundred feet. After another mile passes, another one thousand feet is added from the surface to bottom. This is the same cold, blue water where earlier wooden boats reasoned they had a chance to break through whatever ice they encountered. They were foolish men who ended up paying with their lives. The Griffen intends to not meet the same fate as the earlier ships and crews. She will head north through the Nares Straight and into the Lincoln Sea, and then head west into the Arctic Ocean where, if all goes as planned, its first port of call will be Point Hope in northern Alaska. If her trip is successful, the long sought-out Arctic passage will finally be a reality. Anything can happen on normal water, but the Arctic is far from normal. It has narrow straits, icebergs, and ice that is many feet thick and goes on further than the eye can see. The captain knows her ship, and she has confidence that together they will accomplish what no ship and crew has ever done.

Captain Carolyn Cosgrave, a senior officer with the Royal Navy, has confidence in both her navigational skills and her ship's design. Carolyn's dream of being a naval officer started when she was small, and her father was a fisherman out of Sydney, Nova Scotia. Their house was high on a hill overlooking the ocean, and as she watched ships both small and large come and go, she knew she wanted a life tied to the sea.

Fishing was plentiful, and to the chagrin of her mother, she loved going out with her father every chance she could. Finishing her local schooling, she was accepted into the Royal Military College in Kingston, Ontario. Her next job was as a commissioned officer in the Royal Navy. Promotions came fast for her as she proved her acumen, and within a few years she became the first woman assigned to captain a Royal Navy ship. It was a small ship by most Navy standards, but her leadership and sailing skills caught the attention of the senior Navy officers.

She gives the command, "Ahead full," to the engine crew, and the Griffen heads into more open water that reaches depths of well over a mile. Captain Cosgrave sits at her station watching the bow break through the cold, blue water separating Canada from Denmark. She assigns her executive officer, or XO, to take over while she retires to her cabin to go over the maps once again and to rest up for the journey ahead. The XO, Commander James Adams, is a career Navy man and has been in the Navy as long as Captain Cosgrave. When he was approached by the captain to join her crew, he jumped at the chance to be part of this historic journey. His personality provides the type of enthusiasm she wants to step in as needed.

Rest doesn't come easy as the captain plays over in her head the route in front of her, knowing that if they hit deeper ice than expected, it could be catastrophic for the Griffen. Not from a structural issue, but rather from the perspective that the mission failed, and they had to turn around. She tosses from side to side staring at the Spartan fixtures that make up her cabin. She has only brought a few personal items for her desk, but each means something special to her. Two items have accompanied her on every ship she has ever served on. One is a simple carving of a puffin that her father gave to her when she was six. She had watched him whittle and carve on it while they were out on a fishing trip, and as they docked, he reached in his pocket and handed it to her. Now, every time she looks at the little bird, she thinks of the strong sea man who taught her so much.

The other item is a plain piece of driftwood. To anyone else it is something that could be ignored like a stapler, pad of paper, or a pen laying around. To Carolyn, she remembers it like it was yesterday when she spotted it. As she was boarding her first ship after her commission, there on the shoreline was this piece of nature that had drifted perhaps hundreds of miles to land exactly in this place. She marveled at its journey and decided that it was to be her companion as she drifted to distant shores. Together, these two items are worth nothing, but they're priceless to her. She throws her legs over the side of her bed, puts on her uniform, making sure it is properly buttoned, and returns to the bridge.

"Attention – Captain on deck," cries out a seaman who spots her walking through the door that connects her cabin to the bridge.

"At ease everyone. XO, you still have the helm. I just want to stretch my legs."

She looks at the clock over the front windows – it reads 2200. Because of the Earth's tilt, her crew has almost unlimited daylight, although at this time of night it is a softer glow than in the typical afternoon times. She scans the horizon and as far as she can see, there is nothing but water. She has never tired of watching the spray from a bow plow through the water, and the Griffen cuts a mean streak. The Griffen can make thirty knots in the open water running at full throttle. She knows that once she passes Hans Island and heads into the Kennedy Channel that all bets are off as to what ice the Griffen will start to encounter. Even though satellite images of what was seen from space a few days earlier show some ice, Carolyn knows that everything can change in a matter of hours in the Arctic.

"XO, I'm going to try and turn in again. See you in the morning."

"Aye, Captain. Get some rest."

Nine hours pass and they start to see ice regularly, with spots of dark blue randomly dotting the white expanse. The captain has resumed her duties at the helm, with orders to the engine room to slow considerably. Making only between five and seven knots is important as Cosgrave has to depend on the radar and sonar readings that alert her crew to obstacles in front or below them.

"Ellesmere Islands coming up, Captain," a seaman hollers out. Captain Cosgrave has waited for this moment all her life, because this marks the start of a journey that could put her name in history books. It takes a few hours to pass this landmark.

"Left twenty degrees. Ahead seven. Let's go to Alaska," she orders with a smile on her face.

"Aye, Captain." All feel the large vessel turn and slowly head in a westerly direction and into the unknown. Other ships would now be in mortal danger, as the ice is not forgiving as it bangs against the hull. But the Griffen, with its reinforced bow and thick plates, takes each punishing blow with relative ease. The crashes at first make every sailor on deck stop and look over the edge to see what they just hit, but soon a normality sets in. Her destination is one thousand seven hundred twenty-two miles away, and the Captain estimates an arrival into port in about fifteen to sixteen days.

"What's the thickness?" she commands.

"One point one meters, Captain," comes the quick reply.

"Let me know at one point five and at two."

"Aye, Captain."

Cosgrave leans back in her chair and stares straight ahead. The ice glistens in front of her and her ship, and she hears every blow they give each other. She stands, puts on her jacket that is draping over her chair, and heads to the door leading to the outside.

"You have the helm, Mr. Johnson."

"Aye, Captain."

Captain Cosgrave walks slowly down the length of the ship where she reaches the aft. As far as she can see behind her is a wide swath of broken ice that will freeze back together within another twelve hours, as if she and her ship had never passed this way. She feels the cold and thinks about the explorers who have come before and tried to make a passage in their wooden ships. She shakes her head in awe and considers the foolishness of their thinking but realizes how they were driven as she is now. She inhales a deep breath of cold air and walks to the bow.

The XO and Captain switch off taking control of the bridge, although there is little to do but aim the bow at a precise GPS setting. She sits in her room reviewing charts once again. The ship is performing perfectly, slicing through ice that is varying between two and three meters thick, when over the intercom comes, "We've lost an azimuth thruster; it's not responding."

"My first test, eh, Mr. Ocean?" She returns to the bridge.

"Slow to one knot," the captain orders. "Engineering, tell me more."

"Not sure yet what is going on, captain. We're looking into it. Right now, we show no response from thruster four."

"Keep me posted."

"Aye, captain."

Without the right rear thruster, and with the constant pounding of the ice pushing on the bow, the direction is hard to manage. "Seaman Labrie, adjust and maintain heading."

"Aye, captain."

The captain watches the preset heading compared to the actual direction in which the Griffen is headed, and they are off by a degree. "Seaman Labrie, what's the problem?"

"Captain, the ice is pushing us around without all the thrusters. I'm attempting to keep her on track."

"Well, you aren't trying hard enough, seaman. Get her back on the heading now."

"Aye, captain."

Captain Cosgrave studies the gauges and glares at the seaman trying to maintain the Alaska heading. "Goddamn it, all engines stop. Engineering, what in the hell is going on?"

"Captain, we've found the problem. The good news is that the thruster is working fine. All we had was a controller board malfunction. We have another one, and we're starting the replacement of the failed board now. I estimate ten minutes for us to get this working."

"Good work. I want an update in ten," the captain replies in a calm voice.

"Everyone on the bridge, stand up and stretch. That's an order. We got nowhere to go for ten minutes, so relax. In fact, put on your coats – you're coming with me."

The crew puts on their parkas, and she opens the door and steps out once more into the frigid air. The sun is shining brightly and reflecting off the ice. The air temperature reads minus ten degrees Centigrade. The cold air is invigorating to everyone, at least temporarily, until the cold starts to penetrate their lungs.

"Isn't it beautiful?" the captain asks aloud to no one in particular.

"Yes ma'am," come the answers from all of them.

She looks around to see them all shivering. She laughs. "I can understand sarcasm. Okay, enough scenery. Let's get back where it's warm."

As everyone takes their positions in front of their consoles once again, the captain requests an update from engineering. "We're just tightening up the last screw now, captain. There, all done. We're firing her up now." The captain waits for a final okay. "Testing complete, captain. All thrusters operational."

"Good job," the captain replies. "Helm, ahead three, to original heading."

The engines strain to move the ship, but it doesn't move. The helmsman increases power, but still it's like some giant vice has slowly clamped down on the Griffen. Slowly, the helmsman increases power even more, and the ship creaks under the strain. "Captain, no forward speed," he says.

"Maximum power, helmsman."

"Aye, captain."

The helmsman does as instructed, but the ship's thrusters do nothing but blow water under the ice. This is one of Captain's Cosgrave's worst scenarios, as she realizes that her ship is now frozen and wedged tight. She pictures in her mind the previous explorers in their wooden hulled ships experiencing their ships breaking up under the crushing ice, and for a brief moment she feels a sense of helplessness. She closes her eyes to focus on the problem.

"We will not let this happen, goddamn it," she says aloud. "Helmsman, all stop. Get me Lieutenant Bird up here."

A few minutes later, Lieutenant Dick Bird comes up from below. "Dick, you ready for hot water and air jets?"

"Yes, captain."

"Then do it."

On that order, Bird picks up the phone and gives orders to others on the other end. A minute later Captain Cosgrave sees steam billowing around the front half of the ship. The Griffen has been outfitted with a system that allows cold sea water to be pumped in, routed through special boilers, and then, at ninety-five degrees centigrade, shot through outlets just above the water line onto anything surrounding it. Pirates or ice – whatever is below the jets – will be scalded with very hot water. The ice is reacting by generating steam high into the sky, and the bow of the ship is now enveloped in a white mist, which itself freezes on anything it touches as it falls.

Additionally, the Griffen was equipped with high-pressure air nozzles under the keel that can be extended underneath the ship, and then can be directed up slightly. This had only been tested in a controlled lab environment, but the engineers who designed it had assured the captain that it would work in circumstances exactly like this. Their theory was, that if compressed air was shot right at the ice, the ice would eventually crack from the added pressure. The captain looks at her watch and starts a timer.

When fifteen minutes passes, she gives the order, "Stop all nozzles." She waits thirty seconds. The crew is anxious, as they are not sure what is going on in the Captain's mind. Then the order, "Helmsman, ahead full," is given in a normal rhythm.

The Griffen strains against the ice, and then lurches forward, free from its trap. Underneath her firm exterior, Cosgrave had been gripped with fear that the ship would be stuck, and she would have to radio for help – something that would ruin her career. She could not, and did not, show this fear outwardly, but her stomach was in knots. "Helmsman, resume three knots on course."

"Aye, captain," as he turns and gives her a thumbs up and smile. The captain nods and smiles back.

The next ten days are slow, but at times, five, and even six, knots are made as the ice sheet is found to be thinner in places. The Griffen is performing beautifully. The engine crew keeps the engines purring, and the rest of the crew goes about their jobs with precision. Every day brings the Captain and her crew closer to her goal.

The XO is sitting on the bridge when the sailor eyeing the radar reports, "Ship, straight ahead, sir. Approximately fifteen kilometers."

"Get the captain," the XO orders to another sailor standing behind him.

Within minutes, Captain Cosgrave steps through her door and onto the bridge. "What do you have?"

"Not sure yet, captain. Should we stay on course?"

"Why not? It's a big ocean out here."

"Give me a satellite feed," she orders. On a TV monitor is a live image of her ship and anything within five miles. She studies the images as they are downloaded to her. As they near the other vessel, they receive a message on the loudspeaker. "Canadian ship Griffen. This is the Russian icebreaker Artika."

The captain picks up the phone. "This is Captain Cosgrave on the Royal Canadian Griffen."

"Hello, Captain Cosgrave. Here Captain Vladimir Chenkova. Welcome to Chukche Sea. We break up last part of your trip. Keep your course. Follow path made for you. Very good history moment. Congratulations."

"Thank you, Captain Chenkova. This was very nice of you. Please feel free to fall in behind us if you wish. I will make sure the port will clear you for arrival."

"Spasiba, captain. We turn and do you ask. We want visit city too."

Captain Cosgrave hangs up the phone, then turns to the XO. "Trust me, they want to share the glory, or they wouldn't be here. Shit, they tracked us all the way from Thule – they probably knew our positions better than we did! If they had a ship like ours, they would have cracked the sheet, but they couldn't. They went as far as they could and had to stop. We did it, James! We did it!"

As the Griffen approaches the Artika, the Artika blasts its massive horns three times in a salute. Around the Artika's deck stand what appears to be her total crew, and as the Griffen comes within a hundred yards of the Artika, the crews salute one another as both ships pass. Captain Griffen issues orders to stay in the broken ice channel that the Artika has made.

"Ahead nine," she orders, and the Griffen slides into the broken ice channel. At first the channel is easy going, but within a mile, the ice has already started refreezing. "Slow to five," Cosgrave orders.

Her ship performs beautifully as it plows forward. The Artika, with its thrusters at full capacity, keeps perfectly behind in the channel.

The Griffen is showing the Russians that it is the best of the Canadian fleet, as it breaks easily through the ice. "So much for the Artika clearing us a path, eh guys?" she retorts to those around her.

"Yes, captain. Aye, captain," the replies come back.

Three more days pass when the lights of a distant town are spotted – Alaska. The Arctic Ocean has been successfully crossed from east to west, across the top of Canada for the first time by a ship on top of the water. The possibilities for establishing another shipping lane will have a dramatic impact on the world. The warming climate has opened up tremendous opportunities for shipping cost savings, as well as other opportunities for drilling minerals and oil and gas.

July – Worries

Having no link to the state of Colorado other than in name, the Colorado River meanders through central Texas. Fed by the Texas high plains and creeks, it has always provided enough water year-round for towns and for recreationists. Now, it is almost dry except for small pools. Two years ago, a university southeast of Austin successfully drilled a well to hit the water table, so it was hoped that an unlimited amount of water would be supplied to them. But the university learned that nature has its limits. Ongoing attempts to continue extracting water is bringing up little to nothing at times. Testing by their engineering department estimates that the underground water reserve has fallen five hundred feet. San Antonio and other large cities are also now using this reservoir as their water supply, and in so doing, are draining it at a rate no one has expected.

Tired from a day of standing on her feet lecturing, Dr. Marsha Oliver walks to her car. Another scorcher, she thinks, as she is half-way to the parking garage and can already feel the sweat beading on her forehead. She wipes the droplets off and looks around at the dead grass, which the university had stopped irrigating a month earlier.

After driving home, she spends a relaxing evening with her daughter and husband, then readies herself for bed. She is restless during the night, so gets up and pours herself a drink of water.

"Was my snoring that bad?" John asks as he ambles into the kitchen early in the morning.

"Yeah, it was pretty bad. I'll be fine – just a tough night. I think we both have some allergies. Keep taking your pills for it. Also, don't forget I've got a new class starting at six tonight, so I won't be home until about nine-thirty."

"Everything is under control here. Have fun."

"Yeah, right. But I never know what a class will be made up of – could be some smart folks, or kids just wanting some credits so they can move on. I'll know within ten minutes."

On her way to the office, she decides to whip into the campus medical office that treats students for scrapes and bruises. "Could you work me in?" she asks the nurse at the desk.

"Maybe – who are you?"

"Sorry. Marsha Oliver. I'm a professor here, and I've got classes all day; I'd like to get to them if at all possible. I've got this allergy or something. I just need someone to check me out to see if I have a respiratory problem to be worried about."

"Just a minute. Have a seat and I'll see if someone is available."

As Marsha sits down, she looks around the crowded room. No one looks particularly sick, and for all she knows, the students are mostly here to pick up condoms or birth control pills.

Ten minutes go by, then ten more. Marsha looks at her watch. "Ms. Oliver?"

"Here."

"Come on in."

Entering a small examination room, the physician's assistant asks, "So what's going on? The nurse said you were having an allergy problem. Lots of that going around. Welcome to Texas."

"Each night seems like I'm only sleeping a few scattered hours. Just can't breathe and sleep well. I feel like I'm getting more sleep-deprived with every day."

"Well, let's have a listen," he says, putting the cold, chrome stethoscope to her back and chest while asking her to take deep breaths. It feels good on her warm skin. "Well, I don't hear any rumblings. Your lungs sound clear. Have you been sneezing? Pollen is high from the dead weeds."

"Not a lot. My nose isn't running. I do feel a little plugged up at times when I try to breathe through my nose, but…"

"Say no more. Go to the drugstore and get some saline mist and keep your nose moist. I think you'll be fine. If you find it getting worse, see your regular doctor – which I assume you have, right?"

"Yup. I thought I could drop in since my office is close by – that's all."

"No problem. I think you'll be fine. Anything else?"

"No, thanks again."

Relieved to know that her ailment is nothing serious, she drives to her office and resumes her typical schedule – lecture, consult, lecture, consult, lunch, lecture, consult. Walking into Dr. MacLean's office to drop off some papers, the phone rings, and she notices the caller ID. Where is area code 672? She makes a mental note of it out of curiosity. It's not her phone, but she's there, and Dr. MacLean is her friend.

She answers, "Good morning, Dr. Oliver here. Dr. MacLean has stepped away for the moment. May I take a message for him?"

"Hi, Dr. Oliver." There is lot of static on the line, so she asks the person on the other end to repeat what they are saying. "Yes, it's a bad connection. I'm calling from Antarctica – McMurdo Station to be exact. This is Dr. Walker – an old friend of Dr. MacLean's."

"Nice to talk with you. I was wondering where 672 was – now I know. May I take a message for you?"

"I had some news to pass on to Bob. We're old friends and I thought he might be interested in some research we're doing. Also, I have some bad news about a common acquaintance we had. A colleague, Dr. William Moore, is missing and his plane is presumed down. Dr. Moore had what was thought to be an appendicitis attack, and the local surgeon couldn't operate on him given the medical supplies on hand. It's the dead of winter here, and an emergency flight was scheduled from Punta Arenas." He pauses to make sure he was being heard.

"Yes, go on," Marsha says. "I'm getting this all down for Bob."

"The plane did make it in to pick him up, but on the return to Chile, the plane disappeared somewhere. The government thinks that they had an engine problem and went down in the sea. The water temperature is below freezing, so no one is holding out hope for any of them to survive."

"Oh, dear. I'm so sorry to hear this," she replied.

"Can you pass this information on to Bob for me? He and Dr. Moore and I were working on some stratospheric data, and I'm sure that Dr. MacLean would want to know this news."

"Yes, of course. I've written it all down. Anything else?"

"No. Thank you. Please give my best to Bob. Nice talking with you. Goodbye." The phone went silent. Dr. MacLean's desk is a mess, so she is unsure where to leave the note for him. Instead of leaving it, she slips the message in her pocket while making a mental note to give it to him later.

Returning to her office after her last class of the day, she hears, "Marsha – got a minute?"

"Certainly, Bob. Come on in. Oh, by the way, I've got a note for you. I was in your office dropping off some papers and a strange caller ID popped up on your phone. I hope you don't mind – I introduced myself and asked if they wanted to leave a message –

that's all. I have to tell you, I was pretty excited to actually talk to someone at the South Pole – it was a Dr. Walker. He asked me to take a message, but I'm afraid it isn't good news. Sorry." She hands him the note.

"Thank you." He studies the note. "I would call or email him, but honestly I never know what time it is down there. In fact, I'm not even sure if time is relevant there."

"Sorry to hear about your friend. May I ask – what kind of data were you and Dr. Moore working on?

"He had taken some new measurements of the atmosphere – the stratosphere to be exact and sent them to me as a regular update. The good news is that all of the data looks perfect with what we expected. There has only been a slight variation in the data for the past three years now, so I think we have turned the corner on global climate change – seems like all is stabilized. He, Dr. Walker, and I are – sorry, were – going to publish a paper for the EPA. I will, of course, include William's name in the paper. I owe him that for his data collection and analysis."

Dr. MacLean continued, "I had never actually met him – only phone calls and email. Seemed like a nice man – and very smart. I always wondered what kind of person heads to the South Pole." He pauses, "Yes, I'm sure he was a nice man. Too bad about the crash. Regarding the paper, it should be nice, boring reading to everyone outside our field, but it will allow me to put a checkmark on my published papers this year. You know, Marsha, you're a little behind in getting articles out there. If you need some ideas, let me know."

"Yes, yes, I know. I've been swamped with family things recently – although everything has settled down a lot. Getting something in print is certainly on my list." Marsha starts to excuse herself. "Bob, can I get a copy of the email from Dr. Moore? Who knows, maybe it can trigger an idea for a paper?"

"I deleted the email, but I saved the data for analysis. I'll send that to you– is that okay?"

"Of course – that's all I needed anyway. But you stopped me – remember? What's on your mind?"

"I just wanted to say hello and see how you were doing. I've scheduled a department get-together in two weeks. Nothing major going on, but just wanted you to be the first to know. It's going to be at Bill's Fried Chicken at five in the afternoon."

Marsha replies, "Got it. I'll put it on my calendar. Things are going well, overall. Off to my evening class." Bob gives her a nod and smile as she departs.

The next day she opens her email and sees a link to the data in an attachment from Dr. MacLean. She downloads the data to a database where it's merged with previous atmosphere data, where now she can see several years of data at once.

"Interesting," she says to herself as she scrolls the data up and down and left to right – and reverses several times to make sure she is interpreting the data correctly. "Now, why would someone send data like this? It's the same as before? Crap, what a waste of time and data storage." She closes the database, and heads home.

As Marsha's sleeping improves over the next two nights, she is less worried that something was wrong with her body. Rather, she chalks it up to pollen, or something she picked up from someone. She is feeling refreshed at her classes, and overall, her old exuberance is back to where she expects it. On the third night, however, she's restless again. She rolls over and looks at the dim numbers that read 5:05. "Damn it," she thinks as she rolls back and forth. Her mind is wide awake, so she rises and heads to the kitchen.

"What was it about the data?" she mutters. She can't put her finger on what she missed, but it was something. She puts on some jogging clothes, then heads quietly out the door so as to not awaken anyone. Even at this hour the temperature reads 99, so unlike running as she used to do, this will be a slow jog just to clear her mind.

When she returns, John is sitting at the breakfast table reading the newspaper. "Morning, sleepy head," she says sarcastically.

"Morning yourself. What time did you get up?"

"A little after five – just couldn't sleep. Hey, do you still know the guy in IT for the campus?"

"Yeah, I run into him every now and then – why?"

129

"Dr. MacLean deleted an email by mistake, and I thought it would be a nice gesture on my part to help recover it. Every brownie point helps, you know."

"I'll ask him to call you, then you two can work the specifics."

"Thanks."

At 2:40 that afternoon her phone rings. "Dr. Oliver, Eric Hardin here."

"Sorry, I can't place the name. What class are you in?"

"Oh, sorry – I thought your husband had given my name to you. I work in the university's IT area. Your husband said something about recovering an email – is that right?"

"Oh, yes, Eric, and thank you for calling. I would really appreciate your help in recovering this email if at all possible."

"I'll do my best. Do you have a name and a date it was sent?"

"It was sent sometime in the past month – I think. It was sent from a Dr. Walker – Chris Walker to be exact. It was sent to Bob MacLean."

"I'll need Dr. Maclean's signature to do this. I can't legally look at emails that I'm not authorized to see – unless the NSA orders me to," as he laughs. "And good luck to them if they piss me off, as I can make things disappear rather quickly." He laughs even harder

"Eric, I understand security issues. Dr. MacLean and I are colleagues, and you know my husband. Dr. MacLean is swamped with some research, and I'm helping him with this. I – make that we – could really use your help with this. I can sense your hesitation, Eric – and I appreciate that."

"Dr. Oliver, I know your husband really well. Just send me an email explaining that you are working with Dr. MacLean so I can have a paper trail in case ... well, you know, there was ever someone wanting to know why I did this. You do that for me, and I'll see what I can find."

A week goes by before she sees an email from Eric. She downloads the message along with its data attachment to her database. Then she runs the data. The data input to her analysis program graphs the data showing PPM measurements, along with levels of various gases in the atmosphere and numerous levels. This time the data looks skewed considerably.

"I must have made a mistake," she mumbles out loud. She reloads the data once again, then reruns her analysis and graphing program. The results are the same and are strange compared to the data from Bob that she had analyzed. She leans closer to the screen, then back; she has never seen data out of the norm like this before. The graphs show a five-fold increase in the amount of pollutants from her older data.

"Good god, if this data is actually correct in Antarctica, what's it like in the Arctic?" she thought.

The last time she looked at data from there was over a year ago. She knows from past conversations with Dr. MacLean that he had not brought up any anomalies. In fact, just the contrary – that all data collected was as it should be and well within the norms of atmospheric data.

"What's going on?" she ponders while rubbing her eyes as if some answer would manifest itself. "And why was Bob's data so different from this data?" She makes some notes, then thinks about who could help her triangulate her findings.

Norway has, over the years, taken responsibility for monitoring the atmosphere in the Arctic, and she digs through her notes for her contact in Longyearbyen.

"Goddamn it, I know it's here somewhere," she rambles as she sorts through a pile of papers that hasn't been touched in several months. She stops as she sees the sheet bearing the name Anniken Bergensen. "Gotcha." She remembers the time she met her at a global climate change conference in Brussels, and this is exactly the person she thinks might be able to help her.

Swinging around to her computer, she types an email: "Anniken, I hope this finds you well. I am not sure if you remember me, but we met in Brussels last year. I am doing research on atmospheric changes, and would like to know if you could share your monitored raw data with me? Best regards, Dr. Marsha Oliver." She looks over the message before clicking the "send" button. She doesn't want to give away too much, but at the same time, wants to make it clear as to what she is asking. Knowing that Dr. MacLean probably has access to this data already, she sends an email requesting it from him also.

A day goes by and then MacLean stops by Marsha's office. "Knock, knock."

"Hi, Bob – good to see you. I've been swamped."

"Yes, I know. Decided to start a paper, I see. Good for you. What's it about?"

She wants to say, "Duplicity in the university," but instead answers, "Thermospheric layer effects on the auroras during summer months."

"Sounds like fun. Do you have some journals in mind?"

"A couple. While I have your ear, though, is there a problem with the server that holds the data I asked for? I am anxious to get a look at it – you know, for my research for the paper. I know there is a lot of data to look at, and I haven't defined my hypothesis very well, so I've got a lot of work ahead of me. It could be a couple of months – maybe more - before I'm done. That data certainly would help me."

"I had forgotten about that. Thank you for reminding me. I know there was some IT technical issue at one time. Let me check on it, and I'll let you know what is going on. Just making the rounds with my excellent professors and wanted to say hello. See you later."

The Last Breath

Marsha's mind returns to what she saw when comparing Bob's data to her own data. At this point she is not certain what she is seeing in terms of the effects it could have – both short-term and long-term. There is definitely some anomaly being shown in the data. Maybe it's simply a technical glitch. Maybe some data was lost? After all, the data had to be transmitted from the South Pole to here – hell, all kinds of things could happen in between. Her inquisitive mind fuels her to provide concrete and empirical answers, but before she confronts anyone with her findings, she wants to cover all her bases.

August – Pesky Little Bacteria

For the first time that anyone can remember, Lake St. Clair, which separates Detroit, Michigan, from Windsor, Ontario, reeks of an odor so nauseating that all but the brave or drunk boaters dare to run through it. Usually at this time of year, this area is rife with recreational fun, but not this summer. If the smell was not enough, to make matters worse, the water appears a dull red color. The *Detroit Voice* has interviewed scientists from local universities, and their consensus so far is that pollutants are being discharged at a heavy rate into the fresh water. People shrug it off as nothing new here, as car manufacturers and other plants supporting them have used the streams and rivers as dumping grounds for years. A few fish die at first, but eventually the toxic gunk settles to the bottom and eventually the water returns to a semi-acceptable state.

But this time it is more worrisome, as the economy of two countries is being affected. Not only are both country's governments blaming each other, but while the excuses and non-excuses continue, people are not spending money. In weeks of searching, neither side can locate where the discharge is coming from. While never actually using the term "liar," they are accusing the other city of not being honest with the findings. The pictures of the red water, along with pictures of tens of thousands of dead fish showing up on the internet daily, are making the local inhabitants angry.

In a fit of frustration, both countries agree to let unbiased scientists from outside the community examine, test, interview, and do whatever it takes to find the cause of the stagnant water. As their search proceeds, each government hires scientists in the field of aquamarine issues and gives them carte blanche to investigate what is happening to the water.

Weeks go by as the data is analyzed and reanalyzed. In this relatively short span of time, though, the odor and odd color of the water has now spread into Lake Erie. Ohio's governor has declared this a state emergency and has asked for the Center of Disease Control and the Environmental Protection Agency to get involved.

As in any government department, the wheels can move slowly getting a response. After interventions by politicians who were brought to task by newspapers with headlines such as "The New Red Sea" and "Economies in Shambles Because of Governments' Inaction," the U.S.'s CDC decides to take action on its own and flies in a team of specialists to examine what is going on. Two weeks go by as water samples are taken from fifty locations.

Usually a report summarizing the findings would take months or perhaps a year to produce, but because of the dire situation, the mayors and governors of both areas want answers immediately. The CDC complies, and behind closed doors a meeting is being conducted that includes scientists from the CDC, politicians from mayors to senators and members of Parliament, city managers, as well as several people from the Royal Environmental Department based in Ottawa.

Their findings are summarized and published to the attendees as follows: "Industrial and commercial waste continues to contribute to Lake St. Clair, but no one significant discharge was found. Rather, the totality of these wastes is causing the water to be deprived of oxygen, which leads to the *Chromatiaceae* bacteria forming. This outbreak started in one small area but spread quickly as the bacteria encountered less and less oxygen across the lake. The rust color is actually the bacteria itself. In summary, the lake is considered temporarily dead for all practical definitions."

"So, how do we fix this?" asked the mayor of Windsor. Others echo the same question, but less politely.

A spokesman from the CDC approaches the microphone. "We don't have an answer yet, but we are considering options. One recommendation to fix the problem is to somehow ingest oxygen into the water. This has never been attempted on this scale, so none of the scientists have a solution on how to do this other than to wait for the cyclical rains to ingest clean water and thus provide oxygen into the bodies of water. Another recommendation would be to drain most of the water either from Lake Erie or Lake Huron."

The audience laughs at this recommendation because there is no physical way this can be done.

The spokesman continues, "Yes, we know that would be hard to do. But on a small scale, like ponds or lakes of less than ten acres in size, it has been quite effective. Any solution we would suggest would have an immediate effect on killing the bacteria and restoring the lake to its natural color, and fish can be reintroduced.

He pauses and looks at his notes, then to the audience. "Even the river that feeds into the lake comes from Lake Erie, and already the bacteria are spreading up the channel. Small reddish colors are starting to appear along Holiday Beach in upper Ontario. Our bottom line, or finding, is this: This is not a disease problem per se, but it is a commercial issue. And therefore, it is up the locals to do what they think is economically feasible for themselves."

In the back of the room, a man sits by himself. He is there on bequest of the president of the United States and has introduced himself to their hosts as Dr. David Tarkness, representing the EPA. In reality, Dr. Tarkness' job is twofold: First, to go where he is told to go and report back to the Office of the President; and second, to act as a PR person on behalf of the United States. His job is to witness firsthand the very worst things that can happen in the United States – floods, hurricanes, tornadoes, terrorism, and anything upon which the president wants information. He is not a representative of the United States, as he has told some people when asked about his job, but rather is the president's eyes and ears for anything he is told to go do. He has a lot of freedom in his job, and anything he wants is his for the asking. He has his friends in Congress, and all of them know they can count on each other.

After the CDC has presented its findings and discussions have quieted down, Dr. Tarkness is given the floor.

"Distinguished panel, thank you for allowing me to speak on behalf of the United States. After studying the data from all sources and conferring with my colleagues at the EPA, it is our belief that the bacteria will simply die off naturally as the cooler, autumn months roll around. Every year about this time blooming algae appears at the mouth of the Mississippi, and every year it eventually gives way as the cooler water temperatures flow downstream, and then the Gulf of Mexico is restored to its normal state. This summer has been unusually warm through the middle of North America and, therefore, bacteria such as *Chromatiaceae* is expected. Candidly, we did not expect it to be of this magnitude, but we still anticipated and forecasted it. In other words, we see no need for alarm over this bacteria outbreak."

"But what about the financial impact it's having on both sides of the lake?" the Windsor mayor asks.

"Both your city and Detroit are suffering through this, but like I said, it is simply a naturally occurring event. You are most welcome, of course, to try any program you want to kill off the bacteria, but again, our position is to let it die off naturally. Until then, we realize that tourism and recreation will suffer some, but there is nothing that can be practically done." Dr. Tarkness pauses to gauge his audience. "I wish I could stick around and take questions, but I have another engagement planned back in Washington, so please call my office if you want to discuss this further."

Dr. Tarkness shakes hands with a few members sharing the stage with him and leaves to head to the airport. A limo is waiting for him, and the drive to Detroit Metro Airport should take about thirty minutes. As they make their way through traffic, he stares out the window thinking about how bad the algae bloom actually is. He has never seen anything like this before, and he's worried that this outbreak could get out of control.

At the airport Dr. Tarkness finds a quiet corner in the waiting lounge to make a phone call.

"How did it go?" the voice on the other end asks.

"As well as could be expected," he answers. "The typical gnashing of teeth over lost revenues from recreation, but I told them it would all settle down in the fall when cooler water comes in from the St. Lawrence."

"And they bought it?"

"Yes, I think so. What were they going to do? Argue with the EPA? I sure hope we haven't caused a mess here. I'm not worried about it for now, but if October rolls around and we're still seeing this, we'll have a lot to worry about."

"Thank you for your candor, David. I have no doubt things will be fine and this shit will get back to normal. Great job. Get back here soon because I might need you in a couple more places."

"Mr. President, I hope for all our sakes that we are right in our analysis of this problem." He pauses, awaiting some response, but none comes. "I've got to board in a few minutes. I'll come by your office tomorrow. Goodbye sir."

Dr. Tarkness hangs up the phone and looks around the waiting area and thinks about each passenger – how in the dark they all are of what is going on around them because of bureaucrats like himself – and it makes him sad to think he is caught up in the lies. He goes through security, then waits for his flight in the boarding area. Looking out the huge windows that overlook the runway and jet bridges, in the distance he can barely see the outline of Detroit.

"It'll be fine," he wants to think. But in the back of his mind he is thinking that what he has witnessed could be the tip of an environmental disaster from which there is, at a minimum, a years-long recovery – or worse, no recovery at all.

September – "Out Liars"

It's early Monday morning when Dr. Bob MacLean arrives at the Condor Science Building at the university. The name of the building was given by the university as a way of saying "thank you" to the Condor Exploration Company.

Condor, like Apple or Amazon, is simply known throughout the petroleum industry by one name. The company started small in the gritty West Texas town of Midland. As the oil boom came and went, Condor, through shrewd buying of seemingly worthless land, increased its portfolio of drilling rights. When the next round of oil demand hit the world, Condor started drilling with investor money they had lined up for moments like this. It didn't take long for millionaires to be made, and Condor became the largest independent drilling company in Texas. Through its business savvy, Condor kept controlling interests in all the wells it drilled, and for every dollar they paid out to an investor, Condor pocketed fifty cents. Thirty years after their incorporation and investments that now includes offshore drilling, they control oil and gas exploration that ranks them in the top four oil-producing companies in the world. Condor's generosity is well known at most Texas universities for funding research and scholarships for geology, petroleum engineering, and environmental engineering students.

MacLean opens the door to his office and throws his bag on the table. Five rooms away Dr. Oliver walks over to her window overlooking the campus. She has been in her office for several hours already; she couldn't sleep while thinking about how to confront her old friend and colleague with her new data analysis. She is sure of one thing though, and that is the fact that Bob has deceived her for some reason. Like a downhill skier preparing for a final run, she takes in deep breaths, letting each one out slowly. She walks down the hallway.

"Good morning, Marsha. You're here bright and early. What's on your mind?"

"Bob, I haven't slept well all weekend, and…"

Bob interrupts her. "Sorry to hear that. I hope it wasn't a student. You know, we can deal with issues like that."

"Let me finish, please. No, it isn't about a student. Rather, it's about you." She pauses briefly to be precise about what she is about to say. "I've spent many hours looking at raw sensor data from both poles. I have examined them over and over again to the point that I know their results by heart. Can you tell me why the data you gave me and passed on to others is not the same as I found when I looked at the raw data? Hell, every journal I cross-referenced has shitty data in it. Seventy-five percent of it was what we provided to them. What the hell is going on?"

143

"What do you mean raw sensor data? You have the same data as I do. You know how we get it. It comes directly from Dr. Walker...from McMurdo."

His eyes focus on hers, and he walks over to the window and stares into the parking lot teeming with students scurrying to get from one building to another. He wants her to wait on him, as he wants to control the conversation. Turning, he looks back at Marsha. "Now, what exactly are you talking about?"

"I have sources, too, Bob. I decided to double-check things – you know, the triangulate formula we teach to the students. You're aware of that, I'm sure."

Bob crosses his arms and sits on the windowsill, then speaks somberly. "So, you have sources." He waits momentarily, then continues. "How do you know the data you found was correct? Maybe it was just chaff or scree – just noise with no meaning. Maybe it was wrong. Marsha, this is so unlike you. Before you accuse someone of some dastardly deed, I suggest you get all of your facts straight. Someone is playing a joke on you – they must be. Do you know what Chris Walker has given up in his career to work in that hell hole he has called home for the past several years? A lot. He's a brilliant scientist – one of the tops in my book. So again, I ask, who's feeding you this supposedly 'raw' sensor data?"

"Why do you insist on focusing on that? It's not the issue here. Just be honest with me. I know there is an explanation here –

please. I want to understand what was, and is, going on. But to make you feel better, my data was directly from the sensors. It was clean – it wasn't filtered through your buddy Walker. I'm talking data directly from the sensor. I trust my source, but I'm now leery of data that I am getting second hand. All it took was for me to dig a little deeper instead of falling for the 'trust me' reports that you published. I don't get it – were you intentionally trying to mislead others?"

"So why should you or I trust this guy, whoever he is, more than Dr. Walker? Tell me. Tell me!" his voice rising. "You can't, because Dr. Walker's data is fine. Marsha, I'm not sure what is going on with you?"

Marsha interrupts. "Ever hear of Pascal's Wager?"

MacLean furrows his brow as if to say, "Of course – hasn't everyone?"

"Then why not err on my side here, huh? Just pretend for one moment that I'm right. That what I am seeing is downright scary for us – the world. What if what we are seeing makes people arrive at the wrong conclusions? Nothing added up at first, and then things started falling into place after I started a little digging."

Dr. MacLean moves closer to Dr. Oliver and leans on his desk. "Marsha, look around you. Think about this building and the excellent students we turn out each year. These people go on to do incredible things for businesses, and in turn drives our economy."

She cuts him off – now her voice rising. "Excellent students? Do you mean ones who will grow up and enter the job market and become a business leader or department chairman who might sell their soul?"

She immediately regrets her words. "I shouldn't have said that…sorry. But it's all about the money, isn't it?'

Frowning, Bob replies, "To some extent, I suppose it is. It pays for your car, your house, your food, your child's education, and anything else you want to spend money on. You have built a very comfortable life for yourself and your family. I don't ask any questions – and neither should you. We aren't talking the end of the world here. I care, of course, for accuracy, but sometimes I don't care to peel back too much – it's that simple, and I will go on assuming that all data I have to work with is solid. And if you come to your senses for a moment, you should accept it also. It's not going to change a thing – you understand that, right?"

Marsha replies loudly, "It's not about the money – it's about ethics, Bob – pure and simple. You're damn right I built a comfortable life, but it is built on honesty – at least I thought it was. And you know what? How are you so sure we're not screwing up the climate so much that it could turn into an end-of-the-world scenario? Do you know who is behind this façade and why? Do you have a personal stake in this for you? Is it more funding you're being promised? Maybe a little extra?"

Bob yells at her. "If you think it's some sinister plot by someone, think again. Look, so some of my numbers are, let's say, inconsistent with yours; it doesn't change anything. You need to stop and see the big picture here. There is so much drilling and fracking going on now that it's going to set a course of petroleum independence for the U.S. for decades – maybe even a century. Do you want to give up driving your car? Or how about cooling your house? We get spoiled, and we get comfortable with what we expect. So, who cares if the stratosphere has a little depletion at the poles? It's not going to last. Hell, you've seen the fluctuations come and go like everyone. Get off your high-horse, Marsha, and don't be so naïve!"

Marsha is taken aback. She has never heard Bob raise his voice to anyone.

"Are you sure?" Marsha asks after a few moments of silence.

"Am I sure of what?"

"That it won't kill us. You know how it works – the magnetic poles attract whatever is in the air. How about methane, benzene, ethylbenzene, and n-hexane just to name a few? Those numbers were off the fucking chart! Bob, if I'm detecting this level of pollutants, the ozone layer must be totally bonkers over both poles. The U.S. – hell, the world – looks to us for honesty. I know I must be missing something. Help me to understand this; my mind is spinning for answers. You're a scientist – you know what this means! Did you think this could be hidden forever? Do you really think the ozone layer will keep magically reappearing year after year?"

"Marsha, the ozone can fix itself. You and I both know it varies in its depletion schedule."

"Bob, you know, you're right. But let's not get off on how the atmosphere works – we both know that's science 101. It's about you lying and falsely representing data. How could you – and can you – do that? Do you know what this will mean to your credibility when this gets out?"

Dr. MacLean steps back to the window. "Marsha, I suggest you drop this. If questions start to get asked, well…And then someone wants to take it one more step – maybe the university might want to have me resign – but they will probably ask the same of you. Sort of guilt by association, huh? Could John support you three? Kiss your research grants and publications goodbye. And what would happen to this department? I'll tell you what would happen. Another person will be found that maybe has more ties with the oil industry than I ever had. You think I don't have feelings on this, but I do. It bothers me some, but I get over it when I look at things…how should I say…a little differently than you."

He pauses to let Marsha ponder the answers, then continues as he turns back toward her. "Like I said earlier, Marsha, nature has a way of correcting itself – sort of self-healing – just like this conversation if you give it time. Think about your words. Don't do anything rash, and I won't either. You're a scientist who has a great career in front of you. I think you are making much ado about nothing here. Maybe – just maybe – one or two oil and gas companies have gotten carried away with a little drilling. But they can't drill forever. I agree the chemicals are a little suspect from what I've been told, but it's proprietary to them – I've no right to pry into their business. I will tell you that I've been in contact with some of the largest exploration companies, and they assured me their work will be slowing down over the next year. They'll have enough wells drilled to just pump. New drilling will start to taper off." He pauses to read her reaction. "Tell you what, Marsha – if the data trend over the next year shows an increase in pollutants in the poles, I promise you that I'll be the first one to present a case against them."

"Bob, we didn't take an oath of honesty when we started our careers – it was assumed that our research would always be the best it could be. And here you stand in front of me telling me to chill out – just relax. All will be better soon. You call me naïve. Do you really think drilling will ease up? Natural gas drilling is the cocaine of these corporations – and they constantly need their fix."

"I'm sorry I raised my voice to you. What are you going to do?" he asks.

"I don't know yet. I'm letting this all sink in. Sort of like what the ozone is doing over our heads."

"Think about what I said."

Marsha looks to Bob, but her expression doesn't betray any actions she might take. She walks back to her office thinking of ways to explain this to her peers around the world, but who would believe her? She is an associate dean with no tenure – a person low in the hierarchy of senior scientists. Closing her eyes and sitting at her desk while mulling over the past ten minutes, a graduate student knocks on her door, drawing her away from her thoughts of conversation with Dr. MacLean.

"Dr. Oliver – got a minute?"

"Certainly, Cheryl. What's up?"

"I wanted to show you some graphs that I produced from data you asked me to look at."

A week ago, Marsha asked Cheryl to be an independent source who could examine and verify the new pole data against Marsha's analysis. "Yes, yes, please. I was wrapped up in something else, but I was curious what you had seen. So, tell me, what did you find?"

"Well, you did a good job of throwing a lot of dirt embedded in this data. Although, I have to say it was easy to find as I realized how you skewed the data. It was a fun little exercise. Are you going to give me some extra credit for this?"

"Sure. Can I see the graphs?"

"Yeah, got them right here." She laid them out in front of both of them. "See the red line – that's benzene. I didn't know what that was, but I know now because I looked it up. That was funny that you made it such a high PPM. That can't really happen, can it?"

"It might, but I hope not – or we would be in deep trouble in the atmosphere, huh?" Marsha replies.

"And this other stuff you threw in here – wow. I didn't know what half of that stuff was either. The PPM was off the chart for that, too. I had to recalibrate my graph to adapt to such high readings."

"Thank you, Cheryl. I appreciate you doing this."

"You mentioned some extra credit, right?"

"Yes, I'll take care of it."

As Cheryl leaves, Marsha looks at the charts one by one. She pulls out her own analysis, and they compare precisely. "Okay, step one done," she says as she puts all of the documents into one folder marked "South Pole."

Cheryl pokes her head back into the doorway. "That wasn't real data, was it? I know you said it wasn't, but that was a lot of data that someone put together."

Marsha considers giving her an honest answer, but it would just bring more discussions. "No, it's artificial data. Just wanted to see what you could find. Good job."

Cheryl grins. "Thanks. See you in class."

Shit, Marsha thinks. Now I'm an accomplice to fraud – or whatever fudging data is called. Marsha looks at the picture of her husband and daughter that's sitting on her desk. "Shit. Shit, shit, shit," she mumbles out loud.

She ponders her conversation with Bob. Maybe things will fall back to normal when the drilling companies have had their fun screwing with their chemicals. Marsha wants to be precise in her measurements, and wants her results again validated before she considers any next steps she might take. She decides to do some extrapolations and starts plugging in formulas to start her new analyses.

An hour goes by, and her meeting with two doctoral candidates is ready to start. Usually the meeting is short, and she sends them on their way, but today she has a new project for each of them.

"Hi, Leah, come on in."

"Hi, Doctor O. How's it going?" A student stuck Marsha with this nickname a few years back, and it has stuck ever since.

"Fine, Leah. And you?"

"Busy, busy."

"Hi, Matt – Leah just got here. I've got extra work for you two. You guys up for it?"

Both respond, "Sure."

"It shouldn't take long, plus it will be good research that hopefully each of you can work into your dissertation. It's a quantitative study I need done on some numbers. Leah, here's your assignment. Matt, here's yours. Neither should take more than a few days. How about we meet next Wednesday, and you can show me what you've got – okay?"

"Sure, Dr. O," Matt replies. "Want to give me a hint what this is about?"

"Same here," Leah adds.

"I have some data I've been playing around with, and in the report I gave each of you, you'll find how to access it, run it through your statistical tools, and then extrapolate this out, say, two years. Make that two years, five years, and ten years. I want to see what kinds of trends you might find. I'm going to do the same exercise myself. Any questions?"

Their simple shrugs signify there are none, so she says, "Okay – off with you. Let's see if you can earn those PhD stripes."

Over the next two days and nights, Marsha runs the data through several statistical computer simulations. She makes careful note of her findings, and the methods she used in arriving at them. Wednesday comes around, and at three in the afternoon, Matt and Leah show up with their reports. "Hey guys – come on in and have a seat over at the desk."

"You go first, Leah. Explain to Matt and me your approach, and the hypothesis."

"Matt and Dr. O – my hypothesis was that keeping the same rate of PPM of pollutants will have an adverse effect on the Earth's climate."

She lays out copies for both, giving them time to peruse the graphs. "As you can see from the trend analysis line in figure one, and to summarize, if the same PPM rate is maintained, the Earth will enter into a spiral of non-replenishment of resources. You didn't ask for the consequences, but I gave some thought to them anyway. Namely, fresh water will evaporate at an increasing rate, fish and plants will die off, and, of course, this will have a huge economic effect on many countries. I'm not an economist, so I didn't compute what that number is, but suffice it to say, it will be huge. I assume the ice at both poles will be melting like crazy, but I didn't compute rising sea levels – which I assume would come up a little."

Pointing back to her document, she continued, "Now look at figure two – the correlation matrix. More heat and less water means, of course, fewer crops – well, maybe not crops, but tree leaves. Fewer leaves and greenery in general means an accumulation of carbon dioxide in the atmosphere. Pretty simple how it all came together, as you can see in figure three."

Dr. Oliver responds, "Good job on such a short notice, Leah. So, with the data I gave you, you were able to model a general uptick in the trend line pretty easily. And thanks for taking it out to five years. Very interesting. In other words, you proved your hypothesis. Did I summarize that accurately?"

"Yup – pretty straight-forward really. I just fed the data files you gave me into the modeling statistical software, then looked at the plots. I gave it several different correlation algorithms, and it handled them all pretty easily. Pretty dirty data, that's for sure."

"Okay – Matt, you're up. Whatcha got for me?"

Matt lays out his copies for the others. "Well, Dr. O, let me start with my hypothesis: A reduction of two percent PPM will have a positive outcome for the environment. I took it another step, though. I also modeled increasing PPM reductions of three, four, five, and up to ten percent, just to see what results I would get. As you can see from the tables in my report, none of these reductions would have an immediate effect on the atmosphere. According to my model, it would take an estimated fifteen percent reduction to have even a marginal positive influence on the atmosphere. Most of the report are trend lines and correlation matrices. That's it. Any questions?"

"Nope. Another excellent job on such quick notice. I'll make sure your work is noted for your review committee. See you next week."

Dr. Oliver looks at the reports. She opens her folder and pulls out her own report that has kept her awake for many nights. Almost verbatim, Matt's and Leah's reports confirm her own analysis.

"Now what?" she asks herself.

October – Without

The Herschel orbiting telescope is an amazing piece of engineering. It has uncovered more galaxies in the vast universe that most could have ever fathomed. Like an old friend she can call by a first name, it is simply "Herschel" to Dr. Maggie Sanders. Dr. Sanders is in charge of moving Herschel's gigantic lens via computer commands sent to it. NASA figured out early that if too many were given control of things in space, pretty soon they could imagine those devices spinning in circles from having "too many cooks in the kitchen."

As Dr. Sanders prepares Herschel for another maneuver, she is completely focused on her work, and when her phone rings, it startles her. Scientists like Dr. Sanders enjoy their jobs mainly because of two reasons: 1) they like science, and 2) they are loners who shun crowds. These scientists enjoy their expensive toys, and if truth be told, they would enjoy their companionship over most people. Their computer-driven devices do what they are told, and they return unambiguous data.

She looks at the flashing light of her phone, then back to the computer screen, then again to the bothersome phone. She doesn't get a lot of calls, and when she does have to communicate with someone, it is usually via email. Someone sends her a request to move Herschel, and she does it exactly as requested.

Dr. Sanders' popularity in high school was limited to other nerdy types; to them, she was a goddess. She could recite pi to fifty places, could tell anyone the lowest four-digit prime number, and was so taken with physics that her instructors were always challenged to keep her challenged. She excelled enough to become the valedictorian in her class, and with her near-perfect college entrance scores, she had her pick of any university. She chose the University of Michigan mainly because during her visit there, a professor mentioned that not only would she have access to their twenty-four-inch McMath telescope at Peach Mountain, but also to the bank of many radio telescopes located in the area. That sold her. She had always been fascinated with space – it gave her the solitude she wanted. She did well in all of her science classes, and within only seven years had completed her requirements for her PhD.

Looking closely at the caller ID, she recognizes it as a colleague's number. She finished her command to Herschel instructing it to "stop moving," and answers her phone. "Hi, Jim – what's up?"

"Hi, Maggie – just calling to verify the focal point of the lens setting so studies could begin in the Orion NQ2 10 Auriga constellation."

"Just about to do just that. I'll send them to you in a few minutes. I was just moving Herschel."

"Great – I'll look for your email – thanks."

In the past, scientists had to sit in a cold observatory high on some mountaintop to physically point and record data coming through a telescope lens. Herschel, though, allows scientists the luxury of being in a warm office and examining the data as the telescopes send their data bit by bit to receiving stations like Maggie's. Maggie returns to her calibration instructions on her keyboard. She hates to be interrupted, because she has to double-check where she was in her checklist. No one moves a several-ton telescope, which is traveling seventeen thousand miles an hour and is controlled by many real-time sensors without a detailed list of the steps. Maggie is very precise in her procedures. The Herschel Space Telescope was designed to study far-infrared portions of the light spectrum, and usually it is aimed at specific research targets millions of light-years from Earth.

Resuming the programming of Herschel, she sets the repositioning coordinates, but inadvertently leaves the data recording "on" as it swings around to its new position. For almost two hours Herschel's lens is recording Earth's atmosphere at various points. This has happened before, but no one had cared to look at the data; Herschel's software was not designed to look at the light spectrums that Earth reflected. But in the past six months, a random discovery by Dr. Sanders and her colleagues made them celebrities within their circle of scientists. They had discovered oxygen molecules in deep space.

The presence of oxygen had first been hypothesized by astronomers nearly a decade earlier, but it wasn't until recently that, indeed, these elusive molecules had been detected so far away from any possible planet. This discovery excited scientists because it proved to them that oxygen was indeed scattered throughout our solar system, which, in turn, meant that a moon or other planet more than likely emitted those molecules. If the oxygen was coming from our own solar system, then the thousands of other solar systems in our Milky Way were capable of scattering similar molecules around. In other words, oxygen could be prevalent throughout the cosmos. Maggie is famous to her scientist buddies, but better than that is a feeling of being popular – something she had never been before, and she likes the attention this discovery has brought to her.

Dr. Sanders is dubbed as both brilliant and quirky by her colleagues because of her drive to discover things and come up with new theories regarding how they got there. She is known to be in her office for days at a time pouring over data before she takes a break, so her colleagues usually don't bother her unless it's something urgent. As she settles in to examine the data that Herschel is sending to her, she sees something strange on a graph. She issues commands to have the graph highlighted in more detail, and with each command she enters, more precise information is displayed. She squints her eyes at the data, pauses it from scrolling, and leans in closer to the screen. Oxygen molecules are showing up in the magnetosphere, which is an area outside Earth's atmosphere where magnetic fields start to interact with solar winds.

"Huh?' is all she can keep uttering to herself as she looks at the data over and over.

Dr. Mark Zaidens, with whom she is working on the new constellation study, is a friend she can always confide in. She keys in his number.

"Hello."

"Mark, it's Maggie."

"Do you know what time it is?"

"Shit, sorry Mark. I didn't even look at the clock. Sorry."

"Maggie, you don't even own a watch. What's up?" Mark asks sleepily. "Did something break?"

"No, everything is running fine. I wanted to see if it was okay to postpone your data from Orion for another day. I was repositioning Herschel and saw something – totally by accident. Mind if I swing it back and look some more? I promise to have you in Orion by Friday."

"Sure, sure, that's fine. Remember, whatever you find, we both write it up – we're a team," he says half laughing and half yawning.

"Thanks, Mark. Again, sorry to wake you. Bye."

Maggie looks at the clock on her computer. It reads 4:04 a.m. "Crap – sorry, old buddy." Carefully issuing the commands that will be sent to Herschel, she reviews them once, then a second and third time to ensure they are exactly where she wants to point her orbiting friend. She hits the key to send the commands and waits. Once it acknowledges receiving the commands and then repositions itself, she sends it another command to start sampling data at a precise spectrum. Then, she waits some more. She yawns and rubs her eyes.

Her goal is to keep Herschel sampling for at least thirty orbits of the Earth. As each pass varies slightly from the previous one, the spectrum samples will give her a much better view than the quick one she got earlier. She fights sleep, but finally succumbs to her body telling her it needs to shut down – at least for a while. Several hours later she opens her eyes and looks at her watch – 10:35 a.m. She issues some commands on her keyboard and sees that Herschel has sent almost a terabyte of data already – and the data collection is growing by the second. She looks at her watch again and decides to go home while she lets Herschel collect data for another two hours, at which time she will stop the collecting and reposition it to point to Orion, as promised.

Driving home, she is still sleepy and fights to stay awake. Living alone, Maggie doesn't worry about having to call home announcing she won't be home for dinner. Instead, she comes and goes from her apartment at strange hours with no one except a random tenant noticing. Pulling into her garage, she closes the door, walks to her bedroom, and takes off her work clothes, leaving them exactly where they dropped – and she sleeps.

After a few hours, she awakes and shuffles to the shower; it's the first one she has had in days, and the warm water in her hair feels relaxing. Drying off, she drops her towel on the sink and goes down the hall naked. She always keeps her window blinds closed as she likes the freedom of not wearing any clothes around her house. Hungry because she hasn't had more than junk food for the past several days, she opens the refrigerator to see what is available. With the exception of a jar of strawberry jelly, a stick of butter, some long-expired yogurt, and leftovers that she can't recognize, there's nothing palatable, so she closes the door and grabs a box of snack crackers from her pantry. She heads back to her bedroom and throws herself back onto her unmade bed.

She closes her eyes, and several more hours go by. Refreshed, she gets ready to head back into the office. Looking at her flowers with browned leaves, she pours water on them in the hope that the nourishment will revive them, then stands back and looks at them again. Giving up, she shakes her head with both pity for the plants and dismay at her negligence in caring for them.

After stopping at a fast-food restaurant, she drives another ten miles to her office. Parking in her reserved spot, she heads to her basement office. Making herself comfortable in front of her screen and keyboard, and with a few keystrokes, she has access to terabytes of data that Hershel has dumped for her analysis. The computer interprets her commands and, within a few minutes, reports and graphs are displayed and printed for Maggie's review. She glances at a row of data.

"Now where did you come from?" she wonders as she peers at the data.

She enters commands to drill more deeply into the data, and the results show more detail. The graphs and reports could not be clearer – substantial water and oxygen molecules are showing up outside Earth's atmosphere, especially at the magnetic poles.

"This isn't right," she thinks as she reruns the report just to make sure she ran the report correctly. The second report shows the same conclusion. While the oxygen PPM is not high, even one PPM is worrisome, as there simply should be no oxygen molecules found that high above Earth. In Herschel's capture, though, it was much higher than a few molecules. Oxygen is present where it should not be – it's that simple. But how is getting there? Is it from another planet? Did it come drifting in from some dark matter or comet that scientists have yet to explain?

"Wow, this is exciting! A passing asteroid perhaps? Or are other planets somehow shedding their oxygen. Does it mean that Earth will get an influx of oxygen from some unknown source? This is fascinating! Next, my little atoms, is to figure out where you came from," she mutters aloud.

She pushes herself back from her keyboard and closes her eyes in an effort to concentrate on what she saw and to think up a plan for

163

Herschel. She opens her eyes and stares again at the graphs. Another alternative is to consider a reasonable hypothesis that the oxygen might not be drifting in from outer space, but rather escaping to outer space. "But how?" she ponders. She scrunches her eyebrows and rubs her hands together as if she is on the edge of uncovering something strange, but she can't articulate exactly what it is.

"What's happened to the stratosphere?" she asks her screen. "Shouldn't this have been reported by now?" She rummages through a large stack of papers that have not been filed for several months.

"There it is," she exclaims as if finding a hidden planet. It's an old conference brochure, and she flips through it searching for the speakers' names. She finds the speaker who she remembers lectured about polar cap data collection. A quick search on the internet finds him still associated with the U.S. Antarctic Program. Accessing the USAP website, she finds his email address and sends him a message asking if he's still onsite and gathering data. Returning to the data from Herschel, she runs more analyses of the data asking for more reports and graphs.

Several hours pass while she runs other reports when a small icon pops up at the bottom of her screen alerting her to a new email. She glances at who sent it, but doesn't recognize the name, then goes back to analyzing data. Finally glancing at the clock, she sees it reads 2:14 a.m.

"Shit," she says out loud, thinking of the grocery store errand she promised herself to do the previous evening. Gathering up her personal items to take to her car, she recalls the email that she was going to look at later. She pauses to open it and, to her pleasant surprise, it's a reply from Dr. Chris Walker – the man she emailed several hours earlier.

The email reads, *"Hi, Dr. Sanders. Yes, I'm still in Antarctica gathering data. Quite a place here. – we vacillate between calling it adventure or survival depending upon our mood at the moment. How may I be of assistance to you and what kind of data are you interested in?"*

Maggie ponders her reply, her analytical mind always driving her to be exacting with her words. She has her jacket on and feels pulled toward the door to get home, but on the other hand she feels compelled to answer the email since the sender all the way from the South Pole had taken time to respond to her.

She sits at the keyboard and starts typing. *"Let me introduce myself. I am part of the Deep Space Project, and specifically I am in charge of the Herschel Space Telescope. Well, actually a team is responsible for it, but I can direct where it looks. Recently, and I have to say by accident, we did some sampling of spectrum data around Earth and surprisingly found molecules that we didn't expect. Can you tell me of any anomalies you are seeing in the ozone layer?"*

The Last Breath

Staring at the monitor she waits for a reply, but then realizes that Dr. Walker is probably too busy with other projects to have a real-time conversation with her. She impatiently stares at the screen, and when no email comes back, she stands up and walks over to turn off the room lights and pick up her purse. "Bing" – an email has popped up for her. Her curiosity has her trapped. She turns and reads the message.

"Hello again, Dr. Sanders. No, nothing has been out of the ordinary. In fact, we recently did an analysis of our data for the past three years, and there has been absolutely no fluctuation in the atmospheric properties that we can see. Additionally, we recently recalibrated the sensors to make sure they were functioning properly, so I am comfortable saying that all appears normal on our end. Can you tell me what molecules you saw?"

Her growling stomach, with the thought of the grocery store closed now for several hours, distracts her. She is torn between heading out the door or continuing the conversation with Dr. Walker. Her inquisitive scientific nature wins.

"Dr. Walker, thank you for your quick reply – I know you must be busy. It's good to know that all is stable with the atmosphere, as it is something we have all grown to enjoy. As you know, we expect about four-fifths of the air in Earth's atmosphere to be N^2, with the rest O^2. What I found in some sampling around our upper atmosphere were O^3 molecules, and even H^2O, NO, and even NO^2. I never expected anything like this – it was strange to say the

least." She rereads her message to make sure she was accurate in her labeling of the molecules and clicks "send."

She looks at the clock. Two minutes go by with her stomach growling louder. She stares at the screen, then to the clock, then back to the screen. "Bing." Like a child at Christmas anticipating a present, she opens the message.

"Would you mind if I called you? What time is it where you are?" came the quick reply from Dr. Walker.

"Certainly," and she types in her cell phone number. *"It's approaching 0300, but I keep odd hours. I will look forward to your call."* The thought of getting a direct call from Antarctica is exciting, since she isn't used to getting many calls, let alone from so far away.

A minute rolls by, then another and another as she stares at her phone. She picks it up, checks to make sure she can hear a dial-tone, and then lays it down. "Shit, it's a mobile phone – I can answer in the car," she mumbles and laughs to herself. As she is almost to the door, her phone rings.

"Hello, Maggie here."

Through various degrees of static, she hears, "Dr. Sanders, Chris Walker here. So good to chat with someone outside of our little group here at the bottom of the world. I'm always willing to help another researcher."

"Hi, Chris, and it's good to talk with you as well. Please call me

Maggie. No need for us to be so formal around fellow researchers."

"So, tell me, Maggie, what can I help with? Can you tell me more about what you've uncovered?"

"Well, it was something strange," Maggie begins. "We only detected O^2 once outside of Earth's atmosphere, and it was way the hell out there. It wasn't even close to the inner planets. That was strange enough, but as you know, Earth's gravity and atmosphere should not let O^2 escape – it simply shouldn't happen. In fact, it couldn't happen – could it? But, there it is. I know your next question will be, 'did you check your calibration,' and the answer is yes – all equipment checks out fine. In fact, I double- and triple-checked the results. My first thought was that something has happened to the ozone layer – but you would have seen this, right?"

Walker replies, "There has only been one slight fluctuation in a reading, and it settled back to the normal range within less than a week. The data we are reporting today is for all purposes the same as the results we sampled two, or even three, years ago. The ozone has stabilized considerably since some anomalies were reported back in the nineties."

"It just doesn't make sense, Chris, that we detected anything outside our atmosphere," Maggie replied.

"Maggie, I'm no astronomer, but how far out in the atmosphere are we talking about? Could it be some stragglers thrown off by, say, a comet perhaps?"

"We haven't had a comet of any size come within a million miles of Earth for over a year. While I can't be precise with the exact distance, I would guess that it is under four hundred kilometers."

"Well, that is pretty close – I agree. Could it have some venting from, say, the space station?"

"No offense, Chris. Herschel is good, but not that good. Do you know what the odds would be of hitting an O^2 in the exosphere not once, but twice?"

"Dr. Sanders...sorry, I mean Maggie...when you say 'we' or 'Herschel,' did someone else verify this data with you?"

Maggie laughs. "Sorry, Chris, it's just me and the space telescope. I just call him Herschel. The answer to your question is no – no one has seen this data yet. I have repositioned Herschel to another constellation now, so literally speaking, I have tons of data to sift through now from the Earth's spectrum capture. It's hard to move terabytes of data around, as you probably know, and few have security access to this data – and I'm sure you understand the security aspect also."

"Yes, Maggie, security of data is always key for us. So, tell me, where are you located?"

"Outside of Portland, Oregon. Our government has built us quite a facility here."

"Ah, yes, and I'm sure it's much warmer than where I am. I have some research colleagues in Washington – Seattle to be exact. Would you mind if they drove down to visit and chatted with you some more? I'll even ask them to bring some external disk drives, and they can mail it to me – would you mind if they dropped in? I'll make sure they have proper id badges and whatnot with them. They would coordinate with your schedule, of course. What you have told me certainly is tantalizing and I'd like to hear more. Maybe something's wrong with our sensors, but I would hope not. I think when all is said and done, and we have compared notes better, I would think that your observations are worthy of publication in a scientific journal."

Maggie is always getting pressure to write reports so her department can continue to get funding, so the possibility of getting something published would get her boss off her back for a while. "Do you really think so? You know, get something published?'

"Of course, Maggie. Whatever it was you saw was interesting. In fact, I'll even help you write it and provide all the data you want from our end."

"Thank you, Chris – that's very nice of you."

"No problem, Maggie. Now, back to my colleagues. These two men just returned from our station here about four months ago – just too cold for them. Again, you wouldn't mind sitting down with them as representatives of mine, would you? I would bet they would be in and out within an hour. Could you spare that?"

"Certainly. Please have them contact me, and we'll work out a time to meet at my office."

"Thank you, Maggie. Oh, one more thing. Before we correlate your data with our data, may I ask you not to report anything just yet? If I can call my colleagues in the next day or so, I'm sure they can be in Portland in a very short time. Another day wouldn't hurt your reporting, would it?"

"Of course not, Chris. I'll look forward to their phone call. It was so nice talking with you. Stay warm!"

"Will do, Maggie, and it was very nice chatting with you."

As Dr. Walker hangs up the phone, he contemplates his next step. His first thought is to contact Bob MacLean and let them handle this, but after William Moore's plane disappeared, he hasn't slept well. He tries not to connect too many dots. Planes disappear more often than gets reported back in the world press; it's just a fact of life when flying in minus-fifty-degree weather. Things freeze up, blizzards happen, and sometimes it's pilot error – accidents happen – period. Chris looks around his lab and can count on one hand everything in it that has not been paid for by donations from a company called Condor, which is also MacLean's supporter at his university. He thinks about the science Condor supports, and he thinks about the journal articles he has written that have given him recognition in the science community – all because of Condor's involvement. If he calls MacLean and tells him about

171

his call with Dr. Sanders, he knows they will investigate, and probably simply quash the report somehow. Maybe with some more donations of money – maybe a new lab for Dr. Sanders? Or maybe Condor would flood the media with conflicting data, and eventually the whole matter would disappear, because anyone who cared would simply be too confused to look further into it? Yes, he would let Dr. MacLean handle it however he wants.

Dr. Walker looks several times at the message he is about to send, thinking about all the outcomes. He stares a lot longer pondering what actions Dr. MacLean might take. Then, with a click of a key, the characters were accepted by his computer, sent to myriad computers that stored and forwarded the message, and finally delivers it to the addressee.

A day passes and his satellite phone rings, showing an incoming number he recognizes as MacLean's.

"Hi, Bob. Thanks for calling."

Walker explains the call that he had with Maggie Sanders and passes along her phone number. After Dr. MacLean says he will work on a plan to help her through this, Walker hangs up, feeling that the issue has been taken care of, and his involvement is over.

Two weeks pass and Dr. Walker emails Maggie "just to say hello." A reply comes back within a few minutes.

"It is so good to hear from you. I did have a nice chat with some representatives from Condor Petroleum. We got everything

worked out. After sitting with these people, I re-examined my analysis, and it turns out I might have had some calculations wrong. Thank you for emailing. Best regards, Dr. Sanders."

He asks himself why she would write "Dr. Sanders" instead of Maggie? He shrugs it off and sends another email asking if he can call her. A few minutes pass and a reply comes back.

"Dr. Walker, I am heading out of town for some well-earned vacation and am right in the middle of packing. I'm going sailing – should be fun. Sorry, but I cannot spare any time at the moment. I'll be glad to contact you when I return – which should be in about three weeks."

He replies, *"Have a nice trip, and I'll call you when you return."*

The Trojan horse program written by Condor Exploration easily intercepts Dr. Sanders' incoming emails and screens them before passing them on – or not – if they want. Dr. Sanders' neighbors never thought anything was out of the ordinary when the quirky scientist, who worked in some strange lab and kept strange hours, was never again sighted coming and going.

November – Rivers of Doubt

Heavy sheets of rain sweep the village of Alvorada d'Oeste, deep in the Brazilian state of Rondonia. A light break in the downpour allows Maria to make a dash for her Land Rover, which will take her deep into the lush rain forest. To her and others in her area, every part in this vast area has a name, but to outsiders it is a name throughout the world simply referred to as the Amazon. Maria works for the Brazilian government, and they have asked her to keep tabs on all commercial work in her area.

She feels her reports on the logging companies' devastation aren't getting much attention from the government departments. Her reports haven't been exactly flattering to what she has uncovered, and she hoped that her government could at least investigate more. But, so far, she has seen no action on their part. Still, she has a job to do, and that is to keep writing the reports. A wonderful side benefit of her work allows her to keep in touch with the nature she grew up in.

When this area was first explored by non-native tribes, telegraph poles were planted to mark progress through the jungle. Eighteen poles were planted per kilometer and each one numbered. Today, the telegraph system is no longer in service – having been replaced

174

by satellite communications and cell phones. On this excursion, though, Maria will be driving to where pole six thousand three hundred was once located.

As explorations had begun and detailed maps started to be made, companies realized the huge potential for the sale of natural resources held in the Amazon – and once the land was cleared, it opened up an incredible number of hectares for crops and mining of resources from ore to trees. Time, and people, have changed her surroundings. Maria used to love the Amazon – it was not only her home, but part of her – it was her family. As she prepares for the drive, she thinks about how magnificent it still is, but how even more beautiful it was in the not-too-distant past.

It was once estimated that three states the size of Texas could fit in the Amazon rain forest. Today, it is but a shadow of its former glory. Logging companies started cutting trees to satisfy the demand for cheap lumber and support housing booms in first-world countries. Land was purchased cheap, and crops such as maize, corn, and wheat are now cultivated where trees once stood. The Amazon's beautiful land is still alive, but it is different – its breath, its smells, its essence is changed. Strangely, though, some of the soil that grows fifty-foot trees, with canopies so large that they intermingle with other trees, cannot grow crops that well; the loggers, though, don't care, as they are driven to produce timber – not to worry about what happens to the land after they leave it. Maria calls the jungle her friend, and it always will be, no matter

175

how it is changing. Friends treat each other with respect, and she never takes it for granted.

She remembers many times looking up at the limbs and vines intertwining like gossamer threads of life from one giant tree to another – hurt but one, and they all wept, she used to imagine. The trees' roots would never take too many nutrients from the soil, and the soil in turn would provide just enough of these nutrients to sustain a tree. Corn and other such crops did not have this agreement with the moist soil, and in a short time, farmers had to revert to fertilizers to supplement the soil's nutrients.

"Os malditos criadores" (or damn creators) is a phrase she uses when she sees their plantings where the stately and majestic trees once grew. The creators, or planters, of these new crops don't know what they are doing to the environment, therefore, her phrase damning them seems the least she can do. She becomes melancholy as she recalls dinners with her friends and how their discussion about their land being ruined made them all sad. Looking down the dirt road as she positions her bags in the front seat, she readies for her drive. The day is clear, and her friend is waiting for her.

Similar to the pioneers moving west in the U.S. and plowing up lands to plant crops, people kept moving deeper and deeper into the bowels of the Amazon rain forest. A town would be built, workers brought in, logging businesses would start in earnest, and once the nearby area was cleared of all trees, the workers moved onward another ten miles – and the cycle repeated itself. The momentum had been started and the only thing to rein it in is if they run out of trees – and in an area as big as the Amazon, no one could fathom that that was remotely possible. With the demand for natural resources increasing, Maria ponders if, indeed, the Amazon might one day completely be gone.

To exacerbate what is occurring with logging, petroleum exploration falls in behind as land is cleared. Sometimes the drilling companies vie with the farming companies for immediate access to this newly opened up land, and in those cases, the former always wins out – and the farmers simply wait until the drilling is over before crops can be planted. Drilling an oil well in the Amazon is inexpensive compared to drilling in the United States, as not only the depth to find the oil is shallower, but roughneck labor is extremely cheap. The jungle, though, never gives up its secrets or resources easily. Everything under the canopy lives for survival – even the giant trees themselves have developed a system to protect themselves and their progeny from predation. Rarely, for instance, will one ever see a grove of the same type of tree – and this perplexed scientists for years. Scientists could not understand why this was so, and finally it dawned on the naturalists that this is simply Darwin's theory about evolution at its best. If trees are grouped closely and a certain fungus attacks them, they will all certainly die off. But if they only allow themselves to live apart, then their survival chances increase as the fungus cannot easily find the tree's relatives. This type of

177

survival plays itself out over and over for every living thing from insects, to reptiles, to fish, to animals, and to the humans who had lived there for at least five thousand years – maybe more.

Maria drives through the nearly barren hills toward an area known as the Madeira. As she glances about, her mind wanders back to her carefree childhood days. But then she thinks about the cruel things that the jungle could do. Her father was once a camarada – a comrade, or special worker – for the exploration companies, and when she was no more than six, he would take her along with him to work, even though it was against her mother's wishes. Maria was an adventurous sort, so it seemed natural that she wanted to ride along to the lumber mills that were springing up everywhere. The lumber mills provided more money than anyone in her village could ever earn by farming or from the occasional tour guide request from a rich tourist. On all of her trips, her father always stopped at a small settlement of wattle-and-daub huts to check the telegraph office for any messages before continuing on. One village was occupied by the Navaite Indians, and although they never fully trusted outsiders, they usually got along with most of the native Brazilians – it was the white man they mistrusted.

As Maria and her father approached the village that humid summer day, all was quiet except for the jungle sounds of a monkey calling another in the distance. Then a branch would fall, or a soft din of simple sounds that came from no specific place, yet permeated everything, would complement the silence. The magic of the mind enables it to store senses once experienced – no one knows how it does this, but today Maria easily remembers the smells of that day when an aroma wafts by. And now, as then, just the thought of that day makes the hairs on her arms bristle in fear. The light falls through at random places, and she is trapped by the color and the brightness as it contrasts with the thick undergrowth. The air, almost unmoving, cuts her nostrils with the smells of decaying wood and other fauna. It is the jungle talking, and Maria's thoughts of that day with her father, who had taught her to listen to all around her, continue.

Her father had parked his old truck, and as he and Maria had started walking toward the telegraph office and passing by a small house, a grotesque image appeared that neither could ever erase from their minds. The telegraph operator was buried up to his waist in the dirt, and his exposed torso had, what seemed to be, hundreds of arrows in it. None of the arrows seemed to have penetrated deeply into the skin, as some portion of the arrowheads were still visible. The agony of death had contorted the features of his face. She had heard stories of how the Indians used potions to heal or kill, and now she could see that result. Each arrow must have been coated with something – probably curare. One touch of curare was said to drive a man crazy and cause a slow death, and this man had been hit by so many arrows that his death must have been beyond any pain level imaginable. On top of the man's head was his Morse-key device that had been pulled from the wall.

Maria screamed as her father scooped her up and ran back to his vehicle. Though hot and muggy as it always was, he quickly rolled up the windows and locked the doors. Their hearts raced fast with panic, and her father knew that if did not leave this place immediately, he and Maria could suffer the same fate as the occupant of the house. The engine started and her father drove wildly out of the village hoping that the distance he was making would keep them safe. Such is the uneasy truce with the native tribes – one day they accept an outsider, and the next day something small and seemingly insignificant triggers their ire. They live by simple rules, but even the most knowledgeable outsiders admit they don't understand them.

Her thoughts return to the present as she thinks about the many years that have passed between today and her childhood. The Amazon never erases its images – rather it keeps releasing them like old movies that keep playing. She looks down at her rifle that she is never without. She still hunts, but never for sport. If she needs meat, the forest is a buffet of food for every animal in the food chain. Her gun was a gift from her father during his last years. It has a patina and scars that do not increase its value, but to Maria it is worth a million dollars.

On her trip before this to the rain forest, she had arrived at the furthest outpost just as a helicopter was taking off. It wasn't unusual for her to see companies use all means to explore, but the somberness of the men standing around told her that something serious had happened. Maybe someone had gotten hurt cutting trees, she thought. She waved as she approached a man she knew. "Is everyone okay?" she had asked.

"It was another frog," had been the quick reply. He hadn't needed to say anything more – the helicopter was airlifting the body out. Every worker had been warned. Even the mighty jaguar or a human with a machete or chainsaw fears this small amphibian. The man had come in contact with a poison-dart frog. Nature tries to warn curious interlopers by marking dangerous creatures red, or bright yellow, or brilliant blue – but nature doesn't play fair at times, and for this lowly frog, its color is an ordinary brown – and those are the ones that are hardest to see. While curare causes an awful death, the poison from this frog is said to be so toxic it can kill a hundred people. A simple touch is often instant death.

She has seen so much injury and death over the years that all she can do is be careful. It is the jungle, and if she learned nothing from her father, she learned to be vigilant at every turn.

On the road she glances at the Rover's vitals: petrol – OK; water temp – OK; other gauges – OK. The road is like any rural dirt road in mid-America in the 1920s. If there hasn't been a rain, one can make a fair pace of around 30 mph – maybe even faster if the potholes are well spaced and can be dodged. After a rain, treacherous isn't adequate to define the path properly; in many places, if you're not careful and don't pay attention, any size vehicle could easily flip on its side.

Today is a good day on the well-beaten path, though, as the last rain has soaked into the ground and the dirt is firm. After more hours of driving, she stops to take a break. There are no petrol stations or places to stop into for a bathroom break. Every driver carries at least five large cans of petrol and multiple rolls of toilet paper for occasions like this. Turning off the engine, she opens her door, steps out, and looks at the chopped landscape. Where large trees once stood, only small trees are starting their growth after the land was raped by the companies. She has passed no other vehicle going in either direction all day, and she doesn't expect one now. She thinks nothing of slipping her pants off and laying them on the spare tire as she takes a long overdue body break. Suddenly, a noise startles her, and it is coming from the area of some bushes where the brightness is lost to the foliage. Her attention is now focused fifty feet away, with her eyes squinting to pick out anything that moves. She stands to reach for her rifle. Panic seizes her as she realizes that in her haste to take a break, she left the gun sitting inside the Rover. Naked from the waist down, she walks backwards toward her car door while focusing on the trees in front of her. Grabbing her pants from the back of the Rover as she walks by them, she throws them in the car, and then slides behind the wheel. With a key turn, the Rover starts. She exhales, realizing that she has forgotten to breathe for the past few seconds. She takes in more deep breaths, calming herself down, and drives away. Looking in her review mirror she sees nothing, but her heart feels as if it will jump out of her chest. Maybe it was nothing. Or maybe it was something – a panther? A person? But the jungle was speaking to her. She drives on another half mile where she stops, takes deep breaths to calm down more and, now feeling safer, steps out to put on her pants. She looks about, nods to her old friend the jungle, and continues on her journey.

The road, or wide path as it has now become in many places, winds close enough to the river that on one side is water and on the other there is nothing but a sheer cliff of greenery that stretches at least one hundred feet high. Her mind returns again to how the jungle can turn on a person. Her younger brother Luiz almost died by the river's grip and it wasn't from drowning or from the piranha, stingrays, or even bull-sharks that somehow make their way up the brackish waters. Everyone knew the risks of swimming, but if one stayed close to shore, the water was thought to be safe and a respite from the constant heat and humidity. Maria and her siblings had been warned of little "things" in the river, but her parents never explained what these little things could do. On his last trip ever to the river, Luiz did something that every child does – he peed – and why not? Everyone did it. Out of the billions and billions of gallons of water that churn through the Amazon, a few ounces of urine would surely go unnoticed. But the Amazon never is easy to figure out.

Why nature invented or evolved the candiru is impossible to say. The candiru is a small fish that is drawn to the odor of urine like a shark drawn to a dying fish that is slowly releasing its odors to the vast ocean. The candiru, once sensing urine in the water and in an amazing surge of speed and strength, literally follows the urine stream until it cannot go any further. Before the person knows it,

183

the small fish has embedded itself inside the urethra. Nature has made this worse for the human, as the candiru has spikes on its back that will not let it back out. Wanting more urine, it works its way to the bladder, where days later it eventually dies. When this happens, the person is no longer able to urinate.

Maria remembers her brother screaming in pain and seeing his belly swell to double its size. She cried in her mother's arms wanting her little brother to get well – but she knew he was about to die. No trained doctors could get to them within two days – maybe more – but everyone knew Benedito.

This medicine man, or pseudo doctor, or whatever title one would give him, had seen the pain caused by the candiru several times before. As he studied Maria's little brother, he explained to her parents what was going on inside the small boy. The only way to retrieve the embedded candiru and to save Luiz's life was to amputate the penis. Her father pleaded with the doctor to keep trying other methods, so Benedito kept trying with many painful probes. Finally, by luck or skill, the small parasite relinquished its hold, and with the parents holding down a screaming boy, a careful tug pulled it from the boy's body. Her brother recovered, and within a week he was running and playing with his friends – but he never re-entered the river again. Maria had learned yet one more lesson of the Amazon – no matter how safe one thinks he or she is, something bad is waiting for an opportunity to hurt you. She has never forgotten that lesson, and this is why she always tries to be aware of all around her.

The rough roads shake her back to the present. The lack of rain on this stretch of the road makes the ride hard, and the rolling of the road pulls her in one direction and then another. Her hands grip the wheel so hard that she forces herself to stop several times to stretch her fingers. Hours pass and, in the distance, she can see some houses that mark her first goal – Tapaua, where she will spend a quiet and safe night in a hotel. The last thing she wants is to spend the night in her Land Rover, so she is relieved that her pushing on has paid off with a bed.

Bigger towns close to bigger cities have neon lights – even old ones that don't work any longer. But not in this town. Bare light bulbs dangle from single cords draped over a board nailed with no care for aesthetics. It is all about function.

They know Maria here, and every time she passes through, the hotel owner gives her a hug and insists on having dinner with her. She knows he has other intentions than just food, even though he has at least one wife already. Still, he is always a gentleman, and she always accepts his hospitality with a smile.

"Hola, Señorita Maria," she hears his loud voice as she pulls to a stop in front of the Tapaua International Hotel.

"Hola, Señor Albreto," Maria responds as she gets out and stretches after driving for such a long distance. They approach each other and exchange traditional kisses on the cheeks.

"Mateus. Mateus. Mateus. You call me that. Why do you call my last name? Señor Albreto was my father. We are old friends! Your

185

room awaits. Please, take the same one you always take. No one is here tonight anyway," he says with a laugh but with a twinge of sadness.

"Si, I will do that. I only have this small bag. We'll talk later – I promise."

"Would you have dinner with me? The restaurant will prepare us a lovely meal."

"Yes, but of course – I will look forward to it."

"Do you need any help with your luggage? I will be glad to come to your room."

"Thank you, Mateus, but it is just a small bag. I can manage it."

"As you wish. The room is all yours."

Her room has an odor that she can never quite place – it's not exactly musty, nor is it a sweet smell. Rather, it's as if dust, flowers, gecko poop, and cheap perfume had contrived to come up with eau du Tapaua. The rod where the curtains once hung is still on the wall as if awaiting someone to return any day and hang brightly colored patterns to brighten up the dingy room. The bed, while having clean sheets, is hard, as it consists only of a four-inch piece of foam laid upon a sheet of plywood. The room's greatest asset though is that it has its own bathroom. The door that separates the areas has no handle – just a hole where one used to be. It is never closed anyway, and the hot water rarely, if ever, works. Still, it is all hers. She takes off her clothes and shakes them to remove the dust. She stands her rifle by the doorway, unfurls clean clothes on the bed, and turns on the shower. Out of habit she feels the water and lets out a laugh as if she was expecting anything different than it to be cold. She steps in, pulling the shower curtain as far as it will go. It hangs listlessly as most of the hooks are missing. She closes her eyes, puts her hands against the cool tiles in front of her, and lets the water wash over her.

Drying off, she lies back on the bed and stares at the ceiling. Not many men, let alone women, would do her job, and she promises herself that one of these years in the not-too-distant future she is going to quit and stay at home where she can tend her garden and play with her chickens – and maybe even start a family. She gets up, raises her eyebrows, and mumbles, "But they pay me a lot," as she dresses, then walks into the dimly lit lobby to find her host behind the check-in desk.

"Mateus, so how have you been?" she asks as she approaches him and lets him kiss her on both cheeks again. "I'm starved. Is that horrible little restaurant still open down the street?"

Mateus laughs. "Si, Maria. The food there is no better, but it is okay if you are hungry. There are other places to eat, but they are worse," and he laughs again, only louder this time.

Every road, in almost every town in the Amazon, is either dirt or paved with rocks put in place by workers who obviously had a poor sense of humor. While each rock is smooth on top, all are at different heights from the adjoining ones. Only a fool would driver

187

over them faster than a mere five miles per hour and walking on them is harder yet. Still, visitors get used to it as they learn to do a sort of jump between steps – the locals call it the rocha passos.

"Come, let's go," Maria commands. Mateus nods and falls in beside her.

Maria asks about Mateus' wife and family and, with other small talk, it doesn't take long to reach the café. The eatery is simple in every manner, with four tables set outside under an awning, and an inside room for cooking. There are plastic tablecloths on each wooden, homemade table, and the chairs are molded plastic that have "Made in China" stamped on them. Maria talks about her work, and Mateus talks about the travelers who have passed through his town. His business is prospering so well that he has bought another business – a small petrol and repair station. Maybe not tonight, but on many nights, he explains, his hotel is so busy that he has no available rooms. Yes, he says, the lumber and oil business are good for him. Tapaua was once a small village of only a dozen huts, but now it covers almost a square kilometer and has close to three hundred people living in it.

Maria is respectful in her listening, but in her mind, she is laughing knowing that other travelers have to put up with the smelly rooms also. Her dinner is almost as it always is – a little lettuce, some chopped tomatoes, some beans, and some kind of fish in a sauce that varies in color depending on the light. Still, it is tasty enough to be edible – maybe the taste has grown on her as it doesn't seem as bad as the first time she ate it on her first stop here years ago. Her attention is polite in pretending to listen, but the talk is tiring as Mateus talks about life in his small town, and she feels her eyes droop from the heat and exhaustion of driving over the bad roads.

"Mateus, I must retire for the night. I'm very tired after a long day's drive."

"But of course, Maria. We will talk tomorrow." Always the gracious host, he walks her back to the hotel where he says, with a wink, "Would you like a nightcap? I know the bartender."

Maria gives him a kiss on the cheek. "Not tonight. Another time, though." They both laugh as they know it will never happen. To Mateus, it isn't about the catch, it's about the flirting – which he finds more fun. Plus, he knows that if he is kind to her, she will return many more times, and each time she will bring more stories of the camps. He knows the boundary he mustn't cross, and he stays well on the other side of it.

The rooms at Mateus' hotel are Spartan by all standards, however, besides the luxury of the private bathroom, each room has a ceiling fan. The cool breeze washing over a sweating body provides a coolness that is so refreshing that the noise and wobble of the twirling blades can be ignored. The screens on the windows are supposed to keep out small critters, but every now and then, a gecko falls on Maria in the wee hours of the morning. At first, she bolted from the bed when this guest first dropped in, but now with

189

a simple wave of the hand, she can throw her little friend off the bed and return to her sleep.

On this evening, she surveys the ceiling before readying herself for sleep. All is clear – at least so far. She lays her clothes on the room's only chair and lies back on the bed. She closes her eyes, thinks about her long drive tomorrow, and falls asleep.

The dim light wakes Maria early. It was a restless night of dreams and fatigue. She would like to remain in bed for another hour but knows that that will make her next stop quite late. She walks to the window and sees the morning Alpen glow fall on the town and trees. She puts her clean clothes back in her bag, and dusty and sweaty or not, she puts on the clothes she wore the day before. She grabs some coffee, a pastry, and two bananas from the desk in the lobby.

Mateus is not around, so she leaves money on the counter with a note that reads, "Thank you for the room. See you soon. Maria." The money will be safe no matter how long it sits there, since there is no crime in the small town. She backs out her Land Rover, checking her fuel level as she drives down the jarring street heading north. She knows there is a petrol station only a few streets away, so she heads there to have her tank topped off.

A giant of a man by Amazon standards comes over to her vehicle. He has on green overalls that exhibit such a layer of grease and dirt that they must not have been washed for weeks – maybe months. Like most people living in small towns like this, it is about survival, and clean clothes don't help you survive – especially if you work at the only petrol stop for 150 kilometers in either direction. His demeanor is like his overalls. He looks into the Rover as if to take inventory of what Maria is carrying, then undoes the gas cap and sticks in the nozzle to pump the petrol. He makes no eye contact with Maria nor does he say anything to her, but instead stares at the passing numbers on the petrol pump. He's bored with his life, but it pays a small salary – enough for a beer or two, some food, and a cheap room in the back of the business. When he sees a vehicle like Maria's, he knows that in his wildest dreams he will never be able to have a nice car, nor probably ever own anything other than a beat-up old motorcycle that has been handed down for decades in the village. He would like to leave his town, and if someone asked him where he'd go, he wouldn't have an answer other than "anywhere." The click from the pump pulls him back from his dreams, and he replaces the nozzle and walks to Maria's window.

"Four-hundred Reais," he says as he holds out his hand. She pulls out the money from her bag and hands it to him, then drives off thinking of how the same petrol back at her home would only cost half that. She knows that the petrol has been brought upriver by special boats, then moved overland by several people. The petrol is worth whatever it costs, so she is always glad it is there instead having to use her own emergency cans.

Her next three days will take her deep into the Amazon, with two more small towns almost identical to the one she just left before she will reach her final destination. Some of the road has been paved a short distance with cheap asphalt laid down by some company, but the majority is the typical hard, clay dirt. Every irregularity from rut to smoothness jars her to the point of making her butt sore, no matter how padded her trusty Rover seats are. Sometimes, she crawls along at no more than eight miles per hour, and on some lucky stretches that she knows from memory she can hit fifty. For the past day, though, a rain had swept in and out of this particular area, leaving puddles that are deceiving as to their depth. Carefully, she approaches each one to test them before going forward too fast. Her years of dealing with such impediments and having faith in her dependable Range Rover keeps her calm, and with a steel-edged focus she makes it through.

Her last day of driving is a little longer than the others, and finally she arrives at the newly created town of Sao Gabriel da Cachoeira at 11:30 p.m. She is tired and hungry, and all is quiet except for the hum of generators randomly spread throughout the village. In the distance, lights are on, showing that men are working into the night. There are no street signs, as everyone knows how to get wherever they are going according to landmarks. "Turn at the yellow house," or "At the broken tractor, go left," and other similar directives are the norm here. She makes the turns she knows by memory, and at the end of a road pulls up in front of a house that's green on the bottom and yellow on the top. She shares this house with several other women working here, and she always has a room kept clean for her whenever she might arrive. Like every hotel and house, it has no air conditioning. It does, however, not only have a ceiling fan, but also netting around her bed, which provides relief from the relentless gnats or stray geckos that are always ready to annoy.

As she takes out her bag, she looks in the opposite direction of the working men. Past the streetlights, there is nothing but blackness. In the distance she hears a car start. It is usually quiet, especially around midnight, but tonight the quiet puts her on edge somehow. She couldn't explain it if asked, but yet she feels it. If she listens carefully, she can usually pick out jungle sounds like monkeys, birds, and even the roar of a panther. Turning to see the glow from the workers' lights, she shrugs. Tomorrow, she will worry. Tonight, her bed beckons.

Unbeknownst to Maria and everyone else in Sao Gabriel da Cachoeira, the last remaining Nhambiquara natives in all of the Amazon are close by. They are very quiet as they have been busy stuffing leaves into the holes of trees. They do this for two reasons: 1) they believe that this will muffle their sounds as they approach for an attack, and 2) so the jungle cannot hear the screams from their victims. The Nhambiquaras are a people who have learned how to live in synchronicity with the animals, fish, trees, and all things under the canopy – and to loathe any outsiders, even members from other tribes. Logging and farming have destroyed almost all that they have taken for granted, and now revenge is being planned.

Deep in the forest, many of the Nhambiquaran men discuss what to do with the "others." The Nhambiquara call everyone not belonging to their tribe "others" as they have few words for anything, let alone for a "white man who drives something that makes noise." About half of the men want to attack the workers simply for the honor of killing, and the other half want to attack so they can take their metal and anything they can use as tools. They have no chief – all decisions are made by the group. After a short discussion, all nod in agreement that for whatever reasons they agree to use, the "others" must be attacked.

None of the Nhambiquaran women and children participate in any tribe discussions, although boys from the age of twelve are considered men. They have no words for sexual organs, but they know that a man's penis is important to him. Usually in battles, whether an enemy is dead or not, these warriors will slice off an enemy's penis and stuff it in the dead man's mouth, then start cutting off the ears and the nose.

One boy hollers, "I will kill many of them with you." Other warriors mumble approval in agreement, but not all.

"We have seen their weapons. They can kill us, and they will eat us," another warrior says after the din has subsided. Some warriors agree. A warrior stands up, though, and points to his bark belt – made from the bark of a special tree. He yells, "Nothing can hurt me – I am protected!"

The only clothing usually worn by Nhambiquaran men is the bark from a tree that their ancestors said would protect them. The women wear no clothing. Just as a man shops for a perfect pair of shoes and might inspect each for style and comfort, it is the same here in the jungle where a Nhambiquaran man might spend several days searching for the right tree. Once the perfect bark is found, he slowly peels a section from the trunk. He wraps it around his waist and secures it with a thread made from a vine. The bark usually cuts into the man's abdomen and is uncomfortable to wear, but it is tradition and he wears it with pride.

Other warriors now stand and pound on their bark belts to show that they too are protected. The men inspect others around them, and after many more words of approval by all, they agree that they are invincible. A warrior from the back of the circle of men takes the bodies of two small, white dolphins and throws it in front of the other men. Then a jaguar's carcass is added by three other warriors.

One of the warriors says, "They are devils. Even our fish brothers who breathe now die, and they will kill all fish. The jaguar cannot run any longer without dying. He slows."

With any statement, all of the men say words of agreement. One could say, "The moon is falling" and all would shout words agreeing – it is tradition. There are many of them in their gathering, but they act as one. To the Nhambiquara these animals have no name. Like most living things in the Amazon, the fresh-water dolphin is peculiar as it has gills to breathe in water and lungs to breathe above the surface. In fact, the dolphin must rise to the surface about every ten minutes or it will suffocate. Recently, though, as the dolphins come to the surface, the Nhambiquara saw them struggle to breathe, and eventually almost all of them have disappeared. The warriors in favor of attacking the others see the animals dying as an omen – that if the "others" can kill these mighty animals that have been here for longer than anyone can remember, then the "others" can kill the Nhambiquara also if they don't kill them first. They decide to attack at dawn.

Company guards are always posted by the work crews, even though an uneasy truce is loosely agreed upon with the Nhambiquara. The companies who run the logging operations know how this native tribe could be ruthless, so caution is always given this deep in the Amazon. Months have gone by, though, with no sightings of anyone from the Nhambiquara tribe, even though every now and then a dog was discovered with an arrow through it. Everyone knows the Nhambiquara are watching, but as long as they keep their distance, the workers feel at ease. This will be a regrettable mistake.

Maria awakens early. She is restless and can't get back to sleep, so she makes herself ready for her first day at the camp and walks outside before the sun comes up. Even though it is early, the air is hot and humid already. She looks at the lights in the distance, about where the tree line now starts, and thinks about how the area had once been so rich in a thick canopy jungle that no light ever touched the ground. Now, though, because of fertilizers and just enough rain and sun, the soil will start to grow crops that can be commercially sold for a handsome profit. She is used to the quietness of the early morning, but as her last night arrival made her feel something was strange, this morning has an eerie feel to it also. She recalls a phrase her father had told her many times, "Friends proclaim their presence, but silence marks an enemy."

She walks over to her Land Rover and retrieves her rifle that is lying on the floor. Slinging it over her shoulder she greets two workers who have noticed her and are coming over to welcome her once again to their town. After pleasantries with the men, she goes back into her room. Her head is aching, and she is hungry. She digs through her bag and finds a banana and a piece of bread. She undresses as she lies back on the soft mattress and pillow as she nibbles on the food – and then closes her eyes and thinks about the people she should meet today and get their production numbers.

At the tree line where Maria had just looked, the first arrow flies out and strikes a guard. Then another arrow, and then a dozen more. The guard was dead before he could pull one arrow out or fire his rifle. The next guard is also hit with an arrow, and as he feels the numbness already starting as he yanks on the arrow, he drops behind a log that had been felled sometime before. He can hear arrows hit the wood. Focusing on saving his own life, he knows that firing his gun might scare them. He tries to pull the trigger, but he has little strength left – the one arrow's poison is taking over his body. He tries to focus on the trigger again, and with both hands working together, he succeeds in firing off one shot before he feels his life ebbing away and his eyes fixate in a death stare. That shot alerts other workers of trouble. None know what the trouble is, but all stop working and are trying to determine why the shot rang out. They can see no one running or yelling, so they are confused as to who fired the shot and why.

The gunshot has pierced they heavy morning air, stirring Maria to find out what just happened. Without a thought, she instinctively jumps out of bed and grabs her rifle. As she always sleeps in the barest of underwear because of the heat, she stands there almost naked trying to remember where she threw her clothes. She sees them lying in a pile on a chair, and quickly slips on her khaki pants and grabs her shirt as she runs out of the door barefooted. She sees the others pointing in the distance, and she walks hurriedly in the direction where others are headed.

As she and others of her gun-toting group arrive to the workers, they see the two dead guards. The Nhambiquara are standing proud. A Nhambiquara man stands barely five feet, but his bow towers over him by another foot. The bow is made from a special wood that is so hard that it is doubtful any worker could bend it to pull an arrow. The Nhambiquara have developed upper-body strength, and in one smooth pull can pull the string back far enough to launch their four-foot arrows well over three hundred meters. Although naked except for their bark wrapped around their stomach, their painted faces make them look fierce.

Neither the workers nor the Nhambiquara know exactly what to do next. If the Nhambiquara pull back their bows to shoot, every gun will be fired in unison to try and kill as many Nhambiquara as possible in the shortest timespan – then dive like hell to dodge any arrow that might have been fired. Maria has her rifle ready to fire when four of the Nhambiquara men come forward dragging the dead animals.

Maria is mesmerized by their graceful pace. They are in no hurry, nor do they go too slowly. They are not scared by the "others." Their strides are purposeful, and she watches as they place the carcasses in front of them. As if saying "goodbye" to someone dear, they look down, and then into the eyes of the others as if to dare them to try and hurt them.

"What in the world?" she mumbles out loud. She keeps her rifle pointed at anyone who shows any intention of firing an arrow, but the Nhambiquara stand with their bows next to them – no arrow is nocked.

As with all of the workers standing next to her, Maria is not sure what to do now. She is curious as to why they chose to lay out these dead animals on their doorstep. Breaking the silence, one of the workers, who understands a little of the Nhambiquara language, asks, "What do you want?"

"Others kill these. Others will kill more. Others must leave, or others will die, and we will eat you like monkeys," is the reply

199

from a man acting as their spokesman. All the other Nhambiquarans join in with whoops of agreement.

The worker motions for the overall manager of the operation, Graham Martinez, to come forward. He steadies his rifle to have it quickly ready in case any Nhambiquaran puts an arrow in the bow, as he walks cautiously to the interpreter.

"What did he say?" Graham asks the man.

"He said that we killed their fish and jaguar, Mr. Martinez."

"Tell him that we are sorry, and that it was an accident," Graham tells the interpreter.

The interpreter struggles for a moment trying to say the right words. "What's the matter, man? Tell them!" Graham tells him firmly.

"I don't know the word for 'sorry' or 'accident.' I don't think they have words for that. At least I have never heard them," the interpreter replies.

Both sides study each other. The Nhambiquarans expect a reply or something in response, while the workers aren't sure what to do next. Maria looks around for something – anything she can carry, and spots two workers in the back, holding machetes. She puts her gun down and takes the machetes from the men who reluctantly give them to her, then grabs a hoe and two axes that were leaning against a log nearby. Quickly she walks to the Nhambiquaran man who is standing over the fish and lays her armful of materials at his feet. The Nhambiquarans quickly gather around and pick up the tools. Never has Maria been so close to a Nhambiquaran before, and she can feel her heart race, as she knows that any second many of them could let their arrows fly – several of which could not miss her at this range. The Nhambiquarans back away and gather in a group. Just as quickly as they came, they slip away as silently and invisibly as they had come. No more guns or arrows were fired.

The morning raid had cost two men their lives. Every man who signed up for this work knows that working in the jungle is hard and dangerous. Maria looks down at the animals, and as she rolls each one over, she mumbles, "How did they die? And why blame us?"

She studies the dolphins – they look healthy. "Why did you die, my friends? And you, señor jaguar. How did they catch you? You can run faster than anyone."

She looks up to where the Nhambiquarans had been standing only a few moments earlier. The natives know their old friend the jungle better than anyone – even Maria – and it is speaking to them; someone is hurting it, and they are the protectors of it. Maria feels an obligation to help protect it – but she doesn't know how.

December – More Tipping Points

As the fall turns to winter, irregular events start to occur at regular intervals. Whales are now commonly found as washed-up carcasses on all continents. Countries that had still harvested whales give up once they realize that being at sea for months and never spotting a living one is not profitable. Even the people stationed in Antarctica are getting used to seeing walruses and small fish feed off of these bloated mammals. Scientists guess at the possible causes for the whales dying, but no one has a definitive answer. In the shallower waters around the resorts through the British Virgin Islands chain, more dead fish are washing up on beaches, which in turn leads to fewer tourists in the once pristine waters.

Temperatures are so above normal that people who locate a clean beach and want to cool off find that, even at a depth of twenty feet or more, the water is only about two to three degrees cooler than the surface temperature. As in the Great Lakes area, some scientists attribute the ocean fish die-off to algae blooms –

especially in gulf areas where pesticides wash in. People are fed conflicting and confusing messages, so the accepted solution is to ignore the issue and hope that the problem will disappear with the seasonal cycle.

Up until now, few scientists or governments could get their "maybe we should take a look at global climate change more seriously" story heard. But events like fish dying in the open ocean are happening at such frequency that people are falling into two camps – those who want accountability from some government, or those who just accept the fact and wait to be told what to do.

In lower Ontario, the bacteria that started in one place have now spread at a rapid pace. The coming of the fall season is not providing the promised solution. The Canadian government has brought in expert after expert to find a root cause. Their findings are straight-forward: there is little to no oxygen in Lake Erie – it is a dying lake, even though Lake Ontario should be feeding it with fresh water. Scientists trying to find the source are startled to find that Lake Ontario itself is slowly being strangled by the lack of oxygen-enriched water from the St. Lawrence, which in turn is fed from the Atlantic.

Most people around the world have accepted warmer climate cycles around Earth at times, and governments keep assuring them that with season changes, better temperatures will be coming. In the United States, all states below the parallel of Iowa are experiencing higher temperatures than have ever been recorded.

Utility companies struggle to provide electricity to drive the demand for air conditioning and, in response, these companies are buying old, antiquated coal-powered power plants to put them back online.

Cruise ships to Alaska are enjoying a brisk booking of passengers as reports of massive glacier calving, which was once rare to see, are now an hourly occurrence – providing thrilling pictures and "oohs and aahs" from the tourists. One ship, which was used to settling in about a quarter mile offshore to watch the glaciers fall piece by piece into the ocean, was almost overturned by a large chunk that caused an estimated thirty-foot tidal wave. Only by luck did the ship with its passengers survive. The Coast Guard issues warnings that all cruise ships should maintain a clearance of at least a half-mile from shore and should attempt to keep the bow always pointed toward shore to avoid being hit broadside by a wave. If not, the ship could not only cause and suffer considerable damage, but, if the circumstances were right, could roll over.

As the countries in the Andes are coming out of their spring, the mountain tops usually have snowpack from the previous winter – but not this year. Except for a few peaks in this southern chain, most are devoid of any snow for the first time that anyone can remember. No tourists or workers venture to the high Mayan ruins any longer, since the higher altitude makes it too difficult to breath without supplemental oxygen tanks – something that the tour companies cannot find at any cost; there are simply none to buy from any supplier. Fires are rampant through arid Australia, as little rain makes its way across the continent.

Throughout the Midwest United States, farmers can only watch as their cows suffer daily from lack of food and water. Only a few ponds fed by natural springs have any water in them, and farmers who are lucky enough to have these keep them as secret as they can. Water is so scarce that companies have increased their price per gallon by one thousand percent from the same time last year. For the average farmer with little money to spend, the only solution is to sell the livestock. Prices for meat products drop temporarily as supply overwhelms the demand, but after the glut of meat is processed and the supply dwindles, prices soar for all meat products.

State governments plead for Washington to help with price controls, but the federal government refrains from getting involved. Fast-food chains all respond by raising their prices, which then has a detrimental and ripple impact on their hiring and pricing, and the spending habits of their customers. Economists see this as an ominous sign of inflation, and the federal government is struggling to provide a solution – other than issue their now standard message, "Wait – it will get better."

It has been known for decades that large cities created their own climate because of the reflections from the massive concrete and tall buildings that affected wind patterns, but recently the heat has reached heights where heatstroke is common for outdoors workers, and especially in poorer neighborhoods where air conditioners are a luxury. For those lucky enough to make it to an emergency room, what is not reported is that once the patients are given oxygen, they regain their faculties and feel much better. The influx of patients has a marginal effect on emergency rooms at first, but soon they cannot cope with the endless line of patients waiting to be examined by a physician. It is the norm now that a wait in an emergency room could be more than a day. In any given week it is not uncommon to read about a patient (usually elderly) succumbing to breathing problems to the point of suffocating before he or she can be seen by an overworked staff.

Utility companies scramble to keep their services running. Rolling brownouts are common in most areas, so hospitals have their generators cycling on and off several times per day. This scenario is not unique to the United States, as it plays out across the globe – what scientists, politicians, and the general public have not correlated is that the worst appears to be happening in countries lying between approximately forty-five degrees on either side of the equator. Africa, which had always seen its share of misery because of ocean and wind currents, suffers the most as lakes become dry. Lake Victoria, once one of the most beautiful and largest lakes in all of Africa, barely has enough water left to fill in random depressions that create small, temporary ponds. The larger animals that roamed freely from water hole to water hole simply drop over from exhaustion, allowing the lions, hyenas, and any scavenger animal to gorge on their carcasses.

The Earth is not faring well, with pockets of environmental problems now rising up on a consistent basis. Noting the many environmental issues, Dr. Herman Gunnufsen, from the University of Norway, publishes an article in a monthly geology blog that is noticed by many, but is of special interest to Dr. Marsha Oliver in her office in heat-soaked Texas.

"Simply put, the ability of a body of water to support life of any sort, whether it be plants or fish, cannot exist with these one-celled plants near the ocean surface. I just returned from over six months at sea where I monitored two oceans' supply of phytoplankton, and the results were astonishing to me," Dr. Gunnufsen begins. *"What I have measured is a significant decrease in phytoplankton in both the North Atlantic and South Atlantic. And the decrease is not minimal. Comparing year over year for the past ten years, phytoplankton is down over eighty percent in some places, and they are so minimal in others that they cannot even be measured."*

He continues, *"To the common person these are little, unimportant creatures, but in actuality they take in carbon dioxide just as trees do, and they produce oxygen – also just as regular plants do. They do this with basic photosynthesis. These one-celled plants use energy from the sun to convert carbon dioxide and nutrients into complex organic compounds, which then form new plant material. This is how phytoplankton grows. Some naïve scientists think that trees and greenery we can see on land provide our sustaining oxygen While they are somewhat correct, the greenery is not the only source that we need to protect. Humans –*

207

in fact all living things – get over fifty percent of our sustaining oxygen from the ocean."

"My findings did not pinpoint the cause in the reduction of phytoplankton, but I am one hundred percent sure it is something in the air – or more succinctly, what is not in the air. Some pollution is obviously coming from industrial waste, but most pollution is occurring because of what used to be called acid rain. It's not really "acid," though, but instead is pollution or something in the atmosphere that I believe is getting worse. As my travels from ocean to ocean have shown, our ocean's food supply for humans is dwindling at a rate I have never seen. Herbivorous marine creatures eat the phytoplankton. Carnivores, in turn, eat the herbivores, and so on up the food chain to the top predators like killer whales and sharks. No phytoplankton, no little fishes – no little fishes means reduced big fishes, and less food for us. Fish, though, seem to be adapting to this by diving and living lower – all those that can. I saw almost complete dead zones a half kilometer deep in many places."

"Since the weather is out of my area of expertise, I will defer to other scientists to explain the changes in global weather. To summarize my findings, it comes down to this: fewer phytoplankton means less oxygen, which in turn then causes other food chain problems."

Dr. Oliver pauses to think about what she has read. As Dr. Gunnufsen said, she knew that marine biogeochemical processes have a dramatic effect in the water, but she didn't believe it stopped there. A change this dramatic in phytoplankton abundance obviously has resulted, and is resulting, from the changes in the physical processes controlling the supply of nutrients and sunlight availability. What could the atmosphere be doing? Dr. Oliver highlighted passages to reread. She is about to close the website when the next article, "Photosynthesis and Phytoplankton Doing an Oxygen Dance in the Water," grabs her attention. She clicks on the page.

"As plants die and fall to the ground or sink to the ocean floor, a small fraction of their organic carbon is buried. It remains there for millions of years after taking the form of substances like oil, coal, and shale. The oxygen released in our atmosphere when this buried carbon was photosynthesized hundreds of millions of years ago is exactly why we have so much oxygen in the atmosphere today. We are, or perhaps more correctly "were," spoiled by this abundance of it, and every living creature has evolved to use it. But once it is gone, it's gone. Here is how photosynthesis works."

Marsha raises her eyebrows and rubs her forehead thinking back to her biology class years ago as she continues to read.

"Forests take in carbon dioxide from the atmosphere during photosynthesis and convert it to oxygen – it does this to support new growth. But when those old trees die, those same forests give off comparable levels of carbon dioxide. On average, then, these forests have no net change of carbon dioxide or oxygen to or from

the atmosphere – unless we cut it all down for logging. Well, the oceans work the same way. Most of the photosynthesis is counterbalanced by an equal and opposite amount of respiration. Just as the forests breathe, so do our oceans. The forests and oceans are not taking in more carbon dioxide or letting off more oxygen. We can show this from empirical tests that have been run by many scientists in lab experiments. What we do not know for certain is what the catalyst is for this dwindling supply. Is it the burning oil and coal to drive our cars and heat our homes? Is that what is increasing the amount of carbon dioxide released into the atmosphere? Our scientists monitoring our ozone layers have not seen any anomalies, so the cause must point to somewhere else – and we have not pinpointed what that is at this time. But, our research is ongoing, so hopefully we will have an answer soon."

Dr. Oliver leans back in her chair.

Year 3

The Last Breath

January – Answers Needed

On a crisp winter morning, President of the United States James Barrera is starting his day with his daily press briefing (or DPB as it's referred to by his inner circle) of any newsworthy event that happened overnight, and what, with a high degree of confidence, is to be expected that day. Conflicts abroad usually make up ninety-nine percent of the news, but today it is different.

At his home outside of Dubuque, Iowa, the president and his wife have been staying inside because he cannot shake a constant cough that his doctor is worried about. Everyone in and around the White House has developed the same hacking cough. Doctors haven't been able to find the cause, but surmise that it is pollen-related. Because of the mild winter weather, Barrera is used to jogging with the Secret Service in the early mornings. To protect his health, though, his doctor has recommended confinement indoors.

At this DPB, the secretary of agriculture presents the continuing report on the drought across the United States and how it is affecting supplies and price increases in many areas. This particular report, though, is worse than the previous month's data. The latest fall harvest numbers are in, and crops failed miserably except in small pockets. Costs to buy these few yields are way up, which in turn is driving up the cost of cattle, swine, and chickens for commercial processors of those animals.

The presentation explains that consumers will spend more and do with less – something a sitting president doesn't like to hear. The forecast is that the spiral will continue, with the projection showing inflation will at least double and, more likely, triple over the next twelve months.

After the briefing by the agriculture secretary, Barrera asks, "So when is this drought ending? Is it time to fall back to the Nixon years and put in price controls?"

No one in the room is quick to concur or disagree, as all are at a quandary like the president.

"I think that option might be a little too extreme at this time," Chief of Staff David McNichole says. "To continue, Bill VanLandingham at NOAA says their models indicate a dryer-than-normal year of precipitation coming. Crap happens – the Earth is cyclical in this global warming shit – that's all. Sure, it's tough, but it'll get better. Droughts don't last forever."

"And it's pouring rain in Wyoming – I saw it this morning on TV!" the president exclaims. "You call that a dry year coming?"

"Actually, Mr. President, we do. What we are seeing, and what climatologists see, is intense rain or even snow – maybe several feet at a time. But this will be followed by weeks or maybe even months of no moisture at all. It's a global issue, not just in the U.S."

"I don't care much about other countries – it is ours I am focused on. I was not happy with our meetings with the League of African Countries last month. Hell, you were there. They are requesting a lot more aid, and frankly, I saw in Roy White's report that we can't continue unless we want to print more money. Is that true? Does he just want me to put the mint on overtime so he can print thousand-dollar bills?" Barrera asks.

"They're not talking money, sir. They want more food aid. It's true that our stockpiles are low, but I don't think it's anything for us to worry about."

Barrera's cough interrupts the proceedings. "Sorry, gotta shake this crap in my chest. Okay, let's move along. We've got a lot to cover this morning. We'll revisit this later– put it on the calendar."

Turning to Secretary of Energy Robert Evans, he asks for his summary of data. "It's nothing but good news, Mr. President. Our pipelines are full – both oil and natural gas, and our refineries are running at capacity with no breakdowns to report since our last month. Additionally, gas production is up eight percent over the past six months, and up nineteen percent year over year. Even better news is that one new light gas deposit was found that is estimated to be holding equal to the Barnett Shale – which is approximately seventy thousand kilometers worth of gas. Current oil production is holding steady at 2.4 million barrels per day."

"Now that is a good report, Bob. Don't take this the wrong way, but is that all?"

"I don't understand, Mr. President."

"What's left to find out there? You know my campaign – self-sufficiency was my promise. How close are we?"

"We are there and then some, sir. Exploration is at a high with the offshore drilling and shale drilling that Congress approved. Think about this sir – my department's estimates are that we should be within two percent of self-sufficiency by year's end if just the shale produces all that we expect it to – and there is no reason it shouldn't. We could try to store the extra production, but our reserves are full now. We can continue selling our crude and really put the screws to OPEC. Condor Exploration is showing huge potentials from the test wells they have drilled in the past two years, so thanks to them we should be quite well off for some time to come."

President Barrera looks around the room. "That, ladies and gentlemen, is the type of news we need to stress – let's put some spin on it to take people's minds off of the bad news. Excellent report. Thanks again, Bob."

Barrera dismisses everyone except his chief of staff. "Go out and enjoy your day, guys. Get in some golf. Go down to Maude's Café in town – you'll absolutely love her pies. Tell her I said hello. I'll see you tomorrow at the DPB."

Barrera and McNichole have the room to themselves, so they turn their attention to the news shows on the TVs in the room. Doctors in Denver are attributing local illnesses to some kind of altitude sickness – something they see annually with the flat-lander skiers from the low plains coming into the higher mountains, but not usually this number of cases and at an elevation of only a little over five-thousand feet.

Barrera asks, "Dave, are our disease guys in Atlanta on top of this? We don't need false rumors flying around before my election."

"I'm not sure, but I'll check, Mr. President," the chief of staff answers.

The president picks up one of the dozen newspapers now laid out for his perusal, and as he is glancing through one, his press secretary, Mike Reeves, enters announcing that the top aide to President Napolitano of Italy would like to schedule a call as soon as possible. Barrera looks over the rim of his glasses, then to back the secretary.

"Mike, we got anything planned in the next ten minutes?"

"No, sir – we finished early with the DPB, so you don't have anything for another thirty minutes."

"I love it when other countries look to us for answers. Shows everyone who is actually in control, right? You work it out and get things set up – then ring me when it's ready to go. I'm not going to wait on the phone. Get Napolitano to wait, then I'll jump in."

"Should be just a minute," Reeves replies. The president continues scattering the newspapers so he can see all of the headlines at once, and as he is about to pick up one to read the inside stories, Reeves announces that President Napolitano is on the phone.

"Mike – what time is it there?" the president hastily asks.

"Mid-afternoon, I think, sir."

Barrera picks up the phone, "Buono pomeriggio, Mr. President. How are you today?"

"Mr. President, I am President Napolitano's interpreter, Franca Torellini. President Napolitano wishes you a good afternoon, also."

Barrera can hear conversation going on in the background as Ms. Torellini interprets. "President Napolitano is concerned about many, many illnesses in our northern region. He has been in contact with the president of Austria who has the same concerns. He wishes to know if the United States has been doing any testing of any sort in the northern Italy area, or if the U.S. could provide any guidance for us."

Barrera rolls his eyes at his secretary and his chief of staff. "Please tell President Napolitano that I have not been briefed on any out-of-the-ordinary military exercise going on anywhere in Italy, or in Austria. You can rest assured that I would have alerted him to anything that was brought to my attention about any testing. You are one of our closest allies, and there is nothing we would ever do to jeopardize that partnership."

As the translation occurs on the other end of the phone, the president gestures to his secretary to check into this with the U.S. NATO general responsible for all operations in the western European theater.

"Mr. President, President Napolitano thanks you for your answer. He also has heard about what appears to be similar illnesses occurring in the South America, and maybe even a little in the United States as he saw on the news. He wishes to know if you have determined a cause for this."

"Yes, I have seen the reports also, but it doesn't appear to be related; it's not Ebola or anything like that, so there is no need for worry. Just to be safe, though, I have asked our Center for Disease Control to look into this – and so far, they haven't found anything. From what I've read and been told, the people afflicted are recovering once admitted to a hospital and given rest."

"Thank you, Mr. President." Translations can be heard in the background, and shortly the interpreter returns. "President Napolitano thanks you for taking his call and asks that you update him on any new findings if you receive any."

"Absolutely. Tell him I appreciate the call. Arrivederci."

Hanging up the phone, he turns to the others in the room. "Holy shit, Mike, what was that about? I guess we should get the CDC involved – you know, just to be sure. Make that call and keep me posted."

"Will do, Mr. President."

"Also, get me Dr. Blake. I didn't sleep worth a damn last night."

"Will do that too, Mr. President. Do you want him now?"

"No hurry on the doc. Just tell him."

The rest of the president's day is full of meetings interspersed with trying to grab a nap here and there, but his coughing is making any rest hard to get. Early in the afternoon, Dr. Blake stops in to see him. After a brief conversation and examination, the doctor gives Barrera some tablets to help clear up what he believes is chest congestion caused by a cold.

Later in the day and after a light dinner, Barrera announces that he is turning in with a good book for the evening. A short time after midnight, he wakes up wheezing. This wakes his wife, and after a few pats on the back and realizing that the rasping isn't getting better, she reaches in the dark for a phone that is always nearby. Feeling around for the phone, she hits only one number – a number that alerts the agents stationed around the compound to come quickly as the president needs help. She waits for someone to pick up.

"David here, sir."

"David, it's me, Betty. Get Dr. Blake now – the president needs him."

"Yes, ma'am."

Within seconds, the president's chief of staff and press secretary open the bedroom door, both dressed in whatever was closest to them as they ran out of their rooms. They go to Barrera's side, while his wife sits next to her husband. The president tries to calm himself, but the wheezing and coughing seems to intensify. More minutes go by before Dr. Blake comes running into the room. The president is now sitting up and breathing at a quick pace, with sweat pouring down his face and body. He tries to stand, but the doctor urges him back to the edge of the bed. The doctor detects a rapid heart rate and places an emergency oxygen mask over his face. Within seconds Barrera has calmed down considerably, as he looks to the doctor for an answer.

"I think you had some sort of reaction to those pills I gave you. Some sort of allergic reaction I'm guessing. To be safe, I'll give you a shot to reduce any more possible effects from the medicine, and you should be fine for the rest of the night. Just to be safe, I'll stay in the closest guest bedroom down the hall. If there's anything else that comes up, call me," as he looks to Betty Barrera for acknowledgement. She nods in agreement.

Putting an oxygen breathing tube around his head and attaching it under his nose, the doctor adds, "And wear this tube tonight. We'll get this resolved tomorrow. You feel better, Mr. President?"

"Yes. Thank you, doctor," the president replies with an added nod.

"And for God's sake guys, put on pants next time!" Everyone has a chuckle as they say good night and leave the room.

"Well that was scary, dear. I'm glad the doctor got here as fast as he did," Betty says as she sits on the bed next to him.

"I'm sure it was nothing," the president replies, adjusting the oxygen tube feeding into his nostrils as he lies back on the pillow.

"Now you keep that thing on – you heard the doctor," she whispers.

Without opening his eyes, he mumbles, "Yes, dear."

Two hours pass, and as the president tosses from side to side, the oxygen tube slips off. He sits up in bed and calls out, "Get the doctor again."

In less than a minute, the doctor arrives. He sees the president with sweat pouring from his forehead and attempts to soothe him by telling him to take deeper breaths while at the same time fumbling for the oxygen tube and putting it over his face once more.

"Is he having a heart attack?" Betty asks. The doctor continues to examine him, and orders an ambulance brought around.

"Doctor, what's wrong?" she asks nervously. "Tell me something."

"No, it's not a heart attack," the doctor utters as he keeps taking the president's pulse and heart rate.

Secret Service agents direct the always-on-standby ambulance where to back up, and the agents inside take charge of clearing the path so the stretcher can make its way in and out of the president's bedroom with no interference. On the way to the closest hospital, Vice President Alexandra Smith has been alerted and is now in the process of relocating, with a Secret Service escort, to the White House in case the president's case worsens.

In the ambulance, Dr. Blake adjusts the oxygen mask on Barrera while continuing to monitor his vital signs. When they are less than a mile down the road, the president's heart rate drops to his normal rate of seventy-four beats per minute, and the look of panic in the president's eyes is gone once again.

"Strange," the doctor mumbles to himself as he watches the numbers on the gauges return to what are considered to be in a normal range. "Mr. President, you definitely have a lung problem going on, but I'm not sure why. We'll run some tests at the hospital and get to the bottom of this, so don't worry."

By the time they arrive at the hospital, the president is sitting up and talking calmly to the doctor as the oxygen flows into his system.

"If it's okay with you, I'll just have you walk in normally so there are fewer questions. I'll be by your side. Here, put this in your pocket," as he hands the president a small bottle of oxygen – the kind one might see a scuba diver carry for an emergency.

That night, and for the next three days, Dr. Blake consults with other doctors as to what might have occurred. The only strange thing showing up in the lab reports is a reduction in red blood cells. While on the oxygen, his demeanor and jovial attitude is back, as if nothing happened. He has time to watch several hours of TV, and it doesn't go unnoticed by him that around the country emergency rooms are being flooded with patients having symptoms similar to what he experienced. To allay any fears about the president's health, the White House press secretary explains that the president is getting his annual physical checkup.

Barrera and his doctor discuss what was observed and how the symptoms are abating now that he is given oxygen. Barrera demands that he leave the hospital walking. "It is not protocol that we do this. I'll be glad to wheel you to the curb and you can walk to the car from there", his physician says in a commanding tone. The President looks at him as if to say, "Who do you think you are talking to me that that?"

"I didn't mean that to come out that way, sir. It's a long walk from here to the exit door. What if you were to stumble for some reason? How would that look? Let's just do it step-by-step – nothing will be out the usual. Deal?"

The President ponders what he was just told. Nods his head. "Just remember who is in charge here", he asserts.

No press was even at the door to witness the event, though, but government cameras recorded him striding once up from the wheelchair and entering his limousine. Once inside, his doctor slips a plastic tube over his ears and nose and the President feels the cool oxygen fill his airways.

The next day the President calls a meeting with his chief of staff and other advisors to get ideas on what is causing this problem going around. One person suggests that it could be a foreign government experimenting with some sort of germ warfare.

Another person mentions, "Russia has the means, as well as China. We have contacts within Russia, and nothing is being reported that would make us suspicious. On the other hand, we have no idea, and I mean absolutely no idea, what the Chinese could be up to. We have reports that show Russian people are showing symptoms like those that are showing up here, but nothing coming out of China. Could it be some virus they are turning loose? Hell, they have nothing to lose with three billion people to play with. So, they lose a hundred million here and there? Not a big deal. It is to us, though."

The president asks for other ideas. None are forthcoming.

"So, we have something making people sick, but we don't have a clue what is causing it. Get our embassies over there to find out more. David, can you do that? Let's find out. This virus, or whatever it is, has a source somewhere. Let's put a press release that we are looking into a virus link. Get the CDC onboard with this first, though. We don't want them to say anything to the contrary. Just tell them to stay in line with our message – and if they find anything on their own, let us know." He pauses and looks around the room. "Let's try to stay ahead of any group saying we aren't doing enough."

February – News at 5:00

Time is passing slowly with life around the globe adjusting to this new way of life – heat is continuing to stay at higher than normal temperatures contrary to previous messages that the climate was going through a temporary cycle of change. Medical emergencies haven't abated. Farmers have all but given up on planting, because with little water, the harvest is so minimal that it doesn't pay to work the crops and spend money. Everyone is adapting the best they can to this new norm.

Dr. Oliver has come to the realization that the threat of losing her job at the university or reporting the bad data is really a Hobson's choice – but with a twist, as she has more options. It's been an unpleasant truce with not only Dr. MacLean, but also with herself. She waited as he asked, and the climate has only gotten worse, but she now knows that her dean and her own trust of him misled her.

She searches for newspapers on her browser. Finding the numbers for the "big" papers in Washington, D.C., New York City, and other places that are known for their distribution to many, she sends them emails asking for someone to contact her. She also sends messages to some newspapers in her area. Unbeknownst to her, all of the larger newspapers are deluged with messages claiming to know how to solve the health issue. Some know with certainty how to stop the virus from spreading, but the majority say that it is God cleaning up the wicked ways of the world – that Judgment Day is near and that everyone should repent their sins.

After checking her email several times a day, she gets two replies asking her for more information. Exchanging emails with them, one (a regional newspaper about two hours away) offers to have a reporter call her back. She tells the reporter on their call that he will have to come to her – that she is too busy to break away for a day's drive to his city.

The reporter probes and asks what the urgency is, and all that Dr. Oliver will divulge is that it's scientific news of importance. The reporter leaves her with, "I'll look into it, and I'll call you if my editor gives me the okay."

After she has had time to think about what she has just started, she looks at her hands trembling both from fear and excitement. "What am I doing?" she asks herself as she thinks about the possible repercussions with which her department head threatened her. She looks around and thinks of her family, her home, her career. She knows if a reporter does bite and interviews her, that her name will be in the news, and she knows the university will be brought into this at some point.

"I have to tell John," she mumbles out loud. "He has to agree for me to do this." She remembers when John wrecked their car and didn't tell her for a week while he had it repaired. "I'm having it worked on," was all he would tell her. She laughs out loud at how bad he was at keeping a secret from her.

"I'll tell him tonight," she says out loud.

"Tell who what?" John asks as he opens the screen door and walks into the kitchen.

Startled and taken off-guard, she responds, "Oh nothing – I'm just busy at work. I'll fill you in later. Okay?"

"Sure," John replies with a smile and peck on the cheek. "I forgot my wallet – gotta get back to work. See you around five."

She knows he heard enough to make him wonder what she was saying earlier, so she sits down and puts her head in her hands wondering how this whole issue of lies is rippling through every inch of her life. She thinks about money, work, her next job, and how John will have to start his business all over in a new city. But she worries mostly that if she doesn't say something – anything – then what else could happen to the environment. Maybe others can figure out something to fix it all.

"Shit," she mumbles to the table.

Later in the day, after dinner and play time with Megan, things quiet down after readying Megan for her bedtime. When her child was small, it was different – these bedtime hours. Now it's "Got your homework done?" or "Do you have clothes laid out for tomorrow?"

Giving Megan a hug, she says, "See you in the morning. Sleep tight."

"Ok, Mom. Love you."

Closing Megan's door, Marsha walks down the hall and sits across from John. They look at each other.

"John, I need to talk to you about something – it's about work. It's pretty serious."

"Is that bastard MacLean letting you go?"

"No – at least not for now. But maybe…and that's what I need to tell you." Marsha fills John in on her findings and Bob MacLean's not so vague and overt threat to her.

"There's more. I did something I hope I – make that we – won't regret. I decided to contact some newspapers and tell them of some findings that I think Bob is hiding from the public."

"Wow, that's one heck of a statement. But you do what your conscience tells you to do – the right thing. We'll be fine. Hell, there a hundred other universities who will want you – and I can work anywhere," John responded.

"I know, I know. Thanks for understanding." She sighs with relief and gives him a hug.

"Ready for bed?" he asks. "You'll sleep better tonight – I promise," he says giving her pinch on her rear.

"Not yet. I need to go back into the office to pick up some stuff –

I was so lazy today with no classes on the schedule that I put off looking at some notes I need for tomorrow's lectures. It won't take long."

"I understand – you go ahead. Megan will be asleep soon, and I'll head to bed in a few minutes. I've got the TV and a good book if nothing good is on. Go get your stuff."

"Just there and back. By the way, I don't know when or if any reporters might show up one of these days."

John nods his head. "Yup – it's the right thing, Marsha. I'm proud of you."

It's close to ten o'clock when she arrives at her parking place on campus. She looks around before getting out – something she always did, but now it's different somehow...as if people were lurking – following her. She knows it's all in her mind, but that doesn't stop her from looking twice at parked cars, looking closely into the dark shadows, and being keenly aware of everyone walking close by. The parking lot is lit by several tall lamps, and even at this hour the campus still has students walking around. She places her hand on the door handle.

"What am I doing?" she thinks. "I'll just tell the reporters that I discovered a black hole or something – hell, they won't know the difference." She laughs.

"But the world won't end in a few years if there's a black hole fifty million light-years away," she says out loud. She pulls back the door lever, pushes open the door, and takes in a large breath to relax.

A swipe of Dr. Oliver's university ID has her inside the secured building quickly. Then, after an elevator ride and a walk down corridors lit only by the red glow of exit signs, she arrives at her office door. Her ID card allows her door to open, and she immediately flips on the light switch. She never used to be afraid of the dark, but now the light at least lets her feel more at ease. She walks around her desk to have a seat in front of her computer screen. Logging on, she enters the commands to retrieve the data that will prove her findings. Nothing is returned. She types in the command again. Still nothing. She tries it a third time. She stares at the computer screen.

"Fuck. Did you really do this to me, Bob MacLean? You butt."

Closing her laptop, she notices in the stack of papers on her desk the analyses her PhD students did for her on the data she was searching for. "Gotcha, Bob. I know where I can find the data, and you don't have a clue where it is."

She tucks her laptop into her bag, walks to the door, and looks around the room. This could be one of my last times in here, she thinks, as she turns off the light and heads to the parking lot.

Her mind imagines clandestine people following her as she studies headlights behind her. But one by one they turn, and she is left with no one else on the road for her last mile home. She reasons that Bob might be stupid, but he's not dumb enough to do physical harm to her. She breathes in deeply and lets it out slowly.

She is quiet as she prepares for bed and slips into her side of the bed without waking John. She tries to sleep, but her mind is fixated on the missing data, and what Bob might be up to. After tossing back and forth to try and clear her mind, she finally falls asleep.

She wakes up and looks at the dim light from her clock. Five a.m. Her mind is awake, and the thought of the missing data is all she can focus on. Pushing herself quietly off the mattress she walks down the hallway past Megan's room. She stops at Megan's door and opens it slightly so she can look in and see her sleeping. Megan has kicked her covers off and is lying on her side. It takes a moment for Marsha's eyes to adjust to the near darkness, but she can tell that although Megan's asthma has been recurring on a more frequent basis, she is sleeping soundly with the cool air from the fan blowing across her small body. Marsha smiles as she thinks about how fragile life is, and how much life is in front of Megan to make her mark in the world. Pulling the door closed behind her, Marsha goes in the kitchen and makes herself a cup of coffee while she gets out a pad of paper. She makes a list of what she wants to do today. First on the list is to ask Dr. MacLean if he is aware of her files disappearing. He'll deny it, but it will be fun to listen to him trying to answer that. Number two on her list is to look for another job. No use staying around at a university that won't want me after what I'm about to do.

She stares into her cup and thinks about moving their furniture and uprooting Megan from her friends. She looks up the clock on the wall – 7 a.m. Crap. She yells down the hallway. "Megan, wake up – we're running a little late." Pouring some cereal and milk into a bowl she calls again for Megan.

"Coming, Mom."

Marsha lays out some grapes, then packs a lunch for Megan as she comes into the kitchen in her pajamas. "Sleep okay?"

"Yeah. Did you pack my inhaler in my bag?"

'Yes. If you need to use it, don't wait. Breathing is kind of important to us mammals."

"Are elephants mammals?"

"Yes."

"How about birds?"

"No."

"But they breathe air – right?"

"Yes, but…"

"So, they are mammals. You said that mammals breathe air."

"No, that's not what I said. I said that breathing is important to mammals. But breathing is also important to reptiles and birds."

"So, what's a mammal then?'

"It's an animal that gives birth to…I'll explain at another time – eat up."

"I don't understand why hippos aren't mammals."

"But they are."

"I thought you said that reptiles aren't mammals."

"They're not – but hippos aren't reptiles."

"But hippos live in water – how come they aren't reptiles?"

Marsha laughs. "Okay, they are – everything is a mammal!"

"I knew it!"

"I hope your teachers appreciate your knowledge and that all of this money we've spent on your education has not gone to waste." She leans over and gives her a hug and kiss on the cheek. "Now eat up, then brush, and we're off to school."

"Got up early, huh?" John asks as he saunters into the kitchen as Marsha is waiting for Megan to return.

"Yeah, just couldn't sleep. Too much on my brain, I guess."

"Look, it's gonna be okay. Try to relax. I'm right here supporting you – remember that."

"Thanks again. Not that I doubted it – it's just nice to hear." Megan comes down the hallway with her backpack.

"Ready?" her dad asks.

"Yup – all set."

"I'll be back in a few minutes," Marsha says as she and Megan head out the back door. After the drop-off at the school, Marsha pulls back in and notices John's car is gone already. She wanted to see him again just for moral support, but she feels confident that she can weather any storm knowing he is supporting her. Looking around for her papers, she gathers them up and puts them in a folder. As she is pondering her day in front of students, the ringing phone draws her attention.

"Hello."

"Dr. Oliver, Claudia Ramsey here from the *Austin Star News*. We exchanged some emails earlier. My editor knows I like digging up odd stories, so when can we meet? This virus stuff in the air is scary. By the way, I work with a former student of yours. Small world, huh? She says that you really know about atmospheric stuff – which is all Greek to me. Would you mind if brought her along? Would you be available for an interview sometime soon?"

Marsha tries to hide her exuberance of getting her story out. "No, and yes. Of course, bring her along, and the sooner the better for the interview would be fine with me."

"I've got a list of questions, and usually answers help steer me into the next questions. It could take an hour – maybe more. And I have to tell you, a phone to my ear for two hours isn't fun. I can come to your house, or we could meet somewhere if you would rather."

"My house is fine. I'll email you the address. I think it should be no more than an hour-and-a-half drive for you. I've got classes the rest of the day. In fact, I was about to head out the door – but can you come by today? Would 4:30 be okay?"

"We can do that. It's a slow day here. See you at 4:30."

Marsha hangs up the phone and screams, "Goddamn it, Bob MacLean – this is what you get! Christ, I've got to get organized."

She looks around at her stacks of papers and starts going through them picking out what she thinks is most germane to what she wants to show the reporters. She has to focus on the problem and not get sidetracked, or she knows she'll lose the reporters as their eyes will glaze over with technical jargon.

Her day at school goes normally. She had glanced at Dr. MacLean's office late morning, but there was no sign of him. This was a relief – of all days, she didn't want a confrontation today. Rather, she wanted to focus her thoughts on the two reporters and the information she would methodically lay out for them. She finishes her day and heads for home.

At 4:30 there is no sign of the reporters. She walks to the window overlooking her front yard and curb. She returns to her chair in the dining room and lets the fan cool her. She puts the papers that she will present in order. Like a parent waiting up for her child to return from a date, she starts to worry about all the things that could have happened. Did the reporters get lost? Did they change their mind? Walking outside, she stares in both directions, and with no cars in sight, she sits on the front steps, all the while watching for any slow-moving car that might be looking for her address. Finally, at 4:45 she sees a car slow and stop at her curb. It's them, she thinks with excitement. She stands up to greet the occupants who get out of the nondescript, old Honda.

"Hi. You must be Olivia," she says, extending her hand.

"Yes, Dr. Oliver, nice to meet you. And this is Beatrice Chu. So sorry we're late!"

"Glad you could make it. I remember you Beatrice – good to see you again. Let's go inside where it's a little cooler. And call me Marsha – only the students call me doctor."

"Thank you, Marsha. Lead the way," Olivia answers.

As they make themselves comfortable around the dining table, Marsha turns to Beatrice. "So, you've gotten into journalism. What made you pick this field? I thought, or rather hoped, that all of my students were going out to save the planet?"

"First, I really, really enjoyed your class. But it was an optional class for my major – not really something I wanted to get into. I love writing, so journalism it is."

"So, you said you had some questions, and I've got some stuff I want to first explain to you. And after we go through that, I have some data I would like to share with you. I hope you have time, as it's something that I believe your readers will find interesting."

"I'm sure it is, but more important than my readers is my editor who has to approve everything I submit. And trust me, only about half my stuff gets through him – and the columns that do end up being put in the paper are sometimes edited to make them fit. It's the world of newspapers, but I can tell you that the internet is changing things a lot."

"I understand. So...let me throw out a question for you? Do you think the climate is changing?"

"I think so," Beatrice replies.

"I'm not so sure," Olivia adds. "Well, maybe it is, but I've read where it might not be. It's been hot for a couple of years, but isn't that normal? Plus, I hate to say it, but I hear terms like global warming and global climate change, but aren't they the same? And what does this have to do with the virus stuff? I had hoped you might have some information on how to cure it."

Marsha answers, "Whew – lots to talk about. Here goes. I'm not sure how climate and weather terms got so confused. Global climate change defines all weather changes – whether too much heat, cold, rain, hurricanes, and the like. People who use the term 'global warming' aren't focused on the big picture. And, yes, global climate change is real."

"Pardon my questions, but it's what we have to do as reporters. How do you know it's real? Do other scientists share your view?"

"Okay – now we're getting into it. I can tell you my findings and my hypothesis from that. I'm sure you've heard of the ozone layer."

She waits to see them nod and mumble, "Sure."

"Maybe you've even heard of the correlation between global climate change and the size of the ozone hole?" Again, she waits for them to nod. "Yes, there are fringe idiots who say not to worry, but I'm about to tell you something that cannot be ignored. The ozone holes at both poles are huge, and the amount of heat-trapping carbon dioxide in the air has jumped dramatically, and I have data to prove it. Those of us who are looking at that data calculate that average global warming will exceed five degrees by the end of next year. I won't ask you to speculate what that means, but it's bad – for you, me, and the Earth. The ice at the poles will be melting like snow used to in the Rockies in June. We will continue see hot spots in temperatures around the world. In the Middle East for example, the temperatures could climb to a staggering one hundred thirty-five degrees Fahrenheit – maybe more. Think about that. How could you function in that? Look outside today. Is one hundred twelve degrees normal for this area? We have had that temperature for weeks now. So, what does it all mean?"

Pausing to let her thoughts catch up with what she is telling her guests, she notices that Olivia looks confused. "Does all this make sense?" Marsha asks.

Olivia responds, "But won't the temperature go back down soon? Isn't the temperature spike of a few degrees temporary? It won't stay that hot all year, will it?"

"Average temperatures have risen for several years now. No, it won't stay that hot all year round, and definitely not in one spot only. But what I'm saying is that now springs, falls, and winters all around the world will be warmer than they've ever been before. This is the definition of global climate change. So, let's talk about the side effect of that ice melting. Ice starts to melt more. Less ice means less reflection – and more absorption – of heat by the water. Oceans heat up, algae build up, the food chain changes, animals die, crops fail, water dries up – our climate changes so much that our normal balance of things on Earth is altered forever. And that's the *Readers Digest* version. I can give you more – a lot more."

"You're skeptical, aren't you? As in, 'if this is bad, why don't more people care?' Well, some do. But, as you know, some don't – care, that is."

"So, what's the cause? Are you saying this climate stuff created the virus?" Beatrice asks.

"First, there is no virus. I'm not sure why that explanation is out there. I wish I and other scientists could pinpoint for certain what the cause is – or causes are – for what is happening, but again, it is not a virus. I look at the results – that's my area of expertise. It could be something as simple as cow farts, or maybe China's coal usage finally had the effect the world was dreading? I don't know the answer to your question – I wish I did. You're the reporters. You have been given a story with information and data to back it up. What is happening will continue to affect every living thing on our planet. I can give you more graphs and charts to prove my findings. I will dumb them down so that every Tom, Dick, and Harry can understand them. This is serious stuff I'm telling you so you can start telling others."

Marsha continued, "Look, I know you've heard this gloom and doom before, but let me tell you this is real. My empirical data doesn't lie. Let me give you one example. Carbon dioxide levels jumped by 8.67 parts per million in the past year alone, now totaling to just over four-hundred three parts per million. Do you know what that means?" she asks with her voice rising. She can tell from their looks that that number is lost on them.

"Let me put it in simple terms: It means this is the highest rise ever in carbon emissions since record-keeping began in 1959. And it's not just barely the highest ever recorded; it's the highest recorded by a substantial amount." She pauses.

"So what, you ask? What does it mean to have these high numbers? We breathe in oxygen and exhale carbon dioxide. That's how we humans live. If the carbon dioxide levels are growing at the rate I observed, where is the oxygen? How can we rebuild it? Our oxygen levels are rapidly depleting."

She leans back in her chair, because with that simple statement said out loud for the first time to others, it all becomes clear to her.

She watches their faces. "Okay, now that that is sinking in, let me give you another example. Every body of water absorbs carbon dioxide, as do trees – and they give back oxygen. Most of the chemicals that are pumped into the ground eventually are having an effect on the methane levels – and guess where that goes? Up. Look at the sky – it seems pretty big, doesn't it? It is, but it can't keep cleaning up our mess forever. Can you picture images of companies dumping waste into streams?" She waits for their nods. "It's the same way with our sky. Look, I'm not a politician, nor am I trying to make a political statement – nor am I here to preach to you as an activist or radical. I just want to give you this information and let you take it from here." She watches as both are busily taking notes in their notebooks.

"I'm a professor, but I do keep up on pacts and agreements between countries. In 2009, for example, every nation including the United States agreed on a voluntary goal of limiting global warming to 3.6 degrees over some arbitrary pre-industrial temperature levels. That was a joke. The keyword in the agreement signed by China and the United States was 'voluntary.' Most countries adhered to this limit. Let me be really clear and candid about what I'm about to say. Both the U.S. and China stand out as whores." Marsha sits back down after realizing that somewhere in the middle of her ranting she stood up as if she was lecturing to a class of students.

"We will need those graphs and charts you mentioned. Can you provide those to us?" asks Olivia.

"I can. Also, I will work with any scientist you bring into this discussion. A suggestion for you is to find others to triangulate it

– that's what we scientists do. We have other people look at our findings just to make sure we weren't drunk." She watches their expressions. "I was kidding, folks. I rarely have a glass of wine."

Olivia interjects, "Obviously, neither Beatrice nor I have studied this area much, but I do know that I have seen other articles refuting what you say. You know, stuff like 'This is typical of the Earth's rotation.' Or, 'It was a hot summer and fall, and now the winter is warmer than normal. It happens.' But let's assume what you say is true – now what?"

"I would suggest you ask those naysayers the hard questions, like 'What do you base your views on?' Put them on the spot and have them prove that I'm wrong. They won't be able to. I, along with many scientists, are certain our data and analyses are valid, without question. Reporters dig up answers. Please, take it from here and go write a Pulitzer Prize-winning article. But more than that, let people know the truth!"

Olivia asks, "If what you say is true, do you think anything can be done to fix it?"

"Nothing," Dr. Oliver replies without any hesitation.

March – No Need to Panic

One week after their meeting with Dr. Oliver, the Austin newspaper puts a column on page four that describes how global climate change is affecting the world and truly appears to be a real phenomenon. The article quotes an "unnamed expert in the field" as the source of the data.

Fifteen hundred miles away in Washington, D.C., President Barrera has arisen early like he always does. And since he has been in office, and as requested every day, newspapers from around the country, plus a few overseas newspapers, are laying on his desk for his perusal. Additionally, four TV screens have various news networks on but are muted. The president never reads any newspaper in its entirety, but rather skims the main section of each looking for interesting headlines. If he finds one that catches his eye, he reads it further. On this morning, he stops when he sees the column heading, "Global Climate Change's Economic Effect." Anything to do with jobs and the economy always grabs his attention, so he reads the column with more interest. He makes notes in the margin of the page, then lays it aside as he scans the other newspapers, while glancing at the crawlers at the bottom of each TV screen.

At 8:25 – the same time every day, Press Secretary Mike Reeves, enters the room. The president looks up, gives him a wave, and then continues scanning the pages. Reeves' entrance is a cue that the morning DPB will start in five minutes. Barrera walks down the hall and into the meeting room where most of his cabinet members are waiting. Nothing extraordinary is on the agenda for this morning, but Reeves does remind him of his meeting in a few days with the prime minister of Canada to discuss how the oil and gas drilling has been a boon for each country's economy. As they are wrapping up the DPB, Barrera asks Reeves to go back to his office to find his notes and the circled article from the newspaper he had set aside and make copies for everyone in the room. As the talking points were being exhausted between all in the room, Reeves returns and distributes the copies.

"Take a minute – I want everyone to read this," Barrera says and then waits until he sees all eyes return to him before he says anything.

"Where can we refute this? Give the counterviews, folks," the president demands.

Robert Evans, secretary of energy, answers, "Mr. President, we've had our very best scientists pouring over these numbers now for years, and frankly they have found nothing to cause an alarm. Sir, I will be glad to schedule a presentation where our own research will show this "unnamed" source doesn't know squat. Frankly, sir, articles like this do nothing but inflame and serve no purpose."

"Thank you, Bob," the president says as he nods his head in that direction.

"Anyone else? Come on, speak freely – that's what I expect in a DPB," the president exhorts.

"Mr. President, I agree with Bob," Roy White, secretary of commerce, offers. "Look at our exports. We are shipping more natural gas at higher prices than ever before. Our GNP is going to be through the roof this fiscal year. Hell, this reporter is just wanting column space. We all know that even if some global climate change is happening, it isn't going to last. I don't mean that in a cavalier manner, Mr. President, but the U.S. is doing pretty damned well these days."

Barrera laughs. "Goddamn it, Roy, you always give me your honest answer, and I appreciate it." Everyone laughs along with the president. "So, let's do something about this. We don't the people to get all worked up over crap like this."

"We're working on it, sir," Reeves replies.

"Working on what?" Vice President Smith asks.

"A press release, of course, Madame Vice President. It's impossible for the ozone to simply be broken beyond any hope of repair. We have seen this many times over the decades and the ozone always comes back. When something like this comes out, we have to put some spin on it. It's not our fault China is polluting or mistakenly put some virus out there," the press secretary says.

The Last Breath

The president, who is never far from his breathing apparatus, reaches under his chair, grabs it, and throws it in the middle of the table where it lands with a thud, making a dent in the perfectly smooth and glossy veneer surface, then rolling to the other side where a cabinet member clamps a hand on it.

"Wait until you have to wear one of these. It's not fun."

"Mr. President, even your doctors admit they are still looking into the cause of your ailment. We'll have a nice little five- or six-inch column on the front page of many major newspapers saying something like, 'We are in contact with leading scientists to understand more behind the article.' In the meantime, we can start to look into this further if you want. It just buys us some time – that's all."

"Keep going," the vice president responds.

"We'll say something like, 'The ongoing problem started in Asia, and we are trying to pinpoint the source. We are working with our counterparts in Beijing, etc., etc., etc.' Then we continue with something like, 'The heat wave over the United States has been bad this year, but not as bad as the one that struck the Midwest in the early 1930s,'" the press secretary says. "Then we'll go on to say how everything fixed itself back to normal."

"But is any of that actually true?" the vice president responds.

Secretary of Energy Evans says, "Madame Vice President, the point Mike is making is that we really aren't sure – no one really is. So, in addition to these points, I suggest that, in parallel, we start our own studies. Surely, we can find enough scientists to refute these crazy fringe folks. The fact is that we will, and are, working with other countries to develop clean energy. We provide natural gas and nuclear plant technology to many of them. We can get a bunch of nerdy professors who can help us with this. They always need some funding with grants, and surely we can steer some dollars their way to help us with a study or two."

"Since we're just throwing out ideas, I am pretty sure that our oil buddies are always looking for some good PR – we'll get them to do some gratis ads about how they are helping the environment. If we get the people's mind on something positive, this other stuff will be a footnote in future years," Secretary of the Interior Tom Miller adds.

Looking around the room and listening to the arguments, and thinking about other appointments he has today, the president stands up. "We're done – thanks for your attendance and comments."

The room clears except for the VP and the press secretary. "Mike, get me Hugo over at the CDC. I have to tell you, unsubstantiated articles get a lot of reporters fired – or reassigned." Barrera chuckles. "I wish that reporter in Austin good luck."

A few minutes go by. "Mr. President, Hugo Cortez on the line."

"Thank you, Mike."

Barrera answers, "Hugo, how are you doing today?"

"Fine, Mr. President. Busy as usual, though."

"Hugo, I've got you on the speaker. What have you dug up on this influx of people visiting ERs? You know…the oxygen thing. My folks have given me updates, but I want to hear it right from the horse's mouth. Anything to report?"

"Sir, we have looked into it, and we think we have it linked simply to the heat. We have seen some cases of asthma and other breathing disorders, and it primarily has been occurring in older people who are out of shape. Basically, old age and heat don't mix well. There is an outside chance, but nothing confirmed, that it could be a stray virus. We are still testing for it and asking ER folks to do the typical virus tests for us, but nothing is showing up – yet. Of course, I'll be sending you our press release, so you'll have knowledge of it first, but we're ready to release our findings by the end of next week. The bottom line is what I just told you."

"Hugo, does it look like I'm that old or out of shape?" the president asks.

"Of course not, sir. I was talking about the majority of what we've seen. There are a few exceptions, but…"

Barrera interrupts. "How many exceptions?"

"Not many, sir."

"Hugo, you're not talking to the press. You're talking to me. How many is many," Barrera asks tersely.

"A few thousand cases – that's all. But people with asthma are coping with this worse. I said that earlier."

"Okay, Hugo, give me a number. How many total cases?" the president fires back.

There is silence on the phone, as Barrera waits patiently. "By our count, a little over twenty thousand cases at most, and that's randomly distributed across the country. While that may sound large, it is a really small percentage overall."

"Don't you think we should alert people with existing breathing conditions? Should we say something like, 'Asthma sufferers should head to a clinic or hospital for an oxygen treatment?'"

"We can do that if you want, sir, but we don't need a panic on our hands."

"How many deaths, Hugo?"

Again, there is silence on the line, and Hugo pauses before he answers. "About one out of ten that are admitted. Maybe slightly more, sir."

"So, is a ten percent mortality with any ailment normal?" Barrera asks the CDC head.

"No. Actually, flu has a mortality rate of less than one percent. Tracking this virus has been and continues to be difficult. Our estimate, and I stress the word estimate, is that the ten percent is close. It could be slightly less, or a little more. Sir, not to be callous, but some are poor people who hardly make a blip in the news. They are sick with breathing ailments, and most of their families think nothing of this. And they shouldn't really, sir. It's an incredible heat wave going on across America as we speak. People die, and, while it shouldn't be this way, poor people die more often. That is a basic fact."

Turning to his press secretary, Barrera asks, "Has an inquisitive soul ever brought this up in any press conference?"

"Only once that I can recall, sir. And I answered truthfully – that we are in midst of a heat wave, and unfortunately, weak systems cannot do well in that environment. And if it is an unknown virus, it only makes the problems worse. Then, I got the typical question of government providing assistance, and I replied again quite candidly that the federal government has programs from which local municipalities may request funds for things like free air conditioners."

"So, that is our official position going forward?" the president asks.

"Mr. President, if I may…we at the CDC can assure you that it isn't a new flu strain, but we have not ruled out other airborne particulates. Our research is still ongoing in any outside causes, but nothing has shown up so far. It doesn't seem to be anything more than either direct heat-related deaths or dust-related irritations blowing in from who knows where."

"Have we checked, say, the radiation from Japan? I still think it is China. I remember being over there a couple of years ago and smog over Beijing was horrendous. Are you monitoring West Coast air just in case crap is blowing in from the west?" the president asks.

Before he can get an answer, the press secretary interrupts, "Sir, don't forget we have the governors from Florida, Alabama, and Louisiana in at 1:00 today for a luncheon, then a photo op, then an hour with them that's closed to reporters, followed by another photo op."

"Weren't there four governors scheduled? Where is Mississippi," the president asks, since it's not often the president of the United States is stood up.

The president holds up his hand for Reeves to pause and talks back into the phone. "Hugo, that's all I need today. Keep up the good work and send me your press announcement so I'll know what we will be saying. Good-bye."

Reeves clears his throat before he answers the president's earlier question. "Sir, the governor had a slight emergency overnight. Well, that's what Governor Richards called it – we didn't exactly think it was an emergency. He did call your office very early this morning and gave his regrets but thought it would not be prudent to leave what was going on in Mobile Bay."

"Goddamn it, Mike! Just pretend that I didn't see the news yet and that I've only gotten through three newspapers instead of all fifty. What in the hell is so important that he's not here?"

"Mobile Bay's having some high-water issues, sir. High tide or something like that."

"Mike, do I have to drag it out of you sentence by sentence? Give me the details. Is FEMA involved? Is it some sort of Bay of Fundy high tide?"

"No sir, not yet – FEMA that is. I'm not sure where the Bay of Fundy is, sir. The governor doesn't think FEMA will be needed. The Mississippi National Guard is already assisting. As for details, sir, and according to the governor, two small islands, McDuffie Island and Little Sand Island, are pretty much submerged now during high tides. Another island, Pinot Island, probably has about half of its land above water."

"Is that all? Is that it? Hell, high tides happen. Don't tell me he's worried about some higher water. Anyone hurt?" Barrera asks.

"No sir, just economic damage. Hard to assess the impact at this time, but he's staying close to home for photo ops, we think."

"Thanks, Mike. Just spit it out next time."

"Yes sir."

"What time are those other governors coming in, again?" Barrera asks.

"At 1:00, sir. You're free until then, and lunch will be served outside as you requested."

"You guys give me a few minutes."

That's the cue for everyone to leave. The president walks back to his office and sits in his swivel chair to look out of the large windows behind his desk. He takes a deep breath from his portable oxygen device and looks into the distance at the Washington Monument, and thinks about how he is looked upon to lead the world with ideas and inventions.

Water inundating small isles or atolls is nothing new with rising sea levels; it is simply accepted now as a normal occurrence. St. Louis, Senegal, a seaside town that used to be protected by a long levee, today finds itself completely underwater. The rising Atlantic has made its residents relocate to higher ground. All the ships that used to go out of this natural seaport are gone, as are area low-lying farmlands. Venice, Italy, once the darling of tourists, has given up and shut off one hundred percent of its old town. The full-time residents who used to live on the western side of the harbor have moved inland hoping to be safer from the rising waters. Scenes like these are being played out in both wealthy and poor countries across the globe, and the repercussions to governments and people are having a ripple effect in nearby countries and, in actuality, to entire continents.

May – Muddy Waters

Most people probably read articles related to sports, stock market reports, or local road construction. While "The World's Climate Is Changing" might grab a glance from the average person, the fact is that most people are jaded from reading such headlines and simply shrug it off as just another "the sky is falling" article. Some, though, will peruse it and give it some thought.

Although Dr. Oliver was referenced in the article as an "unnamed respected scientist," she is getting paranoid about her department dean putting two and two together – and she is bracing herself for any repercussions. As she contemplates what she has uncovered, it saddens her to think about what life might be like in another fifty years, long after she is gone. How will her daughter cope with the shape of the world then? She sinks back into her couch and closes her eyes. Maybe it's time for the people to revolt. No, why should they? They don't get it – they haven't before, so why start now? They want to be led and told what to do. It's the leaders who have to change – but how do we change that? She makes a decision and heads to campus.

Meanwhile, Dr. MacLean had received a text message early in the morning asking him to meet someone at a park not too far from campus. He checks his watch and studies the words of the message several times over. He knows who sent it even though the text was not signed, and the sender's phone number was blocked. He looks at his calendar for the day, hoping in some way he could simply reply that he was too busy. He takes his keys from the desk's upper drawer, locks his office door, and walks to his car. It is only mid-morning, but the temperature is already over one hundred degrees. He feels the blast of hot air as the air conditioner starts cooling the car's interior. He's about to put the car in reverse when he is startled by a rap on the passenger window.

"Shit!" he exclaims, as he depresses the button to slightly roll down the window. "You scared me to death. What do you want, Marsha? I have a meeting to get to."

"Are you coming back soon? We need to talk."

"I shouldn't be long. Probably an hour. When I get back, I'll come to your office."

Dr. Oliver can read from his voice and body language that he doesn't know about the article, otherwise he would have been more curt with her. She steps back and watches him wind through the parking lot of cars and students. She is relieved that her conversation is pushed back for at least an hour, as this gives a little more time to prepare herself mentally and to explain what she did and why. As she walks up to her office, she carries on a conversation with herself.

"There actually wasn't much detail. Maybe no one even noticed it. And if Bob did read it, how pissed off could he be? Could he trace it back to me? After all, it's a free country, and I have a right to say what's on my mind without fear of retaliation. I know the data is good. It was a good article."

About three miles from campus, Bob pulls into a park. It's one of those innocuous parks that dot a town's landscape where people pass daily and never pay much attention to – except for those who have kids. It's hot, and the bench where he was instructed to go has no shade. From his shirt pocket he retrieves a cell phone SIM card. He opens his cell phone, takes out the old card, and slips in the new one. He shuts off his car and, sweating, walks to the bench. He puts on a hat that will shield his face somewhat and waits on the bench for the call. The phone rings.

"Hello."

"Bob, have you read the article in the Austin paper?

"No, I don't get it – the paper, that is."

"It's on the web – I suggest you read it. A professor that might be from your department did an interview. The reason we think so is because the data that was quoted is something only you should have. Can you explain?"

"I have a good suspicion who it is. There is one professor who thinks she has found some anomaly with some data – that's all. I will put my data up against hers anytime. Let me find the article and read it – it might not be anything."

"Look in the trash can beside you – you'll find the newspaper. Look on page six. I'll wait."

MacLean does as requested and finds the article. He wipes off the sweat running down his forehead while reading the article twice. "Yes, I read it. Go on."

"I thought you had control of this data?"

"I do – this article is nothing but speculation. I told you – I have the data completely taken care of. There is absolutely nothing I can't handle about this."

"Put this to bed now. We have two months, maybe three at the outmost, to get our funding renewed by Congress – so don't blow it for us now. If something goes awry, remember that shit runs downhill. Your funding can dry up with one phone call, and I'm sure you understand that clearly."

"Of course. I'm not that naïve. It's a reporter and an editor wanting some space to fill in their rag – that's it. Hello…hello?"

MacLean looks at the phone for a moment thinking that it might be a cell tower problem – but it's not – he has a strong signal. He wipes the sweat from his brow again and goes back to his car. He removes the SIM card, puts in the old one, and drives back to his office.

Dr. Oliver's gaze is transfixed on MacLean's parking spot, as her mind races with thoughts of how to defend her actions with the newspaper. Her mind focuses on the data, not whether doing the interview was right or wrong.

"My research was perfect," she speaks clearly to the empty room.

She turns around to make sure no one was listening to her ramble, then as she looks back to the parking lot, she watches MacLean get out of his car. She takes a deep breath as if preparing for battle, which for all practical purposes could prove to be exactly that. She sits in her chair and waits.

Even though the elevator is a hundred feet away, she hears its distinctive ding. The Doppler-sounding footsteps announce that someone is nearing.

MacLean appears at her office door, sweat stains on his shirt and hair damp with perspiration.

"Okay, Marsha, you have my attention."

Dr. Oliver steels herself as she says, "Have a seat."

Bob shuts the door and pulls up a chair. Marsha, who would normally sit behind the desk when discussing issues with students, pulls her chair around to the front of the desk so the two are facing each other with no obstruction between them. She doesn't want any wall, either real or imaginary, to get in the way of their conversation.

He studies her expression. "Marsha, you and I were friends. I take that back, we are friends. I know that you decided to go the newspaper with the hope that they would publish something. You jumped to too many conclusions without facts – something I thought you knew better about doing. You're a scientist who only deals in facts, not speculations."

"Bullshit, Bob. What was there to misinterpret? The atmosphere has almost twice the pollutants PPM as was reported by you and from our station in Antarctica." She stands up, then sits on the edge of desk.

"Friends don't lie to each other. So, are you going to fire me?" she asks.

"No, but…" he pauses to choose his words carefully, "you <u>will</u> call that reporter to tell her that you were mistaken. Marsha, for all you know, the data you were given was as phony as a three-dollar bill. You never told me the source of your data, so how could I reproduce it from him or her? On the other hand, I've told you everything. You are more than welcome to call Dr. Walker now if you want. Hell, I'll dial him for you. You can fix this for yourself, but if you don't, then other actions may be taken."

Marsha bursts out laughing. "You want me to continue the lies? You want a name? I'll give you a name. William Moore. There, you call him. Oh, I forgot – he's dead. What a coincidence. So sorry…I can't dial him for you."

"Marsha, what more do you want me to say? I am not going to continue arguing over and over about this silly issue. You are behaving like a first-year undergrad. And even if the data were different somehow, it could have simply been an aberration. The data could have been skewed for a couple of months because of some summer activity somewhere – hell, I don't know where or why. It was scree – it was rubble at the extreme ends of data. I just saw the raw data sent in yesterday, and you know what? The PPM has dropped almost in half – just as I told you it would."

"Really, Bob? You still want me to believe anything you tell me?"

Bob replies, "Come to my office. I have the latest email from Dr. Walker who sent the raw data. I swear that this data is as pure as it was when it left the sending sensors in Antarctica. You can run as many tests on it as you want, and when you do, you'll see that there is nothing to be alarmed about. You didn't listen to me earlier, and you put this department at risk. And when I say, 'this department,' I mean not only your job, but maybe also mine. You don't think they keep old tenured department heads around forever, do you? Tenure doesn't mean what it used to. Hell, if I parked over the line in the dean's parking space, I could be fired tomorrow. I keep saying this, but you keep ignoring me – but I'll say it again – you need to wise up and trust me. I've been doing this way longer than you have, and I cannot put up with your foolishness again. Anything, and I mean anything, you want to publish goes through me, or yes, you will be fired." He pauses to let all of this sink in, while at the same time studying her body language.

Marsha answers, "I understand your position, and in a way I'm sorry to have put you through this. And you know something, I have tried to convince myself over and over that I was wrong. But I wasn't and I'm not now. You got yourself in this position because I'm guessing that someone was pressuring you. You wouldn't arbitrarily change data on your own for no apparent reason." Her voice quiets to almost a whisper. "But ask yourself this – what if you've been wrong in the decisions that have led you to this point? What if we have passed the tipping point somehow? Then what?"

Bob doesn't reply to any of the questions. Instead he stands and offers, "Let me be direct. You have been warned." Then, he leaves the room.

After he leaves, Marsha takes a key from her pocket and inserts it into the top drawer on the left side of her desk. She turns the key to unlock it, but the key is hung up and won't budge.

"Shit," she says as she jiggles the key some more, knowing that MacLean or someone has taken her notes. Suddenly, she feels the tumblers fall into place, and the key turns to the unlocked position. She yanks the drawer open quickly expecting to find it emptied of its contents. Instead, all of her papers are exactly as she left them. Breathing a sigh of relief, she removes the graphs and places them in a pile. One at a time, she looks at the charts like they are old friends.

She thinks to herself, "Should I just quit? Should I wait to be fired? Bob certainly won't give me a recommendation, and therefore, who would hire me? John has a good job, but he doesn't make a lot."

She laughs – but it is a nervous laughter and thinks, "Maybe the world can hold on another two hundred years? I'll be dead and it'll be someone else's problem – let them deal with it."

Questions and thoughts roll through her mind one after another, but they all funnel her back to her basic questions: "What if I'm right and they, 'the others,' are wrong? Why didn't anyone see that we needed to err on the side of caution?"

Her cell phone ringing focuses her away from her thoughts. "Hello."

"Dr. Oliver?"

"Yes. Who's calling?"

"My name is Hal Monrow. I'm with *Science Quarterly* magazine, and I was sent an email about your research on the increase of pollutants in the atmosphere and the effect on the ozone layer. Would you be available for an interview? I can do it over the phone if that works better for you."

As she listens to the caller's words, her mind wanders back to what she was thinking just before the call. And her caution kicks in as to whether this is a legitimate call.

"Mr. Monrow, I'm awfully swamped at the moment. May I get your number and call you back?"

"Certainly. We writers, and especially our magazines, are under deadlines, so the sooner you could call me, the better. And coincidently, I was pulling together an article on global weather patterns. I know that professors need to get published, and this might be a good article for both of us. Could I get a time from you when I can expect your call?"

"I can't say. I'm in the middle of some research."

"May I call you back, say, tomorrow at some time that you set?"

"Your caller ID is showing up – can I use that number?" Marsha asks.

"Yes, that's fine. Please call me at your earliest convenience, as I look forward to discussing the details behind your article. Thank you."

"Yes, Mr. Monrow. Bye for now."

Hanging up the phone she knows that this is just the start of what she had hoped for – that people might pick up on not only what she had to say, but what others have also said – and start questioning more about what we are doing to our atmosphere. She looks out the open door and thinks about how Dr. MacLean always told her to follow the old college axiom of publish or perish.

"Well, Bob, be careful what you wish for. Here's one you might wish I had passed on."

The Last Breath

All day long her stomach is in knots as she expects MacLean to storm in and confront her again. Late in the day, with high anxiety, she walks to his office to show him that she is not afraid to confront him. But his office is dark. She peers into the empty room, then continues on to her car. Tomorrow, she thinks…we'll talk again. I know I can convince him to see my side. As she is driving home, she hears something on the radio that catches her attention. The governor is at a press conference describing the new drilling he has opened up on state-owned land around San Angelo all the way to the Big Bend area. She turns up the volume.

"People of Texas should be proud of the clean industry we are creating. Over my past seven years as governor of this proud state, we have created over one hundred thirty-five thousand jobs, and there will be more because of this new technology we are using." He pauses for the applause.

"We do not need Washington to tell us how to drill responsibly, because we have been doing this for over a hundred years." More applause.

"Remember the Alamo?" He waits for more applause. "Well, they didn't want anyone to tell them what to do either."

After more applause, he yells, "It's hot today, isn't it? Well, welcome to Texas! Scientists agree that global warming is not something new. There are left-wing radicals who think that because we're having a hot summer or two the world is coming to an end. Those people are crazy – just crazy, as the science simply doesn't agree with that assessment. We need jobs and I'm giving them to you."

Marsha is dumbfounded by what she is hearing. But she is impressed that a little, obscure article has so quickly caused enough attention to make the governor come out with his counterstatement. Scientists? What about the work of real scientists like me?

The governor continues, "The people behind me are all representatives of the leaders in safe and responsible exploration and drilling. They are all committed to this environmentally responsible way of doing business. My staff and I work closely with the Department of Energy to understand our demands as a country for clean and abundant energy. With the technology these men and women are using, the United States is not only self-sufficient for petroleum needs but will continue to be for many decades to come." More screams of approval and loud applause. "Thank you. That's all I have prepared for today. My chief of staff, though, will remain to answer any questions you might have. Good day to you, and may God bless you and the great state of Texas."

"Good job, governor," Marsha mumbles out loud as she drives home. She notices dead grass everywhere and the leaves that have fallen from their dead branches. Rounding the corner on her street, she knows she and a small handful of others are all that stand against the vast resources of governments and businesses.

June – It Starts

For a depth of several hundred feet, algae blooms bob and kill anything that enters them. At heights of over a mile above sea level people are experiencing health problems that are perplexing doctors. Inhabitants around the world are starting to realize the benefit of a "Goldilocks" region (as it is dubbed by the news media) where they can breathe better. No one knows why this is so, but nonetheless, it is drawing the attention of most environmental and health scientists.

La Paz, Bolivia, at over thirteen thousand feet, is being devastated by something that is frightening its people. Some go to bed, and never wake up. Some pass out while on a walk, and never recover. They have given up trying to play their beloved futbol because they cannot get enough players willing to take to the pitch. Word spreads quickly across the world of issues not only in Bolivia, but in other higher-altitude places.

American Airways flight 922 from Miami with 95 passengers and crew is following directional beacons of the La Paz International Airport when the pilot tries to reach the tower. Copilot Ralph Tackitt also tries using different frequencies. He gets no reply.

"Carl, I can't reach anyone either."

Pilot Carl Pemberton, who is in the left seat and has flown this route at least fifty times, checks his equipment and tries again to raise the control tower at La Paz. All he gets is silence. "This shit happens all the time. Who knows? Someone probably tripped over the power cord. They'll get it fixed. You okay with the beams?"

"Roger – Titicaca in sight now."

La Paz only has one runway, and ninety-nine percent of the flights have to land from the west so as to have a clear approach. Focusing on today's approach, all looks good for landing. Detecting a slight side wind from the north, Carl checks the airspeed. In the far distance he sees the glow of La Paz's lights.

"Ralph – any contact yet?"

"No – still can't reach anyone."

"Shit – we'll do a visual then. Keep an eye out for any traffic. I'll line up the nose."

"Roger."

Carl takes the plane out of autopilot mode as the countryside is not conducive for a plane bobbing and weaving through mountain turbulence while being driven by a computer. He cuts the engines some more to slow from around three hundred miles per hour to a little over two hundred. He is aware of the spin-up time needed for his engines, so his hand is on the throttle at the slightest hint of an emergency and if a pull-up is necessary.

"Gear down and locked."

"Roger."

He has the plane in a perfect approach and sees the rotation of the blue and white airport beacon. As he draws nearer, the runway's bright lights come into sight as he cuts power even more and drops the plane to two thousand feet over the landscape.

"Ralph – all clear?"

"Roger, Carl, nothing in sight. Still can't raise anyone – are they on a fucking siesta?"

Carl laughs. "It's a technical problem of some sort. I'm surprised their backup generator didn't kick in, though. I've got the airport in sight, and it's clear. I'm taking her in unless you see something – so keep your eyes peeled. Nothing around?"

"No traffic – all clear. Should we do a go-around?"

"We're fine. I'll notify the home office of this shit when we get on the ground. Being out of contact even in this place is uncalled for."

Carl cuts the engines of the 757 even more and the huge plane drops lower into a glide. His right hand is steady on the throttle, and he adjusts a little more power for some added lift. He glances ahead to keep his heading lined up with the runway lights in the distance while keeping his attention to his speed and altimeter. An alarm's blare fills the cockpit.

"We've lost the left engine," Ralph says giving Carl quick information. The plane jerks to the left as the right engine's thrust by itself is now pushing the plane. Carl corrects the yaw and brings the plane back as straight as he can. Another blare from the panel announces another problem.

"Right engine has quit!" Ralph calls out.

"I've got the controls," Carl says.

"Roger. Trying to restart right," Ralph replies automatically.

"Checklist."

"Roger," Ralph answers quickly.

All of Carl's training from hours and hours in a simulator kick in. With no power, all he can do is to try to glide the plane, given what lift he can coax out of the plane at this altitude. Carl is in control, with Ralph trying to restart the engines. Both pilots are calm, as each focuses on his tasks. Another alarm goes off that signifies low oxygen in the cockpit. Both Ralph and Carl scan the panel that would show a hull breach, but all is normal. Instinctively, they reach behind them and put on their masks that automatically start pumping pure oxygen. They breathe in the coolness and just as quickly focus back on the runway lights still over two miles ahead of them.

"Ralph, kill the alarms." Ralph reaches up and flicks switches to stop the noise.

In the passenger cabin, sirens alert that low oxygen is detected, and oxygen masks automatically deploy from the ceiling. Flight attendants had to practice putting on their masks in their training, but none had to do this while little oxygen was otherwise available to them; today, it's hard for them to concentrate on something as basic as slipping a cup over one's face.

Flight attendant Cristina Sanchez looks over to her right and sees Rosita, her seatmate, collapse. She leans over and pulls her upright, then reaches up to grab the other mask. Quickly, she puts it in on Rosita's face, tightens it as snug as she can, and watches as she breathes deeply and regains her composure. Cristina nods in a reassuring way, and Rosita just looks back at her. Cristina then looks back at the passengers in the cabin. All are breathing through their masks.

"Come on Rosita, they need us."

The passengers are looking at the flight attendants for instructions on what to do next, and she makes the announcement over her intercom, "Remain calm. We have encountered a cabin problem, but your masks will help you."

In reality, Cristina is as perplexed as they are. She hits the button that connects her with the cockpit. The plane is surreally quiet as it glides through the air with no engine thrust.

In the cockpit, Carl says, "Ralph – ignore the cabin call. We have too much going on here."

Outside the plane and unbeknownst to anyone in the plane, a lack of oxygen isn't allowing the engines to ignite the JP4 fuel that's being pumped into the combustion chambers. Ralph continues through his checklist for the second time, thinking that he missed a step. Carl feels his heart race, brought about by a fear that was never real in the simulator. In the simulator, he knew that all he had to do was step out of the box to clear his head – it was a contrived emergency. This is real, and he knows that if he doesn't remain in control of his fear that he will crash.

"Ralph – goddamn it, start one fucking engine. We've got fuel in both."

"Negative, Carl – both engines dead – won't restart."

"Then buckle up tight. I'm going to nurse this sonofabitch to that runway – and if not, it'll be close. Keep an eye out for towers or buildings. Also watch the altimeter."

"Roger." Ralph scans the horizon from right to left, back again, and then once more. "All clear, Carl."

Ralph didn't have to watch the altimeter as the computer announces, "one thousand one hundred feet" "one thousand feet" – but instinctively he does what he was told and echoes each computerized announcement.

The runway is close, and Carl is fighting both stall speed and gravity. He is the master at this moment, and every minute of his twenty-four years of flying experience is focused on one thing – hitting the wheels on the runway.

Carl needs all the aerodynamics of the plane and having the landing gear exposed creates extra drag that he doesn't want. Still,

273

he is determined not to pancake this plane on the runway. For a brief second, he thinks about telling Ralph to raise the gear – but doesn't.

"Five hundred feet," Ralph calls out.

"Stall, stall, stall," the computer blares.

Carl wants to flare the plane by pulling up the nose, but he is not certain if he is over the runway. Instead, he keeps the nose slightly down, and both pilots feel the thump of the front tires touching down first. The manuals and training say never to do this, but these circumstances have dictated otherwise. The tires and the structure holding them roll without collapsing and within a second the back tires also contact the runway. It's a perfect nose-wheel landing – something he has never done before, and never hopes to repeat. Carl still has a lot of work to do to stop the plane, but he relaxes his grips on the controls knowing the hardest part is over. Everyone is safe.

"Ralph, ring the flight attendants. Find out what is going on back there." He rings the call button, but no one picks up.

"No answer, Carl. I'll go back and see what the problem is. I'm sure they were about to shit their pants when the engines quit!"

As soon as he slips his mask off and tries to breathe, he flashes back to a time where he was SCUBA diving in the Caribbean and ran out of air – it's the same feeling. It was only around sixty feet down, plus he had a dive partner close by where he could buddy-breathe to the surface – but it scared him a lot. He grabs the mask and puts it back over his head. What in the hell is happening?

"Ralph, what's going on?" Carl starts to take off his mask, but Ralph stops him.

"No – leave it on. Something is going on – the air is…is gone," Ralph says in a panicked voice. Carl lets the plane coast near the terminal building where he brakes to a halt.

"What did you say?" Carl asks.

"Let me try again," Ralph says and then takes in big gulps of air, throws off his mask, and tries to breathe. Nothing – no oxygen. He holds his breath and opens the cockpit door. He can't believe what he sees – most passengers are in their seats, but some are lying in the aisles, and some are collapsed by the exit doors. Some have their eyes open, and some look as if they are simply sleeping. None of them are breathing, and glancing about, he looks to the flight attendants – also lifeless. It's only been about twenty seconds since he left his cabin, but already he feels his oxygen draining away. He opens his mouth and exhales the carbon dioxide building up in his system, and gulps for air – but there isn't any. Turning, he scrambles the ten feet to his cockpit seat while at the same time grabbing his oxygen mask. His body quickly responds positively to the oxygen, and he looks over to Carl.

"What is going on back there?'

Still in shock from what he saw, he replies, "I…I think they're dead – all of them. It's like their oxygen failed them or there is something toxic on board. Carl, I could not see one person breathing."

Carl takes off his mask and starts to stand up to go see for himself, when he immediately gulps for air and realizes that he cannot breathe. He slaps on his mask again as he looks to Ralph.

"How long does this last?" Ralph asks. "You know, the oxygen. What's our time limit?"

"They're small canisters – maybe twenty minutes, maybe less. Hell, I don't know," Carl answers as he depresses the intercom button.

"Anyone back there?" He waits for an answer. "Anyone." Still no reply. He hits a button to connect him ground control.

"La Paz tower. Look out your window. Do you see a big plane sitting below you? That's me. Anyone there?"

Silence. Carl switches over to another frequency for emergency only usage and repeats the same message. No one responds.

"What do you want to do?" Ralph asks.

Carl is about to reply when he tries to breathe in and feels no sensation of oxygen filling his lungs. He gulps again, and nothing. He knows the bottle is nearing empty.

He looks over to Ralph who is starting to go through the same panic, and says, "We could try to make it to the main building, but there is no jet-bridge. I don't know, I don't know, I don't know. I don't know what to do, damn it."

He takes off his mask and draws in the biggest breath he can, but it is like someone has put a bag over his head, and the oxygen is completely drained away. He pushes the mask tight to his nose and mouth in the hope that a small amount of oxygen can be found. Ralph's eyes are fixed in a stare toward Carl hoping for an answer.

He mumbles, "no, no, no," and claws at the window in the hope that opening it will let in fresh air. Ralph grabs Carl's hand and squeezes it. Ralph lets go and makes a dash to the rear of the plane. Carl throws off his mask, manages to open a side window, and breathes as deeply as he can. Like everyone else on flight 922, all are now dead.

July – Events

In a span of forty-eight hours, the world accelerates in its sickness. Stories are being reported hourly from around the world about how people were at first being diagnosed with what seemed to be asthma attacks, only to see a large percentage die from not being able to get their breath. The death rates are especially high at an altitude greater than a few thousand feet. Doctors and nurses in hospitals fare no better and, therefore, the hospitals are swamped with dead and dying. Some doctors, though, find that high doses of oxygen alleviate the problems all together. Lab techs and nurses are also aware of the issues and discover that by going into a hospital room and attaching a breathing mask to the oxygen output valve, they are fine – at least as long as they stay tethered to the life-sustaining air.

Countries blame other countries – and the excuses range from diseases to poison gas attacks. The president of the United States is demanding that the CDC do something. The president convenes his Cabinet in an emergency session. His press secretary has been fielding calls for several days from other heads of state and has given each the same answer.

"The United States will assist any country that asks, and we are working feverishly to find the source of the contamination." One by one, though, most countries give up asking for assistance, as they realize that the United States is not faring any better than they are.

At his meeting the president is surrounded by his Cabinet, the vice president, and Hugo Cortez, CDC director, whose attendance Barrera now requires. The meeting room, which is a secured room with no windows, is sealed tight enough to allow fresh oxygen from tanks positioned just outside the door to be pumped directly into the room. This allows all the participants to get rid of the portable oxygen masks, which they always have at their sides while not in this room.

The president starts, "Hugo, you're on. What in the hell has the CDC dug up on this? Is it some sort of flu? Is it a poison gas?"

Copies of a report marked "Top Secret/Confidential" are passed to each person as Hugo replies, "Sir, we simply don't have an easy answer. We have seen lab results from thousands of patients, and the only common thing being reported is that something is happening to the red blood cells. The normal blood oxygen levels are a measurement of the saturation of oxygen in the blood, and when a person comes in complaining of something related to hypoxemia or ARDS, we..."

The president cuts him off. "What?"

"Sorry, sir, Acute Respiratory Distress Syndrome. It's when people can't breathe for whatever reason."

"So, what's in the air? It is the Chinese, isn't it? Al Qaida? What goddamn radical group is doing this? Jesus, man, I feel like I'm in some real-life James Bond movie with some mad doctor about to dial in and demand a billion-dollar ransom."

All eyes focus on the CDC director. Everyone in the room is worried not only for the country, but for his or her own family.

"We know it's not a virus or bacteria, sir. It's not Ebola or anything like that. We don't know. We simply don't know. The red blood cells contain hemoglobin that binds to oxygen and carries it to different parts of the body – it's really that simple. When the oxygen levels in the blood fall, it can lead to health complications – or even deaths like we are seeing. Something in the air is reacting with the body – we've seen this in ninety-five percent of the cases. Incoming patients have been tested at less than fifty percent oxygen. After oxygen is applied, normal blood levels are measured, and we see immediate results. Sir, we have a problem that the CIA and FBI should be on. Something insidious is poisoning not only our air supply but everyone's, from what can gather – it's a global issue."

Barrera turns to the CIA director. "What's the chatter? Shit, I know we're hated by some radicals out there, but who would be stupid enough to put this chemical into the air for other countries? Oxygen can't just disappear – it's a big sky out there, folks. Mark, we need an answer."

"Sir, many of our agency's contacts everywhere have been

contacted personally by me – and I can tell you that the only thing coming back is the exact same diagnosis that Hugo just told us. Every country is as confused as we are, and revolts are going on. What is going to be worse is when the revolts happen here – then what? We're going to have a political mess out there to get our arms around. Basically, who is going to be aligned with whom. There are two exceptions to the high death rates – China and Russia. We know they are experiencing problems also, but they're very tight-lipped about what they're testing for and what they're seeing. However, we have contacts on the ground in those countries, and we're trying to find out more from them. Unfortunately, at this time we can't get much out of them."

The president turns back to Hugo. "The world is looking to us, Hugo. Give me something."

"Yes, sir. We know what usually causes a lack of oxygen in the bloodstream, and we are prepared to issue a statement to not exacerbate the problem. I think if we let this thing run its course – whatever it is – things will return to normal. In the meantime, we are prepared to issue these guidelines with your approval: 1) For anyone smoking, stop immediately; 2) Stay away from anyone who is smoking; 3) No strenuous activity of any sort; and 4) Follow some guidelines that slow strenuous breathing."

"Hugo, are you suggesting that we teach a person how to breathe?" one of the cabinet members asks. He laughs, but no one else does, and Barrera stares at him.

The CDC director continues, "We can't shut down the U.S. work force because...hell, we just can't. That's silly to even suggest it. Do you know what this would do to our economy?"

"Yes, Mr. President, I do understand that, but that is exactly what I am suggesting. People have to learn to breathe differently – at least for a while. We are making an assumption also that people are figuring out some of this on their own. We have to change or..." He pauses.

"Or what?" Barrera asks.

"Or people will continue to die."

One of the cabinet members offers, "I've been quietly listening to this about the poison in the air. Can't we just give people bottles of oxygen to use when they start to feel woozy? Or a shot or something?"

Secretary of Commerce Roy White interjects, "Do you know what this would cost? And where in the world exactly do we get three-hundred-fifty million bottles of oxygen to pass out? Or, let's say that we find ten thousand or so – who gets them and who doesn't? And then what happens when those are empty? Do we magically manufacture more? Nonsense. Let's find out who is behind this and find the antidote. Hell, our CDC is the best in the world."

The president focuses back on Hugo, "Well?"

"Sir, we are working on it. That's all I have."

Leaning toward the CDC head, the president scowls. "Hugo, that's not good enough. What resources do you need?"

"Sir, we have access to all kinds of chemical monitoring stations not only in the U.S., but also at the poles – in fact, we have a direct link to scientists onsite there; they report that nothing abnormal is being detected."

"Hugo, while I appreciate your summary, those aren't answers to solve this."

"Mr. President, if I may," the president's personal physician interjects. "With the exception of your hemoglobin numbers being off the chart, all of your lab work came back clear. Frankly, I don't think it is a virus – or if it is, it's certainly a strange one."

Barrera looks at his doctor, nods, then back to the others. "Goddamn it, people, you're not hearing me." He stands up and glances about the room. "Find the source of this problem – it's that simple. I don't care if it is hard – it's what we do. The United States fights hard problems – end of story. Someone, or some country, is out there releasing some type of poison into the atmosphere. Maybe they need help but are too cautious to ask. Maybe it was an accident? Who knows? Stay on your contacts and scientists in Russia and China – let's get their honest answer on this."

There is silence as he sits back down. "Dave will be back in touch to schedule our next meeting. In the meantime, I want updates twice a day from you, Hugo."

"Yes, sir," the director answers as he and the others rise as the president and Chief of Staff McNichole exit the room.

Entering the White House's oval office room, the president lies down on the couch while breathing deep to fill his lungs. Leaving an oxygen-rich room to go to a normal environment leaves him light-headed. He closes his eyes and utters, "God, I wish I had a cigarette."

"Mr. President, I should alert you of something I am just now finding out," McNichole says.

"Shit, Dave, what now?"

"While you were in the DPB, I was handed some notes. The governors of Montana, Idaho, Wyoming, Colorado, Nevada, and, South Dakota all called either this morning or overnight to alert us to incidents going on their states. Apparently, a huge number of deaths and emergency room cases started to be reported throughout their states. They are worried if radicals pick up on this, panic might follow."

The president sits up and looks at the TV screens on the east wall. "What are they asking for?"

"Answers."

"You mean what I just asked the Cabinet for? Jesus, Dave, I couldn't pry any answer from Cortez. If I could do it, I would replace him today."

Dave nods his head in agreement.

"If this gets worse, our economy will drop like a rock. Hell, the market is down almost eight thousand points in the past week already. And believe me, if the economy tanks, and people lose faith in what I'm doing, someone will pay for this – and it won't be me."

"Yes, sir, I agree." As he starts to leave the room, he turns around and asks, "Are you okay?"

"Yes, I'm fine. Doc Blake showed me how to relax and breathe better when I'm upset. It just takes a minute and then I'm fine."

August – An Error in Judgment

At random times, and in random pockets around the world, deaths level off and countries report better conditions. The United States is facing tremendous production problems as companies are completely shutting down from a lack of workers. No factories mean fewer consumables. Food shortages have led to the first price controls in over fifty years. The president reviews his notes from his advisors and asks his press secretary to set up an immediate "state of the country" presentation he plans not only for the American people, but also for other countries to hear firsthand what is facing the United States.

A few hours later, the TV cameras are set up and President Barrera takes the dais.

He is surrounded by scientists his staff has gathered up to support any claim he wants to make. He doesn't dwell too much on what has occurred, but rather how emissions in the United States will be immediately and dramatically reduced to help air pollution. To accomplish this, he tells the audience that drastic measures are needed by all countries. He explains that these changes are planned to only be temporary until the scientists can find out for certain what is causing the health problems. Citing studies from the scientists sitting behind him, he touts the quick adoption of natural gas and long-range batteries as the new standard in all automobiles. He gives examples of how scientists are experimenting with extracting only harmful carbon dioxide in the air and pumping it inside rocks deep underground. He presents slides prepared by the U.S. Geological Survey in which they found thirty-six regions across the United States that could store twenty-four hundred to thirty-seven hundred metric gigatons of carbon dioxide underground. He uses a term called geologic carbon sequestration to describe how the government will be leading the world in this work. The reality is that these are all words he was told to say by his speechwriters, and that the more technical jargon he throws out, the better he will look to the masses.

He references yet more collected data – this time by a survey by the U.S. Energy Information Administration.

He recites, "This group projects the United States will only emit approximately 5.4 metric gigatons of fossil fuel-related carbon dioxide by the end of next year. Based on these estimates, the underground storage we have available for harmful gases is five hundred years."

He ends his speech as upbeat and positive as he can, stating that the United States will provide a clean planet for all, and because of this effort, the air will be cleaner to breathe for centuries to come. He thanks all members of Congress who have supported him and says he has faith in the scientific community working with private industry and government agencies to implement the plans he just laid out.

News programs report the speech, and for the first time in months, some people (at least in the United States) feel like someone is doing something. Unbeknownst to them, most of the scientific studies the president mentioned are still being debated within their respective communities. No scientific project is planned to start for at least two months, if ever, as no consensus is close to being reached by both scientists and businesses that would be affected by these programs.

A month after the president's presentation, the heat is still unbearable, but it seems to have leveled off. There is a collective sigh of relief.

September – It Gets Personal

Dr. Oliver answers her ringing cell phone. "Hello."

"Marsha, it's Bob." She doesn't reply to her boss, but the voice continues. "Can you come over?"

Still no reply. "Marsha?"

"Bob, I've waited all summer wondering when the ax would fall – when are you going to fire me? We owe it to our new students to teach them ethics, if nothing else. You let not only me, as a friend, down, but I think we have caused the harm everyone in the world is experiencing."

"You were right – you are right."

"Now you think I'm right? What about years ago when you fudged the data? Did you really think a few dollars in your pocket were worth not reporting the facts?" She waits for a reply. "Fire me, Bob. I don't care – hell, I really don't. Megan has been sick all summer, and it's worrying me. I've got more important things on my mind than this job."

"Marsha, I understand. No, you're not fired. You can call me any name you want – we don't have to be friends."

She interrupts with a laugh. "Friends? That stopped months ago."

"I hope Megan gets better."

There is silence as her cell phone displays "call ended." That's it? That's what he wanted to say?

She looks at the phone in her hand and, for a split-second, thinks about being dramatic and throwing her cell phone against the wall. Her scientific and rational mind won't allow such bursts of emotions, though, and she cradles the cell phone in her hand and lays it on the table.

Marsha walks down the hall to Megan's room and peeks in. Megan is lying on her back with an oxygen supply tube looped around her head, while a machine sitting next to her bed whirs.

Four months earlier, Megan started feeling weak and complaining of headaches. By that time the doctors had seen these symptoms before, and knew that if caught quickly, a patient could be treated with oxygen and sent on their way. Megan was lucky. At the time of her doctor's diagnosis and a call for a prescription, there were still oxygen canisters to be distributed; now, there are fewer and fewer to be handed out – and those few are rationed to the most critical. With careful rationing and a quick stock-up of extra containers of the precious air, Megan and Bob have been able to keep Megan healthy. Now, though, their cache was down to their last life-giving bottle.

They lie awake at night thinking about what their plans should be if, and when, Megan needs more oxygen. Should they try to move somewhere safer? Reports on social media tell of places where people are living normal lives as if this air problem doesn't exist. Unfortunately, other websites report that almost all of that "Utopian" life is a lie – they don't exist. There are no completely "as usual as it once was" places anymore; rather cities report an index from one to ten that describes their air quality. A one is a dead city, and ten is perfect. No city has an index greater than six right now.

Meagan's asthma has only gotten worse over the past months.

Lewis Trago, the Oliver's neighbor, has been living in the same house for over forty years, and he and his wife were very helpful in helping with errands when Megan was born. Lewis' wife died five years ago, and since then, his enthusiasm for life seems to have drained from his body. He stopped venturing outside his small yard, and except for pulling weeds in his flower garden, he sits in his living room watching old movies. With his health declining, Marsha remembered an oxygen machine brought to him a year ago. She thought at the time about the irony of how lucky he was to be in such poor condition to have qualified for a canister of oxygen. Marsha had watched him a few days ago pulling it along as he ventured out onto his porch. Her plan now is to ask him to share his canister with her daughter if he can. Heck, he is even welcome to move into our house, she thinks.

291

The first morning glow of another day starts to peep through the window shades, and anxious to suggest her idea to Lewis, she throws her legs over the side of her bed, picks up her clothes, and goes into the kitchen. She sits at the kitchen table and waits with anticipation for a reasonable time to knock on Trago's door. She knows she should wait until at least 8:00, as this would seem reasonable given his age. She looks at the clock, takes a sip of water, and waits. As the clock on the wall reads 6:45, she can wait no longer and heads next door.

She approaches his door and raps. She wants to be heard, so she knocks louder. No answer. She knocks some more but with a little more force. She knows he probably is sleeping, and for a moment she thinks about going back to her house. With still no answer, she presses on the door lever. The door opens.

Putting her head inside, she calls out, "Mr. Trago – it's me, Marsha, from next door. You here?" No answer. "Mr. Trago – you here? Lewis – it's me, Marsha. Are you up?"

Still no reply.

Trago's relatives live fifty miles away, and she would have seen their car pull up, or they would have left her a note if they had come and picked him up. She feels awkward being in his house. Very, very quietly, she takes a few steps, then realizes how wrong this is to bother him so early in the day. She turns back toward the door. Why didn't he answer? It strikes her as odd that she didn't at least get some sort of response. Was he sleeping that soundly?

She turns and walks into the hallway and announces herself once more, but even louder this time. With still no response, she walks a few more steps and sees the glow of a light coming from what she assumes is his bedroom. She calls out again as she pokes her head into the room. No one was in there, but she hears the shower running. "Shit," she utters as she retreats to the kitchen.

About every ten minutes she announces loudly, "Mr. Trago – it's me, Marsha, sitting in your kitchen," and she waits patiently for him to appear. She looks at her watch – thirty minutes have now elapsed.

She thinks, "Goddamn it – John's going to be up and wondering where I am. Shit, I should have left him a note." Out loud she calls, "What are you doing back there, Mr. T?"

Marsha mumbles as she gets up from the cigarette-stained table that's holding an ash tray filled to the brim with old butts. She walks down the hall again, announces her presence, and enters the bedroom. She still hears the shower running. She walks closer to the bathroom's open door.

"Mr. Trago – are you okay?" She waits for a response. "Mr. Trago – it's me, Marsha. Are you okay?"

She looks down and sees the oxygen machine sitting just beyond the doorway. Very cautiously she looks into the bathroom. The naked body of Mr. Trago is lying half in and half out of the shower stall. She stares at the lifeless body, which is white except for a few dark areas on the lower side. She stifles her instinct to scream.

293

She moves to him, concentrating her gaze on his wrist and throat area to see if she can see any movement. She touches his skin and jerks away at the coldness of it. She touches him again and takes his pulse. She stands up and stares at the body, then starts to cry. She can't seem to stop her tears for her old neighbor. Thoughts of him always making time to play a game with Megan make her sadder still. She reaches over him to turn off the shower and then walks down the hallway. Back in the kitchen, Marsha sits at the smelly table, picks up his old desk phone, and calls 911. It rings more than twenty times before someone answers.

"What's your emergency?"

"My name is Marsha Oliver; address is 505 Harrison Drive. I went to check on my neighbor. He's not been well. I found him dead in his shower."

"What is his name? And where are you now?"

"His name was Lewis Trago. His address is 509 Harrison Drive."

"An ambulance is being requested. Will you be there when it arrives?"

"Yes. I can show the EMTs where he is."

"Thank you. Do you want me to stay on the line?" the operator asks.

"No, I'm fine. Thank you."

As they hang up, Marsha looks about the kitchen. The coffee pot and counter have spots and rings from past spills, but other than

294

the table where ashes and butts fell in and around the ashtray, the room is tidy with no needless items. She looks out the back door and thinks about how rare it was to ever see Lewis unhappy. He was just that type of person who made anyone feel at ease with his smile and "How are you doing today?"

Marsha smiles thinking about how genuine Lewis was, and how she will miss him.

"The machine!" she utters out loud. She looks out the front door to see if the ambulance has arrived, then walks quickly toward Lewis' bedroom. Her head is feeling light as she steps into his bedroom. She sits on the edge of the bed, breathes in big gulps, walks into the bathroom, picks up the oxygen canister, and heads toward the back door with it in tow. She looks at its gauge; it shows almost half full. She knows she shouldn't take anything from his house, so she sits there staring at the machine and wondering what to do with it. Five, maybe ten, minutes go by. Ambulances are very busy – what is one more old man's death, she contemplates? Out of the corner of her eye she sees the glow of rotating red lights as the ambulance is approaches. She opens the back door and places the machine behind a trash can on her side of the yard. Her heart races as she goes back inside just as a man is knocking on the front door.

Answering the knock, she says, "Hi – thank you for responding. I'm Marsha Oliver – a neighbor – over there." She points to her house. "Mr. Trago is down the hallway to your left – he's in the bathroom. I came over to check on him – he's been sick. I found him just the way he is, but I did turn off the shower. That's the only thing I touched."

Two men in paramedics garb thank her and walk to where Mr. Trago's body is lying, as they themselves take in deep breaths as they go down the hallway.

"Ms. Oliver, that's fine. The police will be here soon, though, since this has to be investigated. Someone did die, and they have to make sure there was no foul play. I'm sure you understand."

"Yes, certainly. Do you mind if I run next door to check on my family? I'll be right back."

"Sure – go ahead. This is going to take a little while."

She exits out the back door, and with a casual motion leans over and picks up the oxygen tank, then makes her way to her house.

John is sitting at their kitchen table. "Where have you been? And what is going on next door. Is Mr. Trago okay? And is that what I think it is?"

"It's an oxygen machine. Mr. Trago died. And he gave us this present." John looks at her stunned. "He had a heart attack or something. Don't ask questions. I've got to go back over and help the police and medics. See if you can figure this thing out. If Megan needs it, use it. Okay?"

She turns to leave, but before she does, she leans over to kiss John. "I'm fine – I'm taking care of it."

By the time she re-enters Lewis' house, the police have arrived. She feels her heart rate speed up, as she knows she stole something. Maybe the police needed it to verify his health condition, she ponders? She explains how she found him.

"Do you mind walking us to the shower?"

"No, not at all. The EMTs are there already."

Mr. Trago's body is lying just the way it was earlier. The paramedics are waiting for the police to give the okay to move him. After a brief analysis of the room and the body itself, the police officer gives the okay to remove the body. They cover him in a white sheet, and the police ask the EMTs if they had noticed anything peculiar about the death. The reply is standard by now for cases like this – that it appears to have been a heart attack. They explain that there is no bruising, just pooling of blood under the skin on the bottom side. They add that he could have slipped and died hitting his head somehow, but that it wasn't likely from their analysis of the scene.

Marsha explains again to them, "This is where I found him – just like that. He's been sick. I came in to check on him and waited in the kitchen for the shower to stop, but it never did. I sat there for about twenty minutes – maybe more; I knew something was wrong – and that's when I poked my head in while calling out his name. He was a good neighbor and a good man."

"I'm sure he was ma'am." Motioning to the paramedics, he says, "Go ahead guys – we have enough. Come on, Mrs. Oliver – let's go back into the other room, and I'll get some more info for the report."

As the report is being finished, she watches them load the body into the ambulance. There appear to be other dead people in sheets already in there – as this was just another stop to make on the dead-person pick-up for the day. Lewis Trago's body was placed on top of them. It makes her sad to realize that soon other bodies will be placed on his.

An officer comes out of the bedroom with a small, black, zippered bag. "What do you make of this? Drugs?" he says to his colleague.

The officer opens it up and inside are new, extra breathing tubes. He takes each one out, examines them, and puts them back. "Go ahead, Ted, I'm wrapping up here. I'll be out in a minute."

Waiting for his partner to leave, the officer turns back to Marsha. "Thank you for your patience, and thanks for calling this in. I'm sure it was the same as we are seeing other places – lots of heart attacks lately with this heat."

"If you need anything, just call me. I live over there," as she points in the direction of her house.

"Mrs. Oliver, you know people are doing strange things these days to give them a little edge to stay well. We've investigated several break-ins where oxygen tanks were stolen. Now, I'm guessing that Mr. Trago did indeed die of natural causes, but we'll let the coroner have the final say. If there is anything odd that went on here, you can bet that I'll be back. Anything you want to add?"

"No, of course not. Mr. Trago was a dear neighbor."

The officer looks at her face to see if he can detect any hint of a lie. "It's just that the times we are in brings out the worst in people."

"I understand. It's fine," she responds. "Do you need me anymore?'

"No, ma'am. By the way, I don't know if you can use this, but feel free to take it. It's just some breathing paraphernalia. You never know when it might come in handy." He tosses the black bag to her.

She catches the bag and nods but says nothing as she walks to her house.

She smiles at her husband as she lays the package on the table. Then, she walks down the hall to look in on Megan. She thinks about what a wonderful neighbor Mr. Trago still is to her.

November – The World Responds

While countries point their fingers and blame others, some groups aren't waiting for any answers. One such collection, known for their radical stance on everything from Nazism to specific religious hatred in the U.S., has determined that there is only one explanation – a virus unleashed by terrorists, and with no proof otherwise, their message is quoted daily as it is spread around the world instantaneously via social media.

The World Health Organization, the United States' CDC, and other health departments in many countries do their best to counter these claims by putting out their own messages, but in a short time these groups have convinced the world that a virus was created by a country or countries banding together to make oxygen levels disappear. The unknown has put a fear into people, and since they are not hearing anything positive from their own government, they take sides against the government. Protests grow, and buildings are ransacked while governments react with force. Both sides escalate their intensity of claims, and the prospect for order is dwindling if concrete answers aren't found quickly.

Medical doctors do agree that health directives must be provided to make the public aware of the symptoms, remedies, and outcomes. They decide to take matters into their own hands and publish their own report on several websites: *"The brain requires approximately 3.3 ml of oxygen per one hundred grams of brain tissue per minute. The body responds to lowered blood oxygen by redirecting blood to the brain and increasing cerebral blood flow. Blood flow may increase up to twice the normal flow but no more. Brain cells are very sensitive to reduced oxygen levels. Once deprived of oxygen they will begin to die off within five minutes. If the increased blood flow is sufficient to supply the brain's oxygen needs, then no symptoms will result. If blood flow is reduced to the brain or blood flow is increased too much by the body over-compensating, brain damage can occur. Cerebral hypoxia is classified because of the reduced brain oxygen. This means that there is limited oxygen in the environment and therefore causes reduced brain function. Aviators, mountain climbers, SCUBA divers, fire fighters, and athletes are all at risk for cerebral hypoxia, and we recommend that these activities be curtailed until a source for the oxygen problem is found. Oxygen deprivation can also cause obstructions in the lungs. Symptoms can include choking, strangulation, and crushing of the windpipe. Severe asthmatics may also experience symptoms of hypoxia. Depending upon the severity of hypoxia, there are four possibilities:*

1) *Aneurysm in a cerebral artery; this is not always fatal, as it could be mild to moderate impairment of brain function due to low oxygen levels in the blood.*

2) *Focal cerebral ischemia; this is a stroke occurring in a localized area; it can be of short duration, or acute.*

3) *Global cerebral ischemia; this is a complete stoppage of blood to the brain.*

4) *Massive cerebral infarction, caused by complete oxygen deprivation due to an interference in cerebral blood flow which affects multiple areas of the brain.*

A silent stroke is also a possibility, so everyone should try and stay aware of how others are behaving. A silent stroke may not have any outward symptoms, and the patient may be unaware they have suffered a stroke. A silent stroke still causes damage to the brain and places the patient at increased risk for a major stroke. Women who exhibit hypertension and/or smoke increase their risk for silent stroke.

If you see any of the above symptoms, or believe a silent stroke occurred, or reductions in short-term memory or the handling of basic tasks, realize that cerebral hypoxia could be starting. Decreased motor control skills will follow, as well as the skin also appearing bluish with a faster heart rate. Continued oxygen deprivation results in fainting, long-term loss of consciousness, coma, seizures, cessation of brain stem reflexes, and brain death. See a doctor for care and quickly get oxygen to the person exhibiting any of these symptoms.

The cause of hypoxia is usually anemia and carbon monoxide poisoning, but we are doctors and not scientists. We do not know if carbon monoxide is high or not, but we do know that people are getting sick, and some are even dying because of hypoxia."

It is a lot of information for most to digest, but it is repeated in newspapers and on a website dedicated to providing medical advice. The message is translated in many languages to make sure people are aware of the symptoms. As the message gets spread, lifestyles change accordingly. Some, though, post messages that this is yet another case where the government wants to control the masses. More protests are met with more resistance, and the circle of fear from both sides exacerbates each day. Hundreds of thousands are laid off work as companies can no longer afford to stay in operation, and this, in turn, makes stocks worthless – which, in turn, makes large banks the only financial institutions standing between simple chaos and total chaos, where governments crumble.

December– I Have Bullets

People are taking extra precautions to avoid contact with others, just to be safe. This has a ripple effect that causes a reduction in trust in almost all pockets of society. An undisputable fact, no matter what the source of the information, is that everyone knows that something is horribly wrong with the air, and oxygen helps solve that problem. Urban hospitals are so crowded that some people, such as the elderly or those with medical ailments, are dying before they can be attended to. Sometimes, people drop off their loved, elderly parent knowing his or her body will be taken care of. Medical staffs are short-handed themselves, and the ones on duty have to make life-and-death triage decisions hourly.

For the religious, they have now placed their fate in their god to save them, or to accept their fate to perish if that is what their god has ordained for them. Fringe religious groups spring up every day wanting people to follow them, as they, and only they, can provide salvation to the mortal souls. People who need something to cling to are attracted to these charlatans who claim to have a connection and insight to God. Many though simply sit and wait with their thoughts and with some hope that a cure or solution will be found to solve the world crisis.

In 1961, during the height of what was known as the "Cold War," a plan was put in place to build a secret bunker that would secure not only the president and vice president, but also all of Congress in case of an emergency. In Seven Corners, Virginia, a sprawling resort promising a challenging eighteen-hole golf course, an eight-hundred-room hotel, and a convention center for over a thousand people was about to break ground. Heavy earth-moving equipment of all shapes and sizes was brought in, and with a typical ground-breaking ceremony with the mayor of Seven Corners turning over the first shovel full of dirt, the resort was started. While the resort was real, unknown to the mayor and others was the fact that under this resort was another complex of immense proportions.

Code-named Atlantis, the underground complex was dug out one hundred feet below the structures above. It was built with three-foot-thick, reinforced concrete walls, and had two doors for access. Each door weighs twelve tons and can be closed within a minute with the press of a button. The complex itself consists of eighteen dormitories, each capable of providing sleeping arrangements for six hundred people. Additionally, there is a dining hall that can feed two hundred people at once. Sixty days of food and water supplies are stored therein, and forty-two thousand gallons of diesel fuel provide three generators with power to keep the complex in electricity for thirty days.

The president, vice president, and senior government leaders are now in Atlantis. Their oxygen is purified many times over to

305

ensure that no virus or contamination makes its way in. For now, the federal government officials are safe. The director of national security issues an order for all state police, military, and National Guard troops to be dispatched to locate and procure at all costs any and all oxygen containers they can find. Once found, the containers are to be delivered only to specific locations provided by the director.

In Maine, the governor receives the directive. He thinks that if anyone deserves the precious oxygen, it certainly isn't someone in Washington, D.C. He lays the paper on his desk. What if the president and vice-president die? Wouldn't that spell total ruin for our country? What if I die? Who would care, outside of my family and a few friends? He picks up the paper and stares at the words, then makes his decision. Before passing the directive along to his state's general in charge of the National Guard, he alters the collection point to be the governor's office in Augusta rather than the state's National Guard buildings. After all, because of his prestige as governor, he sees no reason that he should not be entitled to at least some extra oxygen for himself and his family before he sends the collection on.

Whatever name they are called – radicals, survivalists, or doomsday planners – they have planned for a time where their forecast of some catastrophic event manifests itself. They have stockpiled their own food, water, weapons, gas masks, gasoline, and generators – the essentials and necessities for survival. They had not planned, though, for the possibility of their generators not being able to be run because of low oxygen levels, or for something as simple as oxygen itself to be in short supply. Some did have small oxygen tanks they bought at the local SCUBA shop for minor emergencies, but these hold no more than ten to twenty minutes of air.

A state's National Guard is made up mostly of volunteers who participate in military activities one weekend a month. While they are soldiers in every sense of the word, they are more ingrained in the community with their full-time jobs. Because of their integration within a community, and through their casual conversations at work or in public, people find out that the state's National Guard is being deployed and is seeking out every oxygen tank they can find. The survivalists and some of the general population, when hearing what the government is planning, plan to get a head start to find their own sources of this life-sustaining gas.

The first stores to be ransacked were any retailers offering anything in the way of oxygen containers. Many of these retailers are already wise to the impending scarcity of the oxygen containers and have stashed these away for their own use. Still, medical suppliers, dive shops, and sporting-goods stores are hit by the doomsday planners. As the National Guard is pulling into Bangor with their map and orders to secure any oxygen containers they find, they separate into five convoys so they can complete their work in parallel. As the first convoy approaches Joe's Medical Supplies, they encounter people coming out of the front door carrying baskets of oxygen containers.

"Halt!" comes an ear-splitting command from a speaker of top of the lead truck.

The booming command startles the people, and then a command from their leader tells them to run the alleys.

"Stop, or we will shoot," yells the junior officer who has never had to issue this command before. Mainers are not prone to acts of violence, and this is the first time his men and women have been issued live ammunition. Today will be a test of their military worthiness. With directions from their base commander, the officers in charge of the troops have been given orders to secure any canister at any cost.

A man stands his ground in front of the store. "What right do you have to order us to stop. We bought these in the store. What is going on?"

The reality, however, is that these people did, indeed, break into the store and help themselves to whatever they wanted. The National Guard troops by now are on the ground and have their guns pointed at the lone man. None of the civilians could have ever imagined their own National Guard firing at them. The guard commander orders the civilians to stop, but they look to each other, and in silent agreement continue walking away.

"Fire!" comes the command.

The soldiers who are standing with their guns at the ready, do as ordered. Two women drop to the sidewalk, while the remainder hasten their run into the alleys out of sight.

"Sir, should we pursue?" a sergeant asks.

"No." The captain orders his troops to enter the store and gather up the items they have on their own shopping list. He takes two of his troops and walks over to the people lying on the sidewalk. As he gets closer, he keeps his pistol unholstered just in case. One is dead from what appear to be two bullets in her chest. The captain bends to one knee and looks at the blood pooling around her.

"Can you help the other one?" he asks a private.

The woman is in pain and pressing her hands on her belly as if she can stop the blood from oozing out. The soldier bends over her, moves her hands away, and applies pressure to the site where the bullet entered her stomach. Then he notices blood seeping out from two other holes. The woman's eyes widen.

"God, it hurts!" she utters.

The private attending her is an accountant by trade. He does not encounter wounded, screaming, dying people in his day-to-day work, and he tries to focus on his military training for circumstances like this. To watch a person die in front of him is not something he considered when he departed last evening from home. In training he knew he could defer to a doctor who was always hovering close by, but now he is alone. He is in charge of this woman's life at the moment, and he is alone with his decisions. She will more than likely die from her wounds, and there is nothing he can do to help her.

"Sir…"

"Get a medical kit from the vehicle, soldier. Now!" the captain orders.

The captain looks at the small oxygen tanks scattered about, picks up one, and kneels over the woman. He places the mouthpiece of the tank on her lips and opens the valve. The private returns, rips open her blouse, and puts bandages on the three wounds. He knows it will not help stanch the flow of blood, but he has to try.

"Get a stretcher and get them both onto the truck," the captain orders to the men standing around watching.

"JESUS FUCKING CHRIST! IT HURTS SO BAD! AM I DYING? WHY?!?!?", she screams.

Four soldiers do as ordered and place the women onto the stretchers. Other soldiers are now exiting the store.

"Sergeant, what did you find?"

"Nothing, sir – completely cleaned out."

"Shit." He had his orders to return with a list of supplies, and he has nothing to show for it except for three small tanks on the sidewalk, one dead woman, and another about to die. He had not planned for looters beating him to the store, and he is confused as what to do now. He gathers his thoughts.

"Okay, on to the next store before those sons of bitches beat us there, too."

As the troops ready to load into their truck, shots ring out with such volume that they echo for a full minute after the last shot is fired. The people who were last seen running away had merely taken refuge in the dark and have struck back with a vengeance. Fifteen soldiers drop to their death in a hail of bullets.

"Don't shoot," come the voices from the two privates in the back of the truck. Those words were followed by two rifles thrown out the back.

"Get your asses out of there."

The soldiers do as they were told and stand there sobbing – knowing they are about to die.

A man orders, "Ben, get some help and get Marilyn and Nancy out of that truck."

The man giving orders stares at the two quivering soldiers. He is a mean-looking dude who would invoke caution even in the daytime, but here, in the early dawn, he looks even more menacing as he points his gun at the soldiers.

"We were trying to help them. We were just doing as were told. We didn't fire our weapons. Check them – just check them, please," a private stutters.

The leader orders his men and women to lower their guns and walks over to the quaking soldiers. "Tell your superiors what

311

happened here – that citizens who meant no harm were shot dead by his men. And tell him that if they ever shoot at any of us again, this will be the same outcome," he says pointing to the dead bodies. "Get in that truck and drive away and thank your god that today was not your day die. The people to blame for this run our government – not you. Now get the hell out of here."

"Can we take them with us?" one of the soldiers asks pointing around to his dead comrades.

"Hell, I don't care. If you want to waste your breath on these people, go ahead. Just don't follow us – or else."

The privates examine each soldier to verify that they are indeed dead and decide to leave them as they lay after taking their dog tags.

The men and women watch as the truck disappears. "What the hell is going on in this world? These were soldiers in <u>our</u> Army," one of the men says.

The leader of this rag-tag group stares at the dead soldiers. The day before they might have been having supper with their families, and now because of a bad decision by their officer, they are lying here dead. Others are standing around looking to him for orders. He turns to them.

"We are at war now – with everyone including our own troops. If our troops would shoot at us, it shows how desperate our country is. This is what we have prepared for but hoped would never happen – but it is." He picks up a gun from one of the dead soldiers. "Let's go home."

Home is some forty miles west-northwest of Bangor, just north of Dover-Foxcroft and off a two-lane road half-way to Greeley's Landing, where twenty couples and their children established a community many years ago in preparation of what is happening today. Jerry Smith had not set out in life to be branded a loner; but rather by choices made along the way, he found himself moving from place to place and never found someone to accept his roaming ways. He finished his university degree in business over twenty-five years ago and has used that training to find good but not high-paying jobs with small companies – which figured out quickly he would probably be moving on in a year or two, so it was a mutual decision between those companies and Jerry when he was asked to leave.

He was the third person, or family, to settle into this little community. Not knowing anything much about them, it was appealing to him that he could buy a cheap mobile home on which someone else had stopped making payments to the local bank. Plus, the house came with a small plot of land where he could finally start that vegetable garden he always told himself he was going to have one day. He moved in and found his neighbors welcoming. Jerry had the skills of being both a doer and an organizer, so when small things like car or house repairs came up, he volunteered to help, and surprisingly, he could get others to assist if he asked. He had a charisma about him – he was a natural leader that others in his little community respected.

As more people moved close by, the new residents accepted Jerry as the guy to go to for suggestions and to solve small issues. He didn't seek out this notoriety, but he liked this position of authority – something he never got from all of the jobs at which he worked up until now.

Mobile homes of varying sizes and colors with their well-manicured lawns dot a small area of approximately twenty acres. A gravel road goes down the middle, with ten houses on each side facing each other. There is no restriction on property lines in their little area, so people just parked their homes where they thought it might look good. Most are lined up in a neat row, but two are slightly askew – and no one cares, as their community isn't about properly aligned homes but rather about being a part of community that accepts them with no questions asked. None belong to any religious sect, nor do they associate themselves with radical groups. Gradually, though, their disenchantment with the politics and policies they saw going on in government and businesses have driven them farther unto themselves. At first, the gathering of supplies was done as a necessity, as the nearest grocery was over twenty miles away. But as their buying went on, Jerry had the idea of developing a common warehouse to share goods. Once that was in place, supplies seemed to naturally grow as people brought back supplies in bulk from their latest shopping.

They had not set out to be branded as survivalists, but by most definitions this is what he and the others have become. The men and women work normal jobs during the day and return to live in a tight-knit community of common values at the end of their work shift. Each house has bars on its windows to keep out intruders, and each family has its own store of guns, ammunition, gas masks, and some with homemade bombs that Jerry made from plans he found on the internet. If any house is overrun by outsiders, not only do tunnels connect a house with at least one other, but there is also a cavern at the end of the street ten feet underground that has been equipped with sleeping quarters, two generators, and enough food stuffs to last ninety days. They have gotten along fine with the neighbors, and the neighbors have left them alone as people are wont to do in Maine.

As the men and women return from their foray turn onto the gravel road that leads them home, they are somber – there are few words spoken on their long drive. The adults who stayed behind see the dust and come out to greet the three pickups.

"We ran into trouble," Jerry says as he exits the cab. "Nancy and Marilyn were shot. Nancy was killed in town, and Marilyn died on the way here."

All is quiet until Joseph, Nancy's husband, drops to his knees and screams, "How could this happen?"

During the drive back, Jerry had tried to come up with words to explain how their plan for a few bottles of oxygen had gone so bad. Now he looks to those in front of him.

315

"The National Guard opened fire with no warning. I'm so sorry. It was my fault. I should have been more vigilant. Maybe guards. I just never expected our own troops to fire on us." He walks over to Joseph and attempts to give him a hug – but Joseph pushes him away and walks over to the truck with the bodies.

Jerry turns to everyone else. "Neighbors and dear friends, our own government took it upon themselves to shoot at us like we were wild animals. All we were doing, and are doing, is trying to survive from the virus they have heaped upon us. In return for them killing our people, we retaliated with a vengeance. These are desperate times for us now, as no doubt word will be getting around that some crazies are out there killing soldiers. It will be prudent to be prepared and vigilant, but I do not believe that we will be in immediate danger, as no one knows who we are or where we live. For now, we should be focused on helping each other – we'll deal with other issues as they come up."

The group is quiet. By now the other mate of the slain woman has made his way through the crowd to where she lies. Other members walk up to the men and give them words of comfort and hugs. Jerry walks over to the first truck and passes out the oxygen containers equally among all families.

"Let's meet in the morning at 9:00 in front of my house. Come over to my place any time tonight if you want to talk about anything or ask any questions. Use the oxygen as you need, but that's all we've got until we find some more."

The next morning, after most have had their coffee and the kids are watching TV and playing video games, the adults gather as requested. Jerry speaks. "I didn't sleep a wink last night. I thought I could put it out of my mind, but I couldn't. It was something I never thought I would see and what we would have had to do, but I'm proud that every person stood up for our own lives and our group."

"Jerry, now what? People know us around here."

"The Guard didn't track us, Jeff. If they had, we would have copters and all kinds of shit aiming down our throats. I think our government has bigger issues to deal with, and no one is telling us what is going on. That's why we have to be prepared to be on our own until we know more from them."

Another says, "Of course, we'll fight to the death to protect our own. But I was talking about this virus thing. My kids…well…what about them? Sure, those little canisters help, but where can we get a big supply of oxygen?"

Another neighbor interjects. "I've been thinking about that. Welding shops, medical supply houses, old folks' homes, and hospitals always store that stuff. We'll hit every damn one."

The other men and women offer "damn right," "you betcha," and other affirmatives.

"And then what?" Jerry asks as the words quiet down. "And then what do we do when that runs out?"

"Hell, Jerry, it won't last forever, whatever this virus is. It'll die if it can't find a host. That's what viruses do. We can all breathe now, can't we? I'm getting by. It can't get worse."

"I hope you're right, but what if it does, Joseph? What if we suck every ounce of oxygen we can get our hands on, and it still isn't enough?"

"Jerry, that's silly. You telling me the whole damn planet will lose all of its air? That's crazy."

"I don't know. I just don't know. I was just asking. We all agreed to make a run on the store yesterday – and I'll take as much blame as to what happened as anyone. Hell, I never knew the National fucking Guard would show up. I thought maybe a security guard might be there, and we could handle him easily…but this shooting…this is an ominous sign that they will shoot at us again if they see us going into stores. We'll make runs into towns to find what we can, but we'll do it earlier in the night if we go at all. I think, though, that we need to prepare to hunker down here and do the best we can with what we have."

He looks around at the members gathered. "This is a community of many – that makes us a community of one. I'm going to come up with some plans for some more runs. They will be as safe as we can make them. We'll do better next time – I promise you."

One by one they disburse back to their homes. Jerry sits on the top step of his small porch, scans the horizon with a rifle across his lap, and takes in a deep breath.

On the Rez

One word, "Tókheškhe yaŋ he" is spoken. Loosely translated from Lakota Sioux, it is a greeting. A man alone standing in the middle of field utters as a greeting to the Spirit that embodies all of their land and waters for their people. He waits for an answer as he looks to the sky. Then he says, "Ómakiya yo", a simple phrase meaning "help." For two centuries the Sioux have been pushed from the high plains of the central United States and lush woodlands of Minnesota and Canada to parts of the Dakotas.

Pine Ridge, in South Dakota, is the home of twenty thousand Sioux. They have watched as their lakes and rivers have dried up to dust just as others have seen happen, not only across America – around the world. The great American bison used to roam freely bringing food and bones to make arrows, cooking pots, and anything they could find a use for. One hundred fifty years ago, those mighty herds were slaughtered by the whites (the name they give to all outsiders, no matter what color of skin) in order to rein in the Lakota and keep them from attacking outsiders. Once reduced to a few thousand animals throughout North America that grazed majestically throughout South Dakota, Wyoming, and Montana, now there are none. The last Great American Bison, or buffalo, has died. Even the hardy cottonwood trees that used to grow wherever they found any water are wilted and leafless. Its wood, once pliable enough to make a hundred uses for the Sioux, is now brittle and breaks to the touch.

Always adapting to whatever nature and the whites have asked them to endure, the Sioux have learned how to survive. In these past years where they have seen the earth die around them, they have slowed down their pace and looked to their Spirit to watch over them. A few Sioux from Canada stumble into Pine Ridge hoping for help or some guidance on what to do. No Native American, no matter from what tribe, is ever turned away. Whites, though, who might come to the reservation looking for help are shunned and escorted away. Violence has struck up more than once over the past two hundred years because of the whites pushing themselves onto the Sioux ground that had been given back to them through treaties. But the whites rewrote the treaties, and each time that was done, the whites learned that bad feelings were never forgotten. The rural areas outside of Pine Ridge are littered with cars from the trespassers – with no one asking what became of their passengers.

The internet has always been spotty throughout the reservation. Cellular service for phones, which most take for granted, was bad before the prolonged heat, but now rarely works. The local radio station, KILI, has its own solar array to provide power to the building and to its transmitter – although the signal is significantly degraded because of the high wattage the transmitter requires.

Randall Little Horse is at KILI at 7:00 a.m., ready to send his message to all within listening range.

Mixing English with Sioux, his message is, "We have been shown by our Great Spirit that the whites no longer own Sioux land. We have held on to the Black Hills for one hundred fifty years after they were stolen from us, and today we reclaim them. Look to the east and pray for the Spirit of light to guide us. To the north, the hills and land welcome us with no others. In the west, the Black Hills with Deadwood and other towns are now ours once again. Go there if you can. If you find whites, tell them they are on our land, and they must move. The spirit of that area will protect you. The south brings more land and the spirit of the buffalo and horses. You may follow the Spirit in any direction. We have some food and some water stockpiled at Pine Ridge and at Porcupine – all are welcome to share it. Today, we reclaim what is ours and was taken from us. We have word that other places in the United States have food shortages and rioting is going on. We will not have any crime here."

Randall is the current chief of the Oglala Sioux. He not only traces his lineage directly to Red Cloud but can recite twenty more generations back from there. At the time a child is born on the reservation, he or she begins to learn of his or her ancestors. It is a tradition so that everyone will remember those who came before and pray to the Spirit for their guidance. Although a council of political leaders run the business of the reservation, Randall is the person all look up to for guidance.

The Last Breath

After his broadcast, Randall bids farewell to the people working at the station and steps out into the heat. It is 7:30 a.m., and he has a full day crossing the heart of the reservation in front of him. He is shirtless with three strands of beads covering his chest. His jeans are cut off to make cooler pants, and he wears old tennis shoes with no socks. His dark, long hair is braided into one majestic strand that reaches the middle of his back. His Sioux features are strong, showing his pure lineage. He grabs the reins of his horse, and as he throws his right leg over the saddle, he sits upright and looks to the west. With a kick in the side of his mount, he trots off. Twenty other tribe members on their own mounts follow behind and around him.

In normal times, to get from any part of the reservation to another was always by road. To go from his starting point to his final destination would take the usual circuitous route following the roads; this would total close to fifty miles. Today, Randall and the others will stay on an approximate straight path that is only sixteen miles. To the southwest they will walk and ride over hills and gullies and dried-up stream beds – they will have their Spirit to guide them. Their speed is slow – they have no time limit on when they have to reach their destination. A single person starts a Lakota song. All recognize it as a song they have heard throughout their lives; it is a song of the land. He sings for twenty minutes as others sometimes join in with sounds – not words, but a grunt or holler to acknowledge the words they hear.

After no more than a mile, the horses slow down considerably given the terrain and heat; their breathing is labored. Randall stops his mount, undoes the bridle and saddle cinch, and removes all equipment from the horse. With a slap on its rump, he sends it trotting away. Another man offers his mount to their leader, but he refuses it. "I will walk." The others dismount, disencumber their horses from their saddles and reins, and send their horses away as Randall did. All will walk.

In another half mile, a group of twenty more men and women awaits and joins in the march. This repeats itself throughout the whole walk, until the group numbers several hundred.

As they come to each arroyo, their strength is challenged to continue. Out of respect for Randall's leadership, no one precedes him even though some are better climbers over the rough terrain. The reservation is over thirty-two hundred feet in elevation, thereby causing breathing difficulties. Coupled with only a little protection in the upper atmosphere to shield the sun's waves, each step is difficult – but Randall and his tribe are driven with each step to reach their goal.

On flat land, many of the men and women could easily run a mile in six minutes or less. A leisurely walk of a mile can be done in ten minutes. But today, because of complexities of the terrain and breathing problems, they have spent over nine hours to travel the sixteen miles. Finally, Randall's goal in sight.

A few miles north of the city of Pine Ridge on a ridge overlooking a vast plain is a cemetery of many Sioux. On the southern edge of it, on the boundary of the hill, sits a grave marked by an obelisk that is slightly taller than others nearby. Surrounding it is a dilapidated, faded picket fence. On the grave itself are tokens left by a few who had come to pay their respects. It is grave of the great Lakota Chief Red Cloud.

Randall sees the small hill from about a half mile away, and he quickens his steps even though breathing has become harder. He also sees many others waiting there, and a stand of teepees already at the base of the hill give the appearance of an Indian camp from two hundred years ago. Many of his tribe lag back because they cannot keep up with Randall's pace. But all know that Randall will wait for them when he arrives at his goal.

It is the middle of the afternoon, and the temperature is one hundred twenty degrees. With each step his lungs feel like they will burst, but Randall climbs to the top of the fifty-foot hill. Once there, he regains his composure and takes in deep breaths – then strides purposefully to where the remains of Red Cloud lie. He looks out on the land and waits for all of the others to catch up. Some remain at the bottom of the hill and look up to him, while others have made the hard climb to the top to stand next to him.

"Tókheškhe yaūŋ he" he offers – and waits. A man below starts a Lakota prayer song.

A few minutes later, Randall continues, "Great Spirit of the Earth and Water, watch over us and protect us – your people. All that you have given us has made us a strong people."

He pauses as another man starts another prayer song. When he finishes, Randall begins again.

"We are tired. We want peace with all and do not understand what the whites have done to us and your land."

He stops and a woman sings a Lakota song that her mother sang to her – the same song that was passed down for many generations before that. Randall waits, smiles to all around him.

"My people, the Great Spirit's people, go where you want. Pray to the Spirit to protect you, and I will pray for you, too."

He sits down next to the sacred grave, while others erect a teepee over him encircling the grave. Red Cloud, the last great chief of the Lakota, and Randall, the last chief, will be together forever.

January – Migrations

As recently as twelve months earlier, politicians and a few hold-out scientists were arguing against climate change. Now, almost everyone is admitting that something must be done to solve the world's problem – regardless of the cause. The goal is to survive. One continent is faring better than the others – Antarctica; the problem is getting there. If anyone can make it there – and it is a huge "if," as it's not an easy journey over the water since no pilot wants to try flying since officially all aircraft are grounded. And what supplies will be available if a traveler makes it? And how long will supplies last? Are interlopers welcome if they show up, or are they turned away?

In the central U.S., people have started their journeys from higher elevations to lower ones in hopes of finding relief from their constant fear of simply getting through a day without pain or the fear of death from lack of oxygen. From Gilpin, Colorado, and surrounding mountain towns, folks head to what they once jokingly considered the big "low" city of Denver. At first, it was only a few people, then hundreds arrived, and now a steady stream that has swollen the city by an estimated five thousand men, women, and children adds to the chaos.

Community services to handle the influx of people are stressed, and irritation of the newcomers causing real and imagined shortages spawn anti-social responses. Signs like "NEWCOMERS GO AWAY – KEEP GOING" and "NEWCOMERS NOT WELCOME HERE" are spray-painted around the city. Residents of Denver were already having to adjust to this new life, and now the influx of people has added to the problem. True, the added people are using precious food supplies, but many residents share what they can and hope the newcomers move on after seeing that Denverites have little to offer them.

Natural Guard troops are mobilized, but many troops don't respond to the request; rather, they opt to stay at their homes and deal with family issues – and why wouldn't they? The governor pleads with the leaders of the National Guard troops to help restore order, but they either don't return his calls or say, "I have no troops." The few that have shown up are not sure what to do, as their ranks are so minimal that usually a patrol of one or two soldiers is all that can be disbursed to any location at a time.

In Denver, an ad-hoc militia is formed. They agree that they must be the first line of defense for their families and for the city, so they gather material and form barriers on the interstates and most roads leading into Denver. If someone doesn't have a Denver address on his or her ID, they are told to turn around. Most travelers comply, as they are not prepared to fight against people with guns. But survival has a funny way of making a person act in an impulsive way.

The Last Breath

As the cars are turning around, the drivers in the queue behind them ask what was happening up ahead. In defiance of the militia, and after a quick discussion among themselves, they decide that it is better to confront the barrier police than to turn around to await their fate outside of the city. At least in Denver they might find a little food and maybe a place to camp. Out along the interstate, they have little to nothing.

No one knows who fired the first bullet. It could have come from the overpass at Route 40 overlooking I-70, or it could have come from an occupant of one of the cars. In a matter of minutes, though, over fifty lie dead. Men, women, children – some running away in panic as they are brought down.

Cheers spread through the militia, and then the scavenging of the cars start. It is the worst face of humanity. A shadow of a figure is seen running away in a ditch. Two men give chase and fire multiple shots to stop the escapee. A baby cries as the mother falls, and two more shots bring silence. They stand over the bodies and catch their breath as sweat rolls down their faces. Neither wants to look at the other to acknowledge what they did. They back away and return to their group.

Cars are stripped of any foodstuffs and guns, and bodies are left strewn on the road as a warning to others. Two guards remain to make sure no one else makes the same mistake as the previous interlopers.

In rural areas, crops wither and are replaced by weeds. Cows have

328

long stopped producing milk. Those are the lucky animals. Most cattle simply lie down and die. Chickens, which don't seem to be affected by the heat, peck the ground for morsels. Their eggs are a source of protein, and if not laying, the old hens are a delicious source of meat.

In Deer Trail, only forty miles away from Denver, there are few, if any, options to transport produce to Denver or Colorado Springs, no matter what prices are offered. The few hundred that live there are now a community unto themselves, and as small-town people are wont to do, they help each other. In Denver, where chaos is now the norm, gangs roam the streets collecting food, and barter what they find for what they deem is important. People are scared to wander out, schools are closed, and the police and the few National Guard are helpless to respond to every call.

Options are limited to the many inside the city – stay and fight to compete for waning resources or leave. But where to go? "Lower" is all that people say and hear. Deer Trail, so seemingly safe by its remoteness to the turmoil going on in Denver, unfortunately is on "the road" east. It used to be a town that people always drove by without more than a glance. Now, though, it is a town that potentially could offer a tidbit or morsel to a traveler. It has become a stop for travelers. Some want directions or maybe a glass of water for a child, but usually all move along as they see just how poor Deer Trail is as a city. Chickens, though, disappear. Then, stores are robbed at gunpoint. Locals retaliate by firing back, and bodies from both sides lie on sidewalks. While it sounds gruesome to the local townsfolk, it has the benefit of acting as a warning to others to keep driving on.

And cars with families do continue on – to places like Garden City, Amarillo, Abilene, Fort Worth, Dallas, San Antonio, Houston, Corpus Christi, and Midland. Rumors say how wonderful these places are – people can be safe there. But driving to anywhere is a fool's journey. A few have packed Jerry cans or some container with gasoline, but eventually they all will come to realize that no matter how much they had planned, there is little chance of them arriving at a safe city, let alone finding support along their journey.

All gas stations are shut down for lack of deliveries. Cars stall, and drivers beg others to stop and sell them a gallon or two with the hopes of making it to at least the next town. Fifty dollars, one hundred? How much is offered for a gallon of gasoline has no limit. A person might barter something for a gallon or two, but then what? Another twenty or so miles to nowhere. Quickly people learn that no one stops to help – they can't if they want any chance of survival for themselves. Stranded drivers – some with families – aimlessly wander down roads or across fields. Across Europe, South America, and Asia, the same scenario is playing itself out. Survival on Earth is failing.

March – Guns at Sea

President Barrera, in his secure bunker, is getting briefed by his secretary of the interior on store break-ins and vandalism across the U.S.

"What is the National Guard doing? Do they need regular Army?"

"Yes sir, I'm sure they do. Several governors have already made the request for federal troops, and according to General Beasley, she is responding as fast as she can with troops. But, sir, there is a problem."

"Give it to me, Tom."

"The fact, sir, is that a lot of our troops are on a stand-down mode because they are waiting for oxygen containers. They can't be deployed if they can't function. According to the general, and from what she has been told, the troops become winded and almost incapacitated after only about twenty-five to thirty minutes of active work."

"Jesus Christ, Dave, what does this mean from a security aspect?" the president asks, turning to his chief of staff.

"It means we have riots and the states are pleading for our help –

and we can't handle them all. My last reports show that we have been able to respond to about fifteen percent of the requests."

"Dave, get me General Bernstein on the line – I need to find out what's going on with our missile crews and flight crews. Our Air Force is about the only thing protecting us now."

"Yes sir. But let me remind you that most jets are grounded – at least for now. We lost over twenty of them in the past week – pilots reported flameouts, and all branches agreed to cancel flights until we find the exact cause of their failure. We have the NSA working around the clock to identify if there was a hack that was doing this. Or…"

Barrera puts his head in his hands as he leans over the table. "Holy crap – we have no defenses then, do we? Hell, even if we fired a rocket, would that fail too?"

"Well, no sir, that's not exactly right. Our missiles have propellant on board – at least that's what I understand. They should be able to fly and hit their target."

"Thank you for that correction. So, we're not completely helpless – that's good to know. I feel so much safer now," he replied sarcastically.

While this exchange is going on, the chief of staff hits a button on the phone, connecting him to a secure switchboard. "The president wishes to get General Al Bernstein on the line – connect him, please."

As the president and a roomful of department and Cabinet heads wait until a voice on a speaker phone interrupts the silence. "General Bernstein here."

"Al, give me your assessment of our silos and air defenses."

"Not good, sir. Within the past thirty minutes I have officially grounded all aircraft, including helicopters. I have asked my staff for an assessment of our solid fuel missiles, and contrary to my original assessment, the best answer now is 'unknown' – but my technicians believe they will not function. I have scheduled a firing at seventeen hundred today. We've programmed it to go about one hundred miles over the Pacific, so we'll understand more after the launch. In a small-scale test of a very small rocket we did earlier, though, whatever is going on is sapping enough oxygen to stop the sustainable combustion needed for our rocket to fly barely a mile. The rocket ignited well enough at the surface, but quickly stopped functioning at around five thousand feet. We're still investigating if it was a mechanical issue or something else."

"Thank you, General – that's all I need now. Keep me posted after the launch, please." The president hits the button to hang up the phone and looks around the room.

"I am told that every nation is experiencing the same thing, sir. We have nothing to fear in the form of an attack," General Beasley is quick to add.

"Really, General? How do you know that?" Barrera asks

333

incredulously. "What if this thing in the air is just attacking us? Or us and Russia? Or us, Russia, and say China? Could North Korea be behind this? Do you honestly know what is going on with them?"

"No sir, we don't know for sure, but since every country that we have tracked has reported the same symptoms, I thought it would be reasonable to assume that they would have the same issues that are facing us."

The president continues, "From what I am told, this thing, whatever it is, is worse at higher elevations. If you're at sea level, you're okay – or at least better. Correct me if I'm wrong, but doesn't most of North Korea fall around one hundred feet in elevation – especially the capital?"

"No, sir. I'm pretty sure Korea has elevations much higher."

The president, frustrated about forgetting a basic fact, is agitated. "Goddamn it, don't you think we ought to find out more about what the North Koreans are doing there?"

"Yes sir – we should – and we will. We've had satellites on them, and within the past thirty minutes our satellites have picked up something unusual. We aren't sure, though, what it could be or mean. But, it does appear that a large number of ships have been dispatched from Nampho to Arang-dong. We think they are DPRK flagged, but not one hundred percent positive."

"So, give me a percentage that they are North Korean ships. More than fifty percent? What else is going on over there?"

"Sir, yes, we are fairly sure they are North Korean, but our eyes were only looking at port traffic, not the countryside. Those ships we spotted were tracked and are now in international waters. I don't think there is anything we can do," the vice president inserts.

Barrera answers, "Alexandra, I think the old adage 'desperate times call for desperate measures' applies here. Plus, it will show that the United States is doing something. Mike, how can we spin this?"

Before his press secretary can answer, he is interrupted by the vice president. "We can't just willy-nilly attack another country. We don't have any proof that they did anything. We have ships sailing out to see what's going on – that's it. I suppose we could interdict them under some pretense or the other. Like you said, 'desperate times.'"

"Damn it, Alexandra – what if they're spreading germs to more places?"

The general interrupts, "Ma'am, I think the president is right on this. If the North Koreans have nothing to hide, and the rest of the world is suffering from some sort of virus outbreak, why would North Korea have so much sea activity? And what would they have to hide?"

The vice president answers, "General, with all due respect, I

disagree. It could be cars, or grain, or commercial goods. You tell me with one hundred percent certainty that they are spreading something around the world, and I'll back you one hundred percent. If not, then my vote is that we don't engage. Hell, we can watch them almost minute by minute – where are they going to go that we can't find them? Nowhere. We can track wherever they go and then see what they are up to."

"Alexandra, I understand your point – but we have to find a cure for this," the president says as he looks around the room. "I want more ideas on this."

A phone call is picked up by the press secretary. "Sir, General Windsor, UNC/CFC on the phone."

"Put him on speaker, Mike."

"General Windsor – good to talk with you. I have Tom Miller here, along with others."

"Yes sir, I was trying to reach General Beasley. We have confirmed that it is a large armada of DPRK Navy ships. We have no word on any exercise they wanted to do, so this is strange to us. I have instructed my ships to stand by and to track them at ten kilometers. Do you have orders?"

"General Windsor, what is the situation at this very moment?" General Beasley asks.

"Nothing unusual."

Barrera interjects, "General Windsor, please stay on the line." He instructs his press secretary to mute the line so those in the room can discuss freely what is going on in the Yellow Sea.

"I say that first we interdict the ships, and second that we land troops in Pyongyang once and for all. They have weapons on those ships, and we know it," the president says loudly and animatedly as he leans forward to make his point. "It's time we put an end to this world calamity – I think they are causing it. Who else could it be?"

The chief of staff interrupts General Beasley, "Do we have time for that, General? Of course not. Every minute counts. Hell, who knows what weapons they are sailing with now to points unknown. More viruses? Maybe. Maybe not. We won't know until we see for ourselves. Mr. President, I agree wholeheartedly with you. Let's show the world we will lead through this crisis."

The president looks around the room and waits for more comments.

"Should we notify Congress?" the vice president asks.

"No. I am Commander-in-Chief, and I don't want to spend time tracking down congressional leaders. I'll tell the press that it was a national emergency – that time was of the essence," Barrera replies.

"Excuse me, sir, for interrupting, and maybe it isn't my place to get in the middle of an international situation, but I don't think there is anything for you to be worried about. There is precedence for you doing just that," Secretary of Interior Miller interjects.

337

"What do you mean, 'doing just that'?"

"We have a long history in this country for the president to make hard and quick decisions in times of crisis. Call a couple of folks in the Senate's Foreign Affairs committee, let them know what you are doing and why, and you're free to go on with this. You can act and then address the American people to let them know that you did inform Congress. End of discussion. The fact is that we have a country – maybe it's the DPRK, or someone else, hell, I don't know – that is threatening us and the world as never before, and the DPRK is sending an armada out for who knows what? I agree that we aren't sure what they are up to, but it can't be good if they didn't notify us first with their intentions. Have we had any confirmation of any illnesses or deaths from North Korea? If so, I certainly haven't heard them. Maybe they've developed an anti-virus serum and their people can't be infected?"

"Mr. President, I think Tom has some valid points. We don't want to waffle on this while people needlessly die in this country. If North Korea is up to something, we're all with you. If they have nothing to hide, they'll let us at least stop them and search their

ships. If they have something to hide, we'll soon find out."

"Alexandra, Tom, and the rest of you – let's lay out our plan." Barrera knows that calm and clarity is called for in times of possible armed confrontation, and his words and pacing show exactly this.

The Joint Chiefs commander interrupts. "Sir, this is an easy interdiction. We just stop the ships and search them."

"And if they don't stop?"

"Sir, they will. We'll have so many guns aimed at them that they will have no choice."

The president looks around the room. Alexandra, his loyal vice president who has supported him steadfastly for the past six years, nods her head to show agreement. Barrera stands and walks around the large table making eye contact with each. No one says a word. He stops back at his chair and looks at a map of the world. "General, exactly how many ships are we talking about?"

"The latest satellite data show thirty ships."

"Jesus, general. What class are they?"

"Small – no bigger than escort destroyers."

The president looks around the hushed room once more. "You have my order to interdict. General, I don't want anyone hurt on this – none on either side. You understand me?"

"Sir, I will do my best, but anything could happen. You have my word that I will endeavor to avoid any armed action."

"Thank you, general. Alexandra, you have a lot of calls to make to the Hill. I suggest you get started."

Within minutes, United States war ships in the Yellow Sea are dispatched and making headway toward a rendezvous with the DPRK ships. Most of the U.S. ships quickly reach maximum cruising speed of twenty-five to thirty knots. As the U.S. ships close the gap to the DPRK armada, satellites show on a large screen in near real-time the meeting of the two forces. Crews aboard the American ships are put on high alert, and tensions run high with everyone from the crew down below to the captains at the top in the bridge. The DPRK radar keeps them informed also of the ships headed in their direction.

Three hours go by, and the president has retired to his office to catch up on other issues. The government has secretly stockpiled every canister or bottle of oxygen they have found from any military organization. The stockpile was moved close to the President, and with some inventive engineering special pipes carry this soothing elixir to specific rooms. His Cabinet has been moved to special quarters underground, and they sleep and work in comfortable surroundings thanks to the oxygen. Pipes also carry pure oxygen to all of the President's quarters. At four in the morning, the president is awakened by his press secretary. As Barrera pulls himself together, he makes his way into the briefing room where all of the Cabinet is waiting.

"What's going on, General Beasley?"

"Sir, the North Koreans did not heed our warning that we wanted to board them. We fired warning rockets over a few of their bows, but two of the rockets failed in midflight and slammed into a cruiser."

"My god, general – get me their president on the line now."

"Sir, there's more. The cruiser was sunk. The other DPRK ships retaliated before our captains could respond – we think as missiles were being launched simultaneously from both sides. The data coming in are conflicting, but from what I understand, at least five DPRK engaged us while the others made an oblique turn. I am told from captains that between fifteen to twenty DPRK ships were sunk, and two of our fleet were damaged. We had several sailors killed. The remaining DPRK ships surrendered. Many sailors from both sides were rescued, so I don't have any exact casualty figures, sir. An initial estimate, though, puts the death toll at around two thousand."

The president stares at the general in disbelief that two countries could be at war at a time like this. He shouts, "Goddamn it, goddamn it. You better have an answer for what they were carrying!"

"From our first inventory, it's medical supplies – oxygen containers being delivered to Dalian, China, we were told by one of their captains."

"Did we recover any of them?"

"Yes, sir. A lot from the water, and the holds on the other ships are filled with them."

"Very well, general. Take every goddamn one of them. And if there is resistance…well, take care of it. Then I want every canister brought back to the U.S. Let the Koreans go back home or on to China – their choice. Get our ships out of there, now. I want those canisters here, so figure it out."

"Yes, sir."

April – Generating a Solution

Scientists rarely look at any situation and give up – it isn't in their DNA to believe they can't come up with an answer. NASA scientists have had to figure out all kinds of sticky issues in the past; otherwise, people would have died at an alarming rate in the race to space. Solving the oxygen dilemma in the space station was something they tackled at the onset of the U.S. space program, and they have refined it every year since.

Barbara Bacon, who is NASA's senior technical scientist, convenes a meeting at NASA's Houston base. Like a proud mother, she looks at her engineers and scientists as the best of the best. They are problem solvers. One person might have an idea, and others would run with it. With caution she feels that her little team of smart people can figure out something to confront the air problem – something, anything – to buy the world some time. As they gather in a room deep in the heart of a huge building twenty miles south of downtown Houston and a few miles north of Galveston, she stands next to a metal table on which sit two small metal containers. Each container is surrounded by an improvised heat shield ("borrowed" she tells them) from a lunar mock-up that

343

she retrieved an hour ago.

As each member takes a chair, they look at Bacon's containers and wonder what she has in store for them, as she is not one for drama. Rather, she is one hundred percent pragmatic and focused on accomplishing a goal. Barbara has remembered from one of the earlier missions the first inhabitants of the early Skylab had wanted to somehow generate oxygen while in space. Some space jockey had wanted to use these canisters that now sit on the table in front of all of them – but smarter minds prevailed and convinced the cosmonauts that setting something on fire in a closed environment was not a good thing. The burning-candle exercise was short-lived, but the idea came from solid physics.

She addresses the assembled group. "Like you, this oxygen problem is scaring the bejesus out of me. So, let's try to solve it. Let me show you a little demonstration. Watch how I mix sodium chlorate and iron powder – then, with a simple little match, ignite it."

She touches the flame to the mixture, which then ignites and sustains a flame. She waits a minute, and then explains what is happening.

"The sodium chlorate and iron powder are now smoldering at around one thousand one hundred twelve degrees Fahrenheit. At this point, it is producing sodium chloride and iron oxide – and it releases at a fixed rate of six-and-a-half man-hours of oxygen per kilogram of the mixture to be exact."

344

She had struggled to recall where she had last seen these canisters stored, but once she started rummaging through some dusty cabinets, it was just a matter of time before she put her hands on them. She smiled to herself when the mixture ignited as if on cue. In reality, she had no idea if it was actually going to work.

"I've seen this before – we did this in a research class I took. We can also use potassium and lithium chlorate, or sodium, potassium, and lithium perchlorates to do the same thing, as I recall," one of the scientists says excitedly.

Some of the other scientists' nod in agreement and study the burning candles even more closely – while breathing in pure oxygen for the first time in weeks. "So, what do you suggest, Barbara? Gigantic candles spread every mile across the world?"

"Hardly. But, who knows? Maybe. I first wanted to see if they would ignite after all of these years – and they did. Then, after lit, could they still provide oxygen? And you can see for yourself they can. Now that I've done my part, you all tell me how to use them practically."

Another scientist is looking up anything written about these candles when he comes across an article about an explosion in a British nuclear-powered submarine while using them.

"Hey, let me read this to you...." He scans the article, and summarizes the reading with, "'A chlorate candle had become contaminated with hydraulic oil, which caused the mixture to explode rather than burn.' Holy shit – I bet that was fun. He sunk the whole submarine!" He laughs, but no one joins in his merriment, as others fail to see any humor at the thought of several hundred sailors killed.

"So, that was an aberration. These do really work. Do we build a bunch? What can we do, people? Let's get some ideas," Bacon commands.

"What's causing this O^2 problem anyway? The reason I ask is that let's say we come up with something – will this virus thing just destroy it?"

Another scientist joins in. "I have no doubt that we can create something in a closed environment, but let's face it, the Earth is not like that. Now, with that said, could we get everyone contained in close quarters? Say, in large cities only? If so, we might be able to do something."

Another chimes in, "Bullshit. It's impossible. Granted, the space station is a closed environment. So, here on Earth, first we feed it with pressurized oxygen. Exactly where are we going to get that much to seed, say a building? Or two buildings? Or some gigantic apartment complex to house one hundred thousand people? And are those buildings airtight? Of course not. So, we're screwed right from the start."

Bacon interrupts the discussion. "Let's break this down before we throw in the towel. Hal, you know more about the environment of every command module than anyone. Give us a breakdown, please."

Hal Johnson is a brilliant scientist who had gotten his PhD in environmental studies at twenty-three. Growing up in his home country of Norway, he had always been fascinated by space travel. His parents sent him to the University of Michigan where he excelled and finished near the top of his graduating class. Armed with his diploma credentials and his bubbly attitude, he sought out NASA's employment office. The person interviewing him was so impressed that they offered him a job on the spot. Four years into his work, he volunteered for the first mission to Mars once he found out that funding might actually happen for it. They told him that he would be put on the short list of people to reconsider at a later date. While waiting for an actual opening for Mars training, he was given the position of director of the Marshall Space Flight Center, which works on the Environmental Control and Life Support Systems (ECLSS) project – Mars would have to wait. Ten years later, he still has his exuberance for creativity.

Johnson approaches the white board. "The primary source of oxygen up there is water electrolysis, followed by O^2 in a pressurized storage tank. As you all know, each molecule of water contains two hydrogen atoms and one oxygen atom. By running a current through water, we cause these atoms to separate and recombine as gaseous hydrogen and oxygen. It's simple, really."

"Go on," Bacon nudges.

"Well, let's talk about Earth for a moment. The oxygen that we breathe also comes from the splitting of water, but it's not a

347

mechanical process like we have up there. Earth is abundant in all kinds of things to help speed up the oxygen process. Plants, algae, cyanobacteria, and phytoplankton all split water molecules as part of photosynthesis. The oxygen released goes into the atmosphere. There – that's it. That's oxygen that we know and enjoy – or at least used to. I've always wondered why nature didn't evolve to a point to produce oxygen directly – it certainly would have saved a lot of steps. So much for a benevolent and wise God, huh?"

"Hal, focus on the oxygen problem, please," Bacon prompts.

"Right. So, what we built is a much more compact, less labor-intensive, and more reliable system than a plant-based system. I started on a plant-based life support system design for our Mars trip, but presently it is at the basic research and demonstration stage of maturity. I've had a lot of challenges to make it viable."

"Go on. You have our attention," Bacon prods him once again.

"Well, we do have some other things in mind that we are working on. Our plan is for the hydrogen that's left over from splitting water to be vented into space – I suppose we can just toss it into the atmosphere – shouldn't hurt anything. I did start looking into a machine that combines the hydrogen with excess carbon dioxide from the air to make a chemical reaction that produces water and methane. The water would help replace the water used to make oxygen, and the methane would be vented to space."

Another scientist interrupts. "Hal, you have just described a major dilemma. Again, up there it's a closed system for all practical definitions of the word. Here on the ground, it's not. We don't need to make more water, and we surely can't vent the methane into space."

"Wait a minute, John. There's more we need to discuss Why vent into space? What if we vented the methane into underground? And who cares if we make more water in the process?" Bacon asks.

Hal replies, "Look, the oxygen that we breathe on Earth is produced by plants and other photosynthetic organisms – you know, like kelp and other slimy stuff. Yes, we're looking to close the loop completely in space, but we're doing that so that everything can be reused. It's less complicated here on Earth. I've even been tinkering with a way to use the generated methane to provide power to the rockets. In space, nothing should be wasted." He pauses and stares at the candles. "Ah…but it all starts with oxygen, doesn't it?"

Bacon interjects, "And we have it if we can gather enough sodium chlorate and iron to get our planet back into shape – or at least create some bubbles while we work on a longer-term solution and find the damn cause for this virus. Does anyone want to put a pencil to this?" She knows her question doesn't need to be asked, as scientists being scientists, they are way ahead of her and already scribbling numbers and notes.

"Can't be done. We would need about two hundred billion cubic yards of both just to supply Houston with enough oxygen to last about twenty-four hours," Hal offers after working on his calculator.

"Has the virus, or whatever it is, spread underground?"

"Does it affect different cultures?"

"What about altitude conditions?"

"Great questions, folks," Bacon replies to all of them while trying to summarize the questions on the white board. "Let me add 'super candles' to this, just to keep Hal on his toes." Everybody laughs – including Hal.

"Yes, yes, yes – a candle the size of Dallas would be fine – it should generate enough oxygen to last at least ten years," Hal adds sarcastically.

Bacon sits down and leans back in her chair to stare at the list she has scribbled for them all to ponder.

"Guys, let's assume it isn't a virus, but something we've done to mess up the whole environment."

"What do you think?" someone asks.

"About what, James?"

"What is causing this? I read that the virus is deadly above five thousand feet. That's silly – is it a 'light' virus? There are no such things, and anyone who believes that is an idiot. I suggest we consider what else this might be."

There is silence in the room as people ponder the last words.

Bacon starts to answer and then catches herself and writes 'Can we fix it?' on the board.

"I think we're screwed," one of the scientists offers.

"Hey, I thought we were here to come up with answers!" Hal interjects quickly.

Bacon looks at Hal, and then at everyone else in the room. "Well, do we give up, or should we continue? Before you answer that, I've got a suggestion. Let's not veer off and think about what is causing this air problem. Virus or not, let's discuss and focus on how to generate oxygen. Agreed?" With affirmatives from all, they proceed.

"Let me start," Hal says as he walks to the white board, picking up a marker from the tray and looking at the words 'Can we fix it?' He draws a crude picture of a tree and stick figure. He adds an arrow from the tree to stick figure, and another from it back to the tree. "It's almost that simple. Stay with me and let's walk through this again. In general, through photosynthesis, oxygen is generated, and we humans generate carbon dioxide. It's a nice little closed-loop system nature presented us with. As we said, in space we have all kinds of nice little tanks and water we can force together to generate oxygen – not so simple on Earth. Somehow, here on Earth the oxygen is either not being generated, or..." He pauses, then continues. "It is being generated and this virus, or whatever it is, is sucking it away. But is it creating too much carbon dioxide?"

"Let's do an experiment," a colleague suggests. Bacon nods in agreement, as does Hal.

"Easy enough to do," an engineer says. "Shit, I have sensors so delicate I can detect an atom at one hundred feet. How do you think we found nitrogen on Io? I did that!" he brags.

"So, set it up, Charlie. How long will it take you?" Barbara asks.

"Give me thirty minutes."

"We'll be here – you need any help?"

"Yes, the equipment is not that bulky, but I need power to the outside – somebody meet me by Door 5 with two hundred feet of cable."

While waiting on Charlie to return, Bacon reaches under the desk and brings out two more candles. She lights them and immediately the room is filled with more oxygen. She looks at her watch and waits for the engineers to return. Ten minutes pass, then fifteen. She looks at her watch. Finally, at around forty minutes, the door opens with all the men literally breathing a sigh of relief as they enter the oxygen-enriched room.

"My god, it feels good in here," one of the men says.

As they relax, Charlie steps to the whiteboard, takes the marker from Hal, and puts a big "X" through the line from the tree to the stick figure. "Hal – what is your calculation for oxygen PPM levels in the space station?"

"We aim for what is normal here on Earth – about one hundred ninety thousand."

Charlie lays down the marker. "I ran nine tests. I know my machine was calibrated. None exceeded ten thousand."

A pall falls over the room. "Don't you think our government would have tested this already? What is this bullshit about a virus eating the oxygen?" someone asks.

"Like I said – let's focus on the cure if we can. We've screwed up the cycle – how's that? Now, can we move on?" Barbara asks to the room. "Come on folks, don't give up."

"To generate oxygen in space, we have to jumpstart things – as in having some oxygen to start with. It starts with a compressor – we filter out the bad stuff, and then feed the flow of air into an absorption chamber, coming up with the oxygen stored in a receiver. Once that's done, we force the compressed air into a cylinder," Hal describes to all. "The problem starts on the front end. If the compressor can't pull the oxygen it needs normally, it will run for days with little to no output. I would bet you that there are no SCUBA divers with fresh tanks just sitting around, and the ones who do have them are hoarding them. You'll never see another tank filled again until we solve this problem."

"It can't be done," an attendee, who has been quiet up to now, speaks up. "I'm sorry to be the bearer of bad news to you all, but we are out of air. It's what would happen in the space station if the compressed tanks ran out and the water-generation system failed.

The Last Breath

The astronauts would have nothing to breathe. It's what is happening to us on Earth. I can tell you right now that there isn't a man, woman, or child alive above five thousand feet. And our government has lied to us. Virus – hell, there's no virus!"

Bacon was expecting a solution, not a digression into politics. But there it is. "Okay, let me have your minds for a little longer, please." She waits for the side conversations to settle down and focus on her – just like she does when they are trying to solve engineering issues while their problem is in a space station fifty miles overhead and going seventeen thousand miles per hour.

She asks, "So, what do we do next? I am not leaving this room until I know that when I walk out that door, we have exhausted all possible solutions. Will we have oxygen to sustain us? If so, where is it or how do we make it? There has to be some answer – it can't just all dissipate."

"We'll find more oxygen at lower altitudes – the lower the better. Sea level. Next, cool climates. Hell, either pole would be the ideal place to be. Definitely at the equator," one of her engineers says.

"Great, we package up everyone on Earth and ship them a pole," Charlie says sarcastically.

Barbara interrupts the conversation. "He doesn't mean that literally, Charlie. But what else can we do?"

"Nothing will work," another engineer interjects. "I said it before,

354

and I'll say it again – any idea we have is useless now. It's too late."

Bacon looks at him and raises her eyebrows as if to say, "Keep talking."

"Okay – you want the hard facts? How about this for starters – how do we sustain food? You've seen the crop reports; it's dismal. Every morsel in my house comes in a can. I haven't seen a ripe vegetable in months. Everything is dead or dying. And our government has said, 'Don't worry – it's only temporary – it's just global climate change,' or some such nonsense as that. Plants aren't growing. No plants, no food. And the oceans? I would bet that any shallow water is empty of all life. Hell, look out to the gulf behind us – any of you been out to Galveston Bay recently? Every report we've heard for a year is that an algae bloom has killed the fish. That's crazy, now that I think about it. Why didn't we put two and two together? Hell, the only fish alive now are the weird ones living around the vents at twenty thousand feet in utter blackness."

No one says anything. The summation they just heard is something they all had theorized at one time or another, but not until now, gathering in this room with other learned colleagues, did it all become clear.

"Thank you for your candid assessments," Bacon says as she inhales deeply and closes her eyes to focus on the air. No one in the room says anything as they concentrate on her. She looks around the room.

"I said I didn't want to leave the room without a solution. But, do each of you agree that there is none?"

No one says a word, but by their actions she knows their answers. "You are a magnificent bunch of men and women." She pauses to make eye contact with each one of them. "Okay. I understand."

She pauses again to look at them. "Let's go home. But...before you go, each of you take two candles from a box from under the table – they'll help for a while if you need them. Take more if there are some left over. Oh, and two more things...don't come in to work again – stay with your families. And go find that cool, low place. Get on the first boat to Antarctica if you can find one."

In silence, one by one the engineers get up, look at the box, tuck a candle in each hand, and leave NASA for the last time. Dr. Bacon sits down next to the last burning candle and takes in a deep breath.

Dr. Bacon leaves her office and walks out into heat. As she reaches her house, she sends a text to a number she had been given six months earlier. "Are we still on?"

She anxiously awaits a reply. A minute goes by, then another. She lays the phone down and sits in the shade on her porch. A hot breeze is blowing, as she thinks about what lies in store not only for herself, but also for the whole planet.

Her phone chimes announcing a message.

She picks up the phone where a voice says, "Yes, seventy-two hours. Confirm or your seat goes to another."

"Confirmed," she answers.

She has a bag packed and loaded into a car that she has never driven. She opens the side door to her garage and rolls back the cover that has hidden the auto for over six months. After manually opening the garage door, Dr. Bacon unplugs the car from its tether, and with a push of a button the electric motor engages. She pulls out of the garage and looks in her mirror at her open garage. Smiling, she thinks that at one time she would have stopped and shut the garage door, but not this time. On the freeway she encounters only a few cars. She looks at the large GPS readout on her console, and it reads "1,443 to final destination with 4 scheduled stops."

Dr. Bacon drives north to Houston, then continues on I10 East. She stops every few hours to stretch and take a bathroom break. Her car announces, "First stop; exit on right, third house on left." She follows the instructions and pulls next to a garage. She grabs her bag from the back seat, enters a side door, raises the garage door, and rolls back a cover to another car exactly like the one she has. Starting the car, she pulls out and follows the pre-programmed instructions.

Two more stops that are the same as the first one pass with no incident. Everything has been prearranged perfectly for her. She's drowsy from staring down an almost straight stretch of highway for many hours. She pulls into a rest area, makes sure her doors are locked, and falls asleep with the cool air conditioner keeping her comfortable. It was a restless sleep and she jars awake realizing that she has overslept.

"Damn. Goddamn it." She is sweating as she glances at her watch – she has only slept two hours. She breathes a sigh of relief, slaps her face to fully be awakened, then continues on her drive.

Another change of cars brings her into Florida. She is tired and knows her body needs a rest, but she pushes on as her GPS readout tells her she has five hundred eighty-two more miles to go. She looks at her battery gauge, and although it reads low, she trusts the people who have arranged this for her. Another two hundred miles and her car announces her last stop. She pulls off the highway, locates her car, and continues on to what she hopes is the last leg of her drive.

Signs announcing "Kennedy Space Center" bring both a smile and a sense of dread. She follows the directions on her car's GPS, and it directs her to a small road off to the side of the main entrance. She continues on it for four miles where an armed guard stops her.

"Name?"

"Barbara Bacon."

A minute goes by while the guard relays her name to someone.

"You are clear to go. Drive to building A."

"Thank you," Barbara replies.

"Ma'am, we know where you are going. Have a nice journey, and remember us here."

"Thank you. I will."

She drives on and, in the distance, sees two large rockets in the gantries. She pulls up to a large building marked with a huge A. She waits and thinks about what is ahead of her. She thinks about friends and family, her childhood memories, and all that was once, by all standards, a wonderful life. Being a scientist at heart, she is excited, though, on what lies ahead – and the possibilities that she can do to help the human race continue. Taking her bag, she stands and looks behind her at the flat scrub trees. She takes in the biggest breath she can, exhales, and walks into the building.

A little more than a day goes by, and Barbara finds herself wearing a spacesuit and strapped into a seat in one of the rockets. She has had no other space training or what to expect other than what she was given in the past twenty-four hours. The solid fuel rockets need no oxygen to ignite their engines, as the one holding Barbara fires and slowly rises from the ground. Faster and faster the propellants increase her rocket's speed and within ten minutes she, along with others assigned to her capsule, are headed to their new home estimated to take two hundred ninety days.

Thirty minutes later, the second rocket is launched, and now both of them, containing twenty people, are on a very long journey together.

In China, three days later, two rockets launch – each carrying ten people. Russia launches their rockets one day after the Chinese. Both countries' rockets have the same destination as the one carrying Dr. Barbara Bacon.

In Central Texas, a mere one hundred fifty miles away, Dr. Oliver also knows it is some made-up propaganda that describes a virus. She knows that the world's oxygen depletion was caused by the ozone disappearing. It's all too apparent now not only to her, but for all of the naysayers who argued against her and her colleagues who asked that something be done earlier. The burn-off of Earth's atmosphere and the escape of oxygen into the mesosphere and thermosphere is beyond repair. Every tree in her town is bare as if in the middle of winter, and even the weeds are dying. She knows, along with scientists such as those at NASA, that oxygen can't be magically regenerated.

Year 4

The Last Breath

January – Plans of the Rich

The lack of oxygen in the atmosphere is continues to have a cascading effect on all living plants and animals – both above water and below. Even if crops could grow, there is no machinery nor people to harvest them. For a while some crops that managed to grow were harvested by hand, but that soon stopped because of the exertion needed by the laborers. As crops fail, prices soar and warehouses can't keep up with the demand to replenish shelves with products – whether canned, frozen, or fresh. And even if supplies could be found, there are no workers who want to venture out and expend energy for others.

The stock market futures indexes rise astronomically with the forecasted increase of demand. Soon, though, the people driving up the prices realize that even though the demand is exponentially increasing daily, there will be no more crops to sow or reap anyway. Shares rise, then fall headlong into an abyss as stocks become worthless. There are, though, speculators who profit – but for what? Money becomes worthless as inflation rises astronomically.

A dollar that could buy something yesterday can only buy a portion of that same item the next day. And the next day the same is true, as are the successive ones. In a span of thirty days, the U.S. dollar has lost eighty percent of its buying power. People with little or no money before now have nothing with which to purchase anything. But money is just a bartering instrument, with trust in a government to put a value on a piece of paper. Since the governments cannot guarantee the paper any longer, it has no value. It is now common for people to revert to the barter system that was in place five hundred years ago. People trade anything of value for food stuffs, gasoline, and medical supplies – including oxygen.

Bible zealots are calling what is occurring the final "Judgment Day" and are asking everyone to repent their sins so their souls can ascend to Heaven. Many still believe the rumors that a virus is somehow causing people to die in masses, so they hide in their houses for fear of being contaminated. Fueled by unsubstantiated and silly claims, such as sleeping with a copper necklace that absorbs germs, and social media websites reporting false messages about how government germ-warfare testing has gone horribly wrong, there is an acceptance that any hope, no matter how frivolous has to be tried. Militaries, or what is left of them, are impotent to deal with insurrections by their people. Some governments collapse simply by locking their doors and going home – leaving their respective countries to whoever wants it.

The Earth is sick as sea water rises over eight feet around the world. Houston, New Orleans, Miami, Singapore, Hong Kong, and other coastal cities are in the process of vanishing, while the

South Pacific islands of Kiribati, Tuvalu, and the Marshall Islands can no longer be found – including the people who once lived on them. People trying to survive at all costs move inland – thus creating massive housing shortages and even more food shortages. Hospitals are overwhelmed with people pleading not for themselves, but universally to save the lives of their children. The once amply supplied hospitals with their life-giving oxygen have no more to give. A few doctors and nurses bravely try to assist people, but they realize it is a futile effort. One by one, medical staff stop coming into work – but before they leave, they take any oxygen container they can get their hands on. Soon the waiting rooms become piles of bodies – first made up of the elderly, but now once-healthy adults and children.

A few TV stations continue to broadcast as best they can, thinking that if some solution breakthrough is found, anyone watching can take some action. But a screen with the message "stand by" does not attract a lot of viewers, so any old movies or stock footage of world events are played with no other aim but to provide a sense of focus while the world collapses around them. A few stations at lower elevations have live programs where they discuss world events. None report any miracle breakthrough, but still each broadcast tries to instill hope by using phrases like "Scientists are working to find a solution...," or "The CDC reports progress...," and similar positive phrases.

One station in St. Louis, after laying blame for the crisis on all politicians, announces it is ceasing live broadcasting. Its management decides that putting "The Three Stooges" shows on a constant twenty-four-hour-a-day loop would be a fitting and final statement to make.

Crimes, or as some call it "survival," start as people take everything from food stores. Then, thieves move to unguarded banks. Alarms go off as people break into businesses, and at first the police try to provide some semblance of law and order. But as the responses become slower and then nonexistent, all alarms go unanswered. Cities give up, and with that message to its citizenry, chaos reigns.

And then a strange thing happens. Pilferers and robbers stop breaking into places. They realize how worthless the things are that they are stealing. It does no good to steal a new car if there is no gasoline to put into it. No one wants any material goods, no matter the price. People are practical, if nothing else; they are finding that it takes a lot of work to walk somewhere, break into an establishment, and try to cart something off – so why not save their energy?

The president of the United States, the U.S. Surgeon General, and the director of the CDC hold a presentation that is broadcast over any remaining commercial TV stations, cable networks, and the internet for anyone in the world to see and listen to. They admit what many scientists have already figured out – that the world is running out of oxygen. They give no reasons why, and there are no press members to ask questions. Instead, the Surgeon General discusses the symptoms of oxygen deprivation and techniques to breathe more fully. The TV cuts to a screen displaying these words and being read slowly and calmly by a woman's voice:

"As your body loses all oxygen, it will most likely show the following signs in any order:

- Your lips and fingernails will turn blue.

- Your words will be slurred.

- You will experience a headache.

- You will become drowsy.

- You will experience panic and anxiety with sweating."

These words stay on the screen for thirty minutes. There is a pre-recorded message from the president that he and his departments are still actively looking for a solution. He offers a prayer, then the newscast repeats itself.

There are no more discussions or any descriptions of who will live longer or why, or how to deal with dead bodies, which are already overwhelming morgues. Rather, bodies remain where they fall. With little oxygen, bodies decay more slowly. A benefit for the lack of air to breathe, if it could be called that, is that the stench from corpses is barely noticeable, as those still alive lose their sense of smell. The wealthiest from around the world, including princes and princesses, business moguls, film actresses and actors, and anyone who has made what they consider a fortune, hoard food and oxygen the best they can. But once they have no more oxygen, they fare no better than every other person trying to survive.

Everyone holds out for hope that a cure or remedy will be found for what is causing Earth's illness. The wealthier, though, have more to trade than the poor, and they send their minions to gather up as many oxygen cannisters as they can find, no matter what they have to surrender in exchange. A single oxygen tank used for SCUBA diving at first cost a hundred dollars; this was before people understood the need for them outside their intended purpose. As the supply got scarcer, the price for them went up rapidly. Within a week, a typical-sized diving tank that would last someone about forty minutes costs ten thousand dollars. Within two more weeks, a tank is up to one hundred thousand dollars. Then, it becomes apparent to the sellers that even if they are offered a million dollars a tank, they have nothing with which to increase their own life spans – so they hid the tanks away for their own use, knowing that their use will ultimately provide only a little extra time for themselves.

A few employees of the rich, in exchange for food, make their way back to their employers with their booty. The smart ones, though, realize that it is a fool's errand they are on, and if they find someone willing to part with his or her oxygen, the errand runners simply disappear with their precious elixir. Everyone wants to extend his or her own life, but there is a realization that unless the crisis is averted somehow, the extension will only be for a few minutes, or hours, or days, or maybe months at most. Therefore, many make plans for their own deaths or those of their loved ones. Murder, if it can still be called that, occurs regularly as a husband, wife, father, mother, or other family member kills their loved ones to spare them the panic and pain of trying to breathe. Whoever is left invariable commits suicide.

In the Cascades, Tom Hardin, a man who made his fortune manufacturing computer circuit boards and microprocessors, has foreseen such a worldly calamity and has planned to bide his time in a specially built underground bunker. His bunker is equipped with food, water, and generators to last more than a year. The bunker itself is an abandoned mine that the owner had excavated and enlarged years earlier. Both a stairway and elevator take people one hundred feet underground where they find ten bedrooms, three bathrooms, a kitchen, and two common areas. The bunker, by all definitions, is close to a duplicate of what is found in the International Space Station. When word of the oxygen-consuming "virus" was making its way across the planet, the owner of the bunker, along with his wife, their three children, his wife's parents, his mother, his brother and his family, plus his brother's daughter and her husband, meet at a prearranged time and are escorted by the owner through a secret entrance that takes them into the bunker.

At first it is like a weekend camp-out – the kids are having fun, and the adults are relatively calm and taking a respite from the events happening above ground. Occasionally, an "I wonder what is happening in the rest of the world?" is uttered by someone, and he or she will focus on one of the large TVs to hopefully get some news – but there is none. People are somber, and any semblance of fun comes from the kids. The adults know how lucky they are to be in this bunker and cut off from the outside world where the virus rages, taking the lives of most of the people left on Earth.

After two weeks underground, however, even their breathing is becoming labored, and several family members have extreme headaches and nausea from the lack of oxygen. The group looks to the owner to find a solution; after all, they have all trusted their fate to him, and this bunker is his design – so he should be able to figure out what is going on. Indeed, he does know how it works, as he was the lead engineer every step of the way.

As he thinks about what could be causing the air problem, he lays down his pencil after studying the blueprints. Although he planned initially to take his immediate family, he had never planned to accommodate the extras – family he couldn't say "no" to, but maybe he should have, given their situation now. After all, it is all about survival. He initially figured that with careful planning they could ration water and food, and all would be fine – at least for a while. He never considered, though, rationing something they take for granted – oxygen. He has built in filters from outside to rid the incoming air of pollutants, but he has always counted on oxygen molecules being there. Extra people are using up valuable oxygen, and he is worried about how to address this problem.

"Come on," he prods himself. "Come up with something."

He looks around at the computer wizardry surrounding him. Then, he remembers the oxygen containers that he stored for emergencies. He opens the pantry marked "Medical Supplies" and on the bottom shelf are four green oxygen tanks, each measuring approximately fifteen inches long and containing enough oxygen to last about fifteen to twenty minutes if regulated via a control valve on the top of each.

"Whatcha looking at?" Tom's sister-in-law, Janice, asks.

"Just counting supplies in case we need something," as he closes the doors. "That's all. It's been a long time since I've been over here to verify our supplies, so I needed to do an inventory."

"Any idea what is going on with the air down here? I thought you said the filters would help?"

"Yes, they should be."

"Are they clogged?"

"That was my next stop. They can be shut off entirely if need be – but then it would get really stuffy down here. Come on – we'll check them together."

"Okay – lead the way."

In a far corner is a concrete room containing the generators that vent to the outside, along with the air intake valves. The room is noisy as he opens the door, and everyone within the bunker hears the extra din and looks toward him and Janice. Tom checks the valves, then hits the power switch, and the motors stop immediately. He then examines each filter carefully. He turns them end over end and looks for any blockage.

"All clear. No contaminates can get through these filters – these were from NASA. It's the same stuff we use on the space station." He looks at some gauges that monitor the air quality, and all read zero. He knows this is bad, but he doesn't want to alarm Janice, so he doesn't say anything.

"So, what's going on? The kids have headaches and are cranky. Hell, so am I."

"Not sure yet what is going on. I want to get everyone together, though. Can you get Ben? Are the kids okay to leave alone for a few minutes?"

"Sure, they'll be fine. Do you want me to help get the others?"

He turns on the power, and they step out of the room as he closes the doors behind them. "That would be great. I'll meet you over in the kitchen area."

Over the next few minutes, Janice and Tom pass the word for others to meet, and one by one they congregate and pull up a chair around the large dining table.

Tom looks around and smiles to each before he starts. "I'll get to the point. The oxygen levels are bad in here – that is probably what is causing some headaches. I checked the filtering machines, and although they are fine, they are not registering any oxygen coming in."

"But can't you turn on some air supply down here?" Janice's husband asks. "Surely you didn't build this with no air in mind."

"Frankly, it was planned for five or six – not twelve. But I'm glad you are all here. You're all family, and we are in this together. The good news is that with rationing we will have enough food and water to last us a very long time. That isn't the problem."

"So, is it an air quality issue, Tom?" his mom asks.

"Mom…and everyone…the filtering machines will absolutely filter out any virus – nothing will get through to us. We are safe from what is plaguing above us." Tom hesitates before continuing, and everyone is focused on what he is about to say next.

"We simply are running out of air. There is nothing coming in. Maybe, just maybe there is something plugged in the intake pipe. I doubt it though, as I have those secured from tampering. So, I'm not sure what is going on top-side."

He continues, "We have a little air, but it's going to get worse. A lot worse. I feel I've let you down. I never in a hundred years would have thought that I could not pump enough oxygen in here."

"Surely it's a mechanical problem. I'll help you find it," his brother suggests.

"Like I said, all of the equipment is running fine. In fact, too fine. The filters drawing air in from the outside have been replacing what good air we had in here with oxygen-depleted air. I need to

373

shut them off entirely, soon. They can run a little longer, but not much."

"Shit, Tom. Now what?"

"Here is what I know. The more we breathe, the worse for everyone. I can rig up fans to try and exhaust any carbon monoxide, but there is simply no oxygen behind it to help us." He looks to his wife Marie.

"We need to talk about our options." He waits to make sure he has everyone's attention. "Our comfortable life down here is running out." He waits before he continues. "We, I, have to try to find out what is going on above. I'm going up top."

Marie knows in her head that this makes sense, but in her heart, she doesn't want him to go – to leave them alone with all of the uncertainty scares her. "Isn't there something else to do? You know – down here. Is there no other way?"

"If I stay down here without finding out what is going on, the worse it will become. I'm a big person who uses up more air – it's really that simple. Look, I might be able to find some tanks of good air somewhere, or maybe it is a simple fix with the pipes somehow – I just won't know until I'm up there."

"No, you will not leave me," his wife yells.

"Marie, there is no other way."

Marie looks around the room at the others, expecting someone to raise their hand and volunteer to go instead of Tom. Then, two guys make an offer, but it's not as she expected. "We'll go with you, Tom."

"At least we'll find out more if we go out there firsthand," one of the men says.

Tom adds, "Great to have you along, guys. There is no use to postpone this. The quicker the better, and the less air we'll take up down here. Fifteen minutes, okay? We'll meet at the elevator."

Each man walks away with his wife to say his goodbyes in private. Tom calls his kids in from the play area and explains to them that he and two others are going up to the top to see what they can find. He hands Marie a note telling her to open it only if absolutely necessary. He kisses them all and gives them tight hugs. He stands back, smiles to them, and walks to the elevator.

He looks at the other two who have said their goodbyes. "Guys, you can stay if you want. It's okay. But I've got to go. I have no idea what is up there."

They look at each other, then all step into the elevator. They stand shoulder to shoulder, smiling the best they can as their weeping loved ones cry out, "I love you – be careful," as the door closes.

The elevator rises and each man's heart races not knowing what they will find in a few minutes. A ring announces they have arrived at the top, and the door opens. As the men step out, they immediately feel the influence of this slightly higher elevation.

"Fuck this shit. I'm going back down," one of the men says as he draws in a big breath only to feel little air fill his lungs.

"No, you're not," the other man says. "If being up here can give our wives and kids ten extra minutes, then we do it. End of story."

Both nod in agreement and one says, "Tom, where are those supplies you were talking about?"

"Just above us. Up those stairs over there," as he points to the opposite corner.

By now they are all taking in big gulps of any air they can force into their lungs and are already feeling lightheaded from the minimum exertion of walking only forty feet. The men make their way across the parking garage and get no more than thirty yards when they stop – none can go on. Sweat pours from all of them, and they can feel their hearts race. Tom sits down, closes his eyes, and holds onto a railing. He takes in big gulps but very little fills his lungs. He buries his head in his arm as if to find some pocket of air, but there isn't any. Another starts running back to the elevator and drops. The other man remains seated as Tom stands and takes a few steps up the stairs before he falls back. The lone man looks down at his friend who by this time is clutching his throat and chest. Then it his turn. He closes his eyes and leans back and claws the space around him.

After an hour has passed with the elevator not returning, the people below realize something is wrong. All knew this could happen, but the meaning of this is sinking in. Another hour goes by, followed by one more. The reality sets in that if the men were successful in finding any supplies, they would have returned by now.

A day of personal grieving passes when the remaining effects of oxygen deprivation start to take a toll. All retire with their families and keep their movements to a minimum. One of wives and her three children form a group and sit and hold hands, and whisper about how they will go on a nice vacation next year to some wonderful place in the mountain. Marie has gathered her two children and her mother-in-law to form another group.

"Mom, are we going to die?" her youngest asks.

"I don't think so. Your dad will be back soon. Don't be scared," Marie replies in a comforting voice. She looks over to her mother-in-law and sees that she appears to have stopped breathing. "Shhhh, let grandma sleep," but Marie knows that she will never wake up.

Marie can feel the sweat of panic start, and she reaches into her pocket for a tissue. She feels the piece of paper that Tom had given her, and she pulls it out. *"In the cabinet in a room off of the kitchen, there is a door marked 'medical supplies.' Inside are three oxygen tanks and masks. Use them. I love you all so very, very much. Tell the children I loved them with my final breath."*

Marie closes her eyes and feels tears pouring down her cheeks, wondering what his last moments were like. "Come on girls. Let grandma sleep."

The Last Breath

One by one, the three of them struggle to catch their breath as they get up. Marie almost passes out from being so light-headed, but she regains her composure and leads them to the cabinet. Inside she finds the green containers. She takes them out and says, "Let's play a game."

She places a mask over each of her girl's mouth and nose, then turns the valve slowly to start and regulate the flow of oxygen. She does the same for herself, and all of them sit and smile and point and laugh at how silly each of them looks.

"Breathe easy, girls. Not too much giggling, okay?" Marie knows their enjoyment will only be temporary, and she is already thinking ahead about what will happen when each bottle runs out.

She closes her eyes and prays. A minute passes. She is comfortable for the first time in days as the oxygen fills her lungs. She opens her eyes and looks at her girls sitting quietly, enjoying their fresh air too. She takes off her mask and smiles at them as their eyes smile back at her.

Twenty-five minutes pass when Marie starts to feel her lungs pulling harder. The girls appear fine, which is comforting to know that her girls are okay – if even for a few more minutes. Sweat breaks out on her face, and she pulls harder and harder for air. She takes off her mask and smiles at her girls, hugs them, and lays her head between them. Marie fights all of her survival instincts to panic. She closes her eyes and says a prayer.

378

"Mommy, mommy," each says as they shake her…but they get no response.

Spring – The Last Breath

Circling high above Earth, the International Space Station crew members look down on Earth and wonder about the life they left. The bright blue below doesn't betray the Earth's sickness, but the blackness above does. While the astronauts have all they need for at least another six months, they were told that communication to them would be stopping, but that people were still searching for a solution. One by one their families have had a chance to say goodbye. Each video connection with them brings anguish that rips them to their souls. How can this be happening? How can I get to them to comfort them?

In the astronauts' last communication, they are informed that no resupply shuttle can be launched. Supplies, including oxygen, should be rationed, and they should all prepare for the day when their oxygen completely runs out. The astronauts make a pact that as their final day comes, they will put their spacecraft into a lower orbit. This will cause Earth's gravitational tug to pull them into a faster and faster spiral where after an estimated five orbits their spaceship will disintegrate, and their deaths will be fast as they are torn apart in a blazing funeral pyre.

What they haven't been told is that governments and scientists –

ones who at one time took firm stands on both sides of climate change – are now in agreement that the ozone layer is beyond repair. While solution after solution was proposed, none were deemed effective in fixing the catastrophic problem. Earth, indeed, has a virus, but not the kind that can be combatted with antibiotics or eradication. Rather, Earth's ailment was made by people ignoring day-to-day signs: glaciers melting at a rapid rate, oceans rising, famine from crop failures, and the most critical one – that the atmosphere surrounding the planet had changed.

The Himalayas are ninety percent void of snow and one hundred percent void of inhabitants. The Amazon that once spoke with life but was cut, burned, and drilled for decades without caution, is hardly recognizable as a jungle.

Those people who were once-considered rich are now equal to the poorest person on the planet. Presidents, despots, and those who thought they were more important than everyone else have recognized that they are not.

In Antarctica the generators have enough oxygen to fire the fuel, but the kerosene that was scheduled to arrive doesn't make it. The maintenance crew jiggles the throttling needles to the furnaces to try and keep them running the barest of fuel/air mixture. The massive furnaces stop, then start, then stop, and the cycle continues around the clock as they need full-time monitoring. Without electrical power, though, the furnaces cannot restart. Everyone pitches in to scavenge and drain anything with fuel, rig up solar panels, or do anything to help conserve heat.

As the power sources wane, McMurdo Station becomes a place for desperate people. A few rig up a snow cat with some stolen fuel. They cram into the cabin with an aim for the closest coast, and once there, hope to be rescued. They know it is foolish to try, but at least they want to try something – anything instead of staying where they are and freezing to death.

Dr. Walker, who helped perpetrate the charade that all was good in the atmosphere, knows what he and others have done. He walks down a cold, quiet hallway and pushes the door open to enter the cavernous outer shell. The cold hits him hard, like a weight placed upon his chest, and between the frigid air and reduction in oxygen, he coughs loud and long. Someone has left a door open and a cold wind from outside has turned the once safe zone into a hazardous area with biting cold. At one time, someone would have been held responsible for this infraction, but it makes no difference now. Walker has on his heaviest parka, boots, and gloves, and he struggles as he trudges out into the snow. He stops no more than fifty feet away and looks around at the snow and back to the exhaust stacks that once showed the warm air dancing into the sky. Now, they emit nothing. The air is clear with no eddies of warmth. He sits down by a post, and gazes up at the brilliant stars, and makes a final decision. He unzips his parka. The rush of cold air makes his body shiver, and he fights the urge to pull his garment together. Shaking so hard that he can barely feel his chest, he pulls the zipper down more. Within minutes his heart stops and cannot pump any blood to his brain. He feels no pain as he dies.

Whether married or single, rich or poor, educated or not – the world is making no distinction. Eight thousand miles away in Central Texas, Marsha Oliver faces what everyone else is facing. Her husband feels the tug of oxygen deprivation. He has always prided himself on being athletic, but even his extra lung capacity does him no good now. All it means is that he can take in deeper breaths, not that there is more oxygen for him than for anyone else.

"John, how are you feeling today?" Marsha asks.

"kay Ellnot eely. Can't sleep. Bod shut ng." Tears run down his cheeks. "Megan?" Marsha is unsure of all his words, but she knows he is asking about their daughter.

"She's breathing okay. She's resting now. Do you want to go back to her room or want me to bring her out here?"

He sobs, with sweat pouring from his face and neck. Marsha leans over and hugs him – he is completely soaked. Marsha lies her head on his shoulder and cries along with him.

"Marsha…I die first…my last…you…Megan."

Marsha cries even harder at this thought. "And you and Megan will be my last thoughts," she responds.

Between deep breaths, he asks again, "Megan?"

"Shhh, shhhh, my dear. I have some sedatives to give her to put her to sleep. I have been waiting until I am almost gone, as I want to be with her until…" Her voice trails off as her tears have not stopped now for several minutes. She leans back, takes John's hands in hers, looks in his eyes, and tries to force a smile.

"Be with her," John manages to get out.

Dropping his hands, Marsha rises to go check on Megan. She promises, "I'll be back."

John nods then takes in some deep breaths and focuses on what is around him to distract him temporarily. He looks at *The New York Times* crossword puzzle from an old newspaper that he tried to solve. He used to love doing them, but now has a hard time of focusing on anything. He knows his strength is at its end. He tries to stand but cannot. Picking up a pencil, he studies it, then lays it back down. As if trying to touch Marsha one last time, he holds out his hand and glances around the room, gasping and struggling to draw any air into his lungs. His heart races and more sweat pours forth. Grabbing his throat, he wants to scream but can't. He gasps once more as his life ebbs away.

True to her word, Marsha returns after checking on Megan. When she sees John's lifeless body, she cries not only for him, but also for the fate that awaits her and, especially, Megan.

"Please God, I don't know what to do," she wails as she steadies herself against the wall. Marsha's breathing is longer and shallower. She can get so little oxygen that she is lightheaded and has trouble focusing. She has to get back to Megan. Should I tell her about her father? No. She manages to move next to John's body, sit on the arm of the chair, and kiss him on his forehead as her last farewell. She rises and walks away. Within ten feet she falls and hits her head hard on the floor.

"I can just stay here – it will be easier," she thinks.

"What will she do? She will be fine – she's young. She has to hold on. She can't find my body. How will she find food? She can call her family – her aunts and uncles – yes, that's what she can do. I just don't want her to find me here." She raises herself up to her knees, then to her feet, as she stumbles on.

She reaches the doorway and straightens herself as upright as she can so that Megan will see her being strong. But Megan's eyes are closed. Marsha shuffles over to the bed and sits down. The pillow and sheets are soaked with sweat, and Megan's breathing is deep and gasping just like the time she had no inhaler. They found a solution then, but there are none now. Marsha cries out in agony as any mother instinctively protecting her child would do.

"Mom, can't breathe. Help me. Inhaler. Please, Mom."

Marsha can't offer her anything but puts her hand on her forehead. In the blink of an eye, Megan's chest stops moving. Drawing in the last molecule of air her bursting lungs can find, Marsha cradles her darling, precious, only child into her arms and softly places her lips over Megan's mouth and blows deeply with her last breath – and for a brief instant she sees Megan's eyes barely open. Marsha smiles to her, then lays her head next to hers, holds her tight, and closes her eyes as she gasps for air. The room is quiet.

The Last Breath

Year 5

The Last Breath

The End?

The world has grown silent. No birds fly; no dogs bark; and car, airplane, and industry noises no longer create a din of a civilization that once made a vibrant planet. Blowing winds create a cover of dust that now makes everything uniformly similar in pallor. Waves from high seas lap against new shores a hundred yards inland from where they once were contained. Cities such as Venice and whole countries such as The Netherlands have crumbled since there is no one to turn on pumps or build levees.

No place is immune from the effects of the world dying. No matter how much oxygen was stored for Presidents and their families, it was limited – and when depleted, there was no more. Survivalists had stockpiled food and water, but they could not cope with lack of air. Anyone living at high altitudes either migrated to a lower place where they held out hope, or died where they lived.

From her work location deep in the jungle of the Amazon, Maria saw and felt the changes of the atmosphere roll like a quiet tidal wave. But the force felt was not of water but rather of pain. It is hard to breathe and ignoring her better judgment of staying where she had some comfort, she had gotten into her faithful Land Rover to try and take her back to her home in Alvorada d'Oeste.

The Last Breath

It is a long trek, but she knows that when she is at home, she will be among her friends and family. There, she reasons, she will have time to figure out how to deal with whatever is going on with her jungle friend. She stops at her first regular refueling town, but finds it deserted. A few chickens run free, but there is no other noise. She looks at the petrol pump. She had never paid much attention to it before, but today she will have to figure it out for herself. She picks up the spigot and places it into the vehicle's receptacle and squeezes the trigger that lets the precious liquid flow, but only a few drops trickle out. She squeezes the handle again, and nothing comes out. She looks around for someone – anyone – to help her, but there is no one.

She sits in her seat, turns on the ignition and looks at the gas gauge. Her two extra fuel tanks carry thirty liters each, so she is confident she can make it easily to the next stopping place where she can top off her fuel tanks. She starts the engine, puts the transmission in first gear, and continues on the dusty road.

In addition to not only fueling up as she usually does in each village, she always spends the night rather than continue driving. This time though, whether out of panic or confusion, she drives on, oblivious to the coming darkness. The shadows grow longer, and she turns on her headlights.

"What was I thinking?" she wonders as she looks at her gas gauge.

She stops, turns off the ignition, and takes one of her extra cans of fuel and pours it into the Rover's thirsty main tank. She looks around, and although the jungle is sometimes quiet, it is eerily so in the darkness. She secures the extra can and starts the engine. The headlights brighten the path in front of her, and she pulls away feeling confident of her driving acumen.

She steers around the easily spotted potholes and looks at her watch. It reads 9:30, but it could be any hour of the night because of the blackness. The engine sputters, jolting Maria from her mesmerized driving. She instinctively pushes in the clutch pedal and takes her foot off the throttle. The engine quiets down to its normal sound.

"Don't quit on me now," she says as she pats the dash.

She puts the Rover back in gear and slowly takes off. Five minutes pass and then the engine sputters once again. This time it dies as she pushes in the clutch. She cranks the ignition several times and the engine sputters as if it is coming back to life only to stop again. She looks at the gas gauge; it reads half-full.

She turns off the Rover's headlights, then sits and stares ahead. It is black and quiet. The darkness resulting from the new moon is so intense she cannot tell the tree line from the sky. Feeling tired and sleepy, Maria's mind is telling her that she must find out the engine problem before she falls asleep. She leans back in her seat and takes in a deep breath. With each breath, she feels strange – as if she is strangling. She opens the door, walks a few steps, and drops to her knees. Gasping for air, she grabs the side of the Rover to help her stand. She turns toward the open door and falls face down to the ground.

She awakens as she feels cool water on her face, and she can feel a bed of leaves under her. She gasps for breath and feels a hand on her forehead. More hands touch her. Her instinct is to push them away, but she doesn't. Her eyes dart about her trying to find the source of the comforting hands. Naked, small, dark-skinned women come into focus lit by the various fires in the area. Maria is scared. Are they cleaning me before they eat me? Why am I here? How did I get here?

She is in an encampment of the Nhambiquaras. Maria feels her pulse and breathing race. But there is something extraordinary about the multitude of hands touching not only her face, but also now her arms, stomach, chest, hands, legs, and feet. Knowing that she could not escape even if she tried, she attempts to relax – and does, as she feels her breathing slow. If she is to die in some horrible way, at least she knows they were nice to her before they did it. She prays that it will be quick.

A woman lifts Maria's head and helps her sit up. Maria looks around and sees Nhambiquaran men staring at her. Several of them come over, pushing aside a woman who was standing in front. The woman reacts to being shoved and picks up a rock and hits him in the arm. Everyone stops and looks at the woman holding the rock. Mumbling between the men is heard, and the woman drops the rock. Another man walks over to Maria, bends over her, and sniffs her chest, face, ears, and hair. He turns to the woman who had held the rock, says something to her, and the men return to the far side of the fire.

Maria looks at one of the fires and sees a monkey being roasted over the flame. Maria makes a sign with her hands for something to drink. The women look bewildered, and Maria makes the gesture again. Then again. A woman walks away then returns with a large leaf cradling water. She hands it to Maria. Maria and the woman smile at each other.

Maria looks around. A fire radiates a glow of no more than ten or twenty meters, but beyond that, there is nothing but blackness. Then she hears a noise – a howler monkey calls, and others join in as if to say, "I'm here. Over here. I'll keep screeching until you find me."

Focusing on the jungle sounds, she hears more. All sound soft and distant, but there is a cacophony out there. She looks back to her hosts, and they are talking to each other as if they are so used to the noises that they don't bother paying attention to them. To them, it is food, maybe a hide to make a rope, or perhaps a tool or spear from a bone. The Nhambiquarans have made this home for centuries – maybe more. And they are surviving still.

In its majesty, the jungle has called to her once again. Every now and then a man or woman approaches and touches her, and then returns to what they were doing before. This gives Maria a calmness. They aren't eating her yet, she thinks, so maybe, just maybe, they won't.

The Last Breath

She stands up and takes a step, then another, and then confidently walks about the camp while keeping a wary eye on all of those she can see. She walks over to where the men are standing. Every man's eye is on her. She holds out her hand in a motion of friendship. No one moves. Then one man touches her arm, then another and another, until all have touched her. She then faces the women standing behind her. She walks the ten meters to the women and smiles at them. One by one, all reach Maria's face. In turn, she touches theirs.

Deep in the Amazon, a small oasis is alive. The jungle is talking – and breathing.